Evolution Theorem

Part 3

Premonition

Frank Lewseed

For my darling Helen

Evolution Theorem

Part 1: *Psyche*

E.B.Mad

Part 2: *Pre-existence*

Frank Lewseed

Part 3: *Premonition*

Frank Lewseed

Maybe from these volumes my grandkids can begin to know Helen and why she was the best thing that ever happened to me.

Preface

There's a fascinating scene in the film 'Field of Dreams' where a writer disappears into a cornfield to experience the afterlife, and then returns to write about it. What an excellent idea! There's also a reality which incorporates a pre-existence, a mortal existence and a post-mortal existence. Subjectively, such concepts are both simple as well as extremely persuasive. These three volumes [Psyche, Pre-existence and Premonition] won't be the most exciting reads you'll ever pick up, and they certainly won't be the next creative addition to English literature. However, they can provide a reader with something collectively important. Together they'll offer a purpose in life, a human history, and a crystal ball into the future with an afterlife – hence the three parts.

The first part [Psyche] begins with real life scenarios, followed by a temporal prequel planted within the fascinating concept of a pre-existence, and finally a sequel [Premonition], which remains dependent upon how humanity chooses to write our history. The way we decide to behave could either create an exciting and possibly beautiful future, or alternatively quite an alarming or onrushing sequence of scenarios. I'm personally not interested in fortune-telling nor predicting world events, since that's generally the domain of deity to understand or influence, yet fictional future is a lot of fun, and more importantly, there are factual things we do know, things which can form the framework of a crystal ball.

Ultimately, it wouldn't matter if the entire universe disappeared into a wave of electromagnetic radiation tomorrow, or nothing whatsoever of this physical dimension was left intact. In fact, history, life, wealth and physical matter could all be destroyed. All that's required is for individuals to remember what's important, then carry the memory with them into the next dimension or the afterlife. Interestingly I can't pretend these volumes are coming up with anything new, but what I can point out is they're packed with decent or modern arguments in favour of a reality which many currently believe is true. It's a situation that one day everyone will discover is real, yet for our life and times, we can only write about it or relate our experiences.

The majority of stories I've used are autobiographical, some are 'family and friends' biographical, whilst other parts are acquaintance biographical. I've deliberately mixed up events whereby anyone (apart from my wife) might struggle to identify unique incidents or any part of their life within the stories. Character portrayals are generally composites of my different and rather excellent friends, so I can at least shuffle behind a useful degree of historical impunity. The same rationale applies to cited venues. Some of the storyline that threads it all together is purely fictitious, such as the 'Book of Wars', which is included as an explanatory or fictional example going beyond pure literary licence. Strangely though, a lot more of the storyline is simply describing life's events. I could have included notes to specify which bits were real or which were fictitious, but I'm guessing readers will be able to see the difference. Most of the incidents related were in fact both accurate as well as very real. My wife's kept detailed journals of our life together, although I've really only recorded stories. Our writings were originally intended for our family because every family has ongoing stories to tell. Useful or otherwise, if you do manage to read it through to the very end, you have my apologies. All I can say in mitigation is it'll perhaps be good for you, but I wouldn't bother trying to track me down and then moaning about what I've written, because I agree with you now. What I will say is I've gone to the effort of using pseudonyms, with two thirds of a pseudonym for each volume. My guess though is that after the first volume, whilst a reader might appreciate some of the facts I've merely described, they may also wonder about the author, and conclude it could be that E.B. Mad!

E·B· Mad

[… who in time, became Frank Lewseed.]

Introduction

There comes a time when you get the feeling things can either go terribly well, or just plain terrible. That's when premonitions come in rather handy. Following or heeding premonitions is probably the next step forward in personal evolution. We're not alone in this dimension since deity is a reality.

CHAPTER 1

"I get the feeling we'll hear from Adam Hut again," Frank suggested
"What makes you think that?" Siggel inquired.
"Just a feeling."
"Like a premonition."
"I guess so."
"Well, we'll see," Siggel replied, bringing in the drinks.
They didn't wait long. Frank's mobile began to ring.
"Oh, hi Adam, we were actually just talking about you." There was a pause. "Don't worry, it was all good, but not much content really because we were just wondering." A longer pause followed. "OK, sure. We can do that. At the same café? Sure, we'll see you there."
Siggel's eyes were out on stalks as he peered over his glasses in Frank's direction. Frank said nothing.
"OK, come on then..."
"Come on, what?" Frank asked.
"What does Adam want?"
"I'm not entirely sure," he replied resolutely.
"So when are we meeting with him?"
"Whenever you like."
"Well, the others aren't due until this afternoon, so let's go see him now and hear what he has to say."
"Good."

"Good what?"

"Let's go."

"Where?"

"To the café of course. It's already arranged."

"You do realise, you can be really annoying."

"You're a good teacher."

"Yes, very drôle."

"Let's make a move because we need to be off..."

Adam was waiting for them at the far corner of the café by a window, and had three cakes sitting quietly, almost waiting politely on a plate in front of him.

"Aghh, excellent!" Siggel remarked as they took their seats, each in turn reaching over for a refreshment.

The café was an interesting venue, because it was an offshoot of the local tourist centre in the city centre's guildhall. It was spacious, albeit neatly laid out, with tables, chairs and a collection of more comfortable seats to one side. The work counters for staff were modern or fresh, whilst the level of service appeared to be well managed. Frank judged how Adam had made a decent choice in opting for this same venue once again.

"So what's new, Adam?" Siggel asked, rather eagerly or possibly too eagerly.

"Things are more or less the same. When the CVS constructs a case and it's your case, it's not just the business which fails, but obviously a profession is lost. Financially there's a significant loss, then your reputation also takes a knock. I guess I find it quite amusing, reading what the press have to say about my situation."

"Is it really amusing?"

"No, not at all. I'm trying to be sarcastic."

"What are you doing now?"

"I've moved onto something else."

"Are there any regrets?"

"I've made plenty of mistakes in life but this business venture wasn't one of them, nor subjectively was my professional behaviour at the time. I probably could've been more patient though. The CVS took their opportunity to remove me as a political nuisance, so I guess the outcome was normal. The CVS actions were most likely corrupt, yet nevertheless quite normal."

"I read about Kris Klermunsky, who was a vet working for you, wasn't he?" Siggel added.

"Yes, he was good with cattle."

"But didn't he appear as a witness for the CVS against you?"

"Yes, he did. The CVS has been criticised for prosecuting vets via lawyers they engage, but without permitting an independent panel or jury to decide upon the verdict of cases. Kris was a thoroughly pleasant man, although probably not an appropriate witness for them."

"What d'you mean?"

"Kris had falsified financial travel expenses he'd submitted to the practice accountant, similarly when he'd X-rayed a fracture, he'd suggested he could take another radiograph at the end of the weekend to monitor healing, although it takes about six to eight weeks to heal."

"Why did the CVS use him as a witness?"

"I'm not really sure. Kris testified he'd left a note on my desk to transfer a case he'd handled and misdiagnosed, whilst I'd been handling other cases. The CVS suggested I was responsible for Kris' case as the practice owner, although every vet is responsible for their own work because they hold individual licences to practise."

"And how many cases did you have?"

"Thirteen."

"It's a lot in comparison."

"Yes, I was fairly busy that day, but cases can't be transferred by a piece of paper on a desk. I never actually found Kris' note."

"Hmmm. I heard he reportedly speyed a cat which had kittens a few weeks later and the CVS also tried to blame you, didn't they? He said he couldn't remember not taking out the reproductive tract because of high blood pressure, then sewed it back up again before returning it to the owners."

"Yes, I was lucky because one of our practice staff verified Kris had performed the operation. Kris was a jovial chap, even really quite pleasant to be around most of the time, whilst occasionally he was rather an enigma. If I located the reproductive tract for him, he could perform the spey, although he didn't ask me for help on that occasion. The first thing I heard about the operation was when the queen had kittens."

"Does Kris still practise as a vet in England?"

"Yes, he does."

"Didn't the CVS in fact force Kris into being a witness against you?"

"Yes, as I saw it. We phoned Kris to ask what was happening. My wife heard him say the CVS insisted he testify against me, otherwise they'd take away his veterinary licence to practise in the UK, due to the issue with the spey. It's ironic because when the CVS asked me to sack him, I wouldn't do anything until his probationary period had ended. I actually liked Kris and became rather emotional when he was badly destroyed under cross-examination. I was surprised he gave false evidence."

"Did the CVS committee believe him?"

"It didn't really make much difference either way to be honest, because I believe they'd arrived at their decision beforehand. The outcome was probably normal for my type of case. The CVS barrister manoeuvred Kris. She suggested I'd exploited Kris by engaging him for lower wages. In reality he was lucky to gain employment with me where he'd not been able to gain employment elsewhere, and I took a chance with him. It's true trusted vets were paid more, reflecting their level of experience. I'd taken him on when the other vets in my group had watched him successfully perform a calving, after which they were keen to work with him. Kris was paid fairly for his experience or the quality of his work. I believe I paid him more than another vet I'd employed from eastern Europe. The other vet was in fact significantly better, so I believe I was being financially helpful towards Kris."

"Would it surprise you to know how the CVS spent over three hundred thousand pounds in prosecuting your case? They'd used a third of their annual budget, indicating they definitely wanted to ensure you were stopped," Frank intervened.

"Yes it fits because they sent me around three hundred pages to read within a couple of weeks. I replied with about the same amount within a couple of months and they said I was verbose. I found it interesting, but how do you know about the costings?"

"I can't say, although my sources are very well informed."

"Fair enough. I suppose the suggestion in my CVS Council election manifesto wouldn't have helped," Adam replied. He paused briefly, seemingly giving himself time to reflect. "I'd proposed outsourcing the CVS legal branch," Adam continued. "It's never easy to escape politics. I guess it was my own fault in trying to reform the system. I wanted to put governance back into the hands of vets, away from lawyers, just as Bob the former CVS President who'd proposed my candidacy had pointed out. My mistake was declaring my hand in the manifesto. It was a little stupid really."

"Perhaps it was more honest than stupid, but where do you go from here?"

"I've concluded there's a time to work at some things, whilst there are some things where the time has just gone, at which point it's probably best to let them move on."

"That doesn't sound very resilient," Siggel continued.

"I actually think it's more practicable."

"Justice never gets old."

"Maybe, but I think we do, albeit gradually. Sometimes justice is a mixture of perspective, emotions, alongside objectives."

"What do you mean?"

"The CVS charged me with failing to run diagnostic tests for a dog which had died, then telling the client her dog would die beforehand."

"Why, did you do that?"

"My strong recollection was that I told the client if she chose not to administer the prescribed antibiotics, her pet could be in danger."

"Did she give the antibiotics?"

"One of my staff informed me she hadn't, whilst later she'd changed vets."

"So the dog died at another practice."

"Yes, the client went to the same competitor group which had opened up a new surgery a few hundred yards away from mine. They probably thought it was fair, because I'd gained about a thousand clients from them previously, although mine was about six miles away at the time. It probably helped the competitor practice quite a bit when they hired the person who'd sold my practice to me."

"So why did the dog die?"

"Mr. Stramon, at the competitor practice, gave the same antibiotics as I'd done, and subsequently ran multiple tests but found nothing conclusive."

"Well that wasn't very helpful."

"Yes, my view was very similar. It was also the view of many clients who'd transferred over to me from the same competitor, because they weren't happy with numerous expensive tests which the competitor practice had previously performed."

"So why did the CVS charge you?"

"The CVS prefers tests to economics. A client desires a solution which isn't going to cost a significant amount of funds, especially if tests possibly return nothing. Medicine is a science, although it's equally an art, so a practitioner applies all of the art they can gather in pinpointing the cause of an ailment before treating it. One test doesn't identify what's wrong. One test identifies whether the practitioner has found the relevant condition or not. The dog I'd examined showed clinical signs of a subclinical illness, and in my training a lecturer had taught me how under certain circumstances, using antibiotics in combination can prove to be more effective. Therefore it's what I'd done."

"And the CVS judged it was a mistake."

"The dog didn't die under my care."

"Fair point."

"The competitor practice believed in the CVS approach to Veterinary Medicine, and their vets were subjectively useful witnesses for them, though there was a conflict of interests."

"What d'you mean?"

"The competitor practice developed unfriendly relations with different local practices in the area, with CVS complaints, letters to vets, visits to other practices, et cetera. It was an alternative approach to purchasing practices which they'd indicated weren't affordable. I had a former work colleague who went into private practice locally. He reported a client came to his practice stating they transferred due to unnecessary costs, and it was shortly after a partner in the competitor practice belatedly declared the dog was 'only ever going to go one way' and die."

"Hmmm."

"The reality is in fact, not everything turns out OK. Sometimes we just need to head off in a slightly different career direction. Which brings me onto our meeting today. I hear you've started up a discussion group. Well if it's OK, I'd like to come along please?"

"Oh, I see. That wasn't exactly what I was expecting."

"Sorry, what were you expecting?" Adam inquired.

"To hear you'd managed to correct the CVS scandal, and you were back off practising again." Siggel paused. "I certainly didn't expect you wanting to join our discussion chats. They've grown quite steadily actually, which means I'm not too sure how many more we can fit into my little house, to be frank."

"Yes, of course you can join us," Frank interrupted. "Here's Siggel's address, and I'm also writing down my email address so you'll know whenever we have a meeting. In fact, we're having one this afternoon if you're interested?"

"Yes, I think I might be," Adam replied.

"Good. We generally arrange things through email, simply because it's a lot quicker that way. It'll be useful to have your input, and Siggel will be pleased with some help in the kitchen."

"It's interesting, because my cousin works for a supermarket. He often asks whether he can help out with providing food."

"Excellent," Frank rejoined. "It'll cheer Siggel up tremendously!"

Siggel was still protesting as they made their way out to the car.

"You've been looking for a new way to fund the refreshments for weeks, which means this will certainly help out."

"Maybe, but Adam is a charity case. Letting him join the group would be opening things up for a whole host of new problems to solve."

"I think Adam is more likely to be solving issues rather than creating them, Siggel."

"Well, I'm not so sure."

"You never are."

"And what's wrong with that?"

"Nothing." Frank paused. "Unless we're looking for solutions, of course."

"Very funny," Siggel concluded, still donning a pained expression as he opened the car door on the front passenger's side.

"Well if it's mega amusing, hopefully it'll cheer you up a bit!"

Siggel refused to answer.

"I think Adam is still hoping for exoneration."

"From what I've observed, such an outcome will never happen," Siggel suggested. "Subjectively, the CVS election rigging was rather emphatic, or at least telling. I'm also not too sure he's actually got the appetite for redressing things, especially through any more corrective attempts. There comes a point when a corrupt organisation is probably best left to run its course," he relented.

"I'm rather convinced the other way. There's always something which can be done in any given situation."

"D'you remember the film 'Bridge of Spies'?"

"Yes, it was interesting. Tom Hanks was in it, wasn't he?"

"Yep. He played the American lawyer. During the film he asks the Russian spy why he didn't seemed concerned about his predicament, and the Russian postulates "Would it help?". When Hanks replies that it probably wouldn't, Hanks duly gets the message, even though he later repeats the same question, even a number of times. In the film, an American spy who was freed from Russia seems to be ignored by other Americans, resulting in him telling Hanks he hadn't divulged any secrets to the Russians. Hanks simply replies how the American spy knew what he'd done, meaning the thoughts or beliefs of others were probably less relevant. The same I believe, applies to Adam."

Frank had brought Siggel along for his logical thinking, and although Siggel's views were subjective, they were indeed relevant. Siggel was most likely right. The case of Adam Hut didn't come up again. Frank did wonder though whether Adam's life would be left alone, because fabricated details or leaked counter-arguments seemed to be the news fashion in some circles. 'Everybody's history is written by someone else, irrespective of the truth. Maybe it's just best left for deity to sort out...' Frank inwardly thought, but then erroneously vocalised.

"Maybe you've got a point," Siggel concurred.

Frank continued in thought for a moment. 'Siggel has somehow acknowledged the existence of deity!' He managed not to vocalise his latest thought though. Perhaps Siggel hadn't realised what he was just saying.

"And yes, I do know what I was just saying," Siggel confirmed.

Frank look across at him, somewhat stunned.

"Watch out!" Siggel complained. "You'll crash the car at this rate. That was close!"

CHAPTER 2

Frank dropped Siggel off at his house before he headed home to Helen. He wondered whether she'd be back from the horse stables because at some point they'd need to go over to Siggel's for the scheduled meeting. Helen was brilliant at social gatherings and he loved seeing her mingle with the other wives whilst he boringly chatted with the chaps in the front room. It meant everyone was happy. On occasions the wives would also join them, although usually they preferred to engage with 'girl talk' out in the kitchen – apparently it was more interesting. Fortunately Siggel's kitchen was rather large, carried over from when his wife Frances was still alive. She'd enjoyed cooking meals and Siggel had been keen to make life easier for her. Frank did sometimes wonder whether Siggel was motivated any longer by cooked meals because his refreshments were excellent, yet invariably delivered out of packets. What was clear however, was the way Siggel and Frances had always been a 'forever couple' with a pleasantly strong marriage, which in turn had become a success story for marriage in general. So too was Frances' food. Frank once ventured to ask Siggel about living without Frances, and Siggel related how he wasn't naturally decent at sports but had entered league competitions for a couple of them. He likened life with Frances to enjoying times in a top league with all the privileges it afforded, whilst life without her was like suddenly dropping down to the foot of the lowest league, or getting used to the loss of a pleasant, contentedly happy existence. Siggel related how once he'd accepted the loss, with a downgrade to far lower expectations, he could slowly become more settled. Somehow though, Siggel never looked truly settled over the loss of Frances.

At that moment Frank noticed a car amongst the oncoming traffic. It had begun to cross the white line in the centre of the road, and when the white taxi ahead of him pulled over to make room, he likewise pulled far across to the left-hand side. He also dropped his driver's window, hearing a significant grating noise as he did so. He looked towards the noise, then observed in fact it was coming from the front off-side wheel of the oncoming vehicle, which probably explained why the driver was struggling with its control. The noisy car slowly came to a halt just as Frank pulled up behind the taxi. In fact their two vehicles were almost synchronised in their deceleration down to a stationary state, virtually next to each other. Frank got out of his car, observing how the small blue hatchback had not only blown the driver's front tyre, but was also sporting some rather significant damage to its front off-side.

"Are you OK?" he inquired, approaching the driver of the damaged hatchback.

The driver tried to restart his vehicle before exiting to view the damage at the front. What Frank saw next quite bemused him. The man was a young chap, probably in his twenties, yet as he circumnavigated his car a couple of times, his gait was beyond the staggering which could normally be associated with alcohol consumption, to the point where it appeared this person might have been consuming recreational drugs of some description. He had no visible bodily insults to possibly explain his staggering on medical grounds, however he re-entered the vehicle, attempting to restart it once again.

'His car's not going anywhere,' Frank concluded.

A large gentleman now purposefully strode over towards the driver from the right-hand side, and began extracting him from the vehicle.

"No, don't do that. Just be calm, and everything'll be fine," Frank suggested.

"He's just hit my car," came back the reply.

'Fair enough,' Frank thought, as the large gentleman nevertheless desisted with the manoeuvre, opting to remove his ignition keys instead.

At the same time a woman approached from the left-hand side, vocalising towards the young chap and quite loudly.

'There's another one?' Frank questioned.

"I've got my four kids with me and he's just hit my car," the woman exclaimed.

"OK, I understand."

In reality he wasn't quite sure whether he did actually understand because hitting two vehicles, subsequently ending up quite some distance down the road seemed incredulous, although this driver was apparently under the influence of drugs or alcohol, so maybe anything was possible. It turned out he'd in fact collided with a third vehicle in a different street, whilst also seriously injuring a pedestrian. An ambulance, followed by several police vehicles attended the scene within two and a half minutes of the blue hatchback becoming stationary.

'That's impressive,' Frank judged.

Subjectively though, the most impressive action was displayed by the large gentleman, who'd originally gone over to remonstrate when his own car was damaged, a little before the police had arrived.

As Frank finished conversing with the woman the large gentleman shouted: "He's got a nail gun!"

Frank now saw the young driver place a nail gun to his left

temple exclaiming "I want to die!" whereupon the large gentleman began a bear hug which cut short his irrational, impulsive act. They both fell backwards onto the tarmac, so Frank picked up the nail gun. The large gentleman had probably just saved the life of the reckless young man.

'Heroism comes in all shapes and sizes,' Frank considered. 'Fortunately this chap was rather a large one.'

As Frank finally drove away from the scene he reflected upon the way alcohol or recreational drugs really could cause some serious damage to everyday lives. He was never a fan of either, and after that episode he still hadn't changed his mind.

-

"We need to make sure the children never experiment with drugs," Helen suggested, as he finished relating the incident.

He agreed.

They arrived at Siggel's home in plenty of time.

-

"You know I wasn't going to go along that road," Frank commented, still quite puzzled over the road traffic incident which had occurred on his way home.

"What d'you mean?" Siggel inquired.

"I felt beforehand I should go there."

"What, like another premonition?"

"Yes, I guess so."

"Well the premonition about Adam Hut turned out to be jolly accurate."

"Maybe, but did I do anything for the young driver? It was the large chap who saved his life, so I didn't have to be there."

"We could all say similar things. We've all wondered what the reason was for our involvement in different events. Sometimes it's just pure coincidence."

"Which probably means the premonition wasn't useful then."

"Not necessarily. It just depends upon perspective."

-

Two men stood together. They were dressed in white suits, white shoes and white ties and were deeply engaged in discussion.

"Shall we help him to see why we prompted him to go along that road?"

"He's making good progress but he needs to become an active initiator for good, more than an observer or a conduit for good. His character development needs a next step, and by learning how to develop faith in the process of listening to promptings, regardless of whether he can see the reason or not... well, it would allow him to become a creator of good, which is a whole new level in his personal evolution."

"So the answer is no."

"Well, yes."

"But no..."

"Yes."

"OK, no."

"Agreed."

"Then he'll never know."

"Not right now. No."

"OK. Then yes."

-

"So it makes me wonder when premonitions are really useful, or more to the point, what's the point of pointed premonitions?" Frank queried.

"It's funny you should ask such a question because I think

I've got just the person, someone who happens to be available right now and who might be able to help," Siggel replied.

"Is this someone I haven't met before?"

"Yes, probably."

"Someone new to our discussion group perhaps?"

"Actually, yes."

"Hold on here, it's not too many hours ago you were moaning a huge amount about the possible admission of Adam into the group."

"Yes, but Ian Gerald is religious."

Frank stopped now to contemplate what Siggel was suggesting. Siggel had just admitted he was softening in his opposition to something theistic.

"Ian, this is Frank," Siggel stated, after eagerly beckoning a young newcomer over and into their conversation. "And Frank, this is Ian Gerald."

Twenty minutes later the young newcomer broke away, seeking available refreshments in the kitchen.

"This young chap certainly had some interesting concepts he was sharing," Frank observed.

"Yes, I thought you might enjoy what he had to say. He's intelligent as well as lateral-thinking, which is a useful combination."

"The idea of leaving the political decisions to politicians, then the doctrinal decisions to Church leaders, the family decisions to parents, and so on and so forth... it all seems simplistically logical."

"And it helps with your previous question about premonitions. Any person with a function to perform, can be assisted with premonitions relating to their respective roles."

"Which would mean religious leaders would also need to be inspired over how to act or advise."

"And so too would parents or politicians."

"In the US, theism is publicly shunned a lot less by

politicians, compared to England. In fact the Americans have little compunction in declaring their inclinations to pray."

"Yes, I suppose you're right." Siggel paused. "And now that you've met Ian... I'd like you to meet James."

"Who's James?"

"Another addition to the group."

Frank was beginning to suspect how Siggel had just attempted to restack the odds in his new introductions to the discussion group. 'But Ian is a strong theist. Maybe he thinks James is a suitable counter for both Adam and Ian. Why would he invite along a strong theist such as Ian Gerald? Mind you, Reg brought along Logan as well as Elijah, which is pretty much the same thing... in reverse. Perhaps it was for the discussion? After all, he's just pointed out how Ian had decent answers over premonitions... which is clearly theistic. Perhaps he's having some mixed thoughts?' He couldn't really tell. Nevertheless, what he could guess was James' inevitably strong position against theism. 'I don't reckon there's any mileage in it, yet why does Siggel believe it?' Frank was soon about to find out.

-

Two men stood together. They were dressed in white suits, white shoes and white ties and were deeply engaged in discussion.

"You see, we sometimes just need to wait a while for events to unravel. Freewill or discovery are important."

"He certainly seems to appreciate the reasoning for promptings a little better."

"So it's been successful then, prompting ZygL to bring Ian along."

"Yes, I believe that's true."

"Although James might raise some difficult questions."

"There's a reason James is also there."
"Good."

-

"The clock stops in the next dimension James, when the test of life is over."
"So where is this other supposed dimension, or this make-belief afterlife? No one's ever come back to tell us about it."
"Actually your statement's not quite true."
"What, are you referring to these near-death experiences which some evangelical people happily relate? They're all just an in-built concept to make people cope with dying. It's not real because there's nothing really there. It's hard-wired into our consciousness, but it's just a hope. I prefer living in reality rather than trying to kid myself there's an afterlife... when there actually isn't."
"You really don't get it, do you?"
"Get what?"
"I guess you've never seen anything or heard anything connected with the next dimension, have you?"
"Actually, I have. And I also allowed myself to be fooled over believing it was real... until I woke up to reality."
"Hmmm. So you don't have faith in what you've experienced."
"I didn't fool myself any such thing was real, if that's what you mean. I want to enjoy the present, rather than live for a future which is just pure make-belief."
"I can see you're sincere. You haven't got an understanding yet though. Here, let me show you this," Frank said, passing James a small piece of white card with a mixture of dots plus irregular shapes on one side.
"Yes, I've seen these before. There's a 3-D picture behind the dots, but you've got to focus your eyes properly."

"That's right, and you have to keep at it for a while because it can be tough... getting the picture sometimes..."

"OK, I'll have a go," James agreed, as he began to stare at the card. After a few minutes he eventually gave up, abandoning his attempt to find the image. "Aggh, this is no good. I just can't get it. If I tried it for long enough, I'm sure I could get it."

"You do need to try it for a while though, otherwise you'll never see the picture."

"I'm not sure it's worth the effort at the moment, to be honest."

"Oh, it's definitely worth the effort. What you actually see each time is excellent."

"Well, thanks for the chance, but I think I'll give this one a miss."

"Sure, no problem."

"Why did you want to show me this 3-D image anyway?"

"It's the same as seeing the afterlife in the next dimension. Once you know how, when you've seen it... then you can even forget how to see it... although you still know it's there. It never changes."

"Hmmm," James replied reflectively. "I'm not sure I quite agree with the idea."

"It's possibly because you haven't experienced it yet."

"No, you're not quite right because as I mentioned, I've experienced spiritual impressions, even though I don't believe in them anymore."

"Then it comes down to belief. You've chosen not to believe what you've experienced."

"I choose not to believe the spiritual is real."

"However, spiritual reality doesn't change, even if you choose not to believe it."

"Logically without evidence there's no reason to believe in the spiritual."

"And now we've come full circle, because spiritual experiences are proof of the spiritual."

"No, I'm talking about physical proof."

"Sorry James, how can physical things provide proof of any spiritual matter? It's not logical."

"Well until there's proof, then I won't believe."

"And that could be too late."

"Late for what?"

"For the test of life, or the limited time we have in this physical dimension. We all die eventually."

James wondered what Frank meant by the 'test of life', but he considered all religions regularly preyed upon people's fears since throughout history religions had exercised control over the minds of believers - at least, until science finally broke down the yoke of religious superstitions.

"The next dimension has nothing to do with fear, James," Frank added. "We all pass through the gate called death, then into the next dimension. What's more important, we could be dead for a mighty long time, so it's slightly illogical not to prepare for the inevitable change. If you prepare, you won't fear. Only the unprepared have fear. The effort of preparation is always worth it."

James wondered how Frank had guessed what he was thinking. He concluded that whilst it was uncanny, it was just a coincidence. Or maybe Frank, quite frankly, was more used to this type of conversation than he'd been? He decided he certainly didn't care for it, because he definitely wouldn't be pursuing it again in the future. James left Siggel's house before the rest of the group arrived. Adam also arrived. James didn't return to the discussion group for many months. When he did return, there was a very good reason.

CHAPTER 3

Frank decided if Siggel would attempt to stack the odds, then he'd also have a go. He admitted to himself Siggel had indeed brought along Ian, so it was a significant concession and in fact an excellent one, yet at the same time he'd also brought along James, which indicated the gloves were off. Frank decided to call for LaMar and Ernie, a reaction he considered was probably one of the most proactive moves he'd made in a long time. Not only were LaMar and Ernie a well-rehearsed entertainment team who could've steadied the Titanic (if they'd have been born in the right era), more importantly though they were older, older than Siggel, which naturally gave them an edge. Usefully, things were never quite the same with the discussion group ever after, because Siggel needed to be outmanoeuvred. Frank also considered it as something fortuitous and timely, since he'd recently decided to take a trip back to eastern Europe.

-

"Well you'll have to go on your own!" Helen stated resolutely.
He didn't reply.
"Did you hear me?"
"Yes dear."

"I mean it."

"Yes dear."

"I'm not joking."

 "No dear."

"Right then."

"OK dear."

"Go on your own then, if you don't want me to come along!" Helen frustratedly replied.

"I've got us seats on the plane by the windows, just exactly as you like them." He waited briefly, to let the news filter in slowly, before resuming. "And I've got the same hotel room next to the chiming clock tower, with the figurettes which come out on the quarter-hour."

Helen looked satisfied. Frank was now satisfied. Everything was planned.

He decided to go out to the aviary before it got dark, giving time for his birds to settle down then roost. As he changed his clothes he noticed a stream of birds pass across the view from his bedroom window, and he recognised them as rooks, more of a clamour than a parliament, making their way as a disorganised, spread-out group, skimming the tops of the trees as they wearily yet nosily flew past. After the initial clamour sauntered into the distance, a second group followed them, and then a third, with each successive group becoming progressively smaller. He tired of watching them, so went down to check on the feedstuffs in the aviary. As he approached the double doors to exit the aviary, he noticed a large rodent positioned on the top ledge of the outside door, clearly waiting or observing his actions. He wasn't quite sure why it was up there, and he wasn't quite sure what it was doing, but it was definitely an inconvenience, so he hesitated a moment as he thought over what to do next. The large rat took the initiative, launching itself off the door ledge, then straight towards him, teeth bared whilst squealing loudly as it acrobatically hurled itself in his direction. Instinctively he flattened his body position so that he now faced the screeching rodent side-on, watching it lose height as it catapulted over to where he was standing. The rat seemed to have some control over its intended direction of movement because after it landed onto the floor right next to his feet, it sharply entered a hole which he suddenly noticed in the side of the aviary flight wall, quickly disappearing. He didn't realise there was a rat problem. He did now though. The concrete walls had been deliberately lined with thick gauge wire to keep out rodents since their bodily waste could carry diseases. More importantly though, they'd also hunt his birds. After a rat had taken a hen Kakariki with its five chicks from a nest box, he'd been keen to ensure they couldn't gain access to any of the flights he might build in the future: however, this rodent had found a way in. Consequently he needed to remedy the situation, and quickly.

"I've got a rat in the aviary," Frank announced, somewhat annoyed.

"Well you'd better get it sorted before we go," Helen replied. He agreed. "And that's not the only thing which needs sorting," Helen added.

"So what is it now?" he asked, not really wanting to know.

"The washing machine is making a noise. A loud noise."

"Great!"

Frank put some washing into the machine to commence a cycle, when sure enough the loud noise duly announced itself, continuing to create a racket as it lumbered through the customarily uneventful sequence. In fact the noise became so loud during the spinning towards the end of the cycle, Frank believed the lid might come off. The lid did come off. It came off with good reason, because a concrete block which normally dampened the spinning action of the machine's drum, on this occasion only served to vibrate the entire washer, including itself, until finally it was wrenched from its mountings and smashed its way through the lid.

"Well that was noisy," Helen remarked.

"Yes, and I think it'll end up being a new washing machine," he replied.

"I think there's also a knock at the door. Quite a loud knock."

Frank went to see who it was, opening the front door to find their neighbour there, looking a little worried as well as an interesting shade of pale.

"Did you hear the bang?" Maxine asked, rather concerned.

"Yes, sorry it was our washing machine. Bit of a nightmare really. We haven't had it too long, although the last one lasted for about nine years."

"No," Maxine corrected him. "I meant under the ground."

"Oh, then I guess not, Maxine. I suppose I was preoccupied with our noisy washing machine. Underground?" he queried.

"It sounds a little strange. What's happened?"

"There was a loud bang down below, and my house was shaking as well."

Interestingly another neighbour had also come into their front garden and seeing Maxine, the two neighbours began to converse, albeit in the fading light. Two hours later a news channel announced how an earthquake had occurred in Kingsdever, with its epicentre directly below the village. Frank was surprised their washing machine had somehow become more noisy than an earthquake. He decided they'd better check the local shops for a new one. He mentally revised the idea to 'shops'.

When they'd previously lived in Balton their television had broken down and Frank left it outside their front door for someone to collect. He didn't mind who'd collect it. With other items they'd left outside, invariably by the next day someone had come along and obligingly removed anything at the front door, saving him a trip to the local recycling centre.

It worked a treat. This time however, he was a little surprised over subsequent events. The television once again disappeared from the front doorstep, so the following morning he went along with Helen to a local electrical shop with the idea of purchasing a new one. When they began slowly perusing the various lines of TVs on sale, they were amused to find their old one, the same one which had just broken down: it was proudly gleaming and staring back at them from a middle shelf at the back of the shop. However, the new old TV was seemingly in good working order, so how could he complain? In fact, he was pleased it was back to a decent use. Ultimately, the outcome was as entertaining as it was strange. 'But still kind of strange!' he concluded.

-

As the plane sped along the runway Frank settled down with a decent book. He'd always wanted to investigate LiDAR and what light it could shed on Mayans, Olmecs or Jaredites, so he thought he'd put his own time to good use. Besides, the archaeology had been previously discussed at one of the discussion group gatherings.

"That looks historical," commented a voice next to him, on the opposite side to Helen.

He wasn't quite sure whether the voice was addressed towards him, but after looking around then seeing how Helen was now looking out of the window, he decided it probably was after all. He wasn't convinced though whether he was keen to discuss a book he hadn't actually read yet. He remained non committal.

"Yes, Mayans, Olmecs and Jaredites, they're all fascinating."

"I've only heard of Mayans. Those other ones, were they also ancient religious civilisations with unpleasant pastimes?"

"I'm not too sure, but I'll let you know once I get through the book. I might not have finished it though by the time we land..."

"No matter. All those religions were just the same really, and a lot of them still are."

"What d'you mean?"

"Rather gruesome or a huge waste of time."

Frank wasn't impressed. He decided to comment. "Do you think our pilot today has spent time in a flight simulator?"

"Yes, I hope so!"

"Do you think he's gone through exactly what to do if there's an emergency?"

"Absolutely."

"D'you think there'll be an emergency today?"

"Statistically there's very little chance of anything happening, so no, actually I don't."

"Well was it worth the pilot's time, going through many different possible emergencies in a flight simulator?"

"Yes of course! Important lives are at stake."

"And for the same reason, religion's important."

"Oh, that's completely different. Lives aren't at stake with religion. We all die eventually, no matter what religious traditions people still cling onto, but safety on this plane is more immediately real."

"Hmmm," Frank contemplated. "The next dimension could easily be round the corner for any one of us, especially when we're on a plane. When we get there, we'll be there for quite some time, hence I think it's relatively relevant."

Helen stopped looking out of the window as the plane gained altitude.

"Don't bother the poor man, dear. He's probably just relaxing at the start of our flight."

"Oh, it's OK. I was just talking to your partner about ancient religions."

"My *wife* is the religious one in our family," Frank confirmed, dropping a hint which was hopefully not too subtle - he didn't believe he'd ever subscribe to the new rhetoric fashions.

"Let's swap over dear," Helen suggested. "You can read your book and I can talk to this nice man."

An hour later Frank looked up from his book. They were still talking.

As they disembarked the man handed Frank a piece of paper.

"I forgot to give your partner my phone number."

"My *wife*," Frank hesitated, ensuring the man had ample opportunity to understand the situation, "...doesn't usually make international calls."

"No, it's OK. It's a UK number."

When they'd left the plane, and Frank determined the man was watching them, yet Helen was concentrating on locating the exit, he fashioned the piece of paper into a suitable ball and launched a perfect basket into a nearby bin. He turned back towards the man before grinning broadly.

Half an hour later Helen remarked: "That nice man never gave me his phone number."

"Don't worry, you might see him on the way back," Frank replied, knowing his comment was suitably ridiculous.

"Actually it's OK. I remember now I gave him mine," Helen responded.

Frank decided he'd have a task for one of the kids to perform. He knew one day how all those inordinate number of hours they'd previously wasted on supposedly 'smart' phones, would eventually come in miraculously handy. Such a day had arrived. He wasn't familiar with Helen's phone and he certainly wasn't familiar with the procedure to block phone numbers which weren't on her contact list. Anyway, it wasn't long before Christmas would be coming back round again, which meant he had some leverage to ensure his new 'mission impossible' task would be carried out successfully. Satisfyingly, the catchy theme tune ran around in his head for quite a while, ensuring he was suitably entertained whilst they waited for their luggage to arrive at the carousel. It felt like fun at the fair.

-

The first night of their trip Helen received a premonition.

"What would you do if it snowed with a layer of six inches tonight, so the roads were impassable?"

"Oh, it doesn't look like snow. There aren't any dark clouds on the horizon, which means it might be a bit chilly, but it'll be fine."

When they woke up in the morning he looked out of the window to see a thick blanket of snow covering the entire city.

"What!" he exclaimed.

"What's the matter?" Helen asked.

"Have you looked outside?"

"No, not yet. Why?"

"Have a look..."

A few seconds later Helen returned with a broad smile from ear to ear.

"There, see. I said it would snow. I thought it would."

It took him an hour to walk into the university that morning, and when he returned he was less than jovial.

"I could do without all the walking," he complained, cleaning off his boots.

"I wouldn't bother too much with cleaning those dear, because it could snow another six inches tonight."

"Oh, don't be silly. It doesn't snow really heavily two nights in a row."

The following morning he opened the curtains to a scene of disbelief.

"No way! Totally ridiculous!"

"What's wrong now?"

"It's snowed again and it's twice as deep as before."

"I said it would," Helen said quietly.

His walk into the university took even longer than the day before, hence when finally he got back home he was even more grumpy.

"It's certainly not funny!" he protested.

"You'd better get used to it, because it could easily snow tonight."

"I'm not listening. Any more snow isn't funny! Definitely not funny..."

However, in the morning, as he drew back the curtains he found it hard to accept what now greeted him. Across the landscape he could see how a large, fresh layer of snow had been deposited overnight. He could tell it was most definitely fresh, because the cars which had been cleaned off or had travelled during the previous daytime were once again hidden under a thick, additional, white cover.

"We'll put a stop to all this nonsense," he declared. "You can't mention snow for the next fortnight!"

She didn't and it didn't snow again.

-

"So, what brings you back to Polgaria?" Jozef Kovac asked, as Helen passed the plate of cakes over towards Frank.

"Well, it sounds strange, but I had an inclination to talk with you about my father. A while back you'd said how you felt prompted by him. I'd like to contact him because I think he could answer some questions I have. There's also some project work I still have to do at the university."

"And what about this inclination you had... do you feel it was a premonition?" Jozef asked.

"I'm not sure," Frank responded.

"I think you're right to be unsure. My understanding of how

these things work Frank, is that God is a free agent and whilst we can ask Him for things, He can decide 'yes' or 'no' to our requests, or He could perhaps even come up with something else. Your father may or may not be allowed to contact you because we're not in control of those decisions, although we can still ask."

"OK, fair point."

"I believe differentiating between an inclination or a premonition is helpful. For me, it shows who's driving the communication. A premonition is coming from a source outside of an individual, whereas I believe an inclination is controlled by the individual. Both are important. It's just that one is more instructive."

"The premonition."

"Yes. Inclinations are the first step in raising good questions. Premonitions are the next step in providing good answers."

"So, d'you think I can gain answers to my questions?"

"I don't know. You can ask."

"And if there's no answer?"

"Wait, and just keep asking."

"Hmmm. Interesting."

"No different to a normal conversation. It's also silly to make up the answers. Well, actually you can... but you just end up talking to yourself."

"Hmmm. Annoying."

"Maybe."

-

"Well the visit to Jozef's was interesting."

"Yes, I know it was annoying dear, but at least you know what to do," Helen replied.

"And what's that?"

"Keep asking, then just wait. There's no harm in waiting. You can always get on with something else whilst you wait," she suggested.

"Hmmm," Frank mumbled. He was still mumbling after he'd dropped Helen off at her favourite shopping destination, then headed into the university. He'd not used a rental car abroad before, especially a left-hand drive. It didn't take long though to adapt to a new vehicle or for that matter, driving on the wrong side of the road. Fortunately parking at the university wasn't a problem.

"Excuse me, you're Frank aren't you?"

"Yes, hello. Who are you?"

"I'm Ethan, and I wondered whether I could seek your advice?"

"OK, sure. Please go ahead." He judged this young chap in front of him was probably in his late thirties, although it was unusual to find another Englishman in Polgaria. He was curious as to how the stranger had come to know who he was, yet he was presently more intrigued over what he was about to ask.

"I'm a student here at the university, and I'm very pleased to be here. It's a fantastic experience to travel in Europe by studying abroad, whilst the teaching here is excellent. I've qualifications from England but the Polgarian mixture of theory with practice is a complete pleasure. I have a problem though."

"Oh really. So what is it?"

"The university relies upon an income from foreign students, particularly one country, and whilst I thoroughly enjoy their company, unfortunately they're all cheating on exams. I'm working hard, getting decent exam results, however it's still not enough though when the pass mark is skewed so high by the universal level of cheating. What should I do?"

Frank was slightly taken aback. He'd known of a similar occurrence at a university in the Midlands back in England.

His brother had also exposed cheating whilst he was in English education: the subsequent social backlash from fellow students had been quite severe. Frank's care and respect for this university in Polgaria was significant, since he'd developed numerous friendships, so the news was unwelcomed. He hesitated as he contemplated over a response. The young English student described how the cheating was achieved, yet although the methodology was suitably inventive or devious, Frank wasn't surprised. Indeed, the scheme was elaborate to an extent where a protected business had been created amongst the foreign students, with payments taking place between them. They even had a name for the scheme, which they curiously called 'Newtons' - the rationale behind the name never actually came to light. Frank thought about the name, ultimately failing to uncover its origins.

"My dilemma," Ethan continued, "is my family is in Polgaria with me."

"How's it a problem?"

"One of the students in my group was a policeman, part of its Special Services division back in his home country. He asked for a lift into town one day, and as we drove through the city centre, he pointed out an individual in a thick, long overcoat. He asked me why he should be wearing such a coat on a really hot day, although I didn't have a clue. He stated the individual was concealing different currencies along with weapons inside the overcoat, then remarked I was a 'marked man' since I was intending to expose the cheating. He further commented how my family was here with me in Polgaria."

"Hmmm. I agree it doesn't sound helpful."

"I came into an histology lecture last week, sitting down in my usual place in the lecture hall. I happened to look down, when I noticed something shiny in the seating beneath me. Someone had placed a long, thick needle in the seating at the very position where my testicles would normally be, though on this occasion I'd sat back a little further, so I was lucky."

Frank hesitated once more, whilst he considered what he'd just heard. "OK, leave it with me. I think this can be sorted."

"Can you actually do anything for me?" Ethan asked.

"Don't worry. I believe I can help, because there's someone I know who's rather helpful."

"Thank you. I appreciate it."

"No worries."

CHAPTER 4

Frank learned from a colleague how the Polgarian university had held a Senate meeting to discuss the situation. He cared significantly about the university where the outcome he believed was important, thus he decided it was necessary to make a move quickly in providing some form of assistance. He made an appropriate phone call back to Surrey.

"It's no problem," replied Dr. Richard Klose. "Shimshani, the Chief Medical Officer from that country is in my office in a couple of weeks time. Just let me have the names of the cheating individuals and they'll never work professionally in their homeland after they graduate."

"Thanks Richard, I appreciate it."

"No worries."

"Perhaps we can catch up when I'm back in England."

"OK."

Frank also sent an email to the Dean in Koret asking whether it was normal for foreign students coming from his country to engage in cheating practices. The response was indirect, yet rapid. Yehoshua Yac made contact, requesting nothing was done immediately.

"I know you bring over a significant number of students Yehoshua, but I can't stand back forever."

"I just need some time."

"OK Yehoshua."

"It will be sorted."

Students were transferred to Koret and Frank did nothing more. He cared too much about the Polgarian university to have ignored what was happening.

'Kids these days!' Frank reflected, as he contemplated how the reason he could anticipate their next moves was because his own generation had already tried them out before. 'We're essentially no different,' he continued in thought. 'The secret is trying to minimise any of the bad stuff, whilst at the same time accentuating the good stuff.'

"Personal evolution is critical!" he concluded.

"Sorry, I do not understand the meaning."

Frank had ended up talking to himself again. What had begun this descent into daydreaming was the fact he'd fortuitously met up with Oded on the university campus, or at least just noticed him. He'd always associated the name 'Oded' with a powerful Viking god, whereby it was a fascinating association. Oded was a decent chap.

"Yes, apologies. I was thinking about something else and was busy talking to myself. It's an interesting pastime. How are things? By now, you must be getting well into that study course of yours. How are the others?"

"They are good, thank you." Oded paused. "I heard you caused some trouble with another student group in our year."

"I think they brought the trouble on themselves, Oded. When somebody cheats, they're asking for trouble, and this university doesn't need that kind of behaviour. Besides, they've gone back home, hopefully where they'll all be happy."

"You were lucky because one of those students was in the Special Services for our police force, and he is not a person you want to have as an enemy."

Frank thought for a moment. "To be honest Oded, I'd do

exactly the same thing again. Anything bad needs to be resisted."

"Yes, but there is a good time to resist, or a good time to leave alone."

"Well, I guess it comes back to my earlier, albeit mumbled comment. Personal evolution is a useful way forward, and there's no time like the present!"

Frank and Oded spoke on for a few minutes more before they made their ways to respective destinations. In line with previous encounters he continued to view Oded as a thoroughly decent person. In fact he considered all the students at the university to be decent. He was pleased they'd met up again.

-

Frank made his way back to Helen, this time at a new friend's house. Helen always made friends easily or quickly, consequently it wasn't surprising there was a different venue to learn. The new friend had learnt English from the BBC World Service programmes, which resulted in her English being excellent. He contemplated how foreign travel was made so much easier where most other countries used English as their international language.

'Maybe we're just lazy,' he pondered. He didn't ponder for too long though, since he approached the top of a hillside road which reminded him of the film 'Eddie the Eagle'. He'd previously attended some ice hockey games as well as athletics events, yet despite the fact he'd never watched ski-jumping before, the descent down the hill in front of him bore all the hallmarks of a ninety metre ski-jump. He wasn't keen. His last experience of an icy slope was back in England, during the winter on his way home. He'd driven up to a snow-covered road out in the countryside, but it turned out the snow on the road was in fact concealing a significant ice rink down below. He'd taken another way home on that occasion. This time though he sat staring at the ski-jump ahead. As he deliberated his next move, another car pulled along side before its driver wound down the window to begin a short conversation.

"No worry. You go hill. Good hill."

'Aghh, good old pigeon English he reminded himself. I try.' He steadied himself for an interesting dialogue. "I OK. Thank. I wait."

"See me. I go. You go. You same. You good."

"OK. Thank."

To Frank's amazement, the Polgarian winter sports driver sped off down the hill without a single hitch: Frank was dumbfounded. This driver was clearly as adept at the ninety metre ski-jump as he was also confident, gliding down the massive slope without a hint of a slide, nor a wobble, not even a touch on the brakes. The Polgarian car disappeared into the distance.

"Brilliant. I go!" Frank responded, still in conversation mode.

About half way down the slope, Frank noticed how his vehicle was no longer on the right-hand side of the road, nor specifically in the centre, nor even over to the left. In fact, it wasn't actually pointing down the hill at all, nor supposedly with its bonnet parallel to the centre white line which was customarily painted down the middle of the road. There were some other salient facts though: namely, quite often on Polgarian roads there weren't any centre white lines at all, similar to many of the countries across mainland Europe, and if there had been, they'd have been buried deep under the thick blanket of snow, which was now the only thing he could actually see. European roads also didn't usually have cats eyes. It was rather annoying because he'd come to rely upon them during the dark drives back home. This latter fact though wasn't really relevant since it wasn't dark. All the facts didn't register with him for very long, where he'd suddenly became preoccupied with the car's new driving position. It was really quite a curious diagonal shuffle, or more of an intermittent slide, where the windscreen was revealing as much of the passing roadside buildings or countryside, as it was of the road itself. The car was gliding effortlessly for a number of feet before the tyres regained some grip, throwing the front end back forwards again, then subsequently resorting back to its former diagonal position, usually facing the other way round. Frank contemplated it must have been like watching dancing on ice, with his vehicle impersonating a skater, although he wasn't too sure about the number of points he'd be getting for elegance or style. He briefly considered how many points he might get for technical ability since he was constantly, and he thought quite successfully, manoeuvring then counter-manoeuvring the steering wheel to fight the skid. All in all, this ninety metre ski-jump became one long memorial blur, leaving him particularly pleased when it finally ended. As the car came to a halt, his front windows were still half open. Another Polgarian driver pulled alongside - he was also an expert at pigeon English:

"Be safe. No slip hill. Not brake hill. Drive down, not brake future."

Frank smiled and waved. He wasn't quite sure how the Polgarian had likewise managed to career down the hill, seemingly without any display or degree of difficulty. 'Maybe they've all been practising for years,' he consoled himself.

-

"I just don't get it," Frank protested. "They flew down that hill like it was a Formula One racetrack. I was all over the place. I didn't touch the brakes until the car started sliding, but it was still all over the place. I just don't get it," he repeated, continuing as though the repetition would somehow provide some level of insight.

Helen disappeared into the kitchen. Several minutes later she reappeared.

"I've spoken with Ingrid, and she says they put winter weather tyres on the cars over here as soon as the snow falls. They change back to summer tyres in the spring... after the snow thaws."

The secret to the Polgarian Formula One drivers had suddenly been revealed, and what a revelation it turned out to be.

"It's all in the tyres!"

"Yes dear, so you can stop worrying now."

"Well not really, because it means I'll still be at a distinct disadvantage if I'm in a street race with one of these Polgarians, or if we're running out of..."

Helen had left the room to rejoin Ingrid. Frank reflected how tyres certainly did made a difference, having noticed their evolution when he'd recently purchased another motorbike. He'd never managed to ride out with Helen when the kids were small and he'd owned a GPZ900, but this time he'd got hold of a Z1000SX whilst also improving his riding gear. He planned to enjoy riding out with Helen. Helen still looked beautifully young, and she'd also ridden a motorbike when she was in her early twenties, hence he knew she'd be an excellent pillion. Frank loved being close to Helen – she was the perfect wife for him, and she knew he knew it.

-

"Can we drop in on Jozef on the way back?"

"Why d'you want to see Jozef?"

"I want to ask him something."

"About what?"

Frank played his trump card. He was sure it would result in a green light, therefore he used it, and used it well. "About religion."

Helen said nothing. He was contented the correct move had been selected. As they approached the front door though there was still some hesitation, because he'd not asked this form of question before.

"How can I help?" Jozef asked.

"Well, if I can't rely upon receiving answers from my father in order to solve questions, then where's the best place to look for solutions?"

"I think I'd better ask another question before suggesting any ideas."

"What d'you mean?"

"If you could only ask one question before receiving an answer, what would the question be about?"

This line of thought perplexed Frank. It just wasn't expected, although after a few moments he began to give it some due consideration. Jozef had previously shown his ideas to hold decent merit, so this mental thread was unlikely to prove fruitless. Frank thought seriously. What would be of most value to him if he could only receive one answer to his many questions? 'Well, I've got my own ideas about psyche or where my investigations might lead, and half the fun in research is not knowing what will come out of it all, which means maybe I don't really need to know where the research will take me. Besides, if I find something useful in the research, there's no guarantee anyone else will actually agree with it anyway... even if the evidence is reasonably rock solid. A lot of science is in reality an art since most importantly, science relies upon the art of presentation, where it's vital to present ideas which appeal to whatever an audience is already interested in... or is that actually true? Will truth strike a chord, no matter what an audience is expecting? Surely if there's a deity, then truth will resonate with people? A supreme intelligence must be able to disseminate truth, or short-circuit the massive guessing which science constantly employs and regularly throws out over time?' He paused. 'With all that in mind, what would I ask?' He still paused. 'I'd ask about family or where we're heading. Where will we all be in fifty years, or even a hundred years time?'

"Where will we be in a hundred years time?"

Jozef's expression broke into a smile. "It's a good question. A very good question. If you were the Supreme Intelligence in a universe, or you wanted to answer an individual's question, how would you answer it?"

"I guess it would depend upon what the question was about, who was asking, or whether they would actually bother listening to an answer."

"If an individual didn't know for sure over the fact you existed, would you still communicate with them?"

"Yes, if they'd listen."

"Would you communicate with your full overwhelming power?"

"No, that would be significantly scary or probably pointless. There would be nothing to prove. Only information to disseminate, information which could help."

"Which raises the question, how would your communication be?"

"I guess, simple or clear. Probably easy-going."

"I believe the same thing as well." Jozef paused. "Yet what about someone who didn't believe you existed? Would you easily communicate with them as well?"

"They'd probably dismiss anything I might tell them, so there might not be a lot of point in communicating. I'm not sure though."

"Neither am I."

"If a person was the head of state, I'd certainly be encouraging them to stay calm or not cause wars. I'd show them how to cooperate, then work with other states to benefit each other. I'd attempt to dissuade them from acting selfishly because what goes around usually comes around."

"Would you bother to communicate with different heads of states across the world?"

"Absolutely, because their actions will usually influence a great number of people, and I'd want them to always act for the good of people. Any communications would probably be about their jobs, as the heads of states."

"And what about any situations where heads of states were also parents?"

"Yes, I'd give suggestions on parenting as well. But they'd need to ask about parenting specifically."

"Why?"

"If an individual doesn't ask, I'm guessing they're unlikely to be listening for an answer... whatever or whenever it's given. Conversations are ineffective if you're talking to yourself."

"Good point. So in summary, do you feel that communications from a Supreme Intelligence would be clear, even quiet or not dramatic, and probably relate to questions which were asked by any given individual, or upon any given subject area?"

"Yes, I suppose I do believe your description there could be accurate. I'm undecided though upon how I'd go about delivering my suggestions to different individuals."

"Are we communicating effectively at the moment?"

"For sure."

"Well I see no reason to believe a Supreme Intelligence couldn't effectively communicate with individuals across the universe. There must be many forms of communication, just as there are many global languages, but a Supreme Intelligence would have the experience to use any effective mode of communication. Effective communication can be different for different individuals. The recipient is as important as the provider of information. Some information may simply be delivered as suggestions, especially if there are different, even equally good alternatives."

"So what's the secret in distinguishing between ideas which originate within a person's mind or communications coming from an external source?"

"I believe it's the same as knowing when you're talking to someone else, or merely talking to yourself."

"It's slightly more complex than that," Frank proposed.

"I agree, but the basic idea remains true. For example after my wife died, my daughter began sending me cards which she felt were inspired from her mother. One card said how my wife 'would always be near', and as I read it I heard three distinct taps in my bedroom. I went to the door to see whether my lodger had wanted my attention, although he wasn't to be found because he was still at work. I believe the distinct taps were in fact rooks on the roof, and yet if I was attempting to make my presence known from the next dimension, I would probably want to use something natural. Natural occurrences don't remove the need for faith. Instead they allow an individual to be drawn towards good things by gentle associations. I associated the taps I'd heard with the card and my wife, whilst I don't actually know what happened."

"It could merely have been a fertile imagination, borne of the need to find answers."

"Or more important perhaps, it could easily have been a solution with much less fuss."

"I think we're important enough for a bit of drama... if our psyches were actually born as His kids in a former dimension. A burning bush scene would do just fine... plus a booming voice coming out of it!"

"Which would generally lead to a neighbourhood forest fire, because as you say, everyone's psyche is born of Heavenly

Parents, so we'd all want the same thing. If it happens, the voice is also likely to be a still small voice, because it means the recipient needs to be listening."

"Yes, but from Biblical accounts the neighbourhood forest would never actually be consumed, which would make quite a spectacular show! That's entertaining!"

"With the result our mortal lives would only end up as an entertainment show... for most of the time."

"Well what's wrong with such a thing? It would certainly be fun."

"Fun for some, although no work would probably get done. We need to exercise faith, or to have an opportunity to do things which we couldn't do in the pre-existence. Evolution is forever about personal change or progression."

"What's particularly important about faith? In your experience, why couldn't your wife have just made contact?"

"Sometimes those things can happen, although most of the time in mortality we're here to see how we'll act when God isn't present, because we spent aeons of time with Him in the pre-existence. This mortal life would prove little if we could see Him all the time once again. We need to love goodness for the sake of goodness, not only down to the fact we were familiar with it in the pre-existence, or because we frequently associated with God as our spirit-body Father. My guess is God's constantly looking at the right moments for us in mortality, to let His good ideas come our way."

"Fair enough. As you say though, it would mean we'd need to be open to premonitions whenever they came."

"Yes it would. Quite often we spend too much time concerned about what other people think of how we're doing, or how many honours we've won, or how much money we've gathered. God doesn't compare His children, so I don't believe He wants us to compare ourselves with each other. God's objective for each of us, is to become the best version of ourselves, whatever it means."

"Yes, I can appreciate those are interesting ideas," Frank concluded. He was pleased things had come to a sensible conclusion.

-

Two men stood together. They were dressed in white suits, white shoes and white ties and were deeply engaged in discussion.

"At this rate our work will soon become redundant."

"But he's doing a rather good job though."

"Yes he is, and I don't want to be reassigned onto someone new just yet."

"Maybe. Although there are some things which are only possible from this dimension, so maybe we're not in the realms of redundancy for the foreseeable future."

"What do you have in mind?"

"I'll show you."

"Mind you, I haven't really thought about the future for quite some time. In fact, probably since I passed through the veil from mortality."

"It's what mortality does for you. It places time limits on things, where everyone is concerned about how much time they have left."

"If mortality went on forever though, the test of mortality would go one forever. That would've been too much for me!"

"Good point. I agree."

CHAPTER 5

Frank walked around the building for a second time with Helen. The surrounding grounds were immaculate, with botanical greenery creating a stunning contrast against the pristine impact of this massive white edifice. Rows of beautifully nodding bulb blooms filled columns of perfectly neat flowerbeds. An ornate wooden bridge spanned a small, man-made lake in the centre of luxurious lawn carpets, and a Tudor mansion house in the distance displayed a spectacular backdrop of historical preservation. This visual scene provided its own wonderfully anachronistic setting to their picturesque evening stroll.

"So why would anyone spend so much money on a building like this?" Frank commented.

Helen thought for a while. "I view it as a little piece of heaven on Earth."

"I bet the homeless could do with some of that money in their pocket, if nothing else, to buy some food or to find a place to sleep for the night."

"Yes, you're right. Charities are very important and I support charity. I want you to come along with me to our next charity walk."

Frank suddenly went quiet.

"But in answer to your other question..."

"Which question?" Frank interrupted.

"The question about the temple."

"Is that what it is?"

"Yes, and without a temple, we'd find it more difficult to focus upon the eternal goals we have for this life."

"What goals?"

"To be together as a family after we pass into the Spirit World."

"The next dimension, you mean?"

"Call it differently if you like, but we need to be together as a family. You don't want to go there alone do you?"

"No I don't." He took hold of Helen's hand. "What's a temple got to do with family?"

"In a temple families can be sealed together, and we could be married."

"Well that would be daft because we're already married."

"Only for this life."

"No, I don't believe it. We stay married in the next dimension."

"But our Chapel wedding said 'married until death, do we part'."

"Well I don't agree with the idea."

"About being sealed together?" Helen looked suitably concerned.

"No, about not being married in the next dimension."

"That's what we agreed at our Church wedding."

Frank became quiet again.

-

He woke up with a jolt. Helen was sleeping quietly beside him.

"I've had another dream."

Helen turned over towards him. "It's not unusual," she said, turning back the other way.

"Have you ever seen a temple?" he asked.

"Yes, in London," Helen replied gently.

"What did it look like?"

"White and large. With lots of flowers and an old house nearby. There are lawns around the old house."

"Was the old house Tudor style?"

"Yes, I think it was. Why?"

"Then I've seen it as well."

"When did you see it?"

"Just now. In a dream. You've described the same thing I saw."

"I keep telling you but you never listen to me. If you have a little faith everything is possible. You can get answers to anything you want, if you take the time to ask or pray about it. You can..."

Frank had stopped listening. How could Helen describe what he'd experienced in his dream? How could it be possible? He'd had dreams before but this was a whole new experience. This was curious.

-

Jozef's expression broke into a smile, as Frank finished details of his dream. "You're becoming better at this," he commented.

"Better at what?"

"At receiving answers."

"What answer have I received?"

"Last time, you asked where you'll be in a hundred years time."

"How did you know I was talking about family?" Frank queried.

"The way you held onto Helen's hand. I'm guessing you feel about her, in the same way I feel about Doris."

"How long ago did Doris die?"

"Sixteen years ago."

"How do you know you're still be married to her in the next dimension?"

"Because I've been sealed to her."

"When was that?"

"Forty-six years ago."

"In a temple?"

"Yes."

Frank became silent. "I'm not religious. I'm just interested in the future."

"That's good."

"Are you always religious?"

"I'm probably more like you, because I'm interested in the future, although also my family's future."

Frank became silent. He finally voiced what he was thinking. "I don't believe in predestination nor the implications of time travel. Time could theoretically hold a recorded map which might be re-travelled, but changing a reconstructed recording won't affect the past. I'm fully signed up to the concept of recorded history by deity, or human or psyche memories, yet I can't accept our future is mapped out. Every individual acts independently with freedom of choice, choosing what they'll do or what they'll follow. So how could deity see into the future of humanity?"

"Perhaps it's a little like the way we guess what our children will do. When we've seen our children react to different situations, quite often we can anticipate what they'll do in similar situations. It doesn't mean we're controlling the future, it only means we're becoming better at predicting the future."

"Yes, I suppose your point's a useful one. With the disease models I've developed, it's been interesting because many diseases have a subclinical form which is infectious before clinical signs appear, so the disease may be transmitted extensively before it's diagnosed. Subclinical transmission can mean that many individuals show clinical signs together at first diagnosis. Consequently, the disease incidence in the first time period of an outbreak or epidemic, usually correlates closely with final prevalence for diseases with a subclinical form."

"Therefore the level of subclinical disease can predict the future," Jozef repeated back for clarity.

"Yes, it can... and quite accurately." Frank nodded slowly, as much in recognition of Jozef's previous example, as in recognition of his last comment.

"It's still probably worth remembering how sometimes even the most unlikely outcomes become reality, where deity will work with anyone who's willing to try. It doesn't matter too much what people have done in the past, if they're still willing to change in the future. Evolution is about change or progression."

"What d'you mean?"

"During my time here at the university there was a colleague who constantly criticised religion or numerous points of church life. Parky was a fascinating person but after a while his moaning became tiresome, with the result I began to avoid him. Then one day he approached me stating he had been inside a temple, which I found hard to believe because it would have required a recommend pass. I remembered though how temples hold open days for the public before they are dedicated, meaning it was possible. Then came something not expected. Parky related the fact whilst he was inside the temple he felt something, or a goodness which he could not explain. I could not believe it. I was amazed. I realised deity could contact any man or any woman at any moment, in any place, and the only thing which a person needed to do was to listen. It was a revelation for me at the time, so one which I have not forgotten."

Frank marvelled at Jozef's level of articulation, and his skill with languages. He wondered how he might purvey his own rationales in Polgarian, if only he had a single inkling of how to purvey anything in Polgarian. Frank paused, before relating a story of his own.

"I had an experience with a good friend. He was excellent company, which meant I was shocked when he was diagnosed with Alzheimer's. His future didn't look good and I wondered how he'd cope, because he had a deep belief in deity. Anyway, whenever I met with Eric, along with his wife Marcia, he seemed a little worse than before. In the end communicating with him became virtually impossible. Then I noticed how he'd become very frustrated, because he couldn't reply coherently whenever he was attempting conversation. One day I wanted to find out what was really going on, and it was at his birthday party... I believe he was about eighty at the time. Anyway, I said to Eric, "I reckon you can understand exactly what I'm saying. I think the problem is you just can't get a reply out, therefore I'll be the one talking for a while. I wouldn't worry about a reply, as I think you know what you want to say." What happened next surprised me. I watched a tear fall from Eric's right eye, followed just a few seconds later by a second one. Maybe I'd guess correctly. I'd like to hope I did."

Jozef gave due space for Frank's story to settle into a satisfactory conclusion, after which, he commented: "I am grateful that deity has allowed more methods of communication beyond speech."

"Yes, I guess it was true with Eric. I suppose it's also true with dreams, or with new ideas which can suddenly arise from quiet contemplation."

"And it is all free!"

"I suppose it is," Frank agreed.

"Deity will always communicate with any person who will

listen."

"Hmmm."

Frank became silent. He wondered how Eric was doing in the Spirit World.

CHAPTER 6

"Callum, come down here quick! But make sure you say something first."

Callum uttered his doubled worded speech, then sprinted along the corridor towards the finish line, which ended up in the lab room.

"Come on, sit down or you'll miss it. Here we go. Wait for it. It's coming..."

They both sat glued to the computer screen, staring intently with anticipation.

"Goodbye. Bye."

Dusan looked across slowly, half contentedly yet half in disbelief. He wasn't quite sure what he should address first. "Was that it?"

"Well yes, because I was thinking quickly."

"You said the same thing twice."

"Well yes, because I had to think quickly."

Dusan wasn't impressed. "OK, never mind. It was still excellent though. D'you realise that you're faster than yourself?"

"I knew I was pretty fast."

"Well there you have it. You can travel faster than the workings of a CCTV system. But next time, look up at the camera."

"I was concentrating on getting down here."

"The camera was right above you. All you had to do was look up and grin."

"Well maybe, but I was getting ready for the sprint."

"I'm only pleased you're not repeating the same excuse about thinking quickly."

"Yes. There's that as well."

Frank began clapping, slowly but quite loudly. "Well done gentlemen, a nice display."

Dusan was the first to react. He spun around, seeking out the unexpected introduction, an introduction offered by two individuals who were now seated towards the back of the room. He almost toppled over in his own chair, stumbling under the exertions. Callum on the other hand, adopted a more vocal approach.

"Wooooowww! What the....!?!"

"Well held Callum. You didn't use bad language," Jozef observed.

"Sorry. We didn't know you were there."

"Yes, quite clearly," Frank added, rather amused by the reaction of the two young men, somewhat crestfallen after the exuberance of their experimental success. "I thought you said the people who worked with you were sensible as well as hard-working, Jozef?"

"Well, there is always an exception to a rule."

"Yes, quite."

"But these two are OK. Sometimes."

"Where did they get their English from?"

"Dusan is my nephew's son. He spent about one year in the United States. Callum is one of the friends he met while he was in the United States."

"So they're here to be trained then."

"Well that was the idea, but I'm not too sure whether it is working very well."

"Hmmm. These two could certainly take a while."

"That's the worrying thing."

The two laboratory technicians had endured enough, quickly making their hasty exit through the door to the right, slightly ahead, yet the same door which had just doubled up as a finishing line for the athlete's CCTV experiment. They disappeared with no more fuss.

"Excuse me briefly Frank, I believe the phone is ringing in my office."

"Sure."

A few moments later Jozef reappeared. "This phone call is for you."

"For me?"

"Yes, I believe it is."

"OK, thank you," Frank replied, a little surprised.

A few moments later Frank reappeared. "I think you'd better speak to him."

"You'd like me to speak with him?"

"Yes please."

"OK, I will."

A few moments later Jozef reappeared. They both look surprised.

"I think we had better go over there."

"Yes, I think so," Frank concurred.

The following morning Jozef accompanied Frank along with Helen on a plane back to England, but before they left Frank sent email messages to Richard Klose from his laptop.

< Richard,

I hear there's an epidemic back in England and the Prime Minister's asking for ideas on a website. You know a fair amount about the subject. How about sending him a few ideas? >

A reply came back unusually quickly.

<< Yes, I actually saw him last week. >>

< What do you mean when you say you saw him last week? That was a joke, yes?>

<< I'm advising the government, so I travelled down to number 10 with Alex. We also saw the minister Nick Green beforehand. >>

< I was only joking btw! Well that's interesting. What did you tell them? >

A few emails later Frank understood the situation a little better and was pleased the epidemic was in good hands.

-

Over the next few months Frank watched his colleague or mentor become frustrated over the use of mathematical modelling, although more significantly over a level of politics which he never realised existed within academia: at least, he'd never anticipated such seemingly close associations between various academics and politicians. Frank accepted that in some respects he still remained quite naïve. He'd not been quite sure what to take seriously when he'd previously watched the television series 'Yes, Minister!' followed up by its sequel 'Yes, Prime Minister!' Both series were highly entertaining, yet little did he realise they'd become a perfect introduction to the stories or events which Richard Klose would later relate to him, all in rather fascinating detail.

-

"Remind me never to become a politician, Jozef!"

"Yes OK, I will."

"When?"

"Whenever you need me to do so."

"Agghh. Good answer." He paused. "Let's meet the others in

our discussion group. We've been debating philosophical issues quite regularly now for some time."

"And it's a good venue for a decent meal," Kieron added. "So is this Professor Jozef Kovac? How did you manage to get him over here?"

"I'm visiting England to observe what happens with your epidemic. It will likely reach my country, so I can bring back some advice with me."

"Well that was a decent slice of luck Frank, eh? We finally get to meet Jozef Kovac."

Dave leaned over towards Kieron before quietly whispering: "Why didn't he just pick up the phone and make an international call? Surely, it's got to be cheaper than an air ticket."

"Perhaps because there's some additional reason he's over here."

"Fair enough."

-

Two men stood together. They were dressed in white suits, white shoes and white ties and were deeply engaged in discussion.

"Well this won't be pretty."

"What do you mean?"

"Allowing this virus to cause disease amongst the mortal population is certainly going to cause a huge amount of hardship."

"I'm not so sure that's true."

"What do you mean?"

The questioning had been swapped around.

"You know how many diseases have been held back and carefully prevented from taking their natural course of action."

"Yes, I know. It's good, isn't it?"

"I have to agree it's been good in the past, but maybe not though this time around."

"Well why not... if it was good in the past, then surely it's good again now?"

"There are many mortals at this moment in time who either need to come home to the Spirit World, or would just like to come home. Every mortal life has its testing period, and when such a period has ended, mortal life can sometimes be extended further, but the test has still been completed."

"So are you suggesting many mortals are due to come into the Spirit World, perhaps all at the same time, plus right now?"

"It can be good for mortals to come through the veil of mortality together, as they graduate into our dimension."

"So why now?"

"There's always an appropriate time for a test to become completed. Others have to stay and come along later because families don't often leave mortality as a group or at the same time. If that always happened it could mean entire family lines would cease to exist."

"OK, maybe it's true. Yet why do so many have to come across together? How many will come over this time?"

"There will be many, although not as many as previously have come over at times like these."

"We'd better get ready."

"Yes, I think we probably should."

-

He saw them come from every stretch of the Earth, from every land, farm, even hilltop, from snow-capped, freshly cleaned mountains and wide open, sun-kissed grasslands disappearing as far as the eye could see. He saw them gather from deeply uncharted rainforest, lush and green, humming to watery white rapids as they cut paths through nature. He saw them gather, and they came in thousands. They came, and they kept coming. Thousands upon thousands, tens of thousands. From populous and magnificent cities, from beautifully picturesque village homesteads, from modern, metropolis strongholds and classical, even historically ancient venues. Initially a stream, quickly a flash flood, eventually a vast sea, forming an ocean of souls pouring out relentlessly across the veil which spanned between mortality and the next dimension. He could see the next dimension clearly, quite photographically. There was little need for an imagination. He could see it all precisely in strong, touchable reality. The dimension was termed a Spirit World by those who occupied these realms because he'd heard them previously refer to it as such. The realms were bounded by a spiritual jacket fitting more loosely or expansively around the Earth, compared to the physical boundaries which mortals were accustomed to, or confined within. It was strange he'd never considered how the Earth could be bounded out much further than he'd envisaged, beyond the hard but beautiful surface he travelled upon. It was a useful surface, however spirits were privileged with more freedom, freedom to roam at quite some distance from the Earth, 'not unlike an astronaut's craft' he thought. They were unfettered, moving rapidly across the expanse which was open to them, perhaps more so during journeyings. He wondered what they were doing? Whatever it was though, it seemed important. He watched as they were gathering from mortality. He was curious, stopping to observe for a moment, one particular individual who'd made a tardy passage across the veil. He was interested.

He was a frail man, probably in his early seventies, clearly worn down by mortal worries, so worn down in fact, he was hooked up to a ventilator and heart monitor from his hospital bed. This was fascinating, or at least it would be when this chap finally passed through to the Spirit World. He expected him to trudge wearily out of his body, then slowly float up towards the ceiling, but he was out of that old mortal frame in a flash. Suddenly someone appeared next to him, dressed in white, with a neat suit, white shoes and a white tie. They seemed to know each other, so they chatted a while before making their way over towards the veil. He could usefully see both dimensions. The veil from the mortal side looked beautifully white, pristine, almost brilliant in its radiance. He was captivated. Looking back from the Spirit World the veil was greyish, less appealing, less refined. He wasn't sure whether the view into mortal life was the better one to be honest, and he concluded that he preferred the view looking slightly up into the Spirit World. Anyway, the moment of truth had arrived. The old mortal gentleman, who was somehow beginning to look quite a fair bit younger already, was suddenly about to make the transition across the veil. He passed through without much fuss, but once he'd arrived into the Spirit World realm, then all the fuss certainly began. A whole crowd of people were waiting on the other side of the veil, positioned at the exact place where he'd made the transition. It was as though they knew the precise point where to place themselves. He came through and a woman happily bounded over towards him, wrapping herself around him. This had to be his mortal wife and the chap was astounded, totally thrilled, his eyes were extended out on spiritual stalks.

It seemed as though he couldn't believe himself. He grasped onto her in an embrace suggesting he hadn't seen her in decades, which was probably quite true. He certainly wasn't going to let her go again - at least, not for a few millennia! Tears ran freely and soon they were all off to a family's spiritual party. Frank wondered what such a party would be like, whether they'd have any food, or balloons or music. Frank woke up with a jolt.

"You've got to be joking!" he exclaimed. He looked over at Helen. She was still sleeping, which rather surprised him because he usually managed to wake her up whenever he woke up during the night – it was as though she was tuned into anything he said, especially whenever he dreamt about psyches or something connected with the next dimension. He never did quite figure it out.

"Yes, I'm awake, and no I don't want to know this time, because I keep telling you that if you only listened and had a little faith you could find out all sorts of things, but you never listen to me so why should I bother, and it never gets me anywhere because you never listen, and as much as I tell you, you never..."

Frank thought she was cute when she was angry, although he also believed Helen was cute most of the time. It was quite hard for him to take any of her tirades too seriously.

He was asleep again. He came into what he believed was a celestial Albert Hall, decked from top to bottom in the most beautiful white marble. True to form there was an orchestra in the centre of the hall, with seating and galleries wrapped around the central focus of this new occasion, yet the scale of the celestial building was beyond anything he could possibly have imagined, let alone seen during his mortal lifetime. This was vast, truly vast and he marvelled at it for quite some time. He now instinctively knew why so many souls had been gathering in his last dream. They were gathering across the veil for the occasion which he was about to witness, yet 'what could it be? What's so momentous that thousands upon tens of thousands, maybe millions of souls would be gathering into a building such as this one?' He wasn't left wondering for long. What happened next would probably stay with him for eternity. Immediately before this juncture, he noticed how he felt extremely good and comfortable in the presence of the people around him, where each was emitting a very cordial and friendly, plus caring or cooperative aura, even an ambience from the building itself was extremely pleasant. He wondered how a building could create such a good atmosphere, but he remembered other places he'd visited which he'd also enjoyed in the same way. These were good people and they were in a very decent place. At that moment a massive force for virtue entered the building, with a power of kindness, surrounded by goodness which he could only describe as inescapably larger than all the forces within the universe. He judged this power was greater than everything powerful in the universe combined, and it was overwhelmingly excellent. It was full or complete, and governing or fantastically evolved. In fact, it was simple in pointing towards perfection. 'Well, that's a relief!' Frank told himself. 'I'm pleased. I can rest more easily now, because with such limitless goodness, everything has to work out OK. Nothing bad could be so strong in the universe!' This focus was actually rather hard not to notice. Yet as he observed, he perceived the power was a being, a Being whom somehow he was also familiar with, albeit he felt the familiarity was remembered from a different time, seemingly beyond his mortal existence. A time perhaps before mortal time? It reminded him of the previous dreams he could remember concerning a pre-existence, or someone he'd met during such a period of existence.

"You've got to be joking! This is... this is the Father of our spirits."

"Yes Frank, you've remembered. It is Him. Who is He?"

Frank turned towards the person now standing next to him. There was his earthly father, and suddenly he noticed another person was standing next to him on the other side. There was his earthly grandfather.

"You've got to be joking!" he repeated.

"We only joke once!" remarked his grandfather. "So who is the person we're observing Frank?"

"It's..."

"Yes, you can say it."

"It's... the Father."

"Yes. Or God."

"I didn't say that."

"No, but I said it for you... because it'd be easier. And quicker..."

"Yes." Frank kept looking forwards. This was unimaginable, and unimaginably divine. He wasn't quite sure what to say. He came up with something. "The light from the Father is the most fantastic light I've seen. The feeling from the light is pure, and hugely or goodly powerful. I don't think what I've just said, actually makes sense."

"Don't worry. It makes sense."

Frank had never known his grandfather in mortality because he'd died nearly forty years before he was born, yet from their encounters he was coming to appreciate his sense of humour, mixed strongly with a level of kindness. He grandfather was OK.

The next thing he noticed was the Father wasn't alone. In fact there was another who almost looked or seemed exactly like Him, and was with Him.

"There's two of them!"

"Yes."

"How can there be two?"

"Well, who is the second person, Frank?"

"It's..."

"Yes?"

"It's... a relative of the Father."

"Yes. You can say it. He's Christ."

"Yes, He is." Frank paused. "So why are we here?"

"To listen to some music."

"Really?"

"Yes. And to celebrate."

"Celebrate what?"

"Our graduation."

"How have we graduated?"

At that moment the music commenced. It started slowly, carefully, intricately, moving gently outwards on distinctive layers of floating musical finesse, at the same time unravelling various acoustic gems in exquisite interest, with themes playing out their respective stories, touching on synchrony with tales coordinated above, below and around them. The harmony created was captivating, motivating, whilst the musical details were mesmerising. Frank realised how the graduation was heavenly, and it was perfect, but he felt inadequate. Indeed, this was Helen's domain, yet he was far less certain of his own position. The music came to a section where everyone began to join in. He'd never had much of an inclination for song, but he too wished to join in, along with everyone else. The mood was close to a final song of Last Night at the Proms, and yet the desire to sing along was more of an affirmation where everyone was choosing all that was good, with everything which spelt peace, cooperation and pleasant conformity. These types of feelings couldn't be forced or manufactured, because they had to be experienced freely to be real. The feelings were real but were also strong. Strangely enough he had a similar type of feeling at the Shed end of the Chelsea Football Club stadium, although this heavenly event was a little different though. 'For one thing, there aren't any away supporters,' he reflected. Such an event was so very good. The Chelsea matches were good, but in a slightly different way...

Frank woke up with a jolt. Again. He didn't say anything. He wasn't quite sure what he'd just dreamt or experienced, whilst he knew he'd easily recognise the feeling which had accompanied it. It felt quiet, peaceful and definitely good. That word seemed to come up a lot. "Good," he repeated to himself.

CHAPTER 7

"Jozef is taking us up to London."

"Oh really?" Frank replied with a half question.

"Yes, he wants to show us something, and afterwards we can go onto Kew Gardens. Robert wants to come."

Frank didn't reply, so Helen knew he was OK with the arrangements. He enjoyed going to horticultural venues with Helen and Robert. Robert had recently graduated with an Extended Diploma in Horticulture from an Agricultural College, whilst Helen had gained an interest in plants from her mother during childhood. Frank had begun to develop a liking for gardening from their youngest along with Helen's interest, so slowly or gradually he'd started to join them in the summer months as their back garden grew into something quite delightful. He was proud of Robert's achievements. It was a pleasure to see. He reflected how all his kids had done well - Robert in Horticulture, Jane as a reporter, and the other two as lawyers. His own father had suggested half the secret to a good working life was to choose something enjoyable, which inherently would be different for different individuals. He passed the same thought onto his own children.

As they drove along the main road A22 from the motorway, he suddenly became aware of a spire appearing in the distance, just above the tops of the trees.

"There seems to be a cathedral spire in the distance," Frank commented. "It's useful how we seem to be going towards it, because we could pass by quite soon."

"Yes, we could," Jozef replied.

In fact they did. They passed so close to the building Frank caught full view of it from the roadside, where they drove slowly alongside. It was a large white edifice with a tall spire, which at first looked greyish or even black, but a second more careful glance showed the way it was in fact green. The white limestone contrasted uniformly against the spire. There was another much older building to the right-hand side, throwing large, dark wooden beams across a wattle and daub theme which created the walls. A combination of such history situated proximal to a newer, fascinatingly pristine, more modern structure, somehow only served to announce the importance of architectural complement, and Frank felt it worked really quite well.

"It's curious the spire is green," Frank observed.

"Yes, it's a copper layer that creates the green fascia. It is unusual and I like it."

"So do I," added Helen as they reached a small roundabout a few hundred yards further along the road.

"A left turn here please," Jozef asked, and which Frank obligingly performed.

"Then left again."

"But that'll take us through the entrance."

"Yes please."

Frank was curious now. As he drove in through the entrance gates, subsequently into the car park, the Tudor building was over to their left, with the large white modern looking cathedral situated ahead, now slightly to the right. The gardens were immaculate with lawns laid out in verdant uniform sections, showing off fantastic splashes of flowerbed colours, and yet still modestly, interestingly, perhaps excitedly -

although more to the point, carefully. Alighting from the car, something seemed strongly familiar about the scene he'd begun to observe: the Tudor house in all its historical majesty, the white modern cathedral alongside, the flowerbeds with lawns. A peaceful, quiet calm was gently enveloping the entire site, and Frank wondered what it could be?

"Flying spuds! This is remarkable!"

"Yes it is, isn't it?"

"Well actually, I meant about my dream."

"Yes, I do know."

Frank paused. "That's why we've come here, isn't it?"

"Yes it is. So you could have some time to see what a temple is like."

"So it isn't a cathedral then?"

"It is similar."

"What does it do?"

"It allows families to be together forever."

"They are together... I don't understand."

"For the next dimension."

"I believe such a situation is true anyway."

"And the ceremonies inside a temple are like your belief, because people make contracts, in the same way that marriage is a contract."

"So it's another marriage being offered."

"Yes. Amongst other things."

"What other things?"

"In the Odes of Solomon, Christ is reported to have access to other dimensions, as well as other worlds within the other dimensions. Christ gives us access to them because He is the gatekeeper. He set up and created other worlds, as instructed and directed by God the Father, who is the God of many dimensions. In this way, Christ can grant access to other places according to His will, just as long as it is OK with the Father. In the temple, information is given to people which will help them when they pass into the next dimension after death, when they will seek access to their families in other places."

"Interesting. And what type of information is given to people?"

"Members of the Church of Jesus Christ are allowed access to the temple, as they start to make formal contracts with Christ in the Church He has set up for such a purpose. When they show they are honouring the contracts they have made, they go into the temple to make more contracts at the better level. It is similar to moving from a school to a college or university, where there are exams for every person passing between them."

"What's in these exams?"

"There are questions of being honest, being faithful to a spouse, not taking drugs for fun rather than for medical reasons since drugs can be dangerous when used unwisely. Also there is a testing in making Sundays a set time to study, read, or learn about godly things, or how to evolve character or psyche, in the similar way we all learn at school, or study at college or university."

"What's studied?"

"Theology, as we would reasonably expect for the Church of Jesus Christ. But in addition there are things like how we can make marriages and family life work, how we can be honest when other people around us might not be honest at some times, and how to not steal from others when other people take things dishonestly or corruptly."

Frank was occasionally reminded how Jozef was conversing in a foreign language, a fact which still amazed him.

"Have you been inside a temple?"

"Yes, I visit them frequently and go inside."

"Why?"

"The first time, we go through for ourselves when we make

more contracts with Christ, but after that, we can go through for other people who have already passed into the next dimension, because they no longer have the opportunity to go into temples for themselves or make the other contracts."

"Why not?"

"I believe temples in the next dimension will be situated in a part of the next dimension where the very good spirits reside, so others may not have access to them, in the same way that only people who behave well in this dimension have access to temples in mortal life."

"OK, it seems logical. But what happens when you make more contracts with Christ for someone who's died? Will they talk to Christ about these contracts, or do they eventually go along to temples in the next dimension?"

"Those are good questions, and I'm not sure about the answers. But we can find out those things when we're in the Spirit World."

Frank noticed Jozef had begun to truncate some of his words again. As he reflected on their previous meetings in Polgaria he seemed to remember Jozef had also done the same thing, yet more recently he'd lost the habit. It was now coming back once more on his current visit to England.

"How often d'you get to go into a temple?"

"Not so much recently. We still have to travel abroad because Polgaria doesn't have one, so we all visit temples in other countries, and it's more difficult at times. For a while my wife and I spent some time working in a temple, which we did in another country."

"What language do they use?"

"Generally English, because it is the international language, but there are electronic translators available for most languages in the temples now."

Frank had suddenly found the reason for Jozef's understandably fluctuating habits with English.

"Did you enjoy working in a temple?"

"Very much so. The feeling is excellent and it's very relaxing. Both my wife and I enjoyed it."

"So what about the psyches who don't make contracts in temples, because no one's ever performed the work for them? Surely it's unfair isn't it?"

"Well, eventually everyone will have the chance to make contracts, or accept, even reject any contracts which have been made on their behalf."

"Some may have to wait a jolly long time."

"The time they might spend waiting can still be put to good use, because to enter different dimensions after mortal life, an individual needs to be living worthily, or living the laws which operate in that dimension."

"Hold on a minute," Frank insisted. "I can accept the idea of multiple dimensions, as well as passing from this dimension into another one after death, but are you suggesting there are multiple dimensions after death?"

"I was in the Air Force, and similar to the Army or Navy, there are many ranks within each service. We didn't just have Generals with Privates. There were, and there still are, many ranks in the middle. It is not logical that the same level of order, or maybe a far greater order, doesn't exist in the eternity which God has designed for us. In the New Testament, John 14:2 says: 'In my Father's house there are many mansions.' I think it is logical."

Frank hadn't considered this idea much before, if perhaps at all. He was again curious.

"But what about other planets?"

"What do you mean?"

"I can't believe God only made one earth."

"Neither do I. He must have made many earths in the universe, including many other planets, ones which are different from earths inhabited by human people."

"Well are there humans on other planets?"

"Most likely, yes. I believe there will be."

"What about them?"

"In what way do you mean?"

"If the atonement of Christ was infinite, does it cover humans everywhere as well?"

"I guess pure logic would say how it does... at least for our God or for our universe, yes."

"Then do they have different dimensions after death, with mortal tests as well?"

"I believe the same logic would say they do."

"So, would they pass through their mortal tests at the same time?"

"Logic would again say that perhaps they don't."

"Then how could the atonement of Christ work for them, because He came to this Earth, and there would be many humans passing through their mortal tests before this single earth?"

"I believe such logic would say an infinite atonement could work backwards as well as forwards."

"Hmmm, maybe it's possible." Frank paused. "Are UFOs real?"

"In theistic terms, anything is possible, but I would see no reason why God would allow other mortals to interfere with the mortal tests which we experience upon this earth. It doesn't seem useful. An exam room is usually quiet, because the exam has enough distractions within itself. Lucifer is very good at creating distractions, whilst I have always found God to be clear in communicating, as well as calming and helpful."

Frank's mind turned back towards his own extended family. He thought about his mother along with her strong faith in deity, or her position in the next dimension after she died. He remembered one of the experiences he'd encountered with her, before she'd died.

One day he'd been travelling home from work when he felt an inclination to visit his mother. He dismissed the idea because he was in a hurry to get home to the family. She didn't live far from their home but it was late, so he wasn't keen. As he drove on, the idea was repeated. He ignored it again. The idea surfaced for a third time, at which point he turned the car around then headed for her flat. When he arrived he found the front door open, so he went inside. He continued on into the kitchen, finding his mother lying face down on the kitchen floor.

"Are you OK?" he asked quickly.

"I fell over last night and I couldn't get up, so I slept here last night."

He called a neighbour and they carefully lifted her onto the living room settee, talking for a while before he called an ambulance - it seemed only sensible on that occasion to have her fully examined at hospital. The local social services subsequently investigated various care homes where his mother could usefully reside. Frank related the incident to Jozef.

"You can go into a temple at some point in the future to make the higher contracts for anyone who's passed through the veil," Jozef suggested.

Frank didn't reply.

Jozef knew he was contemplating the idea.

Helen stayed back a little as Frank pushed ahead to explore.

"You've done something which I've been trying to do for years, Joseph. Frank never really listens to me about God but he listens to you."

"Sometimes it takes someone else to come along. I think it's true for many people, Helen."

CHAPTER 8

As Frank sat holding Helen's hand in the airport lounge, he noticed Jozef was talking to someone he hadn't seen before. This had to be a total stranger, which meant Frank was curious what they were talking about. He strolled over towards them to find out what was going on. He was surprised to hear the way their conversation was unfolding.

"So how d'you know God exists? What evidence d'you have there's a god?"

"If I told you, would you believe me?"

"No, because you'd be making something up, or you'd be deluding yourself something has happened when in reality your mind has simply made it up. Your mind would have been doing things subconsciously to enable you to cope with your undesired reality."

"Fair enough. I understand your reasoning, and therefore I won't tell you."

"OK, you're too scared to tell me because I can easily prove you wrong."

"I do accept that you hold such a view."

"But it's correct."

"I don't agree, although that's OK."

"Why don't you agree?"

"Because my experiences allow me to conclude differently."

"How?"

"Quite logically," Jozef sidestepped.

"Give me an example."

Jozef paused a while in thought, before resuming. He contemplated how he might provide an example without desecrating personal experiences, since Darren seemed sincere in his persistent questioning. He resumed.

"I've read, and sometimes contacted those involved with NDEs or near-death experiences. One gentleman was in a car crash with his wife, when his wife was killed. He survived but saw his wife's spirit whilst he was still in a coma and before she passed permanently into the next dimension. Later it was revealed how an attending doctor also saw his wife's spirit, roughly at the same time. The husband from another married couple similarly went into a coma due to a medical condition after which his spirit left his body. His spirit was given a tour of the next dimension by his grandfather. During the tour he visited some of his children as well as his wife. He also visited his father in the US Senate building, because his father was a US Senator. Just after he'd recovered from the coma he was able to tell his wife, as well as his father, along with the children what they'd been doing over the past hours; he could give details about where they were, plus where they were travelling, with accurate descriptions of the events which had occurred for each of them. I believe it's difficult to explain away events when they're corroborated by multiple individuals."

"There's always an explanation for everything. The problem is you're not prepared to face reality or tackle it head on. I used to be a Christian but I've moved on since then to the next level. You have to be willing to say to yourself, 'what would it take for me to not be Christian, or not believe anymore?'"

"Yes, the simple explanation for the incidents I've related is they're true. I'd suggest I've described real events. What do

Frank Lewseed

you want me not to believe? Can you give an example?" Jozef felt justified in the request, since he'd just provided Darren with a couple of examples.

"What would make you believe Christ didn't actually live, or early Christians made up the New Testament stories. Or if he did live, he was just a persuasive character who didn't perform miracles because they were made up later."

"OK, how about if we both answer questions, one at a time. I'll answer your questions if you'll answer mine?"

"Sure. What would convince you not to be a Christian?"

"If God came to me and told me how Christianity was wrong."

"That's not an objective answer. It's an answer you know can't be given, and it's why you're comfortable with it. You have to look at possible evidence or what evidence would convince you Christianity is wrong."

Jozef was bemused. He'd made an effort to give Darren examples, yet now Darren was asking him to disbelieve his knowledge. "It's not objective to suggest my answer wasn't objective," he countered.

"Why not?"

"Because it's a possible answer."

"No, it's not."

"Why not?"

"Because God can't appear to you."

"Why not?"

"Because He doesn't exist."

"He exists as much as you or I exist."

"How do you know?"

"If I gave you my evidence would you believe it?" Jozef knew he was now turning this revisit into a blind alley, yet he still felt justified since Darren seemed closed to any spiritual insights.

"There are plenty of people who've had delusions."

"You don't know what evidence I might give."

"Go on then."

"What would it take for you to believe my evidence was correct?"

"You haven't given me any evidence yet."

Jozef raised an eyebrow then sidestepped again: "This is my question, which we originally agreed to grant each other."

"But you haven't answered my question."

"I gave you an answer."

Darren thought a while. "It would need to be evidence with a clear set of facts which stood up to rigorous examination from an independent group of people."

"That's not an objective answer. It's an answer you know can't be given, and it's why you're comfortable with it. You have to look at possible evidence or what evidence would convince you Christianity is correct."

Darren grinned. He realised he'd just received the exact same answer he'd previously given himself, with only one word altered. He was impressed his answer had actually been remembered. "We're not going to give each other answers, are we?"

"Not ones which will lead anywhere at the moment."

"I could have asked 'what it would take for you to believe God didn't exist?'"

"Well, for such a question I would've answered in a slightly different way. I would have said I'd need to see everywhere in the universe at the time, just to be sure I'd not missed anywhere where God might be. Of course, it would naturally mean I'd have to be a god. Which in turn would mean I must have been made a god, by God."

"Hmm, that's definitely a backward step. Let's get something to eat."

"Sure, I agree."

"I know a decent café just down the corridor from here which sells jolly excellent lunchtime meals, and they're not too expensive."

"It sounds perfect."

"Shall we go?"

"Sure."

The two men exited the lounge area before slowly making their way up towards the cafés on the next floor.

"Are you coming Frank?" Jozef called back to him.

"I'll just get Helen."

As Frank came back to Helen and took hold of her hand again, he couldn't resist the question which was now playing on his mind.

"Why does Jozef spend so much time talking about religion?" he asked his wife.

"Maybe he thinks it's important dear," she replied.

'Maybe he does,' he mentally concluded.

CHAPTER 9

Frank sat at his father's old writing desk in his university office, staring out of the window, contemplating the fact Jozef had come over to meet him from Polgaria. 'Yes, he could've picked up the phone,' Frank confirmed to himself. 'But he knew I'd never have gone to his temple if he hadn't made the effort.' There was a pause. 'It was quite an effort.' He'd found his own trips to Polgaria were always very interesting 'so maybe Jozef wanted to likewise enjoy another visit to England?' he considered. Whenever he thought of Polgaria he couldn't help remembering the drives out into the countryside, the picturesque villages, miles away from any city or big town, the ballet and vaultage lessons for the girls, and the riding lessons in the university's indoor school. 'Vaultage' was the east European term for equestrian vaulting and Frank found it fascinating. The teachers pushed his girls hard, which produced results. He couldn't fault the work ethic. Helen somehow got Frank to join in with the horse riding lessons, where the group ended up standing in the saddles before walking, trotting and cantering around the indoor school. Frank even managed to fall off. All in all, the university stables plus the indoor school were rather interesting as a venue, even a venue where Frank enjoyed spending time with Helen. Clearly, Helen's favourite pastime with horses was indeed quite alluring.

He also became intrigued with the architecture of the various buildings throughout the university. Many were coloured in gentle pastel shades across their walls, adorned along the respective edges with quite intricate, contrasting patterns, creating a form of visual story between the buildings. The university site or campus had managed to seamlessly merge the new structures into the historic theme of the more beautifully old ones. It wasn't an easy feat, and he'd seen many attempts in other cities within various countries, which to his mind had failed quite comprehensively. Such wasn't the case though with this university in Polgaria. It was rather excellent.

He was suddenly aware of how he'd slipped back into the familiar, albeit semi-professional pastime he'd adopted many years ago, although it was quite a relaxing pastime. Day dreaming had become quite natural. What disrupted things was when a jay flew down onto the top of a hedge which was positioned outside, right in front of his office window. He watched the jay, captivated initially by its dark pink plumage with black, white and blue wings, but then a few seconds later by its curious behaviour. In its beak was a large slice of white bread, whereupon the jay proceeded to push it carefully through the top of the hedge, so eventually the food couldn't be seen at all. He wondered what would happen, though he didn't have to wait too long in order to find out. A couple of weeks later the jay returned one afternoon, to exactly the same position along the length of the hedge top, carefully retrieving its valuable cache of food. 'If only all students could learn to be as meticulous as that jay!' he thought.

Whilst he was busy daydreaming, he was distracted for a second time by a group of sparrows, a little to the left of where the jay had retrieved its booty, but slightly further down, just on one side of the neatly cut hedge. They were really making quite a chatter. Nevertheless it wasn't unexpected, considering the clear mixture of cock with hen birds which Frank could now see from his office. The next incident however was unexpected. A hugely quick, dark dart dropped almost vertically out of the sky, straight towards and into the group of sparrows, and with a speed which quite astonished Frank. One second the sparrows were blissfully playful without a concern in the world, the next second scores of sparrows were tumbling and falling everywhere, scrambling, noisily protesting, seemingly as much out of fear as out of protest. When Frank refocused upon the melee, he could see just exactly why the little birds had suddenly fallen into disarray. Sitting on the side of the hedge, with one lone and lifeless sparrow, was the unusual sight of a hunting sparrowhawk. Frank could never describe any hunting animals as majestic, yet man was carnivorous and regularly hunted, so how could he justify moaning about it? He wasn't vegetarian, 'At the end of the day I guess it's probably better for a bird to pass into the next dimension quite quickly. Everything makes the same journey sometime,' he cogitated. 'Could ecology ever sustain itself without predation?' He knew Helen would probably point towards the Garden of Eden as a good example, an example of just such an environment, but could it somehow be real? 'I suppose we shan't know... at least, not until we die!' He chuckled. Whilst the thought was busily amusing him, the phone rang. He picked it up.

"Oh, hello. Was the flight back OK?" he asked.

"Yes, fine thank you."

"You're lucky you got a flight back quite easily."

"Yes, they're locking down everything now, so you're right. Which brings me onto the reason for my call. We didn't find too much time to go over why I initially came over to England. I did manage to go along for some useful meetings, but it would be helpful to look at the effectiveness of some different control measures for this new pandemic."

"OK, sure. Are you still consulting for the State Medical Service over there?"

"It's much less than it was, but I still do some work. There are always different academic camps supporting different ways to control epidemics."

"Yer, good point. I'm also trying not to be irritated by the way the press latch onto various 'buzz' words and change them around, such as 'outbreak'. Outbreak only refers to the spread of disease at one premises, but I've never quite managed to remain unirritated by the usual use of 'outbreak' to mean 'national' spread."

"Traditions will possibly always be in place. They might be wrong, but people still enjoy using them, so they'll probably remain popular."

"You're right, I guess."

"I see various discussions which come up on different communications platforms. Facebook, websites, or I hear people discussing various ideas on buses or in cafés. The pandemic is constantly in the news, on television... in newspapers."

"The same thing is happening over here as well. Normally I don't want to get involved since logically it won't change things, but when I hear discussions, all sorts of different ideas are being put forward. Some of them are more accurate or relevant than others, and I suppose I tend to give input if I believe it might possibly help someone, or helps a friend."

"I can also understand that."

"When people can't see what's going on, it can be fruitless discussing ideas with them... especially if they prefer not to listen."

"I think though the media can drive people to think in a certain way."

"Which is another reason why I don't particularly enjoy the politics which can easily enter science. This pandemic is still less dangerous in terms of mortality or morbidity, compared to some other endemic diseases, but whilst it's annoying, surrounding it with fear will only make things worse. Stress generally heightens illness."

"Maybe that's true. Politics though are a necessary creature. Take for example the older, vulnerable age groups which are truly susceptible to this disease."

"They're the ones who should be protected, rather than isolating those who don't need it. Over ninety-five per cent of the population only experience mild disease. If we don't build immunity amongst the healthy plus less vulnerable age groups, then the elderly will be severely challenged, rather than lightly challenged when they do come into contact with infected individuals. Young people need to build immunity so they won't excrete so much virus when they're inevitably infected, which can be achieved via social distancing in place of national 'lockdowns'. National 'lockdowns' will likely cost more lives."

"Yes, I agree. Although there are still more political considerations."

"What d'you mean?"

"Well, what happens if someone suggests how ten per cent of the elderly age groups will still die this year anyway through underlying causes, or alternatively because of the pandemic. Conversely, others could argue that ring-fencing the vulnerable will never actually work."

"The same argument was made against grounding international travel as well as using it as a bottleneck to transmission. Global empirical data suggests the countries which have restricted international travel, have very low per capita mortality rates."

"This will mean a political decision needs to be made, because there are two different strategic alternatives, possibly three."

"You mean, repeatedly implementing 'lockdowns' or social

distancing. Eventually waiting for a developed vaccine, or hope the virus attenuates towards decreased virulence with a subsequent low mortality rate, as it gradually becomes adapted to the secondary human host."

"Or in line with your previous point, ring-fence the vulnerable population groups, apply bottlenecks to international travel, and allow the less vulnerable population groups to build immunity. The challenges against the more vulnerable are minimised."

"But perhaps the third alternative is best, because whilst national 'lockdowns' don't show advantages over social distancing across the world, they can be locally useful. A combination of dynamic, carefully considered local control measures is most likely to give an optimal control strategy."

"Yes, until the vaccine becomes available."

"It's important when the vaccine does become available that it has a decent efficacy. The seasonal efficacy for flu vaccines are generally under fifty per cent, so eventually there could evolve an endemic minimal mortality rate which becomes the norm... similar to seasonal flu, at six hundred and fifty thousand annually."

"Alternatively, another route is to continue using the dynamic local, and effective national controls, along the side of vaccination. But after a vaccinal programme is implemented, it is unlikely there'll be much reuse of other control measures."

"And sharing international information will remain important... if nothing else, to optimise the vaccine efficacy."

"The government listens to many different ideas or suggestions, sifting out the sensible ones from the less sensible ones. We never know what happens during relevant discussions unless we have colleagues who were at the meetings. Even then, there are some discussions which will always be private."

"You must have access to a lot of these discussions. On reflection, perhaps there's a need to make sure any dangerous ideas are anticipated, plus pre-emptively releasing empirical evidence where it can help. It could weed out the nonsensical ideas."

"The data reaching governments can sometimes be pre-sifted by the current advisors in place."

"Then I suppose it becomes even more useful to have friends, relatives or acquaintances in different places."

"Eventually, once the advice has been given, a choice has to be made."

"But as you've already pointed out, the press can play politics or apply pressures either wisely or unwisely."

"Maybe, but governments are usually fairly resilient. And there are many good journalists out there."

Frank paused, contemplating Jozef's last comment. He'd read a fair number of his daughter's articles as a reporter. They were good, well researched, with an interesting storyline which kept the reader's attention through to the end of each one. Jane managed to balance a clear level of objectivity alongside a degree of interest or passion for those involved in the incidents or stories she was reporting. Maybe he was biased, yet what he couldn't figure out, was if his daughter could write passionately as well as accurately, why weren't some other reporters able to do the same thing? He sighed in recognition of an aspiration which probably remained a little too lofty. Jane's descriptions of her interviews with David Cameron, Theresa May, Ed Balls or others were fascinating. She'd been lucky to have had a job in a marginal political constituency, making the most of the opportunities that came her way. He was proud of what she'd accomplished. 'Pity I can't pick up some of these other papers with similar confidence,' he inwardly moaned. The mood inevitably spilled over into his discussion with Jozef.

"There's a discussion doing the rounds at the moment where some people are criticising the government over the high mortality rate compared to other countries. They've suggested how the high mortality rate was due to tardiness in implementing national 'lockdown', but we know from global empirical data that early 'lockdown' doesn't produce a correlated reduction in per capita mortality. A counter has been mounted, stating international comparisons for mortality remain unhelpful because of differential start dates, which in turn have an impact upon incremental per capita mortality rates. However, most of the occult or apparent transmission increases occur within the first few weeks of a national epidemic, so the per capita mortality rate incrementals remain very small. What's more, the country epidemics all started more or less concurrently in the spring. Countries with higher population densities have also exhibited much lower mortality rates. These discussions can relevantly be sidelined by a sensitivity analysis, where for example, population density is shown to impact disease prevalence, but only to a small degree. Vaccinal plus innate immunity come out on top as the most important factors in the sensitivity analysis, whilst focusing upon factors such as population density can be 'red herrings'. The early modelling advice from science advisors initially caused widespread fear, meaning people were happy to garden at home, or spend time with their families, or do DIY because the government was providing financial assistance for people just to stay at home. However, the economy can't continuously support a national, 'stay-at-home lockdown' approach."

"It's true how government advisors can change the direction of a control policy, but they are generally in the position because they have a good track record from the past."

Frank thought for a moment about Helen's knowledge of her religion. He thought of his own insights into psyches and what his findings had suggested. Nevertheless, despite whatever anyone did or didn't know, everyone still had to live a life where nobody was immune from problems. It was one thing to know how things should be, yet it remained another thing to actually do something useful about it. Life was apparently a test and there was no escape from such reality. By living through difficult circumstances it was possible to discover what did or didn't work, or perhaps more importantly what theories were effective in practice.

If life was totally perfect, or if nothing went wrong where would everyone be? The answer was simple... probably back in a pre-existence which Helen's church always talked about a lot. As nice or pleasant as any pre-existence might have been... and 'it must have been decent if psyches were there for aeons of prehistory... anyway, the amount it was possible to learn in theory, re evolving or surviving in a harsh environment... well it must've remained a fair amount of theory. At some point, all that theory had to be put into practice. Helen would say the practice turned out to be mortal life,' Frank reflected. He guessed, no doubt Jozef would likely agree with her.

'Whenever people ask the question 'why me?' or 'why should such things happen to me?' they're simply asking a question they've already answered themselves. If Helen's right every person had previously asked to come into mortality during this pre-existence time... with zero exceptions. But everyone will only find out why, or the purpose behind details in life... when they die,' Frank confirmed to himself. It was still a common saying from the discussion group sessions at Siggel's house, and a saying which now took on a slightly tangential meaning. This was indeed life. What more could he say?

In fact though, what he did finally say was something completely different, because he was still talking to Jozef, although thankfully not about daydreaming...

"New science is only new since no one has come up with the novel ideas before, otherwise everybody would already be using them. When advisors have historical bias, ultimately the advice can become dangerous, as demonstrated in disease control 'overkill' during previous epidemics. The UK Foot-and-mouth disease 'overkill' was a prime example. What's been fascinating to watch has been the political elements involved in some of the decisions when disease control policies have been implemented. It's quite mootable as to whether the fear generated around the pandemic has been justified. Stress is reported to suppress the immune system, meaning logically it could be argued an optimal approach might be to minimise public concerns. The counter argument though against highlighting the positive aspects surrounding disease control and not overemphasising the dangers to public health, would be problems with compliance. The success of disease control measures relies upon collective or cooperative public compliance with any disease control measures. If control measures are pushed too far and become too harsh, or demonstrate unnecessary 'overkill', then the public has a right to call for a respectable level of autonomy in protecting their own health. The national economy is just as important in the long-term as disease control, where both significantly affect people's lives as well as life quality. Similar debate can be applied to population compliance with a national vaccination programme."

"It is not easy for the public to always trust the way government ministers have made their 'best' decisions, but in the same way it is not easy for the government ministers to find a way to keep the public helping with the process of disease control."

"Yer, good point. What's more, scientists will make mistakes because everyone makes mistakes, so why shouldn't a government keep its options open by opting for a dynamic disease control strategy? In such a way, it can choose whatever turns out to be prudent."

"So what would you advise?"

Frank was rather bewildered that considering Jozef's former professional position, he was still asking for additional ideas. 'Logically however, seeking supplementary input can generally be a wise approach,' he concluded. 'But what about God?' he questioned, thinking back over the dreams he'd had, ones depicting some pre-existence wars, where psyches had battled for the cause of freewill. 'God could've easily resolved the issues himself with the power he holds.' He paused a moment. 'He refers to himself as father. Fathers aren't about one man. So if God is the best, or the most intelligent of us all in the universe, someone who's seen everything, experienced everything, completed everything... he'll be the best teacher... and the best Teacher lets his kids have a go... to give them time practising or striving for what's good. Hmmm, it would've been illogical if He'd have intervened.'

Time was a funny old thing. He marvelled how it could be bent to accommodate totally first class day dreaming, alongside a thoroughly interesting conversation. 'Good old time,' he mentally reassured himself, still not completely sure though of the way it worked.

"I believe the much lower mortality rates will become accepted after a vaccine is introduced, as the disease becomes endemic, similar to seasonal flu. Eventually the pandemic will slowly become 'old news'... until flu3 emerges. Vaccines along with virus attenuation can reduce the mortality rates down to a baseline, whilst a combination of optimal, locally implemented control measures, especially social distancing, can ameliorate transmission in the meantime. Whilst I may disagree with the science interpretations of some government advisors, I respect them if they truly believe in what they're doing. There'll most likely be future emerging virus strains similar to the situation with flu. The literature shows a certain level of immunity carried by existing vaccines for new strains, giving some leeway in developing the vaccines further to accommodate any emerging variants. Again it's a similar current situation with flu. Those variants may reduce vaccine efficacies down towards the lower fifty per cent shown by the flu vaccines, yet the baseline annual mortality rate will gradually stabilise, and immunity amongst the young will still ensure the transmission rates are kept in check. The only way to utilise the innate immunity of the young against future emerging diseases is by allowing them to have exposure. National 'lockdowns' won't help the young gain exposure to new variants of old diseases or old variants of new diseases. As we've already discussed, innate immunity amongst the young is a key defence against an emerging disease until vaccines are available, so if they're not exposed to the virus, then the young will likely excrete more virus when they do become infected. In time, the public might appreciate how such high challenges can inevitably reach the older, more vulnerable groups and increase per capita mortality rates among them. My hope for any future epidemics or pandemics is there'll be a more balanced use of the effective contact rate or reproduction number, which doesn't usefully translate into an epidemic threshold value for diseases whenever a high proportion of affected individuals exhibit subclinical or mild symptoms. With subclinical disease any attempts to measure or estimate reproduction number won't indicate the average level of secondary cases per infectious case, where a positive virus test doesn't show that an individual will mount successful challenges against susceptibles, but more importantly any successful challenge can and often will come from multiple subclinically infected carriers. As new strains or variants arise over time, they could or probably would affect the efficacy of the vaccines produced, in a way similar to how the current flu vaccines are seasonally affected. Hence the exposure of the young or less vulnerable groups will remain important for this pandemic or any future epidemics or pandemics."

At this point Frank was grateful no one else was listening to their conversation. If someone had been listening he could imagine their likely facial expressions, plus a phrase or two along the lines of 'what are you two babbling on about?' and to be honest he'd probably have to agree. He could remember his first few weeks at university, when the step up from school lessons was enormous. He sat mentally bewildered for the initial few lectures, similarly wondering just exactly what the lecturers were rabbiting on about. Slowly as he tuned into the way they were talking, he realised the terms they used were indeed useful, because you could say so much more in a single word, especially if it was a specialised word for the subject or subjects being studied. The same was true for any field of study. Most things had a decent purpose.

A lot of people who were new to Helen's church seemed likewise thrown off by the weird jargon being used. Frank also found it curious the way pictures of the church presidency were placed above the blackboards in classrooms. At any rate, this curiosity remained until he saw a few more American films; he noticed how along the same lines, pictures of the current US President were displayed above the classroom blackboards in US schools. 'Yes, it's an American thing. Helen's church was apparently restored in the US,' he realised. The day dreaming paused once again.

"Some people may worry over a perceived need to vaccinate as many people as possible, before achieving 'herd' immunity." Jozef's comment had pulled Frank back into the conversation.

"Yes, such worries are highly likely. It's unlikely though the disease will be eradicated, since the vaccine efficacies are initially going to probably fall around seventy-five per cent, or even lower as more variants emerge. Therefore it's not the same as getting rid of smallpox where the vaccines approached ninety-five per cent efficiency. This disease will most probably remain globally endemic like flu, which means the idea of eradicating the disease through sufficient 'herd' immunity becomes somewhat redundant. Vaccinated people will generally be protected, whilst there'll be a need to assess the optimal intervaccination period to combat waning vaccinal immunity."

"Other people may worry about getting infected even though they have been vaccinated."

"For seventy-five per cent of vaccinated people they've no reason to worry, just as long as they stay away from anyone, or especially any groups of people, who show symptoms of illness. Vaccinal status is not the relevant factor, but rather health status. Vaccinated people shouldn't logically be insisting unvaccinated people receive vaccinations, because the vaccinated remain protected. The twenty-five per cent, or thereabouts, of vaccinated people who fail to boost their antibodies levels to protective thresholds, should be turning towards personal behavioural methods for protection. We all need to respect the rights of others to choose their personal medical treatments."

The discussion continued, eventually reaching a natural conclusion after both men were subjectively satisfied with the relevant factors or control options which had been explored. In the coming months, Frank spoke with other colleagues about the pandemic, toying with the idea of possibly publishing some relevant or collated empirical data. Finally though he couldn't be bothered with the process, deciding to just bore his friends with it instead.

It reminded him of the time he'd spent with Kasta, a mare at the university's riding stables. 'Warning people can be a jolly decent thing to do,' he reassured himself. Over the years he'd spent hours watching Helen with her horses, noticing the things she'd regularly do with them. One of those things involved cleaning the mud off her horses' hooves with a hoof pick. He was very well aware of the fact any horse had a pair of lethal weapons in the form of its hindquarters, to the point where a vet he'd spent time with one summer, would often place a board or old door behind any horses he was internally examining - generally if a cage or nothing else was suitably available. Hence, Frank learnt to approach hoof picking carefully. Kasta was quite a feisty animal, choosing to spook when he rode her around the university's indoor school, consequently throwing him off on one occasion. He took her friskiness quite seriously.

"Frank, what are you doing?" commented another rider, as they both continued to clean the hooves of their horses after riding.

"You're quite welcome to do it differently if you'd like," Frank offered.

He obligingly swapped around with the other rider, continuing with a different horse in the stall next to Kasta. What he saw next he never forgot, finding it hard to ever erase the image from his memory. After about ten to fifteen seconds he caught sight of someone being ejected from the stall adjoining his new one, flying through the air about a foot or two off the ground, posterior first, moving rapidly backwards, both arms as well as both legs trailing behind his posterior in quite a strange airborne stance, almost as though something had suddenly pulled massively hard on a cord which was attached to the back of his trouser belt. In actual fact, virtually the opposite had happened. Kasta had kicked this chap really quite forcefully, albeit full bore with its hind limbs, luckily catching him on both hips rather than anywhere else - it sent him sprawling backwards and hugely quickly, duly landing in one of the stalls on the opposite side to theirs. The chap wasn't seriously injured, although the incident did nothing to change Frank's approach to hoof picking. Frank learnt a lot of things from watching his beautiful wife.

'Now where was I? Oh yer, the Facebook posting with some applicable disease control cautions. Well, this should definitely send them all to sleep!' he mentally noted. 'Anyone getting through these next couple of pages deserves a medal... but at the end, there's a more handy set of conclusions. Not so bad after all!' He briefly considered putting a mental health warning at the top of the post, advising anyone not interested to engage fast forwarding, quickly deciding though how such an instruction could well apply to the vast majority. In the end, he simply hit the 'post' button to make a final Facebook entry. Facebook had its good uses, where he considered this platform to be a useful one. 'Palatable solutions can be more about objective compromise, than attempting to wield science in order to get your own way,' he concluded. He couldn't resist checking it through before he logged off again. He also read the entry out loud. He wasn't sure if it helped, but he did it anyway.

Frank drew breath before starting. "There'll always be different views on approaches to problem-solving, although at the end of the day a healthy respect for alternative ideas goes a long way towards a sensible or measured outcome. There's been a fair amount of discussion re the importance of buildings ventilation for disease control. Nevertheless, whilst the literature shows empirical evidence for the successful use of housing as a physical barrier to ameliorate any regional spread of micropopulation or highly infectious viral diseases, there's a need to examine the path of crude as well as mechanical ventilation through buildings. Logically at one extreme, a sealed building holding freely mixing susceptible individuals will yield maximal viral transmission given enough time, so extrapolating the rationale towards the other extreme, it might seem reasonable to conclude ventilation could do the opposite. However to make such a beneficial reality, any infectious virions would need to pass out of buildings, preferably not across groups of people. It might be reasonably straight forward with mechanical ventilation, whilst at the same time more difficult using crude ventilation. Crude ventilation through a building can be dependent upon the number or positioning of inlet or outlet sources, whereby virus could at times be channelled towards or across protected areas of buildings, or over groups of individuals."

Frank stopped reading for a while, allowing him to consult the literature. Academic papers were generally available online, hence the computer was a suitably decent tool to complete this task. He'd been forwarded a link to some suggestions re ventilation, highlighting a paper which described a theoretical model, incorporating factors such as settling, filtration, deactivation, outflow rates, turbulence, relative humidity, droplet size, etc. Irrespective of all the theory, and he'd seen a lot over the years, there was no substitute for decently controlled experimentation, which could helpfully identify those ideas that actually worked in practice. He resumed reading out loud.

"The design of animal or human buildings can impact the potential for disease spread both positively and negatively. Using animal models for comparative studies of human diseases or epidemiology can be useful, however caution is required when considering some aspects of comparative studies. For example, questions have been raised concerning 'leaky' vaccines. Attenuated live vaccines, or dead preparations are infrequently used in the human population, and not for vaccination programmes where recombinant, vector vaccines, etc. are used to control human diseases. Hence the 'leaky' vaccines issue experienced with Marek's Disease in poultry isn't relevant and no virus excretion occurs from vaccinated individuals, nor excretion of virus with increasing virulence. The fact that vaccinated people can subsequently contract disease plus act as carriers is a 'red herring' with respect to 'leaky' vaccines per se. A similar question has been raised over whether vaccinations can cause the emergence of new viral strains. The question remains irrelevant because an epidemiologist wouldn't suggest not using a vaccine in case another strain emerges, but would suggest adjusting vaccines to prevent the spread of new strains. The situation is different from national 'lockdowns' which can cause the emergence of new strains, where a failure to allow exposure of less vulnerable age groups to circulating virus reduces the boost of antibodies via innate immunity. Vaccines similarly boost antibody production and therefore mimic the usefulness of innate immunity; hence vaccines continue to be useful for disease control despite the emergence of new variants."

The thing now crossing Frank's mind was the sheer level of heated debates he'd recently been observing over vaccination programmes. He'd promoted the use of vaccines for decades. Something new though was appearing, in the form of a slow march towards compulsory vaccination. It concerned him. He hadn't thought he'd ever witness such a situation in the western world, at least not during his lifetime, yet suddenly it had arrived. He read on.

"A common developing theme seems to be the discord between those who promote the use of vaccines and those who don't. There are relevant arguments both ways although there's no reason why the parties can't listen to each other and agree to disagree. Discussions are about learning from each other in order to get as close as possible to reality, which remains a useful outcome. So what are the arguments? The pro-vaccine lobby rightly points out how safe vaccines are the optimal tool to fight the spread of infectious diseases. The anti-vaccine lobby correctly state the phased trials have been cut short, trials which are used by pharmaceutical companies to monitor any new drugs produced for relevant toxicity or side effects. However, the most vulnerable population groups are represented by older people, where the impact of long-term side effects is unlikely to become an important factor. A former government advisor has further pointed out 'it is also likely that there is a narrow structural limit for the virus to develop variants that would escape the existing vaccines'. Evaluating the relative risks in taking or not accepting vaccinal protection must ultimately become a personal decision. Clearly for older and more vulnerable population age groups the benefits outweigh currently known potential hazards. The situation however isn't so clear cut for the younger, less vulnerable age groups. Recently, those promoting vaccines have suggested the anti-vaccine lobby can be viewed as a danger to vaccinated individuals through the excretion of virus. Firstly, any excretion of virus necessitates unvaccinated individuals becoming infected hence infectious; secondly, for a challenge to be successfully mounted against a vaccinated individual would typically require close contact with an acutely infected person or through the cumulative challenge from multiple infected people. All individuals have a responsibility to avoid anyone showing clinical signs of disease whilst equally, infectious people are morally required to self-isolate. Future epidemics which mimic flu in becoming globally endemic, are likely to show decreased vaccine efficacy levels due to emerging variants, so the question of disease spread will probably focus more upon behavioural courtesy than any enforcement of vaccination programmes. This approach has historically been used for flu over many decades. The future baseline global mortality rate for emerging pandemics may mirror flu at 650k per annum, as the disease also becomes endemic."

Nothing was ever simply. Whenever anybody came up with a solution to a problem, someone else would just as quickly throw out another problem. 'I like Churchill's quote,' Frank reminded himself. 'Apparently, success consists of going from failure to failure without a loss of enthusiasm. Excellent,' he concluded. He read on.

"A further query has been mooted re unvaccinated individuals increasing the likelihood of new, more virulent variants, although the basis for such an argument has not been substantiated. A former government advisor has stated that 'the vaccines do not provide a sterile immunity (like smallpox vaccine) so it is just as likely, if not more likely that vaccinated people would encourage new variants of the virus'. Another counter argument points towards the finding of typical morbidity and per capita mortality rates amongst the unvaccinated Amish community, where the antibody protection for recovered individuals can be greater and last longer than vaccinal protection. Moreover, decades of vaccinal flu programmes have not curtailed the emergence of annual new strains, although the flu virus appears to differ in exhibiting significant ability for antigenic drift or shift. Vaccines dampen levels of viral challenge within a population. In turn, the levels of challenge play a significant role in disease transmission, as well as prevalence and the emergence of new strains. Low regular challenges from emerging strains amongst the younger or less vulnerable age groups will further heighten innate and 'herd' immunity."

Frank had taken a long time to learn that no matter how much he thought he'd learnt, there was always a good reason to retain some level of humility. It was quite simple really. Anyone, perhaps everyone, could at times be wrong, and more often than not, the problem would annoyingly crop up at exactly the same time things appeared to be totally right. No one was immune. Experts could be as vulnerable as anyone else, since at times, any historical baggage might render an expert surprisingly vulnerable. He resumed reading.

"Research can reveal counter-intuitive findings. Global empirical evidence during the first eight months of the pandemic indicated national 'lockdowns' were no better at controlling transmission than social distancing measures. Whichever control measures were used, per capita mortality rates were indicative of their relative successes in reducing disease spread, and countries with the highest per capita mortality rates were the least successful. Significantly when the timing of 'lockdown' implementations were plotted against per capita mortality rates, a scatter graph resulted without correlation(s), removing the reason for 'lockdown' failures being due to tardy implementations. Harsh disease control measures may be suboptimal to more targetted measures. Whatever ongoing research uncovers for relevant epidemiology or immunology in the months and years to come, a transparent as well as objective approach is required in the implementation of suitable control measures."

Frank always felt more comfortable when an article, a Facebook post, or really anything written down was neatly wrapped up with a handy sets of conclusions at the end. 'Why explore a number of ideas if you don't end up with a set of summarising suggestions?' he asked himself. He didn't reply. He read through the final set of conclusions instead.

"One. Concentrate on vaccinating people over fifty, whilst encouraging everyone to get vaccinated. Two. Accommodate the decisions of the young regarding vaccinations, since they rapidly build innate immunity, and whether vaccinated or unvaccinated become the first line of 'herd' immunity defence. Three. Healthy unvaccinated young people, as well as healthy vaccinated young people slow disease transmission of different virus strains. Four. Unvaccinated older people generally know the relative risks to themselves, or otherwise. Five. Sick people need to self-isolate. Six. Anyone mixing with a group of people showing symptoms is inviting trouble. Seven. Health status is important to monitor within any group of people from their symptoms, body temperature, etc., whereas vaccination status isn't similarly useful to monitor since it doesn't indicate a person isn't spreading disease. Eight. A high level of vaccine efficiency means that healthy unvaccinated people don't pose a threat to vaccinated individuals, and new strains can arise amongst vaccinated as well as unvaccinated people. Nine. Self-policing has worked usefully with flu for decades. The panic generated by any new or emerging pandemic will eventually even out to a baseline level of global deaths each year. Ten. People don't become panicked each year by seasonal flu deaths and won't remain concerned about any emerging disease as it becomes endemic within the population."

'Yep, this Facebook post's truly a fantastic cure for insomnia!' Frank concluded. 'I'll have to patent it. I could make a fortune!' He considered deleting the post, because for someone who wasn't interested in epidemiology... 'well, it might possibly be boring. On the other hand... it could be worth enduring the boredom! This pandemic's annoyingly affected millions of lives. Anything relevant might become a record for the future... should anyone ever want to read it, of course... which they probably won't. Never mind,' he acknowledged, slightly crest-fallen. One day he'd discover the post would prove to be rather more helpful than he'd have imagined, although not for the reasons he could have guessed. In the meantime it lay hidden within an obscure account of Facebook. Safe and sound.

CHAPTER 10

Things had a habit of not necessarily turning out the way they were expected. Frank went abroad on a trip with Adam on one occasion, since they both had business in the same city at the same time. It was a useful coincidence. Out of interest, Adam took him along to view a veterinary procedure on a cow with a prolapsed uterus.

As Adam commenced by administering the epidural, another vet, younger and confident, happened to make a comment.

"Why are you standing so far away?" he queried.

"You can have a go if you'd like," Adam offered. This reminded him a little of the incident with Kasta at the university stables in Polgaria. He wondered whether there might be a similar outcome. He wasn't far wrong. The young vet took over a position behind the cow, slightly to the right yet somewhat closer than Adam had been standing. He duly plunged in the epidural needle and the cow equally rapidly shot out a back leg, landing a direct hit on the young chap's shin. He was surprised because the aim was not only highly accurate but Frank considered the angle to be really rather obtuse, whereby he was amazed the animal had been successful. The moaning which quickly followed went on for quite some time. 'Yep, almost a carbon copy of the incident at the stables,' Frank assessed.

"These large animals can be a different handful compared to

companion animals, eh?" Frank commented.

"Yes, sometimes you have to be ready for the unexpected," Adam agreed. "The surgical procedures can be identical on some occasions whilst totally dissimilar for other things. I recently had a prolapsed rectum in a British Bulldog. Those dogs are very friendly, though at the same time very strong. Purse string sutures really aren't applicable with Bulldogs. I ended up attaching the intestine to the wall of the abdomen, which worked a treat."

"Fascinating," Frank appraised. 'All in all Adam, I think I'm with you when it comes to suitable caution with animals."

"Works well for me," Adam concluded.

-

When he thought back over the previous pandemic discussion with Jozef, he remembered how things had somehow drifted into religion again, which seemed a regular theme. Over the years, Frank had begun to see the subject material as an ongoing interest rather than an annoyance. It was probably to do with the way Jozef calmly approached their interactions.

"No one believes a partially-sighted person can view the world in exactly the same way as a fully-sighted person, and similarly no one should believe that a person who's spiritually impaired can see the reality of multiple dimensions." Jozef's suggestion was apt. In fact, Frank judged it was uncanny how many partially-sighted people seemed to be blessed with an ability to understand the reality of multiple dimensions, perhaps through an unwritten law of compensations. Frank paused a moment before mentally replaying more of the discussion.

"It will never be a fact that given enough time a bedroom will become tidy on its own, but most parents resort to tidying bedrooms for their kids. Similarly Heavenly parents tidy the universe, and therefore it remains ordered."

Once again Jozef's words seemed good, albeit slightly paraphrased, since apparently the last idea was borrowed from Hugh Nibley, a theistic author. Whatever the origin, Frank was intrigued. He was likewise intrigued by a parallel Jozef had drawn between Christ's atonement, a resurrection, plus the laws of thermodynamics. Clearly, events in the physical world could be observed as moving from a state of the ordered to the disordered, or from cosmos to chaos, or from the organised to the disorganised. Men could reverse such a trend by building or problem solving, or equally in religion, by repenting or evolving personal characteristics. Jozef pointed out how the creation of Earth from matter unorganised, into organised matter, was another example of negentropy, suggesting deity had specifically intervened. The atonement was another reversal from perpetual human mistakes into evolved human characters. Resurrection was deity's natural upgrade gift from mortality into perfected, fully functional, non-decaying human physical forms. Frank found the ideas interesting. He found it curious though the way Jozef had emphasised that resurrection didn't mean entry into the highest dimension where God could be found, because whilst all mortals graduated from the test of earth life with a resurrected body, there remained many divisions within heaven. Those divisions were ordered according to worthiness for additional authority or responsibilities. Frank had long since equated responsibility alongside problem-solving skills. 'With such an idea in mind, perhaps life isn't so much a test, as new opportunities to find solutions to problems or mistakes,' he questioned. 'Are they the same thing?' He still harboured questions about the future of his family though. He was also curious about some of the political questions Jozef had raised, which highlighted the dilemma of what was the best way to find out?

He was no longer interested in knowing about a future with catastrophes, or eye-catching headlines, or 'get-rich-quick' schemes. He'd recently researched a Jewish ancestor who'd left several million pounds in modern terms, to his great-grandfather. His great-grandfather couldn't be traced, so the money along with some land for a London train station, reportedly went to Reuben Twigley and his wife Jermane. Within two years Reuben had lost around ninety per cent of the newly-found wealth, then had died. Frank wondered what had become of Reuben or how the money had been used? He hoped Reuben had gained from it, but decided he probably wasn't an automatic fan of instant wealth anymore. 'I certainly wouldn't turn it down though,' he reassuringly confirmed to himself. 'I hope I might actually use the fortune wisely,' he continued. 'For sure!' In reality he wasn't sure.

Frank was intrigued by Jozef's fascination with the spiritual. He seemed a level headed man of science, yet why did he hold so much interest in the paranormal? Whenever Jozef talked about such things, they seemed normal rather than paranormal. Reg had suggested spiritual insights or knowledge were collectively another source of information to be used wisely, whilst at times sifted, like all information. His view was it remained unwisely counterproductive to be cutting yourself off from any source of good information. Frank agreed with the logic behind such a rationale. He'd once asked Reg what he thought of Morgan Freeman's religious views or Ricky Gervais' opposition to the idea of God or theism. Reg had pointed out Morgan Freeman seemed to be exploring what was possible rather than being opposed to religion, whilst Ricky Gervais appeared interested in philosophy, even if he perhaps seemed unconvinced by the concept of deity. "It's not straight forward for some people," Reg had suggested. "However, someone has to be the most intelligent Being in this universe, which is also true for other dimensions as well. Whatever anyone believes, everyone will get to find out..."

"When they die!" Frank vocalised.

"When who dies?" John asked, entering the office and taking the other seat just inside the door.

"Oh, I was contemplating the views of Morgan Freeman as well as Ricky Gervais."

"Yer, they both have interesting slants on religion. Gervais seems to be on a crusade, which is fair enough, because whenever someone makes a significant noise about a subject, it suggests they're usually exploring ideas. And exploring ideas is important, no matter what the current conclusions turn out to be."

"I never quite thought of it that way."

"Morgan Freeman seems to be open to discussing all possibilities... which is good. His television series on God is a decent watch."

"Yes, I agree."

"When are you going home?"

"Quite soon."

"They say they're opening up football on the continent. They might even have something on the box again quite soon."

"Maybe. This pandemic has gone on for too long now."

"Absolutely. Sometimes I think we've been at this place for too long, as well."

"What, the university?"

"Absolutely!"

"What would you do if you weren't working here?"

"Spending time at home... doing what I wanted."

"That's a double-edged sword. You'd miss this place if we retired."

"No, I don't think so," John replied emphatically.

"We'll see." Frank left the idea to germinate over time, although he wasn't quite sure whether it would actually take root.

As John headed off home, and Frank began to makes moves for his well-earned trek back to Helen, he couldn't help but reconsider what the future held in store for his family. Recently, he seemed to be having more relevant REM dreams as well as premonitions, whereas in the past he would only experience them occasionally.

"You know God, if you're there or aren't too busy, what's Luke 3:38 all about? If you're the Heavenly Parent of psyches, then how was Adam created? Any ideas please?" Frank was surprised he was actually interested in Luke 3:38, although there was a straight forward reason. He'd seen it in Helen's Bible one day, judging it had connotations with family. Recently his family was becoming significantly more important.

-

Two men stood together. They were dressed in white suits, white shoes and white ties and were engaged in discussion.

"OK, so he's finally engaging with some decent questions. How shall we answer?"

"We can't actually answer."

"Why not? This question is simple as well as sincere."

"Because the question wasn't addressed to us. It has to go to the intended recipient."

"Fair enough. Then I guess we'll have to wait for instructions to see what the answer was?"

"Yes, it's a fair comment."

-

As Frank opened the front door and he slipped the keys back into his coat pocket, he loved the fact that Helen was at home.

She wasn't at the horses' field, so she brightened his day as he came in to see her. She always did. It was excellent.

"What are you watching dear?" he asked, noticing the television was on. It was unusual for Helen at that time of the day.

"Oh, I just felt inclined to put it on for some reason. It's Jurassic Park and I quite like it."

"I must admit, I enjoy the music."

"It's quite scary in places," Helen added.

Frank took off his coat, put it away on its appropriate hook then sat down for a moment. He wasn't quite sure why, because he'd seen this film so many times in the past. It was an amusing film though, whilst dinner would soon be ready.

"Are the kids upstairs?"

"Daniel's at Jack's house for a party, Jane's with her friend Izzy. The other two are in their rooms."

"There's a film on kids," Frank called up the stairs.

"We've seen it before," Lisa replied.

"I'll watch it," Robert agreed, bounding down the stairs two at a time.

"Be careful son."

"Don't worry dad!"

"Hmmm." Frank settled back.

"Turn it up dear, so I can hear it," Helen asked from the direction of the kitchen.

Frank reached over to pick up the control box.

Five characters came into what appeared to be a small cinema. Four of them sat down in respective seats. Frank recognised Richard Attenborough, who was playing an older gentleman, wearing a trilby hat as well as using a supportive walking cane. The dialogue commenced.

"Err, Donald. Sit down. Yer. Right, here we go. Or here I go."

"Hello John. But how did I get here?"

"Well let me show you. First, I need a drop of blood. Your

blood."

"John, that hurt."

"Relax John. It's all part of the miracle of cloning," Attenborough's character announced, as the film unravelled.

"Hello John."

"Hello John."

"Hello John."

"Hello John."

There were now three replicants, all screened in the film's cinema, complete with walking canes, but missing the trilbys. The commentary continued through the replicants.

"Oh, Mr. DNA, where did you come from?"

"From your blood."

"Just one drop of your blood contains billions of strands of DNA... the building blocks of life. A DNA strand like me is the blueprint for building a living thing... and sometimes..."

"Flying spuds!" Frank exclaimed.

"What's up dad?" Robert asked.

"Oh, no worries. It's just something which happened at work."

Robert resumed watching the film. Frank was suddenly less interested in the film whilst more interested in what he'd just realised.

"It's all part of the miracle of cloning..."

"What is dad?" Robert asked.

"Oh, nothing. Just something from work."

Robert resumed watching the film.

Frank walked out to the kitchen.

"It's all part of the miracle of cloning."

"What is dear?" Helen asked.

Adam in the Bible could have been more real than I realised.

"Yes dear," Helen replied. There was no gentle tirade this time, which surprised Frank. What surprised him even more was how his question to God had been answered. He had a new idea. It might not be the answer, but his question was answered. That was presently enough. It was interesting.

-

Two men stood together. They were dressed in white suits, white shoes and white ties and were engaged in discussion.
"I liked those instructions."
"Yes, they were good, weren't they?"
"Definitely!"
"He always gives the best answers for each person."
"Yes, it's true."
"So we've got more progress."
"I think we have."
"Long may it continue."
"I agree."
"Good."

CHAPTER 11

Frank slammed the car into third gear, pressing down hard on the accelerator to send the engine revving into acceleration, and pulled round sharply on the steering wheel to launch past the vehicle which was annoyingly still blocking his way ahead. He shot by with little effort, grinning and waving enthusiastically as he sailed into the lead. He was making progress. These were the things which mattered in life – the realities of every day living.

"Excellent!" he told himself, as he sat back, now ready to enjoy the freedom of an open road, or now more importantly, without any tiresome distractions. "Flying spuds, what was that?" he exclaimed, staring incredulously at the vehicle which had somehow just past him. "It's the same car!" He stared at it again. "Right!" He quickly dropped a gear and listened to the revs pile up once more, waiting for exactly the right time to pull out then back around Mr. Formula One, the irksome individual driving this repeated obstacle blocking his way forward. At precisely the right moment, not long after they'd they raced around the next left-hand bend, judging his distance behind the green incumbrance to spatial perfection, he saw the road open up into a decent long, straight stretch of pure acceleration. He lifted his foot off the brake, thrusting down hard on the accelerator. "Ridiculous!" His foot was back on the brake again, yet even harder. A car was now coming the other way. "Maniac!" He suddenly regretted taking his own car in for its service that morning. "This thing handles like a tank," he moaned. Just as suddenly as the offending green estate had reappeared, Helen's voice now popped up: "A tool is only as good as its user," she'd usually point out. "Not now dear!" he retorted vocally. He wasn't quite sure why he'd said it, because obviously she couldn't hear him and he certainly wasn't going to mention the unfolding race later. He stared ahead. The maniac coming the other way slowly passed by, hogging the overtaking lane for an age, even more. "Some people just don't know how to drive," Frank protested, because by now over half of the long straight road had been squandered, disappearing wastefully behind them. He dropped the car down a customary gear subsequently pulling out with full power as he floored the accelerator. He flew around the vexing green obstacle, forging ahead with renewed speed. He glanced left to judge when to glide back in. The annoying green obstacle was somehow alongside. He pushed even harder on the accelerator, looking for more speed to solve the problem. Luckily he got it. Unluckily the green obstacle was still there. "This idiot's speeding up!" He stared towards the shortening road ahead, glaring at the right-hand bend which was approaching, massively rapidly. He glanced back across to the left. The green maniac was still there. He didn't have much time to pull in before he reached the bend. Suddenly the bend was upon them. He jammed down hard on the brake, swinging the car sharply left into the slot behind the green menace, and just before another vehicular inconvenience shot around the corner, coming the other way.

"Great!" He paused. "I don't think."

His patience was tested to the limit as he waited and waited behind countless sharp, repeated blind bends. Finally they were coming to a bend which he knew quite well, having remembered it over years of driving the same, albeit picturesque drive into work each day. This corner was short enough to lull the green aggravation into a false sense of security, but deep enough to slip past, so long as he managed to view a clear coast when he first entered it. At just the right angle there was a perfect line of sight fully across the extent of the curve. He had to catch it properly. He did, and sailed around his assailant with fantastic ease. He just managed to catch a glimpse of the maniac, now shaking his fist with vigour, 'probably out of incompetent vigour', Frank concluded. "Good. Job done. And now to ensure the green menace stays where he should be."

Frank was extremely pleased. He congratulated himself on a further five miles of blocking countermeasures, sometimes giving the green driver hope by slowing to a speed which invited a daring takeover, but quickly slamming the door shut with a burst of speed at the critical moment. He even made use of the windscreen wash. The windscreen wash automatically became a fantastic backwards smokescreen at between fifty and sixty miles per hour, although there were only a few places where he could use it effectively. He loved the way the blue fluid was catapulted over the roof of his own vehicle, driven by exactly the right amount of wind speed, landing absolutely square onto the windscreen of any car travelling close behind. It never failed to slow them down, as they struggled to clear their windscreen from the immediate visual impairment which followed. The final right hand turn for work was approaching, meaning Frank was thoroughly satisfied with the morning's drive. "Maybe this thing isn't such a tank after all," he revised. His mood somewhat changed though when he noticed how the green annoyance behind was also indicating to turn right.

"I wonder where he's going?" Frank paused. It suddenly dawned on him this menace could perhaps be going into work. "What if it's someone important?" The idea hadn't crossed his mind before that moment. As he pulled into the car park, keeping half an eye on the green vehicle, it similarly pulled into the car park before finding a space. The driver he'd seen shaking his fist seemed rather familiar. He could've sworn he'd seen the person somewhere before.

"Wow, Alec, d'you go racing in your spare time?"

The driver of the green car looked equally shocked. "Well you weren't driving carefully, were you?"

Frank chuckled. "Touché! I think we both went for it. The need for speed," Frank suggested.

"You were driving pretty crazily at times."

"I think we both were, Alec."

"Yes, I suppose that's true."

Frank liked Alec. He was the Head of the Maintenance Department where over the years they'd got on well. The success of the drive was significantly dampened by the thought he could've offended his colleague. Somehow the motive behind getting to the front of the queue suddenly seemed pointless, even counterproductive. Frank believed after his race with Alec he no longer held the same fury behind the wheel of a car. 'Maybe it's when I started to get old?' he questioned.

-

Frank couldn't mention the drive into work to Helen. He knew she'd fall asleep, which was OK. He also knew someone would eventually fall victim to his tale of the highways event, since it probably had to be recounted. As he came into his office he wasn't surprised it turned out to be John.

"Well, there you go!" John commented emphatically, not wishing to berate Frank for any reckless abandon of the highway code.

"And where are we going, exactly?"

"In the expression, to be precise."

"What expression?"

"The one you're about to make."

"Huh, that's a likely story."

"Exactly!"

"You do exaggerate."

"And you don't?"

"No, never have done, never do, and certainly never will."

"Well, that's a slight exaggeration!"

"Better overestimated than underestimated."

"And now you sound like the pandemic modellers."

"That'll never happen."

"If they paid you enough, then it would."

"Nope."

"When I was younger I used to think I'd never go out without a shave, because it was only for older people who were too worn out to do all the essentials anymore. Then one day I went into some local toilets, came over to wash my hands, and suddenly I noticed I'd only had half a shave. Everything below half way was like the unharvested half of a half-harvested harvest field, and I was saddled with some selected stubble until I got home in the evening. I asked my brother why he hadn't mentioned anything in the morning, but he said he'd thought it was some kind of new fashion thing."

"Nope."

"What d'you mean by 'nope'?"

"It still wouldn't happen."

"Let's finish this down at the canteen."

"Sounds good." Frank was happy with John's new conclusion. He'd come in late after dropping off his car at the garage, so it was mid-morning already, although he could easily read through the likely stack of incoming emails when they came back. Besides, he invariably finished work late most days. Frank closed the door as they made their way along their corridor, taking stairs towards the adjacent building. En route he mentally rehearsed what'd happened on the way to work, whilst wondering just exactly what did or didn't really matter in everyday life. He hadn't had time for breakfast, so now he needed some suitable sustenance before he could think anymore. On cue, they obligingly entered the canteen.

"When I've looked into my family history, I've found Jewish ancestry on both parental lines, although my family is Christian and I've had some good Muslim friends over the years. To be honest, I see far more things which Judaism, Christianity and Islam share, rather than any differences between them. The only theism I can't follow is atheism, but any religion which promotes the idea of deity sounds logical or decent, even if it's not complete, or perhaps not completely correct. All the details of which doctrine is or isn't correct, they can always be ironed out over time. I believe a deity who remains the Father of psyches will only hold people accountable for what they've considered to be correct, or whether they've been true to those tenets. I can't see a Supreme Being holding an individual accountable for what's not believed."

"I tend to agree," John concurred.

"Science is often right, but often it's also wrong, otherwise science wouldn't progress. Scientism on the other hand, is another faith. So where do we go for correct answers?"

"I'm not too sure," John replied.

"Jozef reckons the only definitive answer is from the most intelligent Being in the universe."

"How can anyone communicate with a god, assuming he really exists?"

"Well that's what I'm intrigued by. There has to be a decent answer, although I've already had premonitions alongside experiences which have directed me in certain directions. It's logical there's a Supreme Intelligence in the universe, simply through common sense or probability."

"But such a supreme being might perhaps only be a little more advanced than mankind."

"Evolution means that through enough time, and there's plenty of it, a godlike species will always evolve. Theists refer to the Supreme Being in the universe as God, who'd also logically be the Head of any such group or family."

"Yes, it's a reasonable idea. Yet if it turned out to be a total fallacy, anyone believing in God would've wasted a whole lot of their lifetime. I'm not too sure it's a risk worth taking."

"The same situation could be assumed for any work we undertake. It pretty much sums up some of the statements I've heard from athletes who've finished fourth in the Olympic Games, or from footballers who've ended up with runners-up medals in the FA Cup. It reminds me of the film 'Chariots of Fire' when Harold Abrahams tells his girlfriend if he can't win, he won't run. His girlfriend replies if he doesn't run, then he can't win."

"That's fair comment."

"These lives we lead, they really are a reflection of who we are, and because of it we need to know whether this life is actually a test of the characters we'd evolved in the pre-existence. We all should be able to communicate with a supreme intelligence in the universe. So much speculation is thrown at UFOs, whilst science invests only scant resources investigating themes around the most likely and most helpful extraterrestrial."

"You mean God again?"

"Yes, deity has to be extremely positive as well as massively cooperative, otherwise the universe couldn't have been constructed. Sam Parnia along with Raymond Moody have done useful work on the existence of psyches. A press release recently described how the ALMA telescope in Chile has found that the oldest disc galaxies were formed early in the universe's history. It fits with the idea of an organising force at work, which logically would be coming from a supremely intelligent Being. The technology required for a Supreme Being to communicate with humans should really be quite easy. Why hasn't it contacted us?"

"Maybe he has." Frank was always impressed with John's level of objectivity. He rarely took any particular side in a debate, but the comments he made were generally well-considered, moreover any questions tended to be concisely relevant.

"I guess it's rather a good point. Maybe we've just never realised it."

"Atheists though would say how this line of thinking is delusional or simply made up."

"Atheists have been saying all kinds of illogical things for hundreds, even thousands of years, albeit in different formats. I've no arguments with them because I just don't believe them, but when we die we'll find out what's real, subsequently what's finally true about different dimensions."

"You can't let go of this fascination with the next dimension, can you?"

"I've been working on it for too long, so I'd like to find an answer."

"Will you be happy with any answer you find?"

"I'm not too sure, because I haven't quite found it yet."

"Fair enough."

"I can only guess everyone receives answers in their own way."

"Which is again OK. Mobiles have different phone numbers. Radio stations use different frequencies. So whilst communications might be similar, they could all still be individualised or personalised. Speaking of which, why were you late today?"

"I had to drop the car off for its service."

"I thought you could drop them off early now though?"

"Yer, I actually overslept as well."

"I thought as much. It's because we're getting older."

"Well perhaps, but also because of what happened last night?"

John looked puzzled. "What happened last night?"

"Annoyingly I was woken up a couple of times, which meant when the alarm did go off, it didn't have the proper effect."

"Well what woke you up, then?"

"I was woken up the first time by a dream of a spider running across my forehead. I turned the light on, saw the spider and duly turfed it out the window."

"That was a bit extreme wasn't it?"

"No, it wasn't a problem because there's only grass down below, therefore no worries. Spiders are generally fine anyway. Which brings me onto the subsequent event.... the grass."

"The grass?"

"Yes, I laid down some grass seeds yesterday to patch up the worn out area on the front lawn. Just as it was getting light at about 4am, a flock of starlings with about ten rooks, then probably every finch in the neighbourhood, suddenly chose to fly down and say 'thanks'. They were making a crazy racket, which duly woke me up."

"Oh, they were eating the grass seeds?" John half asked.

"In the end I had to go downstairs and take all the wheelie bins round the front, just to keep them off the newly laid section."

"OK, good thinking. That's a reasonable excuse, I guess."

"You approve?"

"Yes, I believe I do."

"Good, because I'd better get back soon to read through all my incoming emails."

The two men got up and exited the canteen. Frank enjoyed working at the university.

CHAPTER 12

In the evening Frank reached a conclusion. He didn't know the answer to his question but he knew he'd keep looking. He wasn't sure which religion was the most correct, but one of them had to have doctrines which were the closest to reality. Perhaps some churches had a part of the truth or had built their doctrines around a central truth, yet maybe had some incorrect doctrines in other areas. Perhaps multiple religions were close to the truth in the key, central themes they'd chosen? He wasn't sure. He'd enjoyed Jozef's analogy of global religions being collectively akin to a mirror which had become broken, where good people had taken different parts of the mirror, then built an organisation around them. As a whole, a great collection of religions could hold a great wealth of truth or knowledge. It wasn't clear though whether putting all the pieces of a mirror back together again would produce a decent result, because there would still be large cracks across it. He also wasn't quite sure about Jozef's idea of one church acting as a brand new mirror, but it could be possible. He could accept the idea of a new mirror, mirrored after the old mirror, which would mirror the truths of the first mirror in the second mirror. At that point he got lost. Where could anyone find such a restored or new mirror? He didn't know. What he did know was what he did know, and on such a basis he would go ahead with life. He judged how logically there was indeed a Supreme Being and he couldn't deny that feeling, nor ignore a pure logic behind it anymore for the future. He'd decided the only way he could evolve would be to seek out good things, in good places, presumedly amongst good people. He wasn't sure where it would take him, but it didn't matter, so long as it was with Helen and the family. He was sold on the idea of premonitions as a means of communication with a Supreme Being, so he decided he'd probably look into them going forwards. The idea though, was just about enough. Frank fell asleep on the settee, remote control in hand, watching a television programme which had lost his interest quite some time ago. When he was a kid, the TV screen shrunk into a tiny dot every night, albeit long before the early hours of any new day had crept in through the windows. His modern television never stopped anymore. Life went on.

CHAPTER 13

Two men stood together. They were dressed in white suits, white shoes and white ties and one of them was engaged in deep thought.

John-Paul wasn't in mortality for very long. He didn't in fact leave Helen's physical security, nor live separately from his mortal mother, but his psyche had gained a body of his own. Like all human children who'd died, John-Paul was a good character, needing only a brief passage through earthly mortality before passing into the Spirit World. He found the Spirit World to be generally quite similar to the pre-existent world, yet with appropriate permission he could observe mortality as well as other surrounding dimensions within the universe. He was fascinated by the way the universe continued to expand, progressing in both its extent along with the general complexity. It was truly beautiful.

He did however notice a difference between the pre-existence and the Spirit World. They held differential spatial positions within the universe, where the pre-existent globe was situated in the centre, whereas his new Spirit World location was a realm which remained tightly wrapped around the physical Earth. The structures of these two realms were also quite similar, although he quickly perceived there were things missing. In some areas, there couldn't be found any temple buildings, which meant they lacked such portal buildings to allow travel away from the Spirit World, or at least this was the case in the sections termed 'Spirit Prison'. He found that name quite apt for this region within the Spirit World, or the expanse or spiritual lands without temples. The other section of the Spirit World was termed a Paradise. This wasn't heaven, because heaven remained where the Father resided towards the very centre of the universe, but Paradise was another similarly beautiful location within the Spirit World, where temples were situated. Everything was rather perfect within Paradise. He loved the sense of peacefulness along with the tranquil countryside, as mortals would describe it. The blooms were wonderful. It was the best description he could give. The clarity for any visual experience within Paradise was crisper than a newly produced, colourful photograph: for every minute section of distant observations, there was a depth akin to a three-dimensional hologram, and it was available in all directions. In the pre-existence he'd always loved the visual acuity, but he'd only come to appreciate it once he'd left his physical body and passed through the veil into the Spirit World. He'd looked back, noticing how the physical world seemed quite dull in comparison. It was still beautiful, very much so, although far more obscured and less intimate. The experience had remained with him, since he'd never recognised such a thing before, despite the fact he'd observed the mortal world countless times from his pre-existence home. It was indeed true how some things just needed to be experienced.

He was both amused as well as bemused over how long it had taken his parents to settle upon his mortal name. His mother had chosen John, whilst his father, Frank, had preferred the name Paul. The family prompter had spent so much time coaching both parents, until it became curious when each had chosen different halves of the full name. After they'd miraculously settled upon John-Paul, the need for a name had actually vanished, because his mortal frame never reached birth.

As he commenced his life within the Spirit World, he'd once again begun to observe men in the mortal dimension. His role as a family guardian afforded many occasions for observing men. He was intrigued with man's recent interest or theories on travelling beyond the speed of light. It seemed quite logical to him how psyches had no issues with travelling at light-speed or beyond, since psyches were constructed from different forms of light, as men would one day figure them to be. At least, psyches had bodies involving particles, which were significantly smaller or energies which were significantly different from (or in real terms larger than), those mortals were accustomed to observing and studying. It was no coincidence how near-death experiences as well as spiritual experiences, were generally associated with human psyches. Psyche was essentially composed of refined matter and since it had no limitations in travelling above light-speed, then experiences could be unfolded in a few mere mortal moments. John-Paul was amused how mortals had come so close to reality in constructing their stories of 'Superman', with his vast speed, or the ability to perform so many things in such a short period of time. It seemed logical the Father often chose the psyches of men and women, or in other words the spiritual, to convey ideas alongside knowledge. It could all be done in an instant. Communicating with the psyches of men and women meant relevant experiences could be accomplished whilst mortal time seemed to simply stand still. It also meant the Father, or His administrative Light-Bearers could help numerous, countless numbers of mortals, seemingly all together or concurrently. John-Paul considered time was being used usefully rather than travelled. Time or history was recorded as opposed to travelled, and the future was governed by freewill rather than time.

He enjoyed finding ways to enlighten the discussion group which Frank attended, giving guides or prompts as to where solutions lay, whether for moral or scientific or family or other issues which arose during their discussions. The evolution question was a regular theme, however he couldn't intervene but only prompt. Each psyche wasn't as the world had suggested in the twentieth or twenty-first centuries, merely 'bricks in the wall' of organic evolution, possessing mortal bodies which had adapted into more advanced lifeforms. Any morphological or other biological changes had occurred on planets, at times dedicated for purpose, and the human physical body was a particular case. Each psyche who entered mortality was previously born of godly parents, holding innate goodly desires in tandem with noble intents. Men had always sought the divine, since their psyches were originally born of the divine. Their passage into mortality would allow each individual to become more godly in their own right, acting for themselves, choosing good over evil where evil was present, and so the battle for the souls of men had begun.

The temporary but gigantic struggle between right or wrong, could only really occur away from the protection of God's perfect pre-existent environment. Men or women would not return to the Father after death just to become constant attendants in servitude, since the Father as a father, spent His time assisting his children; rather, men and women could return as sons or daughters of Heavenly Father and Heavenly Mother, learning to act as They act, doing as They do, and on a permanent basis. Such evolution would become important because any deviation from correctness in heaven, or the heaven which governed and maintained their universe, would inevitably lead to consequent decay or ruin of this universe over time, and there was plenty of time in the universe. Everything had to be perfectly perfect after mortality, whereby entered the need for an atonement, or a way to make things right again. Under such a plethora of mortal mistakes, an atonement became a way of allowing men and women to become fully good once more. Forsaking evil or choosing good was a great purpose in mortal life. It was an eternal purpose which needed to be learned or lived eternally, otherwise there could be no passage into the highest heavenly home.

Such an entrance was achieved through temples. Temples had always been or would continue to be the portals between heaven and other dimensions. John-Paul saw one additional advantage with having had such a short earth life: it didn't seem strange how temples could be celestial conduits, whereas the idea for some mortals appeared totally crazy, even quite preposterous. He didn't completely follow their doubts because at the end of the day, temples were buildings, and humans used small metal buildings, which they termed 'spaceships', in order to travel. Anyway, temples in mortality remained schools for those other temples situated in other dimensions, and as such afforded knowledge, as well as places of evolutionary contract for human souls. The temple buildings provided no guarantees of physical permanency, fitting perfectly amongst all other mortal things, but offered permanency for family relationships as well as associations, eternally by contract. Physical permanency would come later, after souls had logically abandoned any inappropriate or imperfect allures of the temporary environment on Earth. The test of mortality was always to build an inward permanency for choosing goodness, and could be expressed in proper behaviour. Such was logical because it would become an evolution of the individual, or an evolution towards the divine, or a growth into a divine potential residing within every human psyche. Such wondrous capacity for copying Heavenly Parents had continuously and beautifully become manifest or recorded throughout human history. History had indeed shown itself to be fascinating, even for thousands of years, and would continue to do so.

John-Paul had sought good ways to guide Frank or his friends towards temples. Whilst Jozef was open to promptings in this as well as other respects, Frank was slowly becoming more open to premonitions, since evolution was always a gradual process, 'line upon line, precept upon precept, here a little, there a little' until a more accurate picture had been revealed. John-Paul considered those lines from a book were probably apt for Frank, or similarly for the rest of the discussion group. The lines suited their efforts admirably and described the best way forward. A progressive or necessary evolution of psyche depended upon them, so John-Paul was intrigued by the group's evolutionary discussions. They'd concluded there was a logical need for the man called Adam as a righteous psyche, becoming the first godly-born, human ancestor upon the Earth, as Frank had surmised from Luke 3:38. This in turn meant there also had to be a break, between whatever occurred previously on the Earth (in its former form, which seemed indelibly reflected in fossilisations) from the placement of man along with modern day animals upon the Earth. Some would disagree, but the group had found no useful alternative. They'd realised God wouldn't leave the evolution of his children to chance, nor could He create physical forms which would die. Evolution involving the souls of His children was His work and glory, whereby Adam was key to the initiation of such a process. John-Paul observed how psyches entered mortal life with such confidence, such excitement or such energy – it wasn't surprising though, considering the aeons of time they'd spent in a perfect pre-existent environment, where everything functioned perfectly and happiness was extensively the norm. Only through the years of mortal life would men or women become worn down by trials or hardships. Yet that was still a purpose for mortal life, to experience an environment with opposition or difficulties, since difficulties had to be faced at some point in existence. For individuals to become a force for good meant evil had to be encountered, then resisted or overcome.

John-Paul chuckled most heartily when he observed men creating heroes in ancient times and super-heroes in modern times. Not that heroes weren't good, because clearly all good things were good, but more eruditely, there were psyches in the Spirit World (and just across the veil from mortality) who were commonplace as heroes or super-heroes, going about their business, holding all the attributes or abilities which mortal men and women so admired. Psyches inherently travelled at great speed through the Spirit World, through the wrapping which cladded the physical Earth. In a moment they could arrive at a chosen destination. In an instant they could communicate person-to-person across the vast expanse of the extended Spirit World: men would later marvel at the sublime effectiveness of this interpersonal telepathic ethernet, albeit achieved without communications hardware. Telepathy was borne upon a more advanced and significantly refined protocol of communications, driven or used by psyches with a knowledge of systems which had previously been embedded from Light-Bearers throughout aeons of time. Perhaps more importantly, telepathic communications were accessible by whosoever could use them properly. Psyches could traverse barriers standing as obstacles in the physical world, or remove threats to mortals before their menace could exact an outcome. Administrative psyches could deliver information in an instant, information which would avert a crisis, or add spark to creative knowledge, bringing comfort to mortal individuals under mental distress. Everything good was ultimately coordinated, even originated from the Father, so the Father took an interest in all the affairs of His children. He knew how to take an interest perfectly, whilst still permitting a complete level of free agency. John-Paul however, couldn't intervene in the discussions of the discussion group. Not only would it clearly unsettle them but it could also change their mortal tests, perhaps significantly. He could only guide or prompt, particularly amongst those family members who asked, or communicated with the Father. He liked the mortal word 'prayer' because it denoted a level of humility or openness, with an attitude affording clearer and faster communication. It was good. It was a prerequisite for any assistance which John-Paul could provide. Usually the assistance was undertaken in tandem with another psyche, and he enjoyed working that way.

"So what are these instructions you've received?"

"We have to place premonitions."

"What type of premonitions?"

"The important type."

"Aren't they all important?"

"Yes they are, but some are just a little more important than others."

"How important is this latest one?"

"Very important."

"Yes, somehow I thought it might be."

Charlie grinned. "It's your family. In the future they'll be be faced with some quite significant things, so we have to prepare them."

"How?"

"We need to train them."

"How?"

"By placing premonitions."

"How?"

"Do you say anything other than 'how'?"

"Only if I know how," John-Paul grinned.

Charlie judged how his mortal grandson was a joker. It was good. "We need to show them how," Charlie parried, "through dreams, or ideas, or via other mortals, or through good books, or from good stories, or with anything good. Good things create more good things. It's evolution at its best. We have to find ways of getting them to listen."

"Listen to what?"

"To us. Through the premonitions we're permitted to plant."

"OK," John-Paul agreed.

"And the premonitions will be the instructions we receive from higher up the authority line."

"OK," John-Paul agreed.

CHAPTER 14

Charlotte grew sleepy as they travelled along the long winding road on their way back home. It had been a relaxing family holiday. The hotel was very pleasant, the food was good, whilst the summer sunshine was exactly what they'd needed. The children had clearly enjoyed themselves, so it had worked out well for the whole family. She glanced over to watch Jack driving, as he usually did, taking them back up home to the north country. Life was indeed good, which she'd managed to pleasantly consider before drifting towards a period of welcome slumber. She'd been tending to the children for most of the day, but she could happily sleep quite well in the front passenger seat. It was important to have the seat was tilted back, just enough to give a suitable resting position, whilst at the same time just enough to allow room for all the children behind. 'It's a good job they're still small,' she noted before commencing her well-earned rest.

-

Jack looked different as he came towards her. He looked younger, probably back to the time when they were first married. Charlotte marvelled at it. Why did he appear different? She suddenly noticed she was now floating above their car, and Jack was too. They were next to each other, but as Jack began to move away from her, she called to him, unsure as to what was happening. A distinct impression came into her mind. She could go along with Jack, then venture beyond, although she couldn't be with their children if she made the trip. Alternatively, she could stay behind, not going along with Jack, yet remaining with the children. There was a choice to be made.

-

When Charlotte awoke from her rest she found herself in hospital. She knew the dream in reality wasn't a dream, because she knew what had happened. A nurse came to Charlotte and began to communicate, attempting to reorient her into the new, unfamiliar surroundings. After a few more days nurses attempted to communicate concerning the events which had happened and why she was in hospital. They tried to relate what had happened to Jack.

"I know," she said. "I've seen him. I made a choice," Charlotte responded. "I needed to stay with Emily and Edward."

-

Two men stood together. They were dressed in white suits, white shoes and white ties and were deeply engaged in discussion. John-Paul stared in amazement. He'd been present as a trainee or observer when Jack came through the veil. He was spending time noting the typical routine as new arrivals entered the Spirit World. There were initial excited gatherings, the greetings, jubilant extended family meetings, the various welcoming procedures and gradually a collection of all the necessary or new dimensional protocols. One thing gripped his attention above all others. He couldn't figure it out. Why hadn't Jack had a premonition about the oncoming vehicle?

"Why didn't Jack have a premonition about the oncoming vehicle?" he asked.

"Because it was his time to leave mortality. Everyone has an ending to a mortal life, and it was Jack's time," Charlie responded.

"Well what about Charlotte or their kids? Why not extend Jack's life?"

"Would it be any easier for them at a future date?"

"I'm not sure."

"Neither am I. But I do know it was Jack's time."

John-Paul thought for a moment. "So how do we know whether a premonition will work?" he asked.

"Oh, we're back with 'how' again, are we?"

"I'm afraid so... for now anyway... until I fully understand, and then I could definitely ask something else."

"Well," Charlie replied. "It's a lot to do with history."

"History?" John-Paul looked puzzled.

"Yes, whatever comes up in family history can be jolly useful for premonitions."

"What do you mean? Do you look into the past, then guess what can be useful going forwards into the future?"

"Absolutely, because you can usually gain ideas on a way to prompt wisely, and particularly from any successes or events with different individuals in the past."

"Is that fair?"

"Sure. Don't forget we're only causing ideas to arise, whereby every mortal has total freedom in choosing their actions or behaviour, or what they'll continue to think about. Planting a good seed is helpful."

"OK," John-Paul agreed.

"Take for example your parents, and the first time they met."

"I've never looked that up on our holographic records. I

suppose I've never thought about it."

"I just happen to know a little more about the event because I was prompting. It was reasonably soon after I'd entered the Spirit World from mortality."

"What did you do?"

"Frank was Abdem in the pre-existence, and he wanted a mortal name close to Helen's, so when Helen had asked to become Helen Frances, he'd asked to became Frank. Eventually he did. He wanted to find her in mortality but he knew they'd both forget each other because the veil of forgetfulness would come down during early mortality. It was agreed to create similarities between their early mortal lives, so that when they did eventually meet they'd become fascinated by the similarities. Helen's father is also called Charles, like me. They called their pets similar names and as parents, we gave them some gifts which were similar. My wife was Patricia in mortality, similar to Helen's mother. Frank never wanted to become a priest in childhood, although he was intrigued by religious ideas or concepts. He actually read quite a lot of books around the subjects of religion or philosophy, and also throughout his teen years. At one point he started to examine different churches, afterwards going along to some church activities, specifically for young adults. A friend of Frank's knew about his church involvement, since he was religious himself. At that point it was really quite easy for me to prompt Dave, then get him to tell Frank he'd probably meet his future wife during the times he spent at those church activities. It's where Frank met Helen, at a church dance or ball."

"Is this the same Dave I've noticed going to the discussion group meetings?"

"The one at the discussion group is actually his son."

"Dave junior?"

"Absolutely. Anyway, in the pre-existence we all knew how

Abdem and Helen loved to dance together, since they spent ages practising in the celestial halls. They became quite inseparable in the pre-existence, so I used this knowledge to prompt them in mortality. Helen's dancing was different to Frank's. She was more carefree and open, inventive and spontaneous. Frank was more staid or formal, yet they somehow just worked together. When she became too vigorous for him he would simply sit and watch her. Obviously in the pre-existence the closeness between Abdem and Helen was born of friendship or interest, as well as loyalty, amongst other things. Love could grow from attractions outside the stronger, physical hormones which would come later in mortality. We weren't born into mortality with those hormones. I can remember my first early attraction to a girl called Carol, during teenage years of puberty which grew over months, then slowly changed me. Those changes can take a bit of effort to get used to and control wisely."

"I didn't experience that," John-Paul reflected.

"Yes, I appreciate what happened for you wasn't the same. But your opportunity will come in the future. There's always a good time for everything."

John-Paul seemed contented. "So you used dancing to prompt them?"

"Yes."

"Did it work?"

"This wasn't a difficult task. They'd wanted to be together in the pre-existence, so Frank recognised how everything clicked immediately for him when he met Helen. There were no gaps, no need to keep on looking, nor any distractions at all. It was complete. Helen also told him that she knew him from the pre-existence. They've still had challenges to overcome during their married life, but their love's never changed. I don't believe it ever will."

"OK," John-Paul agreed.

CHAPTER 15

"Well that was different!" Siggel announced whilst Kieron allowed the film to draw to its natural conclusion.

"What did you think?" Kieron asked.

"It was different."

"But how did it make you feel?"

"Different."

"OK. Great. Anything else?"

"Yes, inspired."

"Aghh, now that's more interesting."

"Why?"

"Because it was different."

"Hmmm, very drôle. So we're back to where we were before we are where we are, are we?"

"But how was it different?"

"I've mentioned how it was different. I believe they were probably listening to my response." Siggel complained, now turning towards Reg. "These young people today, they don't know how to quit whilst they're ahead, or am I missing something?"

"It's true Siggel," Reg concurred. "But they did choose the right film?"

"Yes, you do make a good point."

"We heard how Morgan Freeman referred to the film during one of his programmes in the 'Story of God' series, so we thought it might be cool to dig it out," Dave added.

"There's actually an interesting story behind that film," Reg continued. "When they were attempting to film the part when he goes into the wood, a blackbird came down and flew around the actor's head. The film crew tried to get it to go away, but they couldn't all the time he was walking into the woods, so in the end they cut the film, simply starting again. The second time they filmed the same sequence, the blackbird came back, flying around the actor's head as before; eventually they stopped filming after a while. In the distance they could see storm clouds gathering, but the actual event occurred apparently on a beautiful spring morning, which meant they only had limited chance to film this key sequence, and they couldn't do without it. They'd enough time for one final attempt. The cameras rolled yet sure enough, the same as before, the blackbird came back down to fly around the young actor's head once again. In the end they left the bird in the sequence but if you happen to watch it another time in the future, you can see it quite clearly. Eventually one of the film crew was curious, to the point where she went back to the archives to look into a journal which was kept during the period, a journal in fact written by the young man who was being portrayed in the film. Exactly as had happened with the film crew, he'd recorded as he'd entered the woods, a blackbird came down then flew around his head."

"Oh, that's different," Siggel acknowledged. "What's the name of this film, anyway?"

"First Vision."

"I heard the film was made by a cult," Wyatt interjected.

"Well, the definition of a cult is a system of religious veneration or devotion directed towards a particular figure or object."

"He's got it off his phone," Wyatt objected.

"There's nothing wrong with a decent use of technology!"

"Precisely," Reg continued. "Following on from the phone's, or the internet's definition, since the organisation is called the Church of Jesus Christ, where it venerates Jesus Christ, it means your suggestion isn't too bad. It's wrong in general context, though still not too bad overall."

"I can see how the film had a logical title," Siggel concluded, returning to the previous theme of their discussion. "Very religious." He paused a while in reflection. "The part about the opposition or blackness was quite graphic."

"Yes, there's a definite opposition to anything good down here in mortality," Kieron noted. "I've felt some dark things before," he continued.

"But a key point is goodness will always help its own. Perhaps a more important point is goodness will continue to be the greatest strength in the universe. It's the power by which everything is held together," Dave suggested.

"So where does the darkness come from?" Siggel inquired.

"In the pre-existence God the Father put forward a plan," Reg answered.

"... outlining how we could evolve our psyches, in order to become more like our Heavenly Parents," Dave added.

"Absolutely," Reg recognised. "After the plan was discussed in detail, the Father heard from the Firstborn as well as Lucifer, a Light-bearer. The Father had asked whom to send as a Saviour or the person who'd make an atonement, since it was highly likely psyches would make a fair number of mistakes in mortality."

"All the kerfuffle over religious sin is boring!"

"Well not really, if you're on the receiving end..."

"It just needs to be ignored."

"Would you be happy letting thieves get away with your stuff?"

"Theft is one thing, but worrying about sin is nonsensical."

"Sins are like theft. Well actually, theft is sin, but more

importantly they all have consequences."

"Anyway," Reg continued, pausing to refocus. "A relevant example concerns the way in which psyches would learn how to build families during mortality using physical bodies, since psyches didn't or don't have the gift of procreation."

"Psyches probably weren't matured in the pre-existence."

"I'm not sure psyches can ever have offspring, otherwise Lucifer and his followers would have done. What's more, psyches in the Spirit World would also probably have children."

"Yes, perhaps. Anyway..." Reg interjected, attempting to bring the discussion back around onto subject.

"But the Father and Heavenly Mother could have children in the form of psyches."

"Yes, it's true. Anyway..."

"But why do heavenly parents with resurrected bodies produce psyches, whilst earthly parents with physical bodies produce mortal humans?"

"I believe it's because Heavenly Father and Heavenly Mother have spirit flowing through them rather than blood. Anyway, in learning how to create families, it was clear the procreative power could be misused. Mistakes such as those would have to be settled, and hence the need for a Saviour to achieve a settlement of the mortal exam, getting people back into heaven with resurrected bodies."

"The Father chose the Firstborn. Right?"

"Yes, He did. Lucifer wanted an alternative scheme to force people into not making mistakes, and save them by force. But it wouldn't have worked. Becoming clones would teach individuals very little. Besides, everyone could be saved through the Father's plan of using a Saviour, which potentially held a hundred per cent success rate. A person needs to use the Saviour's atonement contract to correct their mistakes, whilst evolving themselves by rejecting evil or loving what's good, yet still being in the presence of evil. It's evolution, because evil wasn't present in the same way in the pre-existence. Psyches could previously choose to be less or more valiant in terms of effort, but there wasn't open rebellion against the Father's laws in the pre-existence."

"Not until Lucifer rebelled."

"Again, the point you make is true. When he rebelled he was required to leave. There's a section in the Apocalypse of Moses which talks about Lucifer's anger at the status achieved by Michael the Archangel. Michael was reportedly younger than Lucifer in the pre-existence. Lucifer stated that his followers tried to leave the Father's governance, along with him, driven on by the fact they saw how Michael was positioned above him."

"Lucifer though, wanted to usurp the Firstborn or the Father. It was a crazy move."

"Maybe, but politics can be emotive or at times irrational. The political ideas we experience in mortality, probably had their origins in events which occurred in the pre-existence."

"Was Michael as Archangel, a member of the Godhead at some point? He became Adam later though, didn't he?"

"Yes, he did, although I'm not entirely sure about the hierarchical structure in God's government. The Papyrus Bodmer X talks about Lucifer's aspirations for a role in the Godhead."

"The third position of Holy Ghost is never connected to any single person by name. Perhaps it's a rotational role, or perhaps a role for a group of people? Maybe the Archangel was part of the governmental third role, which was termed the Holy Ghost? 'Holy Ghost' sounds like a psyche, or multiple psyches in rotation. If Lucifer kept being overlooked, it might have made him angry enough for rebellion."

"Yes, pride's certainly a dangerous thing where it's allowed to evolve. In time everyone gets their chance, so it just takes patience. Pride is uncooperative or destructive. It's actually illogical, as well as achieves very little."

"Resentment or pride is still understandable though."

"Yes, it certainly can be. What's real however, is possibly the realisation a Saviour couldn't come to an earth until one regressed, where individuals would actually subject a member of the Godhead to physical death."

"Such a situation is pretty bad."

"And it was probably only possible because Lucifer along with his followers were present upon this earth."

"Is it true? There's supposedly quite a lot of information in those ancient texts you've cited."

"Yes, quite often science castigates ancient peoples as superstitious or ignorant, when in reality, since they were chronologically closer to the times of Adam or other patriarchs, they were in a position to record the ancient events with more detailed accuracy. It's only through time that history has become foggy or mysterious."

"I've read some of those ancient scripts you're mentioning. I can't get my head around some of them because they sound so ridiculous, even their style of writing is mega flowery. Quite often they also contradict themselves."

"Which serves to highlight how they've become foggy or mysterious over time. But every now and then you can still see golden nuggets amongst the apparent level of fog or mystery."

"Well, only if you can find some way of cutting through the ridiculous..."

"And that's where the much needed inspiration comes in handy."

-

Two men stood together. They were dressed in white suits,

white shoes and white ties and were deeply engaged in discussion.

"So how do we help them then? When do we provide inspiration?"

"You can only give them ideas on how to find their answers. If you plant a premonition it has to be left up to the individuals in searching out their own solutions, which generally happens before they can work out what it all means. It's when they need to be using prayer. If they don't consult someone about the answers, they can't sensibly expect to receive help or thereby arrive at a decent outcome. The process is logical."

"OK," John-Paul agreed. "Although some mortals feel they've tried prayer, yet things never seem to work out. Consequently for them, it becomes a ridiculous thing to do."

"I used to feel the same way about tennis before I started practising properly. Working out the way things work isn't always easy. Practice is important."

"OK," John-Paul agreed.

"Now, an instruction's been received for you."

"For me?"

"Yes, let me show you. The communication's quite short."

John-Paul listened intently. He was instructed to prepare a future home for Helen and Frank, a home situated down by the sea, one which could provide them with family enjoyment during their more restful times. Helen had often explored the possibilities of a coastal home with Frank, where ideally it would be perched upon a set of chalky, white cliffs at some open, panoramic vantage point. They'd generally envisaged it would become a homestead which could run a path down to their own seaside waters, allowing everyone to easily wash up old, new stories, surfacing from constantly creative waves.

John-Paul was given a clear scene of the land. It featured a dwelling with lush, green lawns, all neatly bounded around by wooden post-and-rail fencing. Whilst the fencing carefully encircled the outside of a matured garden, outer lands revealed a series of layers, layers created from a collection of wide fields surrounding a double-storeyed, rather expansive log cabin. The cabin itself was standing squarely within the centre of the land. There were additional hedgerows, plus an assortment of trees, and the trees divided the fields one from another, with small openings for leisurely strolls between the green spaces. John-Paul had found the home he was looking for, and it was perfect.

'This is perfect for mum and her horses,' John-Paul commented to himself. 'Absolutely perfect.' Moreover, it was in exactly the location he'd been shown. The house was adorned within a gardener's paradise, 'it's no less than a horticulturalist's dream, possibly a garden centre's showpiece. Robert would love this!' John-Paul continued, wondering how close it could come to winning the Chelsea Flower Show. 'That's only if Robert might shrink it, then make an entry of it. Somehow though, I reckon such a thing could in fact prove to be a little difficult!' he conceded. He'd been instructed to prepare the home for both Helen and Frank, but he wasn't completely sure what there was actually left to do. 'Whatever mum likes, dad usually likes,' he suggested, advising himself once more. 'And vice verse.' He soon realised he still needed to personalise their property, essentially with Helen's loves as well as Frank's likes. He also appreciated they'd bring memories with them whenever they happened to come through the veil. He wasn't exactly confident of finding the perfect balance between leaving an open or clean slate, essentially for later tailoring, whilst at the same time including some of those welcome, reassuring features which could make them feel right back at home. He wanted the place to be as close as possible to the feeling everyone had enjoyed for so long, in the pre-existence. At least, he still knew he could always copy those pre-existence designs again. He was quietly confident they'd like it. John-Paul decided to find Charlie, or even Charles would do, since he needed to figure out whether his plans were going OK. He went off to find them.

CHAPTER 16

C hris was just the man for the job. Chris could help out where others had failed miserably. James knocked on his friend's door and pretty soon they were down to business. He was going to get to the bottom of this enigma, even if it took him the whole afternoon, since at Chris's place he could relax. There was simply no pressure, nor any rush at all.

"Just look at the dots James then focus, because eventually you'll see a picture in the dots. Actually it's kind of at the back of the dots, a little in the distance somewhere."

He passed the sheet of paper over to his friend. James began to focus, attempting to train his eyes to see something he'd never experienced before. He wasn't too sure what he was attempting to do because he'd never previously succeeded, so he also wasn't sure what he'd see. He likewise wasn't confident over the instructions Chris which was talking about, but his expectations were still high because apparently the 3-D pictures were excellent. He began looking. Looking for something. He looked into the dots, and there were certainly a lot of dots. 'Help, there are a lot of dots!' he exclaimed, albeit to himself. "There are a lot of dots!" he informed Chris.

"Yep, you're absolutely right. But keep looking at it."

The dots were many different colours which meant they were rather confusing, yet for a few brief seconds, quite mesmerising. He wondered who'd spent so much time in devising this system or how could anyone actually work out which dots to place in the picture, or how many there should be, or at what distance and... in the end he got fed up with wondering. He stared more intently at the dots, determined to experience the experience which everyone said was fantastic. 'Well, some folks say it's fantastic... not everyone, because not everyone has had a go, but some people apparently can never see the pictures, no matter how hard they try.' He paused thinking. 'Help, I hope I'm not one of those people,' he informed himself "I hope I'm not one of the people who can't see the dots!" he informed Chris.

"Don't worry, you'll be just fine. Simply keep looking at the dots."

He did. Nothing happened. He did some more. Still nothing happened.

"I'm going to fall asleep doing this," he informed Chris.

"Don't worry, just keep going."

When James did fall asleep, he was quickly woken up by the nodding of his head, as he nearly butted the picture in front of him. He began to get annoyed.

"I'm beginning to get annoyed," he informed Chris.

"Don't worry, you'll see the picture."

"That's easy for you to say, because you're not the one doing this ridiculous exercise."

"I've been through it though and it took me ages."

"How long did it take you?"

"About three hours."

"Three hours! That's ridiculous. I'm not sitting here staring at this crazy page of coloured dots for three hours! I can just as easily see the 3-D effect at a cinema."

"OK, no worries. Pass back the picture can you?"

James continued staring at the dots, determined to experience what everyone else had said was excellent. 'Well, not everyone else... because some people never actually get to see the pictures,' he reminded himself. 'But what if there wasn't actually a picture in the dots, or people had just convinced themselves they'd seen something when it was simply in their imagination?' he slowly inquired of himself. He didn't have an answer.

"What if there isn't a picture in the dots or it's just in the viewer's imagination?" he inquired of Chris.

"The picture's there. Just keep looking."

"But I'm staring at it and there's nothing there. I can't see a thing. Only dots!"

"It's fine, but you need to keep looking."

"How do you know it's there. Have a look at the dots and see if there's definitely a picture in there, can you?"

Chris took the picture, looked at it for a few seconds then confirmed, "Yes, there's a picture in the dots."

"What's the picture of?"

"I'd like you to tell me. I'll know if you've had the experience, by what you tell me you've finally seen."

"It's not funny!" James protested.

"No, it's not. It's excellent."

James stared at the picture again. There was nothing but dots.

"Does anyone ever lose the ability to see the pictures?"

"Yes, I lost it for a while. Eventually I began to doubt whether I'd ever get it back at all, but I still knew I'd seen the pictures, so when I relaxed I could see them all over again."

"Well that's jolly convenient," James informed him. Chris didn't reply.

As James awoke he found Chris was no longer in the room. James looked at the page of dots and he got past the stage of feeling frustrated. He just looked at the page whilst wondering what the picture was about or why he couldn't see it. He couldn't see a thing. He was slowly concluding how in reality there was nothing there at all, because James was merely playing a joke. He found the joke idea though a little strange, since he had other friends who'd seen pictures in the dots. He began to tire of being fed up, looking at the page one more time, and as he looked a strange sensation began to befall his eyes. In staring at the page, somehow the page began to disappear into the distance, slowly and literally moving away from him.

"That's funny he exclaimed!" as he realised he hadn't in any way moved the page at all. He couldn't understand why it was suddenly travelling back from him, so he looked to the side of the page just to make sure he wasn't moving it. He wasn't moving it. He gazed at the page another time when once more, it began moving backwards from him, quite haltingly at first but within a few moments, more rapidly until it stopped, even at a fixed distance away. At that point he noticed it. The page was concurrently both a little in the distance, whilst also still close to him. In fact the collection of dots was forming a tunnel between what he could see close up and what he could see further behind. 'Help, this is 3-D!' he exclaimed to himself. He could now see a fantastically realistic view of some countryside, with rolling hills, a picturesque country cottage, all bathed in a swathe of rather excellent sunny weather. 'Well that doesn't happen too often!' he commented to himself. He studied the scene for a while. It was very good and he marvelled at how accurate everything seemed. At the end of the day it was possibly quite amazing. 'Help, this is amazing!' he mentally acknowledged. 'There really is a picture here amongst these crazy dots. I never could have believed it... not without seeing it.' "I never would have believed it!" he called out, forgetting Chris wasn't actually in the room. "This is truly amazing!"

"I said you'd get it," Chris replied, having come back into the room whilst James was making his full discovery. "So what's the picture of, then?"

"Countryside. It's countryside!"

"Yep, you've got it. And it didn't take you too long. Only forty-five minutes."

"Yer, and it's worth every minute of the wait. I do agree, this is excellent."

Chris likewise agreed, being rather pleased James had finally joined the large collection of people who knew how a page of dots could carry far more visual information than a page of dots. In all those dots a fascinating pictorial story took refuge, waiting for people to discover its reality. Chris was pleased how his friend had made the leap of faith into a world of brand new reality. He concluded it was probably work enough for one day.

"Let's go to the cinema," he suggested.

"What now?"

"Absolutely!"

"Well what d'you want to see?"

"A 3-D film." Chris paused deliberately. "I'd like to see a 3-D film."

James grinned. "OK, sure. Let's go."

Chris grabbed the car keys and they both headed towards the front door. He knew there were some good films at the cinema that week, so they could just choose when they actually got there. James closed the door behind them as they left. He'd left the 3-D picture on the table. He knew what he was looking for now. He wondered where the premonition had come from though – the one which suggested that if he went around to Chris' place, he'd solve the problem. He didn't know but he'd think about it later.

-

Two men stood together. They were dressed in white suits, white shoes and white ties and were deeply engaged in discussion.

"So now you're getting the idea of how things can work."

"Yes, I believe I am," John-Paul confirmed.

"We planted an idea, then we left it up to him to discover things for himself. It's free agency... with a little help from some friends," Charlie explained.

"And family."

"Yes, because they make good friends."

"So what do we do now?"

"We wait and see what the next move becomes. Helping people is a dynamic situation, since people have free agency, so the goal posts are always moving."

This reminded John-Paul of something. "I didn't get to play football in mortality," he commented wistfully.

"Well let's put it right... and straight away. We'll go gather some of the others and we'll have a game."

"Great idea!" John-Paul agreed. They quickly vanished.

CHAPTER 17

Frank logged onto Facebook. He'd read Mandy's comments on his Facebook post about disease control measures and he was interested. A reply was needed. In fact fifty-one replies had already been posted, see-sawing between different people with different opinions on the pandemic. As he looked through them all, he slowly came to the conclusion that every opinion was valid. Not every opinion was correct, yet everyone had a reason for believing the things they expressed, which meant every opinion was still valid. At the end of the day, people were more important than any point and friends were virtually as important as family. He'd spent so many years researching the existence of psyche, whilst a far more worthy consideration was the likelihood of family as well as friends originating from a logical pre-existence. 'Family along with friends could have carried over from this pre-existence,' he postulated to himself. Previously he'd used his Facebook account to bury an episode surrounding the global pandemic, and now it was taking on a rather 'time-changing' perspective.

'Hold on, hold on!' he protested. 'This isn't earth-shattering...' Silence quickly erupted. 'However, if Helen's Church is in any way accurate, it would mean our psyches were credibly born of heavenly parents, and that would make everyone potentially perfect... which is nonsense, because no one is anything like perfect.' A pause interrupted, balancing the arguments for a moment. 'We just don't need to be... at least, not for the foreseeable future. Evolution is all about progress. And if everyone on earth is in the same family, well what about other earths, or other inhabitable planets, or even other created or organised regions? Is everything evolving? If I ever get around to finishing off that stuff I was doing... about psyches, or a pre-existence or premonitions... I think I'll call it something to do with evolution.' Time waited patiently until he caught up. 'Yes, it's a bit of a collection of ideas in places, so maybe something along the lines of an evolving theorem... or Evolution Theorem... a bit like E.T.... that was a good film. It probably still is...' He'd never thought through such ideas before. He logged off from Facebook to spend some time with them. He was soon asleep.

-

"Let's have a look at that book again please Frank," James asked as he picked up the cup of hot chocolate, enjoying its warmth on such a bleak, mundane morning. "We haven't seen the sun for ages, you know."

"True, it's a bit depressing. That's why I always keep one of my clocks on British Summer Time... in actual fact, all the year through. The tricky bit comes if I've got an appointment, which infuriatingly could result in leaving super early, but generally it cheers me up and somehow seems to work," Frank replied.

"Well I reckon someone should move England down into the Mediterranean. That'll solve both the dark nights as well as the lack of sun. Two solutions for the price of one!"

"Maybe... but then the countryside would be brown, whereby there'd be no green or pleasant land."

"I've also thought about such an additional problem, and I've got an answer for it as well..."

Frank didn't reply but waited patiently for the inevitable solution.

"In parts of America in the mid-west, they've plenty of sun in the morning whilst it then rains for about an hour in the afternoon. After the rain, the sun comes out once again, staying around until sunset. A perfect solution!"

"True, but it's still not green. The countryside's mostly brown."

James fell silent. He wasn't sure anymore whether there was a perfect solution – he concluded perhaps all the solutions, or any of the solutions, was probably correct.

After a while Frank found the book and handed it to James. He could see James was downcast over his attempts to brighten up the weather.

"Look, I like your idea of moving England down to the Mediterranean," Frank commented.

"I thought you said England would be a brown or barren land," James negatively embellished.

"Perhaps... but it would be a bright and sunny one though!"

James grinned. He looked at the cover of the book. "Evolution Theorem... by E.B. Mad..." he vocalised. "Why did you choose such a weird pseudonym?"

"It was my real name, originally."

James started to laugh. "OK, fine... if you don't want to tell me, I guess I won't bother pushing..."

"Read the book and you'll see what I mean."

James opened the book at the first page, then commenced reading from the rear of the book. Within a few moments he looked up before closing the back cover. He stared towards the window on the far side of the room, seemingly absorbed or distracted at the same time.

"Well that was quick!" Frank remarked. "I've seen some jolly good speed-readers but what you've done is impressive. What

I don't get is why you opened the front cover before reading from the back of the book?"

"I was looking for answers. Who wrote the epilogue at the end?" James asked pointedly.

"I did." Frank obliged. "Well actually, not really, I didn't… not entirely. The section you're reading was something which evolved from things I found in my father's old desk. It seems jolly familiar whenever I read it, but I've never truly figured out the riddle. What you've just done is also in there."

"Where?"

"More towards the end of the book than the beginning."

"How?"

"A premonition. Anyway, because I couldn't really figure it out, I stuck it in the book as an afterthought… more of a mid-book conundrum which someone might take pity on, but suitably hidden away. Anyway, why did you ask about the epilogue?"

James opened the end of the book, before re-reading it. He looked back over towards the window and stared out for a long while. The target of his gaze seemed less relevant than the fact that the gazing appeared to assist his contemplation.

"What are you thinking about?" Frank finally intervened.

"It's the wording." James paused, looking around for a brief moment before duly staring out of the window again. "Those ideas seem so familiar... so distinctly familiar."

"What's so familiar about them?"

"I'm not too sure... it's just as though I've heard the ideas before. It's as though I spent a long time considering them... an age ago..."

Frank chuckled.

"What's so funny?"

"Oh, I was thinking how I was in the exact same state you're in, when I first had an experience."

"An experience? What type of experience?"

"An experience involving another dimension," Frank replied. "You're having a déjà vu... which in my English, means you're merely getting a feeling over something which likely happened in the pre-existence. Or a premonition from somebody..." He paused. "For example from someone in the next dimension, after this life."

Frank was rather disappointed when James didn't retort with a suitably sarcastic riposte. "I'm surprised, James, because you're clearly losing your edge here a bit. I was expecting a decent come-back, or more to the point... in timely fashion!"

James continued to look out of the window, but after a few moments diverted his gaze back into the room. "This is different Frank. I've not experienced this before."

"Yes, these incidents are a little... different. That's a jolly good way to describe them. It's also good," he concluded resolutely. "Because they invariably feel good as well. Which similarly makes them good."

"So what does it mean then?" James asked. "Science changes all the time, but time doesn't actually end in the epilogue. Why's it in any way familiar to me, or why would I think I've come across it before, or something like it?"

"You're not the first person, you know."

"I'm not the first person to do what? What d'you mean?"

"You're not the first to get something out of the epilogue. Admittedly other people usually read some of the book first, and don't go straight to the back. They somehow never seem to buy it though. It's jolly annoying because I could do with the royalties..." Frank noticed how James wasn't listening, which meant he decided to stop talking. 'This is exactly what happens with Helen, when she vents her gentle tirades,' he reflected. 'Flying spuds, I'm turning into a woman! No worries though, because if I'm becoming more like Helen, I don't particularly mind!' Frank had successfully countered as he argued with himself, playing both of the respective roles sufficiently well to nearly keep the conversation going. He smiled.

"You're laughing again!" James protested reasonably strongly.

"No, I'm really not," Frank reassured back. "In fact it's quite the reverse. I think there's a group which was formed in the pre-existent dimension and for some reason they're drawn to this bit at the back... or rather the words within it. The key thing though, is a question over what this group thing's about, or what's the need for such a group? The people all eventually seem to end up at the discussion group meetings in Siggel's front room. It's as though the group members are maybe each looking for something... perhaps the same thing, or possibly different things. I'm not entirely sure. The group just continues to get larger and larger at the moment."

James stared out of the window again. Frank wished he'd stop.

"How long did it take you to write it all?"

"What, the book?"

"Yes, the whole thing."

"About twenty-five years... possibly longer."

James began to laugh. "It's an incredibly long time to spend writing a book."

"Perhaps, but I had to live the experiences before I could write about them. Otherwise, I had very little to write about."

"Fair comment."

"What I just don't get though, is why I spent two years editing the book when I could have simply written the last couple of pages, and entitled it 'Epilogue'. I could've spent a couple of years on the beach, so at the end of the day..."

"Frank, shut up a minute!"

Frank looked up, slightly bemused.

"I think I know why there's a need for this group you're talking about."

Frank looked over towards James intently. His attention was well and truly grabbed.

-

James was running late. He had thirty minutes to reach his exam venue whilst it took twenty-two minutes to complete the train journey. He enjoyed train rides because they were comfortable and straight forward, as well as generally hassle-free, but this journey wasn't going to be hassle-free. He began to plan it out in his mind, running through every section of the sprint which he'd have to make, in order to reach the college hall before the exam commenced. He needed to be sure about every bend, every downhill stretch, every pause for traffic lights, even with additional alternative routes if the traffic lights turned against him. He decided he was ready, now only needing to wait until the train stopped. When it did eventually stop he leapt through the carriage door, ticket in hand, eager to present it at the exit barrier to the waiting attendant. Exiting the station he flew along the long, straight main road which ran uphill until it levelled off. He knew he had to put in the effort for the uphill climb, and he'd use the flatter section later with the multiple traffic lights, to catch his breath. The lights went well until the final crossing, which turned green for traffic so barring his immediate onward progress. It didn't matter though because there was a smaller sideroad that he'd used before, which meant he quickly diverted, carefully missing the slow, older lady to the left, similarly the schoolkids coming the other way on the right. He never could quite understand how it worked out that when he ran well he never felt tired, but whenever he was running more slowly he usually felt shattered. He ignored the thought and pressed on. The goal was within sight, then as he turned the final corner the exam hall loomed large across the horizon. He bolted for the entrance.

"You're cutting this late aren't you?" Mr. Gibbons queried, noticing James had entered the hall with barely thirty seconds to spare. He didn't answer but was grateful for the good result. He was equally grateful the invigilators took quite a while to hand out the various exam papers, since the hall itself was packed. He used the additional minutes to physically cool off and mentally switch on. As he briefly scanned the exam paper through for the first time, he was no longer sure whether the trip had actually been worthwhile. The first twenty minutes were spent scowering his overloaded memory for relevant information, and planning the details of his written presentation. This method had generally worked for him in the past, consequently he'd decided to resort to it once again.

The exertions of a sprint along to the exam hall, followed by mental tensions from just not initially understanding his exam questions, inexorably resulted in an overactive bowel, and this was quite irritatingly the case over the following twenty minutes. It reached a stage where James could no longer hold it in. With a relieving release he allowed a significantly loud flatulence to slice through the silence of the exam room, extending vibratory permeations to the outer regions of the hushed hall. Without hesitating James turned around to Harris sitting in the seat behind him, and audibly muttered: "That's disgusting!" In future months or years, Harris was never able to convince anyone that he hadn't actually created the renowned exam room indiscretion.

After about ninety minutes, or about half way through the exam, James was momentarily distracted by a student who rose to leave. 'You've got to be kidding. He can't be finished so early can he? Either he knows far more than I ever will do and he's an expert speed writer, or he knows even less than I do and he's given up!' James dismissed the thought, until a few minutes later another student rose to leave. He glanced behind, seeing him also walk towards the back of the hall. When the fourth student repeated the same action he decided it needed investigating, even if it meant he'd lose time, time which logically should have been spent in getting his answers down on paper. He looked towards the back of the hall and what he saw amazed him - the sight completely changed his thinking, to the point he decided it would need a deeper investigation, or at least once the months of the exam period had finally reached a conclusion. He saw each student in turn, devote precious exam time on prayer mats at the rear of the hall. He judged carefully how these men were Muslims, with sufficient faith in their religion to observe something which was clearly important for them. He found these actions significantly impressive, and didn't forget it.

-

James decided his subsequent course of action would be finding out what actually happened at the discussion group meetings. He'd heard they were reasonably entertaining, which meant he decided he'd go along again.

"It's risible how some sections of the scientism community happily struggle with any possible concept of a short Biblical creation period for the Earth, yet they happily apportion only mere fractions of a second for the creation of the universe. That's really weird!" Dave vocalised.

"It's really a matter of perspective," Siggel suggested.

"How's that?" Dave inquired.

"Well truth can evolve. Or at least, our understanding of the truth can evolve."

"This'll be interesting," Dave ventured to Kieron.

Siggel remained unperturbed. "Frank mentioned the other month about a road traffic accident he'd witnessed where a driver, intoxicated by drugs or alcohol, caused serious injury to a young pedestrian. The person then drove into several other cars and finally appeared to attempt suicide with a nail gun. I was curious, so I looked it up to find the newspaper headline: "Man held nail gun to driver's head and seriously injured teen in hit-and-run spate."

"The last fifty per cent of the headline was accurate but the other fifty per cent was pure Jackanory," Frank intervened. "The intoxicated driver was putting the nail gun to his own head. He wasn't putting the nail gun to the other driver's head."

"He was jailed for three years," Siggel continued. "One of the news outlets said they'd obtained their information from the constabulary statement in the public domain."

"I posted on the constabulary website, reporting how the other driver was a hero for saving the intoxicated man's life," Frank clarified.

"Your post wasn't there when I looked. It must have been removed. I phoned the police and contacted the case officer. He confirmed their witness had agreed with your version of events, although he couldn't comment on the newspaper article. He apparently had no dealings with the constabulary statement, but he did say the 'other driver' felt threatened by the nail gun."

"Well it's interesting, because when I was with them the nail gun was either pointing in my direction or was against the intoxicated man's head. I thought about ducking, but the nail gun wouldn't have gone off unless there was physical contact," Frank added.

"After I contacted the newspaper, I left my email as well as phone details with them, yet they never came back to me. The jailed man's solicitor said he mistrusted press reports. He wasn't too concerned though since the sentencing apparently wasn't affected," Siggel finalised.

"Well, you've been busy. It's crazy, because whilst the jail sentence was fair enough, the truth has been manipulated into a fantasy."

"And that's what I mean by an evolution of the truth," Siggel offered.

"Sounds more like an adulteration of the truth on this occasion."

"We all need to evolve, in order to both eliminate our mistakes whilst overlooking the mistakes of others. At the end of the day, we all make mistakes," Reg offered.

Nobody argued with Reg's conclusion.

-

'I'm attempting to choose good over evil, despite thinking how some nefarious activities can be rather appealing. I can understand the call of the dark side, but I'm aspiring to reject it, even strongly. Its appeal is short-lived or pointless, because at the end of the day, you're always going to have to go back, then undo all those things you know are wrong, whilst you're left feeling guilty about them as well. So I've finally decided to take a well-earned short cut in beginning to learn how to seek out the good, generally more so than any 'appealing' bad. It's simpler that way. The only individuals you need to stay away from are those who never intend to ever feel guilty or never intend to undo what they've done wrong. It's a pointless journey. Those individuals need to stop such behaviour, but they also need to stop themselves so the change can become effective long-term. Generating any more bad things always has to be bad,' James vocalised, although only to himself. He wasn't actually in public going to admit to any of those things he'd just mentally rehearsed, or at least certainly not within the discussion group.

"So is revenge, or more to the point war, always bad?" Tony postulated.

"It can be. Most often, it is. I believe the only appropriate time for going to war is in defence. Otherwise the whole idea is counter-intuitive. If politicians are keen on conflict they should get themselves into a ring against each other, as sometimes was the case in olden Biblical times. My guess is conflict would somehow suddenly become redundant," Chris offered.

James mentally agreed. The rationale seemed logical, but again he said nothing.

"And should we kill people in self-defence?"

"Dying's not the real issue. It's the shortening of life which is the issue," Kieron interjected.

"Surely they're just the same thing aren't they?"

"No, there's a difference. Dying is the loss of the physical body. But the psyche never dies, nor can it, nor is there a reason why it should. Eternally, death is impossible. So there's no worries in death, where the psyche has merely taken off its physical coat. However, the shortening of life is a problem. Any early shortening of life gives psyche less time to finish the exam of mortal life, which is evidently not fair."

"People live for different lifespans, so what's a fair lifespan for someone?"

"Every lifespan is individual. Each individual has their own peculiar set of tests to pass or overcome in mortal life, whereby any artificial shortening of a lifespan isn't fair for any person."

"What happens to the individual's test then, if their lifespan is shortened?"

"Well I guess it's like cricket."

"Like cricket? What d'you mean?"

"Well if rain stops play in one-day cricket internationals, then time is lost and they look at the run rate. They judge the outcome by how the teams were doing at the point when things were stopped. The team with the best run rate wins the match, but extrapolating the principle, I guess if an individual was doing OK, meaning their life was good, I suppose the outcome is good."

"But what about individuals who were about to embark on a fantastic run of change or repentance? How will anyone know if they were about to become much better versions of themselves?"

"You've raised a good question."

"And what's the answer?"

"I believe God could make a decent judgment call but overall, I'm not too sure."

"Well, your idea's not too fantastic!"

"Subjectively though, it is for now."

"But what happens later on then?"

"I guess you can figure out different answers for yourself."

"And how can anyone figure out such ecclesiastical conundrums? Assuming ecclesiastical conundrum's are actually worth figuring out..."

"Your answer is simply by communicating with the universe's greatest intelligence. Most people call him God. The communication is called prayer. Give it a go, or see what you get back."

"Hmmmm. I'm not too sure if I'll get anything back."

"Well I suppose it'll probably depend upon how good you are at using the prayer communications protocol."

"What if I'm rubbish at the prayer thing, or more to the point, the process itself is rubbish?"

"Then you'll need to start practising!"

"That sounds like quite a lot of unnecessary effort."

James was surprised by the verve of the various discussion group members. He didn't see it as a contentious verve because each participant was sincere, but he was still surprised.

"The physical things in life are pleasant, whilst the spiritual things are better," Reg reassured. James thought about the idea for a while.

"And what of virus. How can they be good in the next dimension?"

"Some virus serotypes have been found to be beneficial in initiating the control of cancers, so ultimately all life forms can work together. Bacteriophages have similarly targetted cancers such as glioblastoma. I don't believe God created anything without a purpose."

"Well what about animals? What purpose do they have in mortality? Are there any reasons we can have to kill them?"

"To kill animals without a purpose isn't something I agree with, but meat-eating or an application for clothing makes use of their physical death. I don't believe there's a mortal test for animals in the same way there is for people. Meat-eating won't be detrimental to the future well being of animal psyches, simply because there's probably no overall mortal test for them. There's likely a difference in the mortal probation for men, compared to the mortal lives of animals."

"And what's the purpose of animal life?"

"You've got another good question. I'm not entirely sure of the answer though. Perhaps to act as human companions during mortality? Additionally, human behaviour towards animals will probably be significant in terms of how we develop our characters."

-

When they made their way across the main road towards the field James felt the first few drops of rain begin to fall.

"How far have we got to go before we reach this bus stop?"

"Not far," Kieron encouraged.

"Yer, but we've got to make it across the field first," Dave added.

"What d'you mean?"

"He means this field is renowned for the number of lightning strikes which have been reported."

"Oh nonsense!" James rebutted.

"OK, then don't believe me."

"He's right you know," Tony agreed.

"What?" James queried, suddenly looking a little more concerned.

"Yes, it's true," Ian added.

"Who reported them?"

"People who've walked across this field."

"Yer, very funny."

"OK then, don't believe us."

"This isn't useful."

"But it's true," Ian continued. "Ask Kieron..."

"Yer Kieron, tell James what happened to you," Dave rejoined.

"Why, what did happen to you?"

"And keeps happening..."

"What d'you mean by 'keeps happening'?" James asked, suddenly more inclined to believe this strange meteorological theme which had begun to gather ground.

"Yer, what does he mean Kieron?" Dave jibed.

"He means that Kieron has been struck three times in this field so far," Ian added nonchalantly.

"Oh, nonsense!" James retorted again.

"I'm afraid it's true," Adam confirmed.

"Not you as well!"

"I'm afraid so." Adam stood his ground.

"Well how can anyone survive a single lightning strike and be able to come out unscathed, let alone three? It's not credible."

"Because he had an umbrella," Chris explained.

"Don't be ridiculous!" James still insisted.

"It's true. Kieron's umbrella has saved him three times."

"Yes, it has actually," Adam verified.

"I agree."

"Well I don't! How can an umbrella protect anyone from a lightning strike? If you've got it in hand or you simply wave it around, it might even make things worse."

"Not if you put the umbrella up though," Dave suggested.

"Now you are being ludicrous. How can putting an umbrella up protect you from a lightning strike?"

"Because it disperses around the whole of the umbrella, primarily along the thin metal supports. The umbrella even lights up, and you can see the flash inside."

"Yer sure," James replied, refusing to accept their account of events, or just seemingly at that particular moment.

"Kieron, let's have your umbrella over here please," Dave asked politely. "OK James, hold onto this for a while because we'll see what happens."

"No way, Jose!"

"Aghh, so you do believe it then," Ian suggested. "Can you let me have it Dave, for a bit?" The umbrella was passed over, opened and within a short space of time James witnessed something he'd never expected. Suddenly, or as if magically from nowhere, there was a bright flash within the umbrella, spreading instantaneously across its breadth in all directions. Ian didn't react, but James jumped back in surprise.

"You've got to be joking!" he exclaimed.

The rest of the group began to laugh.

"Nope, we're not joking," Dave confirmed resolutely. "And it'll probably happen again because this weather is perfect for it."

James looked disconcerted. "How can this be right? I don't get it. Lightning doesn't light up umbrellas."

"It does if it's sheet lightning," Kieron explained.

"Expect the unexpected!" Ian suggested. "There's an answer for everything. But it might not be the one you're expecting though..."

James finally agreed, as they eventually reached the other end of the field. James decided at some point he'd get them back and give them their own surprise. It would certainly wait though until later. There was no rush.

CHAPTER 18

Two men stood together. They were dressed in white suits, white shoes and white ties and were deeply engaged in discussion.

"So how did Jack Frost die?"

"It wasn't an accident."

"Yes, somehow I didn't think it could have been. What happened?"

"Let's go and meet him, because he can tell you himself."

"OK," John-Paul agreed, as he followed Charlie's lead.

Jack Frost was taller than John-Paul expected. Psyches projected an aura which was larger than their physical counterparts, yet Jack Frost still rose higher than John-Paul had imagined.

"Hi, I've heard a fair bit about you from Charlie."

"I hope it's all good."

"Oh, yes it definitely is."

"I had to pay him Jack," Charlie quipped.

"Well, don't expect any subsidies," Jack replied.

"Same old Jack!"

"Not old anymore though... in fact, I never actually made it to old age in mortality."

"Yes, it's what John-Paul is rather curious about."

"What, you mean about my mortal exit?"

"I heard you got out at the wrong train station."

"Nicely put! I think 'pushed out' was probably more accurate. One of the scoundrels opened a door, because in those days it was the passengers who had control of the doors, so the next thing I knew, the other rotter had conjured up an unwelcomed exit."

"That wasn't helpful."

"No it certainly wasn't, but one of them regrets it though."

"How d'you know one of them regrets it?"

"Because I've asked him... you can ask him yourself, if you'd like..."

"What?"

"Yes, come on, let's go and see him. I've been working with the chap for quite a while now."

"How did you find out it was him? How did you even find him?"

"Oh, it wasn't a problem. I just looked up the hologram records. The best records are those which are added from a psyche's memory bank. I checked the records for passengers on the train that day, and there were also records from recorders. The recorders usually provide a starting base to kick things off from, so once I had the correct names of the two characters in my coach, then it was quite straight forward from there on."

"Have you ever worked as a recorder?"

"I have for a while actually, and it's really quite interesting. It can all be done remotely. I like the overnight method."

"How does it work?"

"When mortals sleep they frequently run through the day's activities, which results in the relevant daily activities being usefully recorded for themselves, or even for others at times. We might also provide suggestions or even inspirations in dreams, carried over from our dimension. Most of the time though activities are very regular or mundane. Every now and then some interesting progress might be made, so acting as a recorder can be a rewarding assignment."

John-Paul paused, slightly distracted as they arrived at the entrance to the Spirit Prison. He glanced at Paradise before looking back towards the Spirit Prison again. He'd seen this other section of the Spirit World before but hadn't as yet made the trip across. It didn't really look a lot different, although the entrance was very distinct. He remembered how when he'd made the short journey from mortality into the Spirit World there was an escort, accompanying him to his appropriate destination into Paradise. Paradise was beautiful, and not just in the picturesque, peaceful, countryside environment which he'd initially encountered before he met up with other psyches. The environment was made perfect by the company of family psyches as well as former pre-existence friends. Initial entry was followed up by an introductory tour of modest yet beautifully ornate, majestic edifices. These first class structures created spaces for ordered, purposeful, or useful work throughout Paradise. Paradise was unique in being permeated with a heavenly feeling, a feeling borne of deep satisfaction in all which was good or right, or all that was just plus logical; everything became clear and somehow simply obvious.

The entrance to Spirit Prison seemed cocooned, in fact the entire Spirit Prison appeared cocooned. In a similar way to the veil between mortality and the Spirit World, the division between Paradise and Prison was presented differently - it was dependent upon which way the division was observed. From Paradise it became visually darker or less bright, whilst once they'd made the trip across, from the other side the division appeared much brighter, clearer, noticeably more radiant.

"Well that's a contrast," John-Paul remarked.

"Yes, it looks different, doesn't it?" Charlie replied.

"It takes a little self-motivation each time the dividing bridge is crossed," Jack suggested. John-Paul mentally agreed. As they made their way further into the region he observed people, people with varying degrees of aura emanating from them. Within paradise all psyches radiated a good, pleasant aura, consequently it was a pleasure to associate, or spend time amongst the company of others. However the region of Spirit Prison wasn't exactly the same. Auras around individuals ranged from the really rather dark, to ones shining with a level of virtue which could still be felt, quite distinctly.

It didn't take long before the group reached their intended destination. The house they attended was small, where an interesting glow of goodness came from within its structure. John-Paul nevertheless sensed a level of melancholy, drifting intermittently down towards brief splashes of uncontrolled despair - the sliding moods were wrapped together strongly, almost inseparably. John-Paul knocked gently on the door. He watched the door open whereupon a psyche came to the entrance initially deep in thought, looking anxiously for the visitors who might have come to be with him. When he realised who they were his face lifted into a slow, relieved smile. He was focusing upon Jack, intently checking his aura for approval. The man looked unsure. Jack greeted him warmly.

"Are we coming in then Juliano?" Jack asked.

"Yes Jack. Please do." The door was wide open. Inside Juliano's house they found a neat and tidy interior, with furniture plus arrangements which showed care as well as organisation.

"Are you keeping well?" Jack continued.

"I'm looking ahead, trying to forget the past. But I'm not sure how I'll get over my mistakes, because they were so foolish. I've found others who want to know more, so we've been talking. In fact, I'd like you to meet them... if you'd care to?"

"Of course."

"We've arranged to gather and talk. There's so much the

170

others would like to hear about those ideas you've been discussing. They were as astonished as I was, when life went on past mortal death. We've all had a similar experience, because after coming through the process of death with that tunnel, followed up by the reality of life simply continuing... it turned out to be just an extension of our old life... but it was better... reality was truly astonishing. But that's when it all started to become more real. Whatever we'd done which wasn't good during mortal years, suddenly became useless. Completely wasteful of our time. Nothing was achieved. Nothing had been accomplished by doing bad things. Existence isn't fun unless you're with people who make you feel good. And doing bad isn't good. It's depressing," Juliano concluded, looking downwards as he finished.

"I agree. You're evolving," Jack pointed out. "It's useful."

"I hope so." There was a pause. "The others were wondering what the future holds? I was telling them that by making changes to how they act, it's still possible for everyone to improve, so they've asked what the idea meant or how could things possibly work out going forwards? Some say they've seen people like you who've come to visit. Others still say they're mad, and this world is as bad as the last one, perhaps worse because it goes on forever where they haven't seen anyone die. Some think this is hell and they want to escape, yet they haven't found a way out. There are some irrational ideas circulating on how to escape, which range from the ridiculous to the very bad. Some think we've come through a worm-hole or have ended up here by mistake. Others are suggesting we've been abducted by aliens."

John-Paul was rather perplexed by the complexity of ideas being explored. He'd imagined how once everyone knew there was life after death, everyone would logically know God existed because they continued to exist. He was surprised to see this wasn't automatically the case.

"Where do all these notions come from?" John-Paul asked.

"Mildred's told me she's seen some unusually dark individuals who've appeared or conversed with people, who've then begun to spread some of their ideas. The most believable suggestions somehow seem to come from secret groups. The really wacky themes, such as an apparent nuclear holocaust which in some way brought us all here, they don't usually come from these groups. They tend to lose ground over time, with the result they haven't become too popular. Scientists are pointing out we're on a rotating world, where the universe is still visible, suggesting we must still be on the Earth. Other religious people are saying it's just not possible because we're dead, or in other words heaven or hell aren't anything to do with the Earth."

"Would you like us to meet up with your friends and explain how we can all continue to improve?"

"Yes, I'd appreciate that," Juliano agreed.

-

"So which one was Juliano then?" John-Paul asked cautiously. "Was he the one who gave the push, or the one who opened the door?"

"He opened the door, and I recognised his face because I saw him clearly. The other person isn't as open to talking with me as Juliano. Sergio has a longer way to go on his road to progress."

"These guys sound like the Italian mafia."

"Yes, I had an experience with the mafia once," Charlie interrupted. "I was talking to an American woman at a dentist's reception in Cechslovia. Nona and I were about two or three feet apart. Suddenly a couple of men wearing long black coats, black trousers, black shoes, black shirts and black sun glasses, they came walking straight through between us without saying anything, and I could couldn't help it, so instinctively I said: "Thanks chaps!"

I asked Nona, "Who did those two think they were? Mafia hit men?"

Nona replied, "How did you know?"

I replied that "I didn't, because I was joking!"

She then explained there was a mafia café upstairs, which surprised me since I didn't even know the mafia existed in Cechslovia. Apparently they also drove black cars, fittingly with black tinted windows," Charlie concluded.

"I likewise didn't know the mafia existed," Jack confirmed. "Not until I made an exit out of the train."

"So why did Juliano do it then?" John-Paul asked, even more cautiously.

"Apparently there was a second inheritance coming to the family. The first one had gone to Jermane but this time around she'd already passed on, so as it happened, I was the next in line."

"You mean you were taken out for the money?"

"Basically yes," Jack confirmed.

"That's very primitive."

"Maybe, but it's one of the oldest reasons in the book."

"Which book?"

"Any book which matters."

"Oh, OK," John-Paul agreed. "So how did Juliano become involved?"

"Italian mafia."

"What? The Italian mafia came over to England?"

"More like they were already here, but Italians were being shipped back to Italy, labelled as undesirables during the war years. So Juliano and Sergio needed some money to bribe a few people, in order to try and keep their identity safe, as well as their families."

"Was it really that bad?"

"Well, we had a couple of great grandfathers... err, Azario and Spacagna, if I remember rightly... anyway, they were on a boat back to Italy when it was torpedoed and about six hundred died."

"Who sunk it?"

"Not sure, although I believe it was a German vessel. At the end of the day they still died."

"Hmmm, fair enough."

"Is it right then how Juliano can continue to make progress after what he's done?"

"It's not for us to judge. Only the Father can truly know what was in a man's heart at the time he did something."

"It's very magnanimous of you."

"Well, we're all in need of a little forgiveness. Mortality was a test for all of us... in different ways."

"Oh OK," John-Paul agreed, slightly bewildered by Jack's admirable desire for reconciliation.

CHAPTER 19

"OK, keep pushing. Everyone has to push or we'll never get this thing started."

"My thoughts exactly! We're never going to push-start a fully laden removal truck. This is sheer madness."

"Don't worry, it's possible because I've done it before," replied the Pickfords employee. "And it's not as difficult as you might think."

Adam, Chris and James joined the others again at the back of the truck.

"We must be mad," James whispered quietly to Adam. "There's no way this crazy scheme is going to work."

"We'll give it a go," Adam responded. "If nothing happens, then at least we've tried. Besides, the bus doesn't arrive for another twenty minutes, which means we've got nothing better to do. It's stopped raining so it's no problem."

James had to agree with the logic. It probably wouldn't work, but at least they would've done a good deed for the day. He began to push along with all the others. Strangely yet slowly he couldn't help but notice there was a small movement forward.

"It's actually moving!"

"I told you it would. Just keep pushing and the truck will start."

"I hope that driver knows what he's doing," Ian remarked.

"Oh, he's fine. He's been doing this for years."

"Hmmm. Well that could explain why removal lorries never arrive on time..."

"This doesn't happen too often, you know."

No one replied. James was intrigued. He was even more intrigued when the lorry started to splutter, then judder, and finally he heard the unbelievable sound of a deep, revving engine.

"We've done it!"

"Yes, thank you." The Pickfords employee disappeared around the side of the truck before there was a slam of the passenger door. He called back.

"Stand clear everyone."

Ian, Kieron, Dave, Adam, Chris and James made their way back up onto the pavement, subsequently following the path slowly up towards the bus stop, still catching a diminishing view of the sizeable removal truck as it pulled away in the distance.

"That was a big, old truck."

"Yes it was. I'm jolly surprised it actually got going."

"Well, the saga's got to be a revelation in itself."

"I suppose it is. But I can't go along with the idea where all removal trucks take forever to get to their destination."

"No, they don't. It was an exaggeration, probably only spurred on by the general feeling of the moment. Some things do take a fair while though. My brother received a letter which was delivered ten years after it was posted."

"That's crazy!"

"Yes, I thought so as well. It only had his Christian name on the front of the envelope, with simply the first part of the postcode. Nothing else."

"It's even more ridiculous!"

"Yes, I thought so. Yet it got to us... albeit ten years later."

"I guess you're right," James agreed. At the end of the day, he was still sticking with 'crazy' - a good 'crazy.

A bus turned the corner at the end of the road, before pulling up and stopping at the bus stop. The group got on.

As the bus made its way along the usual route through the estate, something caught James' eye. Up ahead at the side of the road, were a small group of young people, and without counting James guessed about nine or ten of them. James could see that one was lying motionless on the floor, whilst the others were gathered around. A couple of young girls left the group and began to wave at the bus, attempting to flag it down, whereupon Adam pointed out what was happening to the bus driver. He obligingly slowed down to let them off. The bus had moved on a fair distance by the time it stopped, so hurriedly they walked back to the point where the roadside group had gathered.

"I thought we saw them just here," Dave commented.

"Yer, it was about here because I remember the white van over there in a garden."

"So where are they?" Ian asked.

"Good question," Kieron added.

They searched around for about five minutes, without finding any sign of the young people, nor the individual who was lying prostrate on the ground.

"Well that's curious."

"Yer, I'm guessing more prank-like than curious."

"You're kidding!"

"Nope. It seems as though those kids have set this up before, giving us the slip," Chris concluded.

"Great!"

"More importantly, there's not another bus for about an hour."

"I suppose it means we're walking then."

"Great!"

"Well I never did any of this kind of stuff when I was a teenager."

"Hmmm, quite a decent joke, really. You were one of the worst."

"Thanks."

"My pleasure..."

"James, don't worry about it," Adam suggested.

"The thought's great, but we've either got to wait an hour or take a long hike back through the rest of the estate."

"They were just kids having fun."

"And if I find them again, I'll have my own bit of fun!"

"We all need a bit of room to make a few mistakes. So long as no one gets hurt, it's not such a big deal."

"So how come you've suddenly become all avuncular then?"

"When I was at university I ended up running the rifle club along with the chess club during my middle year. I thoroughly enjoyed it. It was good and I was grateful for the different opportunities. During my final year I had to give them up to concentrate more on studies, but I was still on the teams. The new captains subsequently changed their approach a little for the local county competitions. When they had some success with their changes, it was quite a pleasure to be involved. The chess captain moved our bottom board player up to the top position, then moved all of us on the other boards down a position. We won every match that year, which meant we won the league. The poor chap who was moved onto board one, well he lost every game, but he didn't mind because he was pleased we became the divisional champions, which meant it was good for him in the end as well. The rifle team captain had a slightly different approach. It was a postal competition, which encouraged him to look at the statistics from the previous year. He got us to shoot off all our cards within a single sitting, then he put in our best scores against the best divisional teams, with the worst scores put against the worst teams. His statistical analysis was excellent, because once again we won the league."

"Was he allowed to do that?"

"No, I believe he wasn't, and it's why I couldn't look at the medals we all got with the same feeling. But at the end of the day, everyone has to learn what's good or what's not particularly good, since ultimately we get to see what needs changing, or evolving. We've all made mistakes, plus we were all young and everyone's still learning," Adam suggested.

"Hmmm," James vocalised, briefly contemplating the advice before changing the subject. "I guess a bit of decent exercise isn't such a bad thing."

"Well, we've nearly got through the estate now. More usefully, it's not started raining yet, and there's still some good daylight as well."

"You really are quite a dazzling ray of sunshine, aren't you?"

"Yep!" Adam confirmed.

James wasn't too sure whether to grin or to grimace. In the end he did neither. They carried on to a point in the road which was narrowed down to one lane by roadworks, with the usual compulsory set of temporary traffic lights in place.

"Someone's always digging up the roads," James moaned.

"Such things are part of the service," Adam replied. James briefly considered this comment could simply be vocalising cynicism, rather than actually being serious. There wasn't much time to give it a lot of thought though, having noticed two cars were driving towards each other, one from either side of these temporary traffic lights. If something didn't happen quite soon, there was about to be a rather traumatic collision.

"Adam," James enunciated, with both a concerned voice as well as an accompanying pointing motion. "Have you noticed how there are in fact a couple of cars approaching us from both sides of these lights. If I'm not totally mistaken they're about to collide at exactly somewhere in the middle... or more to the point, where we are right now."

"Oh don't worry, it's probably a typical mistake from one of the drivers. Someone will back down then reverse."

James wasn't convinced, because by now both cars were carrying on with their apparent collision course.

"I'm not convinced, you know."

"You worry too much," Adam reassured him.

"No, on this occasion, I don't think I am. It's more a case of alarm!"

Adam took the trouble to look behind them, then forwards again.

"You know what... I think you could be right!" There was a brief pause. "In fact, you are right. Completely right! I'm going up the bank..."

At that point Adam began a quick, positively evasive sprint up the grassy bank to their left-hand side, making rapid progress within a relatively short space of time, promptly followed by an eager James. Horns started blaring, brakes commenced squealing and rubber began burning. Thick, palpable noise filled the air immediately to their right, whilst both pedestrians stared back down the grassy bank, observing disbelievingly at what was unfolding below them. James expected a loud, nauseating thud, followed by some form of enormous vehicular drama, possibly an explosion. Adam wasn't quite too sure what to expect. None of the above actually transpired. What did occur was as much comical as it was unexpected. The car originally coming from behind them started to snake and weave, whilst its counterpart chose instead, to violently splay out the cones which workmen had conveniently placed down the centre of the road. The cones flew off in a curious variety of directions, but generally in a firework-like, aerial fashion, all to the right-hand side. The oncoming car slid its nearside rear into a sideways motion, whilst the front end was steered to the right. In the end it took up a fully progressive, side-on forwards advance. Conversely the other vehicle, originally coming from behind, chose to brake harder with a loud, probably more dramatic screaming of tyres against solid tarmac. There was quite a racket as the wheels struggled, even protested over a sudden demand for elusive road grip – at the same time the offside rear decided to adopt a similarly comical drift out towards the traffic cones in the centre of the road, causing them to splay haphazardly, but in what James could only describe as:

"A fantastic demonstration of how to demolish some coconut shies!"

"Yes, quite," Adam concurred.

The two vehicles came to rest a few millimetres from each other, albeit in broadside fashion. What followed next wasn't quite so comical.

The drivers of the vehicles appeared to synchronise exits from their respective cars, and followed up the theatre with a fully rehearsed, rich dialogue of verbal abuse, launched shamelessly with poetic verve in opposing directions. The altercation was capped off with a ritual of threats, escalating into a crescendo which was only going to end up one way i.e. not with any hint of a backslapping peace accord.

Adam made a rapid valiant descent back down the bank, reaching the roadside at the point where where the cars had come to a standstill.

"Hey chaps, I think I've got a solution!"

Both drivers immediately looked over, appearing rather startled by the sudden interruption into their important discussion. For a moment they seemed transfixed.

"We can find out which traffic light was showing red. It won't take a second." Adam pulled out his mobile and began to tap in a number. James joined him on the pavement.

"Ian and Chris are up front and I'm phoning them. Can you phone Dave and Kieron, because they're still behind us? Ask them what colour the traffic light is showing, can you?"

"OK," James obliged, also tapping into his phone. A few

moments later: "It's green."

"Ian, what colour is your traffic light? It should be red," Adam asked. There was a slight delay. "No way! OK, thanks."

Adam turned back towards the two drivers who were miraculously in abeyance, waiting for a verdict to justify their respective anger. "Well chaps, you were both on green, so you both have an equal right to be jolly angry."

"Who's up for trashing the traffic lights?" James asked. Adam stared sternly in his direction.

"Please ignore my friend. He's just recently been recovering from a mental breakdown," Adam explained.

"No, I haven't..."

"Well that's it then. It's lucky there was no harm done. All's well that ends well."

Slowly and slightly reluctantly, or more likely flummoxed, the two drivers withdrew themselves from the confrontation, nodding to each other in recognition of their shared exoneration. The cones were a sight to behold, yet Adam considered this new rearrangement to be quite an improvement, so he did nothing to change things.

James conversely took matters into his own hands, and retrieved a couple of cones from the side of the road. One cone was placed over the top of the first traffic light, then in turn, a second cone was placed in similar fashion, over the other traffic light on the far side. He also manoeuvred both lights towards the roadside bank.

"I reckon it should do the trick!"

Adam agreed.

"Well, at least it wasn't a hole in the road which caused all the trouble," Adam remarked, as they made their way back along the road again.

"What d'you mean?"

"It just reminds me of a trip which Frank made over in Polgaria."

"You seem to spend quite a lot of time listening to Frank's travel logs," James observed.

"Yes, I suppose I do. But in the discussion group, we've all shared our different tales somewhere along the line," Adam explained. "I tend to remember the episodes that are unusual, and this was one of Frank's."

"So what happened?"

"The family was driving along the road in Polgaria, making their way back home in the dark, when they started to cross a bridge. Suddenly Frank noticed a couple of traffic cones straight ahead of them, but only on their side of the road. The way you placed those two cones on the traffic lights made me think of them. Anyway, he initially wasn't going to stop, and was going over onto the other side of the road to avoid the cones, but a car was coming the other way, which meant he had to stop. Since they were stationary, he decided to get out of the car to remove them, and that was when he saw it."

"Saw what?"

"Behind the cones, there was no road at all."

"What d'you mean?"

"The road suddenly ended, hence all he could see was a big gaping hole which dropped down to the ground underneath. The gap on their side of the road was about eight to ten feet long... enough to drop a car through."

"What, a hole in the bridge itself?"

"Yep, absolutely."

"Well that's crazy."

"I thought so, but Frank seemed to take it as the norm."

"I'll have to make a visit out to Polgaria one day."

"It does sound an interesting place." Adam paused as they continued to walk. "Talking of unusual events, why have you decided to come back to the discussion group?" he asked.

"I'm not too sure. I saw a paragraph which Frank had written down and it seemed to resonate." James wasn't prepared to elaborate on his ideas re the group itself. At least, not at the present time. Something additional had also seemed to pull him back to their meetings.

"Aghh, so you've been subjected to some of Frank's stories as well! What he's done is to keep a journal. Everyone has interesting stories to tell. It's a good idea to jot them down though, otherwise family history is simply lost. There's a lot to be said for writing down the things we've experienced. I regretted not taking A-level Latin with Mr. Barber..." Adam stopped, noticing how James seemed distracted.

"It wasn't exactly like that. It was different. As though I'd somehow seen the paragraph before, or might see something similar again."

"Like an unusual form of déjà vu or premonition, you mean?"

"I suppose. Yes, maybe." He waited for a moment. "I've investigated what I saw, and I've found something quite unusual. It's fascinating."

Adam was curious as to what the nature of James' insight might be, yet he didn't want to distract him again.

"However, the part I don't go along with, is this idea of prayer. It seems so childish... almost pagan," James continued. "Why would anyone pray to an unknown, unproven being, which probably doesn't exist. There's no logical reason to believe in a god, because no one's ever come back from death to tell us what's on the other side... if there is another side."

"Well, your suggestion's not exactly correct James, where the internet's now full of excellent near-death experiences. But in the end we all make choices as to what we want to believe." Adam had quickly tangentialised, realising James could properly discover near-death experiences for himself. There was also a better thread to try and explore.

"I'm sorry, I don't agree. Science is about facts. Religion is about stories which help you build up an emotional crutch. But if it helps you, then it's a path you need to follow."

Adam was even more intrigued why James had come back to the discussion group. "Have you seen the film 'Lucy'?"

"The one with Morgan Freeman and Scarlett Johansson."

"Yes, that's the one. It's an entertaining film with an interesting storyline."

"And of course the idea how we only use ten per cent of our brains is wrong. We use one hundred per cent of our brains."

"Well, the film was fantastically embellished for the screen. Otherwise, it would have either been a jolly boring watch, or a very short film. What I was alluding to though, were the questions or answers which can arise. The central idea which came to mind for me, covered the cases of Acquired Savant Syndrome."

"Oh, where people suddenly become highly skilled without training."

"Exactly. There's evidence for untapped capacities or unused areas within the brain."

"Sure."

"For me, a brain with untapped capacities hasn't evolved but was designed, because a dormant capacity can't biologically evolve. I see cerebral reserves as being built into our bodies to accommodate future physical issues which can arise during mortality. And those things interest me. It's why I use prayer. Deity remains the greatest intelligence in the universe, meaning information dissemination can be helpful at times."

James laughed. "Are you serious?"

"Sure."

"Does god talk to you?"

"Absolutely. And He also talked with Newton, Einstein, Archimedes... as well as many other people on many other occasions, supplying them with 'eureka' moments. During his lifetime Einstein referred to God multiple times, although apparently he felt God resided within individuals. It's not surprising though, considering the number of inspirations he received for new knowledge. Whilst they were externally conveyed into his mind, his only natural point of reference for them would've been internal."

"You're just wrapped up in wishful thinking."

"I understand why you'd say that. Interestingly, Einstein also stated how 'coincidence was God's way of staying anonymous'."

"Do you pray?"

"Sure. Whereas science evolves through mistakes, God has seen it all before, and His experience is worth seeking out. He's watched all the mistakes which have been proven possible over time, meaning He's seen what works or what doesn't work. It would be counterproductive not to consult such an individual."

"You make a god sound real."

"Absolutely. But everyone has to choose what they believe... before they can start to do something about it."

"Yes, you're right there," James conceded.

"I choose to believe in something good. I can't blame scientists for enjoying a time of popularity. They were treated badly by theists in the past. Theists should've acted in a more Christian fashion."

"You're absolutely right there!" James confirmed, as they turned the final corner towards home.

"We've arrived," Adam observed.

"Living on the same street has some uses."

"Yes, it does."

They were agreed.

-

Two men stood together. They were dressed in white suits, white shoes and white ties and were deeply engaged in discussion.

"So what has James learnt?"

"Well, I think he can see there's something more than he previously believed there was."

"Very nicely put John-Paul," Charlie assessed. John-Paul felt happy about his comment.

"It's a good job I can read between the lines."

John-Paul wasn't quite sure whether he still felt happy about his comment.

"Well, to put it another way, James has become more teachable," John-Paul added.

"Yes," Charlie answered. John-Paul decided he now felt happy with his additional comment.

"And where do we go from here?"

"We await instructions."

"Yes," Charlie responded. "Interestingly, they've arrived."

"Oh, OK," John-Paul agreed, looking expectantly for a follow-up discussion, which duly took place.

"We need to bring the group together on a more lasting basis."

"Why?"

"To make it more permanent."

"How permanent?"

"Very permanent."

"But it'll break up as they leave mortality."

"Exactly."

"Oh, you mean it should continue into this dimension?"

"Yes."

"Why?"

"Hmmm," Charlie expressed. "Clearly I need to show you something. Let's go."

"Where are we going?"

"Over to Spirit Prison."

"Why?" John-Paul asked, slightly concerned.

"It's not a problem. Trips there are usually useful, similarly this time it's likely to be useful as well."

"Oh, OK," John-Paul agreed, still looking slightly concerned.

The passage through the entrance occurred without incident, as it previously had done and John-Paul suddenly realised he was now familiar with the procedure. It was naturally quite straight forward.

During the journey through Prison, he reflected upon the word. 'Prison' sounded so harsh, yet in reality, the word was both adequate as well as accurate. There were no beautiful temples in this area of their dimension, therefore no means to travel out into the other fantastically expansive dimensions, nor ways to explore those complex spatial systems which surrounded them, nor the vastness of eternities which stretched out in every direction. He briefly contemplated how some mortals had exactly the right idea when expressing travel. "We're off to the city and it's about five hours away," he would sometimes observe them to exclaim. Other mortals considered this was akin to saying how green the grass smelt after it was cut in the summer, but the expressions were absolutely accurate when it came to discussing their long-distance travel, where they described it in terms of time. "I'm just off to Kaeevanrash, and it's about three hundred light-years through Raukeeyang on the way to Oliblish," he could likewise say. In real terms, it was about five minutes travel from the Spirit World, but the same principle still applied. John-Paul was intrigued by man's constant interest with space travel. It was natural as well as good because ultimately, good men or good women who unavoidably entered Paradise would have access to travel. Travel was important for administration, in addition to governance, or knowledge dissemination, or indeed any needful activity which occurred across the cosmos. The activity within the Father's realms was ordered and constant.

He marvelled again how Prison wasn't too different from Paradise, where the entirety of the Spirit World shared similar qualities. Psyches could travel rapidly, exceedingly rapidly, whilst the picturesque landscape ran endlessly in every quarter. Green hills were separated by curiously rocky outcrops, slowly adjoining beautifully carved valleys, all spread across more evenly with tree-lined banks or grass-banked ridges. Sometimes the valleys descended through quite a myriad of gradients down to carefully channelled river beds, balanced between white-painted waterfalls or peaceful, harboured pools. In other places there were more even sections of calm flowing waterways. It wasn't the environment which caused angst within Prison. Firstly, there was no way out. For those who were assigned to Prison, they didn't have an exit. John-Paul wondered how it would feel. He wasn't sure, because he'd spent quite a short period of time in mortality, so he believed there would be many things about mortal life or similarly Prison, which he just couldn't fully appreciate.

Charlie had told him how he enjoyed the 'superhero' powers which all psyches inherently possessed, but this meant there weren't any cars or trains or motorbikes in the Spirit World. Charlie had expressed how he'd wished he could have some of those experiences once again, since he clearly missed the fun of it all. When he was on RAF tours in the Middle East, he enjoyed nocturnal motorbike excursions out into the desert with his friends. They'd go together in groups, sometimes without their lights on when they were in combat regions, and for one particular occasion a friend disappeared off on his own for a while. Sometime later he'd doubled back and this chap used to enjoy daring stunts, consequently when he noticed the group had formed their bikes into a couple of lines, he decided to go up the centre of them to give them all a bit of a scare. The only trouble was, he hadn't doubled back far enough because the two leading lights at the front weren't actually motorbike headlights – they belonged to a rather large truck.

The stunt rider didn't make it. Their excursion that night hadn't actually turned out to be quite as much fun as normal, but most of their trips were enjoyable.

On reflection, John-Paul was rather pleased that his mortal experience had only been a short one.

The second key difference between Spirit Prison and Paradise was the internal state of the psyches themselves. There was plenty of time to think in the Spirit World, allowing any evolved attitude or behaviour to be strongly felt within, and to significantly shape a psyche's experience of internal peace or comfort; from mortality, personal attributes as well as habits had been carried with them. These individual characteristics could in reality be passed over from any previous dimension, although the most recent mortal dimension exerted a very strong and lasting effect. An angry man in the physical world, would enter the Spirit World in similar fashion. A cheerful, helpfully kind man in the mortal world would likewise enter the Spirit World in a similar fashion. John-Paul considered the trick was to turn an angry man into a happy one, hence generally such a turnaround required a fair amount of assistance.

Whilst John-Paul pondered on these ideas he carefully followed Charlie, wherever he was taking them. They travelled deep and far into the Prison sector. He didn't know where they were going but he knew it must have an important purpose.

When they reached their destination John-Paul surveilled the scene. There was a horseshoe rock face in front of them spanning out into spectacular, almost pristine, mottled-white stone, eventually curving back round into an entrance gorge. The scene cast quite a wondrous alpine feel, with a form of stability which could only have been made in solid time. He found they were now positioned outside a door. The door had also been carved from the side of the rock face. It was crafted into rather a neat and tidy fit, where the fit seemed rather perfect. Several windows appeared either side of the entrance, all fashioned inside additional moulds of excavation. This homestead had indeed been sculptured worthily. It possibly could become an abode for ages, yet somehow it bore the feel of semi-permanency.

Charlie knocked before they entered. "Hi Phillipe. How are you?"

"Just the same."

"OK, I understand."

"How's the work going?"

"Yes, I'm observing and prompting according to the instructions I've received. We'll keep working until we achieve a result for you."

"How long will it take?"

"I don't know."

"I've already been here for three ages."

"I know. But at least you have family here. It's different from being all together as men, or all together as women."

"This is still too long."

"I understand."

"I won't go without Rebecca. Our children are mixing with characters here who show them all sorts of wicked possibilities. I thought mortal life was wicked, but those activities are practised and taught here too. Everyone just continues as they'd previously left off, yet now they're telling my children life continues forever, so why shouldn't they just carry on with how they lived their mortal lives because after all, they enjoyed it such a lot. That argument's very persuasive. I'm not sure how I can protect my children from these people."

"No one leaves here Philippe unless they change their behaviour."

"They don't want to change."

"Then they'll remain. Over time they'll notice how others have progressed or gone on to leave, so they'll look to also move on, which won't be immediately possible. Once they start looking for a new future they'll want to evolve, because this endless cycle of repetitive iniquity will become tiresome or degrading. As they start to change, they'll realise how each nefarious activity needs to be undone or discarded. Hopefully it'll dawn on them that they should've started just a little bit earlier because they'd have much less mess to undo. Sooner or later it takes work, possibly a huge amount of work to turn things around, so any enjoyment they've taken from bad habits will be hugely outweighed by the efforts of repentance or evolution."

"They just won't bother."

"Then they'll remain."

"So how can I leave with Rebecca and the children?"

"The time for fast-track was in mortality Philippe. Any possible road to Paradise takes longer in this dimension."

-

"So how long is three ages?" John-Paul asked, after they'd left.

"Three days."

"Oh, that's not long. Why's he seem so depressed?"

"Because it's not three mortal days, but three Kolob days."

"What! He's been here for three thousand years?"

"Yes."

"That's a long time. No wonder he's depressed."

"And it's why we're working on his case. We're probably the right individuals for his particular case. In some Spirit World regions they need the respected leaders to teach them. Those who were Muslim in mortality, they have the best opportunities to teach their people here, similarly African leaders can have great success with their people, et cetera, et cetera."

"But why can't he just come over into Paradise? He seems like he's living correctly, so what's the problem?"

"The authorities have to be sure he'll remain true to his word. If he comes over to Paradise with Rebecca, his wife, and if they have access to a celestial resurrection, in time they'll be able to have spirit children. If they haven't proven themselves to be fully worthy of the privilege, their status as parents of psyches would become untenable. The Father won't permit wickedness nor destruction to tread the celestial realms. So they must wait. It's essential all things are done correctly or perfectly in order. If the time is right, his whole family could move into Paradise as one complete group."

"OK, well what's the hold-up?"

"There are no temples in Prison, likewise no temple sealings for the betrothed, nor for families."

"Maybe we should have had sealings in the pre-existence."

"There were no physical bodies to make the physical unions work, and our spirits can't have children, so it would have been too early. Marriage, children and families are an important mortal thing, as well as for the resurrected who have bodies which don't decay or die."

"And when's that?"

"What, the resurrection, you mean?"

"Yes."

"It's a lot later for many."

"Well, OK. Perhaps Phillipe and Rebecca could go over to Paradise and get married later."

"Things aren't quite like that though."

"Why not? What d'you mean?"

"There are always different possibilities. For example Philippe could go into Paradise on his own, though he's clear on what he'd like to do, because he wants the family going over together, leaving no one behind. You need a marriage licence to go into Paradise as a married couple, where everything needs to be in good order. "

"But why?"

"In the same way your parents needed one. It's even more important in Paradise because it's permanent."

"OK, we need to get them a licence in Prison."

"They don't do marriages in Prison because there aren't any temples."

"Well there must be other people like Phillipe and Rebecca... those who want to be together as a family."

"Yes there are."

"So what happens to them?"

"They get their licence from the physical world."

"I'm sorry, but it sounds a little illogical."

"Why?"

"Because they can't have an unknown person do it in a different location. They need to get one for themselves. "

"Where from?"

"From here, I guess."

"But they don't do them over here. Have a look around. When's the last time you saw a temple marriage taking place over here?"

"I haven't been in this Prison sector very often, to be honest."

"Well, we can always arrange to stay a lot longer if you'd like."

"No that's OK, thanks. I'll take your word for it. But if the licence is back in the physical world, well how are Phillipe and Rebecca going to find out?"

"There were banns issued in the mortal world, so there are records kept as well in our Spirit World dimension. We have assignments to monitor the work done in the temples of the physical dimension."

"What about the huge numbers of people who didn't have

access to temples in the mortal dimension?"

"It's what a millennium period is for, later in human history. There's a time to allow a catch-up for anyone who's been missed out."

"This still seems a little odd..."

"Fair enough. So what's a better solution?"

"People over here could do their own work."

"Have you seen any spirit kids here?"

"No, I haven't."

"So you haven't seen any marriages, and you haven't seen any kids. What does that tell you?"

"Things are different?"

"Exactly. Quite a bit different from Paradise, where we enjoy family groups, as well as access away from, or back into the Spirit World. And with such a thought in mind, some people want to progress or leave Spirit Prison to come over into Paradise, often as married couples. For this depth of progress, you need a licence. It doesn't matter where the licence is issued, the people who want to make the change are simply looking for a permit, and they aren't concerned where it comes from. But like any other new right of access, they do still need permission."

"OK," John-Paul agreed. He hesitated before asking gingerly, "And what about issuing licences from Paradise?"

"There's room for arguing about it that way, I guess. Perhaps for many people, the mortal records are the best proof of a genuine marriage contract, but I'm not really sure. Logically though, when have you generally heard of a permit being organised from a place which you're trying to get into? Permits are usually granted before entry, although after a period of testing, and by an administrator who resides outside of the area. You've observed the educational systems in mortality. When a person seeks to attend a university, they have exams to undertake beforehand at a school. If they leave school without the qualifications, then they can go back to school later if they wish to attend university as a mature student. The same idea applies for Spirit Prison. Mortal life is the place to gain the qualifications for entering Paradise, so whilst teaching occurs in Prison, the official qualifications still come from mortal temples."

"Yes, but universities also have entrance exams."

"It's an unusual route and not the regular way to gain university entrance. Your questions though are good. You can search out someone who knows all the details when we get back into the Paradise area."

"That's OK. I'm not too concerned," John-Paul agreed. A few moments later he asked his final question. "So who sorts out the proxy licences, or what's this prompting you were alluding to, for Philippe and Rebecca?"

"It's rather a long story... but I can tell you on the way back through..." Charlie suggested.

"OK," John-Paul agreed.

They made their rapid passage through the extensive Prison area, over towards the boundaries of Paradise. Charlie noticed something and stopped before they passed through.

CHAPTER 20

"How come we all walked last week, can I possibly ask?"

"Because I needed the exercise."

"Great."

"Well you can still walk this week because I can drop you lot off here, at this corner."

"Yer, ha, ha, very funny."

"So you'll stop moaning then?"

"Nope, we don't agree to that. Besides it's raining hard, which in the end says we've got something to moan about."

"And just exactly what have you got to moan about, considering we're all inside the car?"

"Yer, but we'll be getting out at Siggel's soon. It won't take long before we'll definitely be getting soaked."

"Speaking of which, wouldn't it be weird if we turned the corner and there was a rather large flood across the road. If the car stalls each of you'll be fulfilling your ambitions of getting wet... maybe just a bit earlier."

"Is this some kind of premonition? If it is, I'm getting out... on any corner... wherever you choose to stop."

"We'll see."

"I don't like the sound of that."

"Yer, the water's building up across this road quite badly."

"It'll be fine. Stop worrying."

"He's doing the pushing if we get stuck!"

"In your dreams!"

"Not to worry everyone, because the next street is Siggel's."

After coming across a dual carriageway into a narrower, tree-lined street, before turning a sharp corner, Adam noticed how the surface water had suddenly increased. It was up to a level above the bottom of the car doors. He decided the only course of action was to continue onto their destination, where the worse thing would be to simply stop. 'If water covers the exhaust pipe, the engine will probably stall so we could get marooned,' he contemplated. The idea of getting water inside the car didn't fill Adam with a lot of excitement.

"No one opens up any car doors," he instructed.

"Well, just make sure you don't stall the car."

"I certainly don't intend to..."

Driving further on up the road the possibility however, did cross his mind. The surface water had originally begun as a small stream. In turn, it became a rapidly flowing brook, slowly but gradually transforming into an alarmingly heavy ford, until in the end, all that could be seen was a raging torrent hurtling down the middle of the street. Fortunately though it was in still the direction they were travelling. The car gradually ground to a halt as the engine stalled.

"Hold on, now what did I say about not stalling the engine?"

"Don't get out of the car anyone."

"We're still a few hundred yards from Siggel's house."

"Where has all this water come from?"

"He's up on a slight hill, so his place should still be OK to park."

"Why have we got a river running down the middle of the street?"

"Can someone kindly get this vehicle going again?"

Adam ignored the comments. This was the third time he'd been in a similar situation. The first time was coming out of a bridge near Selby after torrential rain. It took a while but the car had started again. The second time was in Brazil when the vehicle was driven by a family friend on their way to a local church. He was greatly impressed by how calm Tauama had remained throughout that particular episode, initially phoning her brother with his taller vehicle, presumedly to give her car a shunt or a tow out of the flooded area. However, once again the car had restarted successfully. He saw no reason to assume his vehicle wouldn't just restart this time as well. He noticed a lorry coming up from behind, having very little difficulty in pushing through the rushing waters. It was propelled by both the sheer torque of the HGV engine, coupled with its significant height above the force of the waters. For a brief moment as it came up close behind, he wondered whether it was about to push his vehicle out on its way through, but all it did in the end, was to merely bury the car under a wall of water. It seemed like a typical story from Frank's collection.

"Well that was helpful," Kieron commented.

"Don't open any of the doors folks," James helpfully reiterated.

"You can push," Dave retorted.

Ian was asleep, so he missed much of the unfolding drama.

"What are you planning?" Dave inquired of Adam.

"To get to Siggel's."

"How?"

Adam ignored the interrogation. After a while he retried the ignition. It duly started.

-

"Has anyone seen the film 'Bruce Almighty'?"

"Yer, it's good, isn't it?"

"I enjoyed it as well."

"The bit I like is where he's taken on the role of God for a while and he has to answer the millions of incoming prayers.

He hears them audibly first off but it drives him crazy, so he gets everything recorded onto yellow Postit Notes, which immediately fill the entire room. He transfers them over into emails and spends the whole night sending out answers, but as the sun's slowly coming up, his incoming emails are even more than the replies he's actually managed to send out! Eventually he replies 'Yes' to everyone, which means all pandemonium breaks out with rioting, looting or mayhem everywhere."

"Yer, I did wonder what the answer could have been, although the film moved on. They left it as another mystery."

"So what's the answer?"

"I reckon it's like the actions of young superman in the 'Smallville' series, where he can decide to run at lightning speed, or just slow down whenever it's not required. If God speeds up or slows down, then everything can work out. It could be like smaller animal species moving a lot quicker than larger ones, having higher metabolic rates with faster movements or shorter lifespans."

"And a shorter lifespan isn't a problem after mortality, since apoptosis, or disease or death, they aren't relevant factors when there's a properly or perfectly controlled environment."

"True. You're still missing one small point though."

"Yer, what's that?"

"God's not a mouse."

"No, that's not the important point. The important point is none of this is an important point, because none of it's important. It's pointless!"

"The pointed point is rather how God can use any useful principle, no matter where the principle comes form..."

"I think I'm about to yawn."

"Well done!"

"On a slightly different tangent, it's never been clear for me how the environment could naturally select higher human intelligence. I've seen all the stories about man's use of early tools, with cooperative language development, et cetera, but at the end of the day, human intelligence is unnecessarily sophisticated for survival needs. Evolutionary psychologists such as Geoffrey Miller have highlighted this type of problem. As humans we think or we've planned out things which have no benefit for natural selection, and it's been going on for a long time. These over-sophistications suggest the work of an inherent design, leaving a stamp of built-in mental capacity for future expanded use, and it usefully accommodates the continued evolution of psyche, rather than any evolution of the physical body."

"Yes, I follow your point, because human biology evolved creatively billions of years in the past, where it occurred in the universe under controlled conditions, over a much shorter time period. The idea of natural selection for humans is a downgrading of something which occurred that was truly quite magnificent. Creation couldn't be haphazard because deity itself was the blueprint for human biology. I'm still convinced natural selection has been mixed up with the excellent contingency capabilities which species inherently hold, ultimately in dealing with changing environments through adaption. Adaption remains a design, whereas natural selection is rather more haphazard, taking quite unpredictable, convoluted paths. They're similar, but the most relevant evolution remains the personal evolution of the psyche. Which we only get to find it out..." Dave paused.

"When we die!" Everyone joined in.

"What's the impromptu chorus line all about?" James asked, out of natural curiosity.

"Oh, it's just something we've been doing for a while. It suggests a way of drawing a line under a discussion, since we all need to remember how every opinion is valid. Sometimes you just have to respect a difference of opinion. Whenever there's a possibility for contention, then the 'chorus line' as you so aptly put it, usually comes into play. It kind of acts like a release valve before any pressure builds up."

"OK, fair enough."

-

James was still thinking over the discussion at the discussion group, as he went up for the header. He wasn't too keen on Sunday league football, but where he'd done it for such a long time, he didn't particularly want to give it up. He'd still prefer to play on Saturdays though, if he ever had the chance. He wasn't quite sure why he hadn't delivered his preplanned, suitable distraction when he was with Dave, Kieron, Ian and the others, over at Siggel's place. 'They certainly deserved to be thrown out of kilter, especially after those crazy shenanigans with the lightning flashes in the umbrella. I'll have to remember it next time,' he confirmed, as he saw the ball fly past his head, also clearing the chap who was jumping up with him. He was satisfied. In defence, if you couldn't get the ball, you only had to make sure the attacker didn't get it either. That had successfully been achieved.

On the way back down to ground though he saw a rather unwelcomed elbow launched in an ungainly fashion towards his head, and whilst he assumed the action was due to a loss of balance, he quickly decided he had to take evasive action. He just about managed to, albeit before he was struck firmly in the side of the face. It was quite annoying really because he'd nearly got his head out of the way in time, so when they both landed he felt inclined to vocalise his displeasure, even quite strongly. He suddenly found however, he couldn't in fact open his mouth to say anything at all. Somehow his jaw was now frozen. He felt his jaw on the same side which had been struck, and it seemed to be a little lower than normal, perhaps slightly more to the left as well, or at least compared to where it should have been. 'The thing's dislocated!' he informed himself. After the initial shock, he knew he had to figure out what to do about it. He felt both sides again to see whether his mandibular was positioned squarely under the maxilla, and properly in the middle.

'Nope, it's definitely not. It's over to the left. This isn't helpful, because it needs to be back the other way.'

Using his left hand, which he opened out flat, he carefully but strongly slapped the side of his face from the left-hand side, hearing a creak and a pop. Gingerly, he made another attempt to speak.

"Good, that's done it."

"What's done what?" asked the lanky opposition attacker.

"My jaw's back in place again."

"What are you whinging about?"

"Nothing. My jaw's in place now."

"Are you trying to say it was dislocated or something equally ridiculous?"

"Yes, it was."

"What utter nonsense! You can't put your own jaw back in place."

James couldn't be bothered to argue. His jaw clicked badly on the right-hand side for the rest of the match, and seemed loose for about three weeks afterwards. Occasionally in the months or years which followed, he'd have to push it back into place again, usually when he was eating something which required a fair amount of chewing, but he hadn't known it at the time, otherwise he probably would have moaned rather strongly. Besides, this wasn't his first orthopaedic football injury.

His team had played a rather decent army team in Aldershot, and he was playing at centre-half with another ex-army friend at left back. Jim had coordinated the defensive line perfectly, pulling the army's attack offside for most of the match.

Finally however, an army midfielder played the crucial pass over the defensive line with their centre-forward sprinting through to collect the pass, judging his run perfectly, neatly avoiding a repeat of all the previous offside decisions. James was nearest to the action, and spun round to chase their centre-forward, yet as he did so, what flashed through his mind was an England versus Germany international he'd watched on television a while back. Exactly the same thing had happened. To his astonishment the England defender had grabbed the German then held onto him, luckily just before they both reached the penalty box. James didn't contemplate for too long. He masterfully recreated precisely the same scenario which he'd happily watched on the television.

"What d'you think you're doing?" yelled the army player.

"Oh stop moaning," James replied, as he saw the ball rolling along just in front of them and moving ahead quite merrily under its own steam. He decided at the last moment he wouldn't take any chances, so it was time to hook the ball away into the sidelines way over to the left. As he used his right foot to push the ball away, the attacker lunged forward to keep the ball going towards the goal. The next thing he knew, there was a collision, the ball skewed off to the left touchline, and then he heard it. "Crack!" The noise was something akin to a branch snapping. He heard it quite clearly. They both ended up in a heap. When he dusted himself off, subsequently making ready to stand, he suddenly noticed how his right ankle felt awkward. He examined it to see a significant level of swelling beginning to form, especially around the joint.

"It doesn't feel too good," he commented. One of his teammates came over to assess the damage.

"Can you walk on it?"

"Just about. Not sure I can run with it though."

"OK, well the ref is someone I know, and I'll see if you can swap with him for the rest of the match."

"What about one of our subs?"

"They've had to go home, because one of their wives is having a baby."

"What, now?"

"Yer, her sister's come along and they've had to go home."

"What, d'you mean all of the subs have gone home? How did that happen?"

"Well yer, because they were all from the same family."

"And what will the army team say? They won't be happy if the ref is your friend."

"I won't be mentioning it. Leave it to me, because it'll be just fine. Either way, you can't be playing with that swelling. Certainly not in defence, anyway."

James was grateful for the advice at the end of the day, since he later took a trip up to the local hospital where they x-rayed his ankle in the A&E department. His fibula was fractured. A couple of operations later, they'd plated the fracture subsequently removing the plate, ensuring the fibula had healed correctly. It was fortunate he hadn't attempted to continue playing.

"Come on James. Wake up!" yelled one of his teammates. He did, yet this time he wasn't going to be sideswiped nor left with a repositioned jawline.

-

"Oh don't be ridiculous!"

"Hey, that's my line..." James replied, indignant over how someone was using his typical script.

"Not today, it's not."

"What's not?"

"Your line."

"OK, well why's it so ridiculous?"

"Because we can't all be related. It's not just ridiculous, it's totally absurd as well."

"Aren't they the same thing?"

"What's the same?"

"Ridiculous and absurd."

"Well no, because ridiculous is open to derision, whereas absurd is sufficiently mad or wild, it's void of any useful logic."

"What's your point?"

"On the one hand you can make a jolly decent mockery of anyone who's being ridiculous, whereas on the other hand, you can lock up someone who's turned absurd because they've lost far too many marbles to ever be let out again safely on their own!"

"Well not quite."

"Why not?"

"Because this has absolutely nothing to do with it!" James protested.

"To do with what?"

"My suggestion."

"It is ridiculous."

"No, because I've started to look into the group's family history and there are some strong links for many of us... possibly all of us."

"That's still totally ridiculous."

"No... but possibly absurd."

"I think James is right," Reg intervened. Everyone became silent. "Many months ago I raised the idea whilst you young folk were busily having fun."

"I think he means us Dave," Kieron commented.

"Don't worry, he's just being absurd because we never make fun."

"Yes, I agree. Never."

"Actually, does he mean we were making fun of what he was saying, or just making fun? Because making fun per se is a good thing."

"Whereas making fun of someone... well that would be ridiculous."

"Or absurd."

"Absolutely."

Reg ignored them. "James, we should check each others' work to see whether it might overlap, although I'm guessing it should all mesh together quite well. Siggel and Frank found the same overlaps after I'd previously raised the idea. Kieron and Dave are probably just having a senior moment, because they must have been here when Frank last mentioned it."

"He's talking about us again, Kieron."

"Well, we don't have senior moments, so we must've missed that meeting."

"Absolutely, and senior moments are reserved specifically for senior people."

"Just ignore them Reg. Let's get together to compare what we've found," James agreed. James didn't vocalise his next question, at least not to the whole group – he'd decided against it following the reaction to his original statement. "Don't you find it unusual Reg how everyone in the group shares a branch of the same family tree."

"My thoughts exactly. I'm also find it fascinating the way different people in the group are individually coming up with the same conclusion. It's good you've observed it."

James was likewise pleased how a few of the group had similarly seen the significance.

-

"Why is your god so harsh in the old Bible, and then a son of the god tells everyone about love or forgiveness a bit later on... in the very same book? It's incongruent. Someone clearly hasn't read the Old Testament when they've been writing the

New Testament."

"Interesting."

"What d'you mean?"

"It's interesting you've read it like that."

"Everything's there in black and white. Are you arguing with fact now?"

"I understand you might view things a little differently from me. It's fair enough."

"What's your answer to my point? Do you even have an answer?"

"If you knew someone had a jolly ugly hat, perhaps after they'd asked you what it was like, what would you say?"

"What's this got to do with my question?"

"Hopefully you'll see."

He paused before reflecting a while. "I'd say they had a hat which suited them."

Frank chuckled. "Yes, OK. Fair enough. But would you tell your wife the same thing?"

"Probably not."

"Then what would you tell her?"

"I'd probably suggest another hat."

"And I reckon I'd follow suit with your idea as well. It's not unreasonable Dirk, to think God has done pretty much the same thing in the Bible."

"What d'you mean?"

"God knew a better way, but the people in the Old Testament weren't ready to listen to the better way, therefore He gave them something which they would listen to, or could understand."

"What, killing people with a flood was useful? It was barbaric, totally selfish or just a story which someone made up because they felt it was a way to somehow cope with natural disasters."

"Have you seen the film 'Taken', featuring Liam Neeson?"

"It's an entertaining film but it's merely a story. The storyline's not true... exactly like the Noah's flood story."

"If your children lived in an evil environment, would you attempt to take them away from such a situation?"

"Yes I would."

"It's what God did with the flood."

"And that's very harsh on the people supposedly outside the boat."

"I'm referring to the people outside of the ark, as well as the new psyches being born to them."

"Then how did they survive the flood or get away from their unfavourable circumstances?"

"Because they entered another dimension where things were changed, with a chance to start over again. They were most likely never going to progress or evolve any further in their mortal dimension."

Dirk thought for a moment before quickly presenting another example. "Well what of the stonings amongst people in the Old Testament? Or the genocide. How were they anything but simply cruel powers over peoples who often didn't share their dogmatic beliefs?"

"When the Israelites requested to come through the land to reach a destination, they were refused access. They attempted to make peace or pass through without any conflict. Repeatedly on occasions they offered the banner of peace long before any conflict, yet the other side would still choose conflict instead. There's inevitably another side to every story, which means quite often the stories are taken out of context when history is written. I lived through the era of Margaret Thatcher as Prime Minister, and what I see recorded now is nothing like what actually happened in reality. History is only as accurate as the historians who've recorded it."

"And what about the biblical stoning of citizens. How can that be correct?"

"Various debates over capital punishment haven't been confined to biblical times. It was relevant in England during the twentieth century. I personally favour the saving of condemned innocents through jailing individuals, but I can see the logic behind arguments for capital punishment."

James had been following Frank's conversation with interest. He could empathise with Dirk's stance as well as many of his questions, although he felt Dirk could possibly tone down his approach a little, and perhaps listen for answers. 'Maybe he was actually listening? I can't believe I just thought that,' he thought. 'I think I'm thinking too much about what he thought, or what I thought he might think, or I might think...' he thought. 'I'm not thinking about this anymore,' yet he couldn't stop thinking.

"So how many gods are there?" Dirk continued.

"It's an interesting question. Many religions have multiple gods such as the trinity, but others focus upon a single god. Any religion which focuses upon God has goodness within it."

"Religion causes too many wars."

"Some people who do such things will call themselves religious but generally theists seek to build a peaceful future with others. You don't need to agree with other people's opinions, you just have to accommodate them."

As James listened to Frank's answers he wondered whether Dirk was also related to the others in the group. He saw new people arriving from week to week, and yet when he'd investigated the genealogy, he'd found connections for everyone he'd researched. 'How does it all work out? It can't just be a coincidence. But maybe it is though? Or maybe it's not? How did it happen if it's not?' He was thinking again. He thought it was probably about time to go home. 'There's football on TV, and Frank always appreciates football as a jolly good reason to go home.' He was happy with his conclusion. An hour and a half later they left.

Premonition

CHAPTER 21

Two men stood together. They were dressed in white suits, white shoes and white ties and were deeply engaged in discussion.

"Listen to this conversation a moment John-Paul," Charlie suggested, stopping beside a group of individuals who were now conversing within a larger group. There were both male and female individuals, every one dressed in quite a different assortment of attires, all standing alongside a large, grey building with multiple storeys and plain, rectangular windows.

"I'm bored. I've been here for such a long time now. I just want to explore or get away."

"I agree. This is tedious. I thought all my dreams had come true when I found out our existence continues after mortal death. But then I didn't figure on being stuck here in this awful place, or for this length of time."

John-Paul switched off to the expletives, along with various blasphemous cursings which were now being expressed.

"We need to do something fun. I'm not taken in by those pious, religious moaners. If they're so good, then how come they're still here with us? They say they've got all the answers but I haven't seen any of them leave. How do they know what's outside this place?"

"More to the point, we can do whatever we like, for as long as we like. Nothing's stopping us. The elections are coming up soon. I believe I could do better than those idiots who are running things at the moment."

"Maybe, but I'm still fed up."

"Look if you support me, then I'll see to it that you're in a good position."

"What will you do for me?"

"I've heard how your family back in mortal life are talking about you."

"Have they said anything decent?"

"Well, we can find out because I know someone who's found a place where people in mortal life all gather. They gather in groups to call for us."

"What d'you mean?"

"They talk to us and we can answer them back."

"How?"

"At this place I've found. They get their building or a room they choose super dark, after which somehow they can feel us... or sometimes they can even see us."

"Don't be stupid!"

"Yes, it's true."

"I've seen it as well, because I've been there," another individual intervened.

"And what happens?"

"We talk, then they talk."

"How?"

"Come along because I'll show you how it works. It'll give you a chance to try talking with your family. But you have to help me in these new elections."

"OK. If I can see my family I agree, I'll help."

"Good. But don't listen to any of those people who come with big ideas or say they can teach us. They promise to teach us, saying how they'll somehow get us together with our families in the future, but no one gets to see relatives at all. They say it's only supposedly possible once the family die from

mortality or come over into this world, yet we've not actually
seen any families they've supposedly helped join us. The
families which do join us say they've never spoken to these
religious teachers. It's just a sham. They want us to join them
in their own kingdom, but whenever people choose to join
them, they always rule over them, forcing their leadership
onto them, giving them rules to follow with strict 'dos' and
'don'ts'. It's total rubbish because they haven't even been
democratically elected. What I'm offering you happens right
now. It's not later. We've all waited long enough for some
kind of change. Our lives need change and we need it now!"

"Yer, we've waited long enough."

"Far too long!"

"Yer, I agree. We all agree."

"We won't stand for this any longer."

"We need change!"

John-Paul look stunned.

"These people haven't learnt to carefully distinguish between
the good or the bad. If this is the way people can be thinking
here in Prison, how can we possibly know when someone has
truly changed? Without this knowledge, who can realistically
be allowed into Paradise?"

"That's a very good question," Charlie replied. "You've also
been asking why any licences to pass from Prison to Paradise
have to be performed by proxy. I see it as a safety mechanism
where people must automatically choose for themselves
whether to evolve or progress onwards."

"Surely it can't effectively work though if they're choosing
themselves, can it? Everyone will always want to grant
themselves a licence."

"Maybe not. Because to get a proxy licence from the mortal
dimension means there has to be a level of work, a work
which involves guiding mortal men or women towards
genealogy for proxy labours."

"In the same way we prompt people."

"Exactly... in just the same way. Each time someone in Prison looks to be taught the evolution in choosing good things, it means after they've been taught, the promptings for them can begin. Some of us in Paradise can help those in mortality with proxy temple work, prompting them towards the mortal genealogical records of the psyches in Prison. It adds a significant layer of goodness to what needs to take place. Before the licences are granted or bestowed, they still have to be accepted by the intended recipients in our dimension, and through sacred acknowledgements. All that complexity can only happen if numerous people are working cooperatively together, or in other words the people in Prison must also work hard, consistently making the right choices. Being cooperative is good, which in turn means the process can take time, as well as needing proper effort. It's difficult to pass into Paradise from Prison."

"Why didn't those in Prison just do better in mortality? It would've been more far more logical or easier, wouldn't it?"

"I agree."

"Proxy licences certainly seem to add quite a lot of complexity, but then I can see it means you have to be genuinely good to pass over into Paradise from Prison. It can't be a 'flash in the pan' as some mortals would say."

"I can see that's true."

-

When they made their way back to Paradise John-Paul reflected upon how he'd seen quite a fair amount of dishonesty or scheming during their trips into Prison. People we're attempting to 'get themselves ahead' of each other. However, at the end of the day since everyone had similar plans, they all just 'got ahead' for a brief period before the merry-go-round changed many of their respective plans, and someone else 'got ahead'. It really seemed rather pointless. 'All this 'merry-go-round' might possibly achieve,' John-Paul concluded, 'is a lasting feeling of resentment, which would ultimately be futile because it would simply stifle cooperation or retard personal evolution.' He quickly visualised their home in Paradise. 'Everyone in Paradise works together, helping each other, building systems or organisations, at the same time creating beautiful environments,' he reflected. 'Evolution is truly pleasant as well as decent.' Based upon his recent experiences, he was still pleased his own time in mortality had been rather short-lived. As they travelled onwards, the next conversation he overheard only served to confirm such a consideration. He marvelled over the way he could encounter conversations at some distance, even before they'd passed by, allowing him to pick up any exchanges in real time and whilst they were actually being made.

"It was clearly survival of the fittest in the previous life, and it's survival of the smart in this new life!" declared a beaming official, as he addressed the captive audience. They were doubly captivated. Initially it was by the rhetoric, which appealed to their desire to 'forge ahead' in making their individual gains, but also because they were packed tightly into the large and spacious building, which wasn't quite so large nor quite so spacious, once they'd all been packed in.

"But we now know how natural selection supposedly selected individuals to remain in the previous life, when in reality every individual always makes the trip too naturally into this next dimension."

"And those who've used their strength against other people in the previous life, they don't get accepted particularly well over here," added another voice in the large and spacious building.

"I'd beg to differ," continued the leading official.

"How?" came a cry from the back.

"Because we all carry wisdom with us which we don't forget. And such wisdom can be put to good effect in this our new dimension. Anything we've learned or experienced before, can still be used to promote our positions for this time, or equally in this space."

John-Paul became more curious at this last remark. There wasn't too much space in the large and spacious building, increasing his curiosity as to where the conversation could be heading.

"Charlie, can we stop a moment?" John-Paul asked.

"For sure," Charlie replied as they came to a standstill. They were just a little without the large and spacious building.

"What are you suggesting?" asked another occupant, albeit quite sincerely.

"I'm suggesting," added the official, "that we help each other. If we hear of something bad which might be about to happen to any of us, we should tell each other and collect together as one group, looking out for the welfare of anyone in the group."

"It sounds reasonable."

"So the elections are coming up. What shall we do? How shall we cast our votes?"

"It's not so much how your votes are cast, but how your votes can be used."

"What d'you mean?"

"If we mix among the people and let them see what's happening, then they'll choose to side with us because our movement will be sweeping across this state. Before long we'll have friends spanning the vast expanse of this dominion, which means we'll be able to take our rightful places as rulers of all we can see. This is our proper right... it's our time. We must seize our moment!" he roared, to rapturous applause, applause which rippled or cascaded down throughout the large and spacious building. "We will be victorious!" he announced with outstretched arms. "Strength and freedom!"

"Yes, strength and freedom!" came back a reply.

"Strength and freedom!"

"Strength and freedom!" reverberated yet again and again, only gaining in volume or voracity as it spread across the crowd.

"I'm not sure there's too much long-term veracity in his approach," John-Paul remarked to Charlie.

"Yes, I agree," Charlie replied.

John-Paul contemplated that he was learning a lot from their trips into Prison. He might not have spent long in mortality, and he'd simply observed mortal lives before making the excursion down to Earth, yet his observations of Prison had become revealing. It didn't really seem much awry, or especially different from any mortal history. History was interesting because a lot could be learnt from the actions of men or psyches. John-Paul was content at the thought they'd return again. These trips were gradually becoming a fair bit more useful.

CHAPTER 22

J ames was rather concerned. He'd prepared as best he could for this university exam, although he'd had little time. He'd been asked to swap groups which meant he'd had about sixty per cent more subjects to cover over the year, even above or beyond what was normal. He was happy to cooperate but this increase in workload was onerous. 'This might be a good time to test the God theory, the one Reg keeps talking about,' he thought.

'If you're there God, perhaps you could give a hand because there was nothing more I could do in the time available. Thanks,' James concluded.

There were thirty-two topics for the exam he was about to take, where the format of the exam was he'd draw two cards out of the thirty-two, prepare his answers for a while and then orally present them. At the conclusion of his presentations, a question and answer session would subsequently follow with the examiners. James decided to inform them of his position.

"I've only managed to study eight of the topics," James announced.

"Well, you're here now. You may as well go ahead with your questions, because this exam will count."

One of the lecturers fanned out sixteen visually identical cards directly in front of him. As he stared at them, one of the cards was sticking up higher than the rest, quite a lot higher.

'Well, I'm not choosing that one!' he exclaimed mentally.

'Why do you think it's sticking up?' came a searching question into his confused mind.

'OK,' he mentally responded, as he took the card from the pack. He read the topic description on the back.

"This is one of the eight," he announced.

The lecturers looked surprised as a couple of them shook their heads in disbelief. He prepared and delivered his answer. In time, another lecturer approached him with a second pack, fanning out sixteen more cards in front of him. He chose to go right along the deck, whereupon another strong idea became crystal clear, even audible within his mind.

"Go left!"

He heeded the thought, moving in the opposite direction towards the left, duly choosing a card. He read through its details.

"This is also a topic which I've studied," he announced.

This time all the lecturers looked surprised, whilst simultaneously most began to shake their heads. He prepared his second answer for delivery.

The result of the exam was satisfying.

'Cheers for that God,' he mentally thanked. There was no answer, but he was sure his comment had been heard. James decided he might repeat this experiment again in the future. It was a good experience and he was grateful.

CHAPTER 23

Two men stood together. They were dressed in white suits, white shoes and white ties and were deeply engaged in discussion.

"What roles do we perform beyond making trips to Prison? Do any of us go back to mortality at all?" John-Paul asked inquisitively.

"Why do you ask?" Charlie responded, even with another question. "Are you wondering what's happening with family?"

"How did you know?"

"Are we going to be conversing with questions now?"

"D'you think we should?"

"Can you think of a reason why we should?"

"Do we have to make a decision?"

"OK, I'm tired of this now. Some of us can go back as guardians at particular times, whenever it's needed."

"How does that work?"

"You really like these questions, eh?"

"Is that wrong?"

"OK, fine. When someone has something to complete, maybe work, and it's not their time to make a transition from mortality to the Spirit World, but if they're confronted with mortal danger, then yes, guardians can be sent back to provide assistance."

"How does that work?"

"You're pushing things with these questions John-Paul." Charlie's expression clearly conveyed his mounting lack of approval. "Guardians can work alone or they can work together. The end result will be the same, because protecting the individual or individuals is always important... at least until they've achieved what they need to accomplish in mortality."

"Won't the number of guardians actually shape the way they can provide assistance?"

Charlie ignored the question. John-Paul continued instead. "If they work alone then surely they'd need to provide some form of shielding? If they worked together, wouldn't they be able to divert multiple dangers at the same time, because I remember observing men shooting arrows and sling-shots at a man on a wall, who was shouting things down to people below about how they needed to change their behaviour? I wondered at the time, why couldn't they seem to get any of their shots on target, despite the scores and scores of missiles they were launching at him? Multiple guardians could've worked together to divert the different missiles away, couldn't they? D'you think that the man on the wall should've stopped telling them they were misbehaving, because the people down below, the ones who were firing things at him, they just looked to be getting more and more angry? Should he have given up?"

Charlie ignored the questions. John-Paul continued instead. "Is it OK if I change the subject a little, because I've got another question?"

Charlie looked over towards him in disbelief. "Did we choose our gender before we became psyches? I can imagine we were given the choice, because the male protective or administrative roles can be different from female nurturing or teaching roles, but were the differences as clear-cut as that, or were we allowed to make such a choice?"

John-Paul continued to ask questions as they made their way back to Paradise, whilst Charlie had expected him to run out of new queries. Nevertheless, it never actually happened. Charlie was quite surprised. As they entered Paradise Charlie turned towards John-Paul.

"Would you like to take a trip away from the earth?"

"Is that possible?"

"Would you like to find out?"

"Yes, I think I would."

Charlie was pleased. Finally the questions had dried up. "I'll see what's possible," he replied.

"OK," John-Paul agreed, obligingly.

CHAPTER 24

"So how do you occupy your time now Siggel?"

James asked, suddenly more interested in the workings of God or man, following recent events plus the result from his latest university exam.

"I used to watch the series 'Friends' where those six friends spent much of their time together, talking, helping each other, spending time together doing various activities, so the series title was exactly appropriate. After my wife died, I realised how my family were also my friends."

"But I thought they live in different parts of the country now?"

"Yes that's true, since over time all things can change a little. Logically I had to adapt or stay connected with other friends. This discussion group developed from an initial conversation amongst some of you and it's just grown. I guess it's how things worked out."

"But what do you do with your time?"

"When you lose the love of your life, you have to find another thing to love. If it's a good thing then it'll also feel good, allowing the good feeling to come back every day, and eventually the loss isn't centre stage anymore. But there's always an effort."

"What's the new thing in your life at the moment?"

"Well, things have changed over the years, but right now I'd say genealogy."

"Yes, and after plotting with Frank some months back, they've got us all involved with it as well. They just wouldn't stop talking about it," Kieron reported.

"Incessantly," Dave added.

James was greatly surprised. When he'd previously brought up the idea of everyone in the group having a connected family tree, the initial reaction from Dave and Kieron was to suggest he was being ridiculous.

"Have you found anything interesting?" James asked.

"Yes, we've come to the conclusion a great number of us in this group are connected by our genealogy, although some links are quite distant."

James was suddenly almost as smug as he was greatly shocked. He wasn't quite sure which emotion to express, so in the end his face only remained totally blank.

"Do you believe me now then?" he asked.

"Believe what?" replied Kieron.

"How everyone in the group is part of the same family tree."

"We just said that," Dave continued.

"And they were in the room at the time when you previously reported it, James," Reg supported.

"Thanks Reg."

"My pleasure. Everyone is slowly arriving at the same conclusion. We need to compare our research," Reg added. "We'll probably find some overlaps."

Twenty minutes later James felt vindicated over his suggestion, the one which he'd previously made, and Frank before him, and Reg before Frank. Everyone was finally taking it a little more seriously. He was pleasantly surprised the way a decent idea could quickly mushroom, only with a small amount of moral support. He wasn't quite sure why everyone in the group seemed to have common ancestry but it couldn't just be a coincidence. He wondered what had brought the group all together, ending up in Siggel's front room on an increasing and pleasantly frequent basis. There had to be a reason for it, although he mentally admitted it did indeed seem ridiculous.

"Oh, by the way everyone, I'd like to introduce Clare and Ali," Frank announced.

"Hello Clare and Ali!" was returned.

"Who are Clare and Ali?" Dave asked.

"Clare is Helen's sister whilst Ali is her boyfriend... and also our friend," Frank explained.

"Is Ali religious?"

"Yes, I'm Muslim," Ali replied.

"I had a Muslim friend who had a near-death experience," Adam added. "Angus rode motorbikes, but he admits he was travelling far too fast one day which resulted in a rather bad accident. He flew through the air, ending up quite some distance from his bike, although when the emergency services found him, apparently one of his legs was wrapped around his head."

"Wow, it sounds like it was a rather nasty one."

"That's exactly what I thought as well. Yet for a few minutes he was pronounced dead before he was revived, and Angus says he saw things."

"What type of things?"

"Well, he saw psyches. And not just good ones but also bad ones. He said for a few months afterwards he continued to see them, where they were quite commonplace, mixing amongst everyone. Good psyches would encourage people to do good things... whilst the bad psyches would encourage people to do bad things."

"Yes, it sounds logical."

"It's exactly what I thought."

"I didn't know Muslims believed in an afterlife."

"Yes, we do."

"The more I learn about Islam, the more I see things which

Christians share in common with Muslims."

"Those are the things we need to focus upon or discuss. Also for Hindus, or Sikhs, or any other religion."

"I'd agree with that."

"Absolutely."

"Even more to the point, we should also include agnostics as well as atheists in discussions."

"How did you figure this out? Atheists are against all religions, so what can they share in common with theists?"

"People normally associate religion with faith, or science with questions plus answers. I'd like to suggest how science requires faith which in turn, means if you ask the right religious questions you can also get the right answers."

"What d'you mean?"

"If I told you that as a preacher, I was going to build a boat, and then I invited you to sail across an ocean in it, would you accept my invitation?"

"Probably not."

"Well, what about if I told you, before I became a preacher I worked as a marine engineer for twenty years. Would you perhaps accept my invitation?"

"Yes, I probably would."

"But nothing's changed. I'm still the same person and you're still the same person. The only difference is you now have faith in my science."

"Yes, I suppose you're right."

"If I now asked some religious questions, perhaps some logical answers could come from them. What would you say for example, if I asked what it's like on another inhabitable planet, or the life forms which might be encountered there?"

"I'm not too sure, to be honest."

"Fair enough. Alternatively, have you ever wondered why so many terrible things happen on this earth?"

"Yes, I certainly have."

"When the Father told Lucifer he would crawl on his belly down in this Earth, it was another way of saying he couldn't leave the planet to cause havoc elsewhere. Lucifer became mega angry, after which he decided to cause as much angst here as he possibly could."

"I guess it sounds about right."

"With such in mind, what could a planet be like which is similar to Earth, but without Lucifer on it?"

"Maybe not much could go wrong?"

"Yes, your suggestion's a plausible one. But at the same time, men would have to learn about the importance of cooperating with each other, overcoming all the usual problems in temporal existence where things can wrong or quite often do go wrong. It's one thing to be good in a perfect pre-existent environment, yet an environment which is more difficult requires men to cooperatively work together."

"And that's just not easy with some folk."

"Exactly."

"So why would we come to an earth like this if we could have chosen a less harsh earth?"

"Perhaps because this is a fast-track earth."

"Fast track to what?"

"Good question. Maybe a fast-track in evolving?"

"For those who fail, it's a big gamble though. Any fast-tracking progress might not be a decent idea at all."

"Maybe, but I imagine if someone's going to make a big mistake, it would perhaps be made whatever earth they went to..."

"Then what's so important about choosing a fast-track earth life?"

"You've posed another very good question. I'm not too sure. And that's why it's worth asking questions... to gain different views on possible solutions. However, if we can't find an answer the next best approach is to shelve the question, because any question can always be answered at some point in the future."

"I think I follow what you're saying."

"Great. Also it's important not to forget there's always possible communication with the most intelligent Being in the universe."

"You mean God?"

"Yes."

"But I'm not convinced feelings or ideas can be trusted since individuals can get different answers or ideas through feelings."

"What d'you mean?"

"Well, I once heard a radio presenter relate on his radio programme, an occasion when he'd prayed about a Church and got the impression it wasn't correct or right."

"How did it work out?"

"He was asked by Church missionaries to read their literature then pray sincerely afterwards to determine whether the Church doctrine was correct. The missionaries stated if their Church was correct, the radio presenter would feel good about it or reassured."

"So what happened?"

"The radio presenter prayed to be humoured, where he asked for a warmth or reassurance if this Church wasn't correct, and he received the reassurance."

"Well that's like placing your foot on the brake to go forward. It doesn't sound logical to me."

"You make a good point. A Church member who was on the radio programme suggested the radio presenter was indeed being humoured in his answer." Evan paused. "What do you think actually happened in terms of an answer?" he continued, shifting the opportunity for an explanation.

"In my experience, prayers are answered in two ways. A positive 'Yes' answer is received by a good feeling of strong assurance, whilst a negative 'No' feels strongly incorrect, even to the point of a stupor of thought."

"Yes, I believe your rationale's quite logical."

"And it doesn't really work the other way around, because if you have a stupor of thought as a 'Yes', you'd be forgetting an important question which needed answering. Or similarly, if you had a goodly feeling of reassurance as a 'No', then you'd be associating good feelings with something incorrect. It doesn't really add up the wrong way round."

"Then what answer was the radio presenter receiving?"

"Probably he received exactly what he'd asked for. He'd asked to be humoured and he probably was, because his desire to turn things upside down seems to suggest he wasn't perhaps ready at the time to receive the Church's message, so the same or similar message could easily be delivered later. That might occur when or possibly if, the presenter was ready to hear it sometime in the future. Clearly the radio presenter was sincere, but perhaps a little unreceptive at the time."

"Yes, I think you're probably right." Evan paused again. "A question was also raised about the plurality of gods, where Christians tend to associate plural gods with pagan deities, whereas Christianity normally has one God, or a Head God as the basis for its religion. It's similar to Judaism or Islam."

"Would you say those religions uphold families as well as family life?"

"Yes, I would."

"Would you say God is a good example for humankind?"

"Yes, I would."

"So would God ask us to do something which he didn't approve of?"

"No, he wouldn't."

"Then logically, where God approves of families, He will have a family."

"Yes, but humankind is God's family."

"Absolutely. So God is the Father, humankind are the children and logically there's likewise a Heavenly Mother."

Evan paused in thought. "Scripture tells us there is no other god before God nor after Him, nor was there, no will there be."

"Sure, and it's logical because Heavenly Mother is a co-partner with Heavenly Father in an eternal family."

"But humankind isn't eternal as part of that family."

"Well, yes and no. As mortal humans, life is a transitory testing state to see what we'll do when God isn't present, but our psyches which reside inside our human bodies remain as eternal as Heavenly Father or Heavenly Mother, because psyches have eternal parents."

"So are you saying our psyches or spiritual forms had a birth?"

"Yes."

"Then they couldn't be eternal."

"You make an interesting point. Going forwards, our psyches remain eternal, but going backwards, our intelligences are eternal because, as you say, our spirits were born."

"So what exactly are intelligences, according to your definition?"

"Intelligences are individuals before they're born as psyches or spirits. Psyches are a spiritual body, in the same way as in mortality we have physical bodies, with parts alongside passions. Intelligences weren't bodies."

"Do intelligences exist now?"

"Logically they must. God is evolving his children to become better, although only if they'll accept His help. So the process of spiritual birth for psyches will always be taking place somewhere or another, since families have grandfathers and grandchildren, great-grandfathers with great-grandchildren, and so on."

"Are you suggesting the idea God has a father?"

"It's not for us to focus upon because our thoughts need to be concentrated upon our Heavenly Father as our guide through mortality, yet have you ever seen a son without a father?"

"What about Adam?"

"I don't think my question changes with Adam."

"So who was Adam's father?"

"We know God created Adam. Which means the father of his psyche was the Father, whilst his physical body was made differently."

"How?"

"I'm not sure."

"Cloning?"

"I can't rule anything in or anything out, because I'm not sure."

"Did this happen before time began?"

"Another good question. If you take the physical dimension or in other words the universe we can actually see, Heavenly Father made it for testing human mortals, amongst other things. Science says it was created around thirteen billion years ago, where a primaeval atom expanded into gases, dust, forming stars, planets, et cetera. We know from ancient texts things were created spiritually before physically."

"Well what about when the stars run out of hydrogen and helium? Each star has a life cycle, therefore a finite life. The universe will eventually become dark."

"God can find a way of creating more 'big bangs' if needed. I imagine His children who become like Him will have their own 'big bangs' in time, whereby the process renews itself. God has plenty of forward plans, or backup plans if they're needed. There's also plenty of matter, which has to be organised but it's always existed everywhere and will continue to exist forever. The idea of matter forming from nothing isn't sensible, whether declared via religious or equally, via scientific doctrine."

"Yes, your point's interesting."

"Another interesting thing for me is the way Heavenly Father incorporated fantastic detail in His creation of the universe. When it expanded stars, galaxies, clusters of galaxies, et cetera were formed, where everything physical came from the initial primaeval atom. It's quite fantastic. He's also allowed His kids to become involved with the creative processes, learning various different methods or approaches. His Son was a director in the formation of planets from unorganised matter, which resulted after the initial expansion of the universe, and so-called unorganised matter still fills the universe or perhaps beyond. God allows His kids to evolve their creative skills over time, as well as their psyches or characters."

The discussion continued for quite a while, although James left before it concluded. He had ample questions, with some decent answers stored away mentally, all to mull over at a later date. He was tired.

-

James looked up the hill before deciding whether or not to make an attempt on it. It was extremely steep whilst there were no street lights illuminating the way, and the entire road was covered in snow.

"Why are we stopped?" Evan asked.

"I'm not sure whether there's ice underneath all the snow," James replied. "Frank told me how he was caught on this hill one winter, so he decided to take another route."

"It'll be OK. Just go up with vigour, making sure you don't ever brake otherwise you'll roll us back down the hill again."

"We might not make it to the top."

"It'll be fine."

"If the wheels start to spin, we could easily come to a halt."

"Yes, let's not risk it," Emily suggested. "It's not worth it."

"And if we get stuck half way up then we won't get home at all," Anne added.

"It'll be fine. Simply go ahead, but make sure you drive up evenly, without any sudden accelerations."

James remained unsure. He felt that perhaps he shouldn't. Emily and Anne felt they shouldn't. Evan was totally convinced they should. He put the car in gear and gradually built up an even speed as they reached the bottom of the hill, gliding up carefully onto the increasing gradient.

Everything seemed to be going just fine at first, exactly as Evan had predicted, with the car making good progress steadily up the hill. There were no sudden accelerations nor braking to change the status quo. As they approached the small section before the summit at a place where the gradient became a little steeper, James noticed how the car had notably begun to slow, although he'd not changed his depression of the accelerator, nor touched the brake at all.

"Why are we slowing?" Evan asked.

"I'm not too sure," James confirmed.

"Well, whatever you do, don't stop," Evan instructed.

There was nothing James could do because slowly, gradually or without any more ado, the vehicle continued to decelerate, reducing its former slow progress up the hill to the point where ultimately and finally, no forward motion was achieved whatsoever. The car had stopped.

"Hold on. Didn't I just suggest that you shouldn't stop?" Evan protested.

"I didn't. The car stopped itself."

"Yer, like that's possible."

"It is, if there's ice underneath."

"Well if there's ice underneath then we'd better get out."

"Why?" Emily asked.

"Because we'll probably start rolling back down the hill."

Emily opened the front passenger door before exiting. "Come

on Anne," she beckoned, whereupon Anne opened the rear nearside door, then exited.

"Looks like we're all getting out," Evan moaned, eventually following suit.

James exited the driver's side and made his way around the front of the car in order to shut the passenger doors.

"Don't go behind the car," he advised, as he closed the one at the rear nearside. Just as he reached out to close the front one, there was a heavy creak beneath all the wheels, with the car slipping back several inches.

"Come away, girls," James instructed, as a second louder creak was heard, and the car rolled back again, this time though not stopping as it previously had done, but gathering some gradual momentum. James waited briefly for the tyres to grip once again as before, yet it was in vain, because the motion was extended into a continual slide without any abatement, gliding back down the gradient of the very significant hillside they'd only just ascended. For this trip however, fortunately or unfortunately, its driver wasn't now in situ.

At the last moment James realised the one car door left open was rapidly coming towards him, threatening to pull him down the hill along with the car, and for an instant he contemplated jumping inside to somehow direct it back down the hill. He'd already put the hand brake on, so there was little point in attempting to stop the car. It was clearly drifting on the underlying ice which he'd been concerned about from the beginning. He dived to the left, plunging over into the cushioning snow onto the hillside bank, with the flailing door just narrowly missing him by only a few inches.

Everyone watched as the car began to gather speed. James expected it to career off the road, or probably rip off the nearside passenger door at whatever point it might get jammed into the mud of the bank. That never actually happened, since his vehicle inexplicably kept a straight line backwards and all the way down, following the roadway until it slowly, finally came to a halt in a trough at the bottom.

'Phew!' he mentally acknowledged. 'Thanks a lot God... for the extra driver,' he respectfully suggested, not entirely sure what had actually happened, but certainly not prepared to declare in public he'd suddenly developed some new religious inclinations. 'At least that's saved me a substantial repair bill,' he realised, wondering how his student finances could have stretched to include a sizeable garage bill.

"Well that was fun!" Evan declared, looking back down the hill to the event below.

"Not fun in the least!" Emily voiced loudly, unimpressed by Evan's remark.

"Yes, and I'm certainly not coming if we go home this way again," Anne added.

"What, d'you seriously mean you won't come along to the group if we come back via Siggel's hill?" Evan asked.

"How's this Siggel's hill?" James queried. "It's a couple of miles from Siggel's place."

"Maybe, but it'll remind us of a momentous event on a cold, snowy night when the lights were low, and the roads were dangerous," Evan related, drawing out a sense of peculiar mystery now in his voice.

"OK, that's enough Mr. Jackanory," Emily scolded. "Let's get into the car and take another way home." She paused momentarily. "But it won't be back up Siggel's hill!" The hill's new name was cemented forever, remembered as a landmark amongst members of the discussion group, and long after they first got to hear of it.

"How d'you know about Jackanory?" James inquired.

"My mum told me about it. She always mentions it whenever something seems a bit OTT."

"Fair enough."

They clambered down to the bottom of the hill from where the car journey was completed, via a different route.

-

Two men stood together. They were dressed in white suits, white shoes and white ties and were deeply engaged in discussion.

"OK, so does it answer some of your questions about working together in a team?"

"Yes, I think it probably does." John-Paul had been involved with guardian assistance teams before, yet this had required a significant degree of both coordination as well as cooperation. "It was slightly tricky getting him to jump at the right moment."

"And the car wasn't particularly easy to keep in a straight line," Charlie added.

"I was pleased it was possible to keep the door away from the bank."

"And the best part was making sure it didn't slip until they'd all got out."

"Thankfully they listened about going around the front. I was wondering whether he would hear the prompting."

"Yes, fortunately he was listening quite well, although sometimes you might have to repeat the promptings," Charlie advised.

"Yes, everything worked out OK. I enjoyed it."

"So you're happy now."

"Yes, I think I am," John-Paul acknowledged obligingly.

-

James was still contemplating the event on Siggel's hill when he was driving to classes the following week. He couldn't quite figure out why the car had managed to stay on the road all the way back down the hill.

He carefully studied the cars in the queue ahead of him. They were all going along in a perfect straight line. 'Yes, but they've got drivers. What's more, they aren't going backwards,' he mentally argued. 'Maybe the steering lock was on for Siggel's hill?' He paused in thought. 'Then why didn't I have to release the steering lock when I got back in?'

He stared back ahead again at the perfect straight line of cars still travelling in front of his, all evenly spaced whilst moving uniformly...

"To the left!" he exclaimed loudly. He'd just quickly noted how the modified road he'd joined, even quite some miles back, had multiple, small, coned off exits on the left-hand side, again at regular intervals. "This could be an exit!" He pulled the steering wheel sharply to the right, realising he'd already begun to join the left-hand diversion. The diversion was separated from an alternative right-hand route by yet another endless procession of suitably placed traffic cones. His vehicle lurched to the right, not quite making the adjustment in time. It smashed a traffic cone which bounded the start of the demarcation. He knew it was an important delimiter, separating the left and right-handed temporary roadways for the disparate flow of traffic.

"Boom!" he heard, as the cone disappeared beneath his vehicle. He pulled down even further on his steering wheel, hard to the right, hoping to gain some of the extra road positioning he rapidly needed. "Boom!" he heard, as a second cone hit the front of his vehicle and then disappeared again underneath. "Boom... boom... boom!" he heard with successively flattened cones, each suffering exactly the same fate as the previous ones. At this point he was stunned how his vehicle hadn't been thrown off course, nor could he hear any cones scraping the underside. He'd normally have expected some kind of noise. He caught sight of the last cone just before it disappeared, spying that in fact it was one of those thin types rather than a rounded version. Thankfully they were fixed at a bottom edge to the road itself.

'Phew!' he inwardly exclaimed. 'Clearly someone else has done this before, so they've stuck those flexible cones here instead of the usual ones.' Following his encounter with the ridiculously placed traffic equipment, he decided to slow down significantly. He drove along like a P-driver all the way back to the university car park. 'Let's hope those cones made a comeback,' he contemplated, pulling into a parking space before he levered up the handbrake.

'I did have the handbrake on for Siggel's hill,' he slowly concluded.

CHAPTER 25

Two men stood together. They were dressed in white suits, white shoes and white ties and were deeply engaged in discussion.

"Before we take the opportunity to make a trip away from the Earth, we've an errand to do. We also have a little time for some personal things," Charlie announced.

"What kind of things?" John-Paul asked.

"Well I'm going to the library, because I'd like to find an answer about something I've been investigating."

"Can I come along?"

"Sure."

"What are you looking for?"

"I'm puzzled about the Book of Abraham. There was a discussion over the writings of men and how they can be used carefully to benefit those in mortality. That's when the Book of Abraham came up."

"So what did you hear then, whilst you were in mortality?"

"I never paid much attention to such kinds of things. The Air Force, sport and also family life were important, but religious writings or anything beyond the Bible, they weren't particularly interesting for me. Certainly not during those years, anyway. I've used some of my personal time in Paradise to study them a little more closely. Our libraries have accurate information, whilst the role of any records written by mortals is intriguing. It shows why mortals have done some of the things they do, or it also helps to understand why they believe or think in different ways. You can't blame a person for something they strongly believe is correct, since you can always teach them differently. It merely depends on whether they're believing something which isn't true."

"OK," John-Paul acknowledged. He followed Charlie to a large, dome shaped building with ornations built into the general fabric of the construction. The dome itself was perfect in shape, and whilst the details were majestically simple, they weren't distracting from the main purpose of the building. It was a source of learning or eternal evolution. John-Paul loved learning, and evolution was a grand design, integral to the existence of the Father's creations. Personal evolution had always remained a central theme for life. They entered the large central doors, moving through the ingress placed squarely in the centre of this semi-spherical edifice. 'It wouldn't matter where the doors were situated,' John-Paul considered, 'because they'd always be in the middle.'

Charlie moved straight towards a section on the left-hand side, slightly back from the midline across the dome, whilst John-Paul scanned around the surroundings he'd just entered. There were numerous psyches, both male and female individuals, passing carefully through the library, thoughtfully choosing particular sections of the library to visit. When an individual had chosen a volume of interest, it would become extracted from its place of storage, opening at the page of relevance as it rested gently, even motionlessly in front of the searching individual. Each search was prepared mentally by the researcher, with thoughtful search requests directed towards the volume before the extraction took place. Consequently, any selected volume fully registered the scope of the inquiry before leaving its storage niche. John-Paul considered every volume to be a masterful work, an especial piece of art in its own right, expanding records of feelings, objectives and considerations from the respective individuals concerned. Any given record or sets of records constituted a complete history of events along with perspectives. All of these contextual details were carefully and accurately held within the relevant volume, whilst records were telepathically announced to the researcher upon request. They held wonderfully precise descriptions of the surrounding events, either preceding or succeeding a record, as well as the stacked intentions of the event players who'd acted within their relevant time stamps. John-Paul enjoyed perusing the library. He found it peacefully informative. It never failed to engage his desires to understand history, or comprehend science, to appreciate the arts, even gaze into the future and so much more. In fact, endlessly more.

After a while Charlie quietly beckoned to him, inviting him to come over.

"Have you found what you were looking for?"

"Yes, I believe I have."

"What does it say?"

"Well apparently the Book of Abraham facsimiles were significantly more relevant than people had calculated them to be."

"How did that happen?"

"Interestingly, people looked at the facsimiles and thought they were funerary rites taken from the Egyptian Book of the Dead, so dismissed any connection within the text of the book. In fact, whilst some of the important facets were missing from the original documents, understandably after copies had been made and were later discovered, a connection should have been recognised between funerary rites and temple rites. Funerary rites or temple rites share many themes or similarities, whereby the Book of Abraham remains a description of events which were described in temple rites.

The funerary connection was merely a 'red herring'."

"Why did men choose to make the connection with funeral procedures?"

"Because it was simple and there was no guiding contextual information available. The Book of Abraham facsimiles gave details, however the details still related to temples, as well as funeral descriptions. In the same way, any descriptions of our Spirit World could include details of Paradise or Spirit Prison, or both."

"I see," John-Paul commented acceptingly.

"We could start thinking about our trip away after we've finished here," Charlie suggested.

"Can I ask a question before we leave?"

"I wondered when you would," Charlie accepted, grinning broadly.

"What stops unrighteous individuals attacking the teachers who visit Prison?" John-Paul asked, slightly concerned.

"Haven't you noticed yet, John-Paul?" Charlie chuckled.

"Noticed what?"

"The difference in the aura which emanates from individuals."

"What generally, do you mean, or here in Paradise compared to Prison?"

"Yes, both."

"I have noticed a difference. I know what you mean because for sure, there are noticeable differences. The Prison psyches have an aura which is more subdued, probably not as bright as everyone we meet in Paradise or beyond. The administrators who visit from the Father's other realms have especially bright auras."

"That's because there's a change whenever we enter a new dimension. Each dimension has an effect upon our bodies, just as mortal life made our physical bodies temporary or subject to decay. Paradise enriches, enlivens or expands our psyches, whilst Prison doesn't allow such a high level of evolution or progress. Individuals in Prison are left to contemplate their personal situation a lot more, because they struggle to choose their future actions. Basically, the constituent particles of bodies from one dimension aren't affected by the constituent particles of bodies from a different dimension. In this respect, Paradise and Prison are separate or distinctly different, so danger isn't a reality."

"In paradise it's all cooperative."

"Exactly. Either by choice, or by the laws of respective dimensions, there's forever and always a level of respect or order amongst the Father's kingdoms."

"What about security within Prison?"

"Psyches can't be destroyed. It was only possible in mortality, so seeking an advantage through killing had to be taught to men as an idea from Lucifer or his followers, since it was a totally unknown or a foreign concept in the pre-existence."

"Such a teaching is a pity."

"The corruption of good is always a pity."

John-Paul thought for a moment. "It's a big change to move from Prison to Paradise. Multiple changes have to be made."

"Yes, that's true. But it was the same in mortality. If you wanted to evolve or continue evolving, you had to be prepared to change. It's life. What more can I say?"

"Yes," John-Paul agreed obligingly.

"OK, well I think we've just about finished here now. Shall we go?" Charlie asked.

"Yes, OK."

Chapter 26

James opened the letter with one hand, whilst he held his McDonalds hamburger with the other. He began to eat and read at the same time, feeling rather pleased with his multitasking skills. Helen had mentioned multitasking at a previous meeting, so he was attuned to any future possibilities.

Dear James,

Thank you for your questions about our family history. I did find a link you were hoping for, which is good news. Yes, on the list you sent me there's a name for someone who shares a section of our family tree with us and strangely it actually turns out to be Frank. The link with Frank comes from his relatives in Polgaria. I've enclosed the relevant tree section, highlighting the common link in blue.

We were in Polgaria a couple of months ago because Bill took me over to Europe for our silver wedding anniversary. We left the hotel and went out for a drive, and we hadn't gone very far when we were stopped by the police. We didn't understand a word they were saying, because it was all double-Dutch. Then the situation became surreal. The policeman on Bill's side of the car hit him through the window, then we were told to get out. They certainly knew the correct English word for "out!" Crazily once we were out on the roadside, one of them got in and drove our car away! I couldn't believe it. It took us ages to walk over to the nearest town and when we got there, we went into a police station, because we thought the two men must have stolen the police car along with their uniforms, so we wanted to make the police aware of it.

Anyway, we found someone in the police station who could speak English, and we told them about what had happened. They disappeared into the back rooms for a while before coming out with Bill's case. We thanked them, afterwards inquiring about the car. We were told they didn't have any information to do with the car, which was when Bill started to create a bit of a fuss. We were asked whether we wanted the case or not, because if we did, we had to take it and leave the police station. That was slightly unexpected. I've never heard of anything like it before, but we never saw the car again.

We hope to see you sometime. Maybe you could come over and spend time with us? We always have the spare room available.

Bye for now.

Love,

Aunt Alison

James nearly dropped the letter as he read through details of their events abroad. In the end he only managed to drop some of his hamburger bread instead, and as it fell on the ground he noticed something out of the corner of his eye. A blackbird had carefully crept up unnoticed, almost to the foot of the cathedral bench where he was sitting. The blackbird picked up the rather large piece of hamburger which had just fallen down, keeping very low to the ground as it flew off. It quickly disappeared around one corner of the cathedral outbuildings, buildings which were neatly lining the edges of an adjoining lawn.

"Huh, it's lucky it actually got off the ground with all that bread," James chuckled to himself. He was still chuckling when the same bird appeared once more, similarly at the foot of the bench. He broke off some additional bread then carefully tossed it towards the bird. It was a cock, with fine black plumage and in rather decent condition. It disappeared as before, post-haste. He was still wondering where it had flown off to, when it reappeared beneath the bench as previously. He threw down an extra portion of his bun. It quickly disappeared. The process was repeated a further three times until James had finally finished his hamburger.

"Sorry birdie, I've no more left..."

James was convinced the bird understood his situation, because within a few moments it flew off yet didn't return.

"Clever bird," he chuckled. He made his way back to the university accommodation. "Everything needs a home," he contemplated.

CHAPTER 27

Two men stood together. They were dressed in white suits, white shoes and white ties and were deeply engaged in discussion.

"How are things coming along Philippe?"

"Much better thanks. The children are listening more now, which means we seem to be making progress as a family."

"Excellent," commented Charlie.

"I have one question though, because it's one which I can't seem to answer."

"OK, sure. What is it, please?"

"It's about reincarnation. My youngest has been talking to people but she says we can't dismiss reincarnation, because we don't know it's not true. She thinks it's possibly a good way for God to help everyone slowly progress, always at their own pace or in their own time. It seems logical."

"It does seem persuasive."

"Do you believe it?"

"Whatever a person believes is generally important, since an individual is judged upon what they believe to be true."

"So is it correct?"

"I've not seen the Father implement it at any time."

"Is it logical to implement?"

"Evolution is a progression into a better state or a higher dimension. I believe we can progress in ways which will continue to advance every individual. The Father will always want individuals to get better, or become an improved version of themselves in terms of behaving decently."

"What does it mean though in terms of reincarnation?"

"You need to be more experienced or hold more knowledge in order to teach others. I therefore see the evolution of an individual as a process which involves a progression. A system which doesn't involve a chance for the progression of individuals isn't a system which I believe the Father would use."

"Surely any experience is useful, isn't it?"

"Would you want to wear a nappy in order to learn how to change one?"

"No, but everyone who changes a nappy, will also have worn one at some point."

"You're right. However, every individual still needs to learn how to change the nappy. Evolving to be at a higher level remains important. It's an important process as well as an ongoing one."

"Yes, I take your point." There was a pause. "Well, what about reincarnation into another human life? That could be progressive, couldn't it?"

"Each human life is a perfect test for an individual."

"So are you suggesting that a second test isn't needed?"

"Every life will suffice for an individual, because it's tailored or personally given by the Father."

"OK, your point seems logical."

"I wonder what the Father's doing now?" John-Paul asked, interestedly but privately.

"Would you like to find out?" Charlie asked.

No answer was needed.

CHAPTER 28

"Life's reality is the situation described by whatever circumstances you find yourself in, and at any point in time," commented one of the members of the discussion group.
"So can we change reality?"
"We can always do something."

James thought for a moment about the time he fell through the loft hatch. He'd been up in the loft then stepped back without thinking. Luckily he'd landed on the side of the hatch, but unluckily he'd broken several ribs in the fall, and it was agony whenever he laughed over the next six weeks – his friends did their best to make him laugh. It wasn't funny. What was funny though was when his friend had fallen through a chapel ceiling. He hadn't gone into churches too often, but on this occasion he'd agreed to help. They'd been laying down some insulation in the roof, although his friend hadn't remembered where they were because they were too busy chatting. He'd ended up straddling a crossbeam after dropping several feet, so James was astounded when he'd later managed to father his own family. The chap who'd just put up the plasterboard certainly wasn't too happy, since he'd come back into the room to see two legs sticking through the ceiling.
'Reality can be painful but jolly funny at times,' James concluded.

He also remembered the packs of feral dogs which Frank had mentioned he'd seen roaming the streets, just across a border from Polgaria. Some realities really could be changed. Some realities were worth changing.

-

Two men stood together. They were dressed in white suits, white shoes and white ties and had been deeply engaged in discussion.

John-Paul wondered how they'd make the trip, consequently when they entered the building he began to look around. The entrance comprised sturdy double doors - white, large and of fine workmanship. Their surface was pristinely plain yet again majestic, perfectly matched by the carefully constructed, supportive archway. He moved to one side to touch the texture of a nearby wall: it felt very much as he'd expected, smooth and solid, although it wasn't as cold as he'd imagined and in fact, the light within it was curiously radiating its own illuminating heat. The effect was surprising, perhaps slightly perplexing. He'd not been afforded an opportunity to touch stone in mortality, or any structured buildings in fact, so he wasn't sure what he'd expected to expect. It didn't really matter. He gazed along the long straight corridor ahead of them, which also seemed familiar. The marbled walls presented a number of interior doors, even along their entire length, whilst a mirror at the far end was decorated with vibrantly coloured flowers, delicately arranged for a blooming variety in the background. Charlie passed along the passage, taking the last door on the right. John-Paul followed him.

The interior room was comely yet not over-elaborate. A large transparent wall at the far end was glass-like, creating a vista of the cosmos. He paused a moment to view the stellar expanse in front of them, because clearly there was no disturbance from any incoming illuminations which might hide the twinkling lights. There was indeed a glorious abundance of lights, and in all sorts of strengths or formations. Their clarity was excellent, almost as though the transparent wall was refocusing his gaze wherever he directed it.

"That's excellent," John-Paul commented.

"Yes, it is rather good, isn't it?"

"It certainly is... completely. But I have a question."

"Yes."

"How do we make a trip out of this room?"

"Through the portal in front of us."

"It's a wall. It might be transparent, but it's still a wall."

"You need to see what's happening here... let me show you."

-

John-Paul was rather surprised by the way their passage through the portal wall had been so simple, with no resistance in passing across it whatsoever. He decided to ask about that when they returned, but for now he was mesmerised by their subsequent journey through space: he enjoyed the straight line movement which cut directly towards the ultimate or intended destination. He wasn't entirely sure how direct or how straight the travel was in reality, yet he was never aware that they'd either turned to the right or to the left, not at any point in time. He was truly transfixed by the sheer scale of the complexity and the vast structure of the cosmos surrounding them, as they rapidly made their journey through the Father's realms towards His home. John-Paul reflected how it was previously and familiarly his own home as well, so it would be interesting to go back again. Home was always a decent place to visit, even likewise to reside.

They found their Father busily arranging family business in His large domed family room. John-Paul knew it was the family room because their Father conducted His family affairs there. It had many suspended or levitating windows delivering visual, auditory and other sensory reports along with regular updates. All were carefully amalgamated into scenarios, each moving or relocating as outgoing matters were put into action. Incoming or returning reports of the countless family members were continually arriving, specifically showing real-time events or results of actions, every one within their respective frames. John-Paul wasn't quite sure whether or not the windows were just displayed for the benefit of Charlie and himself. They could have been an aid to enable them to see the Father's work, or perhaps they were equally helpful as visual recordings made for other individuals, whoever they might be. 'Maybe they'll be stored for referencing at a later date?' John-Paul considered.

What he remembered of the Father was the way He emanated a magnificent presence. His presence gradually revealed how the Father fantastically held within Himself, all of the equivalent power of the universe, and so much more; He was the author of and from first principles. He could precisely organise, maintain or administer the universe alone, whereas in reality He'd forever chosen to include His children in those matters. He did however choose to answer prayers individually and personally, where His power meant He could do that across His universe.

The Father didn't seem to direct the windows, so John-Paul guessed all of the attention, listening, responses and plans, were performed without the need for any form of external gadgets. Some frames seemed to have clear confidentiality locks upon them, whilst others played freely, showing wonderful, sometimes miraculous events which unfolded within the lives of the individuals concerned. Intriguingly, different events overlapped or unfolded into the lives of the individuals' friends or mortal families. John-Paul was quite transfixed with a number of these stories which he saw playing out. They kept his interest quite easily, and it seemed as though he was watching several films at the same time. He'd never seen films in mortality, because he'd not been afforded a physical age for suitable viewing or comprehension; nor had he subsequently encountered a mortal opportunity to do so. He'd seen many historical recordings of earthly events, with specific stories of possible future scenarios which could unfold. Any future events which might unfold were dependent upon how men or women would choose to behave, or conduct their lives in the future. He found these fascinating, and he'd spent time in Paradise perusing the libraries of human films. Some were delightful, although others were sad, probably because they told stories from human history which at times could become tragic. Other sorts of films simply never gained entry to the libraries. John-Paul was born into a Christian family yet he felt he could understand why Muslims seemed reluctant to create images of God. Human portraits perhaps couldn't suitably convey the presence or power of the Father, although some artists he felt had made rather excellent attempts. The likes or dislikes of art generally appeared to be a more personal thing.

The Father turned to greet them, smiling exuberantly as He responded to their entry, welcoming them into this room which displayed His marvellous workings amongst His family. John-Paul judged that this might be a central family room, so he wondered whether there could likewise be others. All of the regular activities in the family frames were suspended.

"Could I ask how that's possible?" John-Paul asked politely. "When workings are suspended, how does the universe function?"

"Time is different here, John-Paul," the Father responded. "Actions are planned ahead, and with a change in speed, all things can receive attention ahead of planetary time, or equally at the same time."

"I see. Thank you."

"What would you like to ask?"

John-Paul was surprised. He'd just answered a question and yet the Father knew he had a more important question to ask. It seemed logical though, because after all, 'He is the Father,' he concluded. He posed his question.

"How long do we stay in Paradise before we can come back here, or maybe gain permission to travel around?"

"You have a good question. How long would you like to remain in Paradise?"

"I suppose until the work there is finished, when everyone has had an opportunity to choose between good or evil, and everything is concluded fairly."

"Again, you have a good answer."

"I want to stay and work, but I'd also like to travel away at times, whenever it's possible."

"I hear your request, John-Paul."

John-Paul knew the Earth itself would be cleaned and upgraded at some point in the future, or rather restored to a celestial status. It meant some individuals would use the celestial Earth in the future, although he wasn't quite sure or even had any idea when that might be, but the question wasn't important enough to be posed.

Charlie asked some questions of his own and they spoke until they were satisfied.

John-Paul asked to be shown more of the Father's home, so as they left, he glanced at a chair in the centre of the room. It looked very comfortable, coloured gold, with other cushions of light which were fashioned in colours he couldn't remember seeing before; the magnificent furniture piece was showing an adaptive quality that he imagined would fit an occupant to perfection. It could only be a throne, yet there were two of them. John-Paul assumed the thrones must be for the Father and Heavenly Mother, but he didn't ask. He was keen to see more of their home, somehow feeling this particular or special home seemed very familiar. 'Such familiarity must be from the pre-existence,' he decided. 'After all, every psyche's fortunately experienced aeons here.' His pre-existent memory was slowly returning. 'It's taken a while because I was only in mortality for a few months.' He paused. 'It really did have an effect.'

Chapter 29

"So what do people think about the fact we all have a common genealogy?" James asked.

"It must be a coincidence," Grace suggested.

"I thought the same thing as well. I've looked into it, but the likelihood is too low for all of us having a shared family tree, and purely by chance."

"Surely the chances of common ancestors goes up when more people are in the group?"

"The probability of everyone in the group actually sharing a common link, or branching into the same family tree is far too low to be a coincidence. "

"Well it must be possible if it's true."

"It's truly real, which raises the question as to what could perhaps be the reason for it?"

At this point the discussion quickly mushroomed with input from anyone and everyone.

"Maybe we've felt inclined towards the same type of people, I guess?"

"Such a possibility could be true."

"But it would mean we share genetically innate reasons to be drawn towards family."

"Or we made an agreement in the pre-existence, to gather up down here."

"That's crazy. Who says there was a pre-existence, anyway?

And if there was a pre-existence or we made an agreement, then why would we feel inclined to meet up?"
"Maybe some of the group haven't come down yet, so they're prompting us to get together?"
"Or maybe some of the group have already come down, and are prompting from over in the next dimension."
"This conjecture is all just make-belief."
"It's interesting though..."
"It seems like wishful thinking to me!"
"Fair enough."
"But if we did agree to get together down here, what would be the purpose of it? There'd have to be a purpose for everyone getting together."
"Possibly it could be to help each other out?"
"With what?"
"With life..."
"The idea sounds a bit vague to me."
"Well what do we spend our time doing in these discussions? We simply go through what we each find interesting, or can't figure out. It seems like a meaningful arrangement to me."
"Maybe."
"Besides, it's also good for Siggel."
"Someone's mentioned my name."
"Yes, it's good we meet round here at your place."
"I must admit, I do find it entertaining."
"Did you have these types of discussions with your wife?"
Siggel was surprised by the sudden divergence, yet it was a fair question which he was happy to answer: "I did actually, yes. Quite a lot in fact."
"What's it like being married for a long time?" James asked.
"With Frances, my whole life was centred around her calendar. It was excellent, and she had something planned for each or every weekend, with other things through the week. There was constantly something going on, because she made

all the necessary arrangements. Throughout our married years, I'd never really noticed how we'd grown older together but I guess Frances always did look forever young. Thinking about it, I used to have a few motorbikes, and I got a rather decent one, which was probably after we were married about ten years. One day, when I'd stopped at some traffic lights, a brand new model pulled up alongside me. As I looked at it, I suddenly realised how my bike had in fact aged. It struck me that it was also how I'd describe marriage. You don't notice the way you or your wife might be growing older, because you remember the beautiful young girl you first dated and married, so the memory never fades. At least it didn't for me. Frances was always young and beautiful." He paused. "Even when she became sick, just before she passed on." Siggel looked out of the living room window, as though he was expecting to see someone, somewhere outside. If James hadn't known better, he would have said that Siggel was looking outside for his wife. "But you know, you have to work at it, because it's like anything worthwhile," he continued. "When I was younger I used to run cross-country, where at college I was in the team for competitions. I'd started off at school. It was relatively straight forward then, because you'd just go out and run as hard as you could, or whenever it was required. But later on when we were at college, our team won the county championships a couple of times. Half the team went out for regular training because they were jolly motivated, although I didn't pay much attention to it, since the ones who trained were generally those who'd been in the middle order at school. I'd assumed it would have been easy to beat them, similar to before, then I soon found out that if you didn't train, you didn't improve, so quite soon I was the sixth man in the six-man team. By the time I'd decided to actually start training I'd also finished college. It taught me a valuable lesson though. I saw if you wanted to get anywhere worthwhile, you generally had to put the necessary work in. It's equally true of marriage."

"How d'you put effort into marriage?" James asked.

"You learn to listen to your spouse, or try to be kind when things go wrong. You try to stay calm when they're upset, or you look for ways to praise or show affection for them. It all works quite well."

James was intrigued. He stored these ideas away for a later time because it seemed like sensible advice. A chime rang out from his mobile phone, announcing a text had arrived. He pulled it out of his pocket to take a look.

'That's great,' he chuckled inwardly. 'I can have a look on my way back.' "Can you possibly take me via Bertmore on the way home, Adam?"

"What's out in Bertmore?"

"Oh, it's about time I got myself a car. I've been planning it for ages, although I've never got around to it. It's a cheap one, but it should do the trick... at least for now."

"Sure, no problem. So whose was the car I saw you driving the other day, then?"

"Oh, it was one of my parents' cars. It's been very useful. Now though, I need my own."

"Sure."

The vehicle turned out to be a reasonable price and James couldn't find any obviously negative issues with it, so he made the purchase. He picked it up later after sorting out the tax along with insurance.

-

Several more months had passed before James decided to make the trip back home again for the holidays, as soon as the university term had finished. He enjoyed coming home and meeting up with old friends. He'd arranged a trip to the cinema with one of his friends, along with a couple of girls.

"Can you pick up your brother from school please James before you go out?" his mother had asked.

"I'm tight on time, but I might be able to fit it in."

"Please," she replied.

He grabbed his car keys then hurried out of the front door. He was surprised how quickly he made it across town before reaching the school where Jed was waiting for him at the back entrance. When Jed got into the car, something caught his eye from across the sports field, a little over to the right, followed promptly by a rather loud noise. He turned around to see what all the commotion was about. What he subsequently saw, he could hardly believe. A large helicopter had just started to descend after clearing the trees at the far side of the sports field, and was soon hovering above a terrapin hut. The hut was situated close to the first of two rugby pitches, visibly marked out in white across the adjoining field. He wondered whether it was going to land, checking how far away it was from the goal posts, but in fact it was hovering above the hut for a rather unusual reason. Several men were positioned on top of the hut, and James made a double look when he saw that they were standing next to a school minibus. A cable was being lowered down from the helicopter, slowly over towards the minibus, which was now surrounded by the waiting men. One of them managed to grab hold of the cable as it swayed freely above their heads.

"Why's there a minibus on top of the terrapin?" James asked.

"Oh, it's the end of term, and some of the sixth form decided to play tricks."

"What d'you mean?"

"In the dark last night they thought they'd put the minibus up onto the terrapin."

"Well how did they get it up there?"

"They drove it up there."

"How?" James asked, somewhat mystified.

"They used a couple of planks of wood. As the rear of the minibus reached the top of the planks, just before crossing over onto the side of the roof, the planks lifted up behind it so they both stuck out backwards. Once the minibus was fully on the roof, it was simply moved forwards, which meant the planks fell back down and onto the ground below."

"Why did they have to get a helicopter in though, to get it off? Surely the helicopter's got to be a bit extravagant, hasn't it?"

"Because the angle is too steep to drive the minibus back off the hut. I guess they considered it was a bit too dangerous."

"Well the whole thing's crazy."

"Yer, but it was a jolly good stunt though, wasn't it?" Jed replied.

James wasn't really sure whether to be amused or amazed, considering the general recklessness of his sibling's school friends. In the end he was simply astonished, mainly over the sheer scale or likely cost of the rectifications in place. He watched the men for a while as they struggled to safely attach the minibus to the winch, which had been lowered down from the helicopter. In the end he drove away, realising he was already late for the cinema.

"So who put the minibus on the terrapin?"

"Some of the people in my year."

"You already told me that earlier. But who?"

"No one you know."

"OK, but who did it?"

"I can't say."

"Why not?"

"What will you do about it?"

"Probably nothing."

"And that's why I won't say."

"Why not?"

"Because of 'probably'."

At the same moment, James was suddenly distracted by a second noise, although this noise wasn't quite so loud as the helicopter. It was more of a throaty, mechanical growl and it seemed as though it was coming from somewhere behind them. James looked in his rear-view mirror. There were cars following behind them, where they were now on the dual carriageway, which meant it had to be coming from something to the rear. When he heard a thud he looked again in his rear-view mirror, just in time to see a piece of metal exhaust pipe bouncing, subsequently crashing along in the fast lane with several cars swerving in turn to avoid it.

"Well that's ridiculous."

"What's ridiculous?" Jed asked.

"Some complete idiot has just lost their exhaust but more to the point, they've nearly caused a pile up behind us!" James exclaimed.

Jed peered out of the back window to catch the last of the unfolding action.

"It nearly took out that last car. It's finally gone off to the side now," Jed responded.

"At least it's off the road," James commented. "How could you possibly lose your exhaust yet not know about it? Some people really are pathetic," he concluded.

He dropped Jed back at home before making a dash to the cinema, forgetting about the latest incident on the dual carriageway. However, as he pulled into the car park which was situated right below the cinema complex, he noticed a throaty, mechanical growl once again, and it was seemingly echoing from the walls of the underground car park.

'This repeated noise is a bit of a coincidence,' he mentally noted. He wound down his window to look to the side whilst parking, hearing the same growl yet again. As he got out of the car, he left the engine running.

"Something's a bit weird," he voiced verbally, going around

to the rear to locate this recurrence of the previous mechanical growl.

"In fact, it's even more weird."

The growl now seemed to be coming slightly forward of his position, somewhere quite low to the ground as well. He bent down, checking the ground beneath the cars at either side of his, but as he scanned from left to right, he noticed a curious anomaly about his own vehicle.

"You've got to be joking! My exhaust is missing!" he remonstrated, although no one was actually listening. "So how did this happen?" Slowly it dawned on him, albeit very slowly, over the exact place where his exhaust pipe had been lost. "Oh," he concluded.

-

"What's the place you went to, Frank?"

"It was a temple."

"It sounds like a pagan building for make-belief gods... something the ancient Greeks or Romans would have used."

"Or the Egyptians... because they came first."

"They certainly were ahead of their time."

"It's an interesting point. Language was developed from temples."

"Oh, nonsense."

"Take a look at history, then see whether my comment is valid."

"Google will reveal all. Just a moment." A couple of minutes later... "He's right you know. Most of the early writings which we currently have were religious temple rites."

"If you were God, and you wanted to share the benefits of language with your kids, what type of examples would you use to teach them?"

"Obviously, religious ones."

263

"Yes, temple rites would be a perfect example."

"But it's ridiculous, because we all know how language began with cave drawings, and then pictorial writings, until finally the alphabets came along later."

"My kids made a lot of excellent drawings when they were small, with lots of pictures from junior school, followed by cursive writing in secondary school. They could easily have invented language."

"Amusing idea... although just a few thousand years too late, mind you!"

"Not really. Anyone's kids could have done the same thing, even thousands of years ago."

"So what's your point?"

"Cave drawings or related artefacts do tell family history stories, but my money's on the gift of language from an informed teacher."

"A teacher from where? Outer space?"

"How did you guess?"

"I was being sarcastic. You clearly must've lost your marbles on this one. "

"Anyone's kids might have done something like that in the past, but I was thinking though of a slightly more practicable approach."

"Practicable approach," came back the reply. "What are you talking about?"

"The divine teaching of people, in progressing their language skills rather than leaving education to nascent development. There are plenty of teachers who do exactly the same thing every day as they follow their national curricula."

A discussion quickly ensued re possible or impossible connections between divine teaching and language development. The discussion was brief.

CHAPTER 30

Two men stood together. They were dressed in white suits, white shoes and white ties and were deeply engaged in discussion.

"He clearly needs some assistance. Shall we assist him?"

"He's doing just fine, John-Paul. We don't need to intervene."

"But he doesn't know the relevant details of what happened."

"I don't think it's going to be important."

"Why not?"

"On this occasion, the participants have already made up their minds. When your mind is open to more ideas or additional information, you generally seek things out or search diligently."

"And what happens if they don't find out?"

"There's usually another opportunity. Watch what happens," Charlie suggested.

-

"People today believe the Tower of Babel was a childish story, concocted to help men find a way of explaining the origin of different languages," Owen announced.

"Well, it is a story."

"Yes, an historical one."

"In what way? What d'you mean?"

"Some poorly informed individuals believed they could build a tower into heaven to seize control."

"Your suggestion sounds extremely fanciful. It's really quite amusing."

"Yes I agree, because truth can often be stranger than fiction at times. I must admit though, it was rather a ridiculous idea."

"Well, the Tower of Babel was always another primitive fairy story."

"Errr, no it was real. But the episode was ridiculous... to believe they could do anything with a tower. Anyway, as you've pointed out, the Tower of Babel is usually associated with the proliferation of languages. Whilst the temple writings gave consistent or accurate accounts of human history, some individuals wanted to adapt history, so one of the best ways to have rewritten it was to come up with another way of communicating, in essence an esoteric language, beyond the vernacular."

"Why would anyone have bothered to go to all the trouble of inventing another language? It sounds very arcane."

"If you controlled language, then you controlled pretty much everything which was taught from writings, and you could rewrite history however you wished."

"Why would someone want to rewrite history?"

"Because it creates power."

"How exactly?"

"I'll give you an example," Steve interrupted. "I lived through the Thatcher years when she was elected multiple times as UK Prime Minister. People were contented as well as pleased with the Thatcher governments, and so she was repeatedly re-elected. Today, a different generation has re-scripted history to make Margaret Thatcher appear as though she was disliked or tyrannical, yet nothing could have been further from the truth."

"As you saw it."

"And as the people of the day saw it, since she was re-elected multiple times."

"More people voted against her than voted for her."

"Which is generally the nature of democratically elected governments."

"Not if you dispense with first-past-the-post elections in favour of proportional representation."

"Which often leads to unstable, short-term governments."

"Which are forced to cooperatively compromise."

"Forming policies which leave countries constantly going back to the polls."

The discussion continued, twisting and turning through various exploratory directions. James was surprised by the number or forms of convolution which unfolded as the discussion followed its own path. It was interesting, yet he was sold on the idea there had to be a more productive form of politics, a method beyond the adversarial approach which was still popular in the modern era. He believed decent political discussions might always be lively or passionate, whilst contention was simply counter-productive.

CHAPTER 31

Two men stood together. They were dressed in white suits, white shoes and white ties and were deeply engaged in discussion.

"On our previous trip away, did you enjoy the tour of the Father's home?" Charlie asked.

"Yes, very much," John-Paul replied. "It seemed so familiar."

"You know why, don't you?"

"I think I do."

"It's because we've all been through the Father's home in the pre-existence. It's what we remember, although it takes a while for it all to come back."

"Yes, I thought it was," John-Paul concurred. "There were parts though I couldn't recall, so I was pleased to look around again."

"And we'll probably be back from time to time, whenever it's needed," Charlie suggested.

"I think it would be good."

"Have you considered what you'd like to do with your time in Paradise, before everything changes?"

"What will change?" John-Paul inquired.

"At some point, when psyches have passed from the pre-existence then through mortality, the Earth will eventually change."

"How will it change?"

"My guess is the physical part of the Earth will be cleansed of pollutants, the land mass will also probably be joined back together again, creating a general rejuvenation across the physical Earth. The idea only seems logical though once psyches have passed through mortality, usually into this Spirit World dimension of the Earth. The workings behind it all will be intriguing. Hopefully we'll get to see how those events pan out. It'll probably seem very natural, the same as all the other historical earthly events which have occurred, although it might perhaps be a little more dramatic. We'll see."

"When will it happen?"

"I'm not too sure. I'm not sure anyone's sure... other than the Father."

"Oh, OK," John-Paul accepted obligingly.

"And what work would you like to do during your time in Paradise?" Charlie asked.

"I think I'd like to continue working with family. Maybe helping them in this dimension, or still prompting those in mortality."

"I like your thinking. Such work could possibly also continue with extended family members," Charlie advised.

"The opportunity sounds good," John-Paul responded.

"I'm pleased you've mentioned it, because we've been directed to help someone."

"How can we help?"

"I have an idea."

-

James took the book down from the shelf in the living room of his flat and looked at the brown front cover. There was a picture of a family tree, extending, even branching across the reaches of the book front. He followed it around the spine, eventually onto the back cover. 'This interest in family history is fascinating,' he considered. 'But why is Frank on a branch of my family tree?' he queried. As he placed the book back into its rightful place on the shelf he had an idea. 'I need to talk to Frank.' There was a pause. 'No that's crazy, bothering him with something so trivial.' There was a pause. 'On the other hand, he might be pleased to be asked a question about his family tree.' There was a pause. 'He'd think I was bonkers.' There was a pause. 'That's not a problem.' There was a pause. The pause didn't last very long before he grabbed his car keys and headed out of the front door. It slammed noisily behind him.

-

Frank answered the knock at the front door.
"Can you get it, dear?" Helen asked.
"Will do." Frank let James in, inviting him towards the front room.
"Who is it?"
"Just James."
"Make sure you get him something to drink," Helen called back down the stairs. "Actually, I'll come down shortly."
"Good," Frank said quietly, as they made their way into the front room. "So why do we have the pleasure of this visit?" he asked.
Ten minutes later Frank was fully versed re the situation, at the point when Helen entered with some welcomed refreshments.
"That looks nice, dear," Frank commented.
"Make sure James gets some," Helen instructed, as she placed the tray onto the living room table. "You'd better get in quick James, because in a few moments there'll be nothing left."
"Thank you. I will."
Helen left them discussing recent events as she retired to the

kitchen, before going back upstairs.

"So you've had a premonition, or 'a prompting' as Helen would put it, which suggested if you came over here, you'd probably get an answer to your question?"

"Yes, I'd say so," James agreed.

"Well, I'm not sure I've got any answers but we can go through it logically."

"OK."

"Until quite recently..." Frank continued. "By recently, I mean the past two or three years. Anyway, until recently... I know I'm repeating myself here. Anyway, I used to dismiss some of these new ideas as merely rubbish thoughts, or things which had cropped up in my mind... perhaps ones of little value... unless I could see where they might be leading... logically. Helen has always suggested I should trust my feelings, yet that wasn't something which came easily. Eventually I began to have some different experiences making me pay more attention to the whole rationale, but at the end of the day, I believe everyone's journey in life is unique, with unique difficulties or personal questions. Those things need to be answered individually or again, only personally. I see your genealogical question as something of a prompting for you, rather than perhaps being connected with anyone else in the discussion group. Everyone else is slightly interested, but not as much as you are. You're probably the most interested, even more so than Reg, or even Siggel or myself."

"It was a lot of effort to join up our family trees though, wasn't it? If this was all just to inspire me..."

"Maybe. Yet I don't think it's too much effort for God, and I think He probably thinks it's worthwhile. We also need to help each other. Maybe God could perhaps have set up a few plans which are now running in parallel. It wouldn't surprise me if this 'connected family' thing, or our discussion group, was somehow planned a long time ago. I think we'll all be friends going forward into the next dimension. I can't really see it changing to be honest."

Helen came down to join them in their discussion, adding how she thought things might have worked, or could perhaps work in the future.

Several months later, following many subsequent discussions James joined the organisation which Helen attended on a Sunday. James was surprised to find out how Frank had also joined. James decided when he married, he also wished to have a marriage which would extend into the next dimension, similar to Frank and Helen's. When he did get married a few years later, Helen and Frank were witnesses, firstly for the civil marriage, and later on the same day at the temple marriage. James gave his first child the name 'Frank'. It was a good name, since his friend was called Frank. Frank had done the selfsame thing years before, and all decent history seemed to have a habit of repeating itself.

-

Frank became more interested in genealogy after James had married, then finally moved away for work. He spent time back at Somerset House, no longer looking to find the reason for the ridiculous family name he'd originally inherited alongside his siblings, yet more to investigate those branches of the family tree which were connected with his own. He looked up the family link James shared, afterwards following up on the various links to other members of the discussion group. In the end, the common links also inspired him in becoming better involved with genealogical trees, and subsequently family history became a more general pastime. He was made aware of some things which were probably best left to quietly rest, such as bigamy, infidelities, painful stories of family break-ups, even homelessness. However, for the most part, he was intrigued by the successful, uplifting histories which were uncovered through regular research. The more he learnt about family, the more different characters revealed themselves as details of their respective lives slowly emerged. He found it interesting. Family was important.

-

Frank picked up a photograph taken of his father Charlie during his RAF days in Iraq, remembering how he'd suddenly become more involved with religious activities. His father had participated in many different sports during his thirty years of RAF service, particularly tennis, hockey, badminton, boxing and gymnastics. Frank also possessed numerous photographs of his father diving into swimming pools in various exotic, sunny countries. It was safe to say their father had been generally physically fit for most of his adult life. The turning point for Charlie came when he contracted gangrene in his left ankle, despite the years of sporting activity in the air force. He'd been a heavy smoker of strong cigarettes, starting from the time he'd joined the RAF in 1924 as a Halton cadet. Slowly with advancing years, the impairment to his peripheral blood circulation led to complications resulting in gangrene, where ultimately an amputation was scheduled for a Monday morning. Previously, a Church administrator had suggested to Charlie that if he became more religiously involved, he might be blessed to avoid the requirement for an amputation, but Charlie had patted Margaret, the secretary of Richard Le Grand, and thanked her for her kind words. He took no action. However, on the Sunday evening before the scheduled operation, Charlie announced to the family the fact he wanted to join the religious organisation. The family were somewhat stunned. However Frank's mother quickly postponed the operation. Medics strongly advised against any postponement, but Charlie's foot was still left intact as well as in use through additional years of his life. Frank found the incident very interesting. He wasn't totally sure what to make of it, so he decided to simply store it in memory until a later date. It was true how his father had further complications during periods of relapse related to smoking, nevertheless it couldn't explain the way the gangrene didn't cause his death at the time and his foot was saved. His father had always been thoroughly decent, eventually passing into the Spirit World as a faithful church member. He now remembered this incident once again, as he carefully filed the photograph into its respective place.

"D'you think there'll be doctors in the next dimension?" Frank asked.

"Of course, dear," Helen replied. "Spirits might be perfected functionally, but they'll still need to prompt men or women here in mortality, so to be useful they'll need to know the science of how the body works."

Frank hadn't thought of that. He loved Helen's insights, especially the way she could marry up the realities of religion with good common sense. He always found it usefully refreshing.

In turn, this made him think of Siggel. When Charlie had died he'd thought about what it might be like in the next dimension, or how the transition actually worked from mortality into the Spirit World.

After Frances died, Siggel had contemplated whether she'd cope OK, going over into the next dimension. He kept those thoughts to himself, where it was strange because he'd argued so vociferously against the idea of deity. Logically, he had no reason to believe in another dimension. Whatever he'd previously argued, Siggel later remarked that he'd always been concerned over what Frances might be doing, or whether they'd be able to contact each other through the coming days, months or possibly years? Frank as well as Reg had both watched Siggel's difficulty in coming to terms with the loss of Frances. Siggel eventually told him, he couldn't put up with the idea of losing her forever, which became one of the reasons he'd decided to join a religious organisation. It was the same one Helen, and later Frank (as well as James) had joined. Slowly Siggel had found other loves to occupy his time, with genealogy clearly being the latest. Despite these unusual twists and turns, Siggel remained adamant over his need for a future reunion with his wife, even if reality demanded he'd have to wait until the next dimension. There was nevertheless a quiet calm accompanying Siggel after he became a member of the religious organisation.

Frank realised Siggel's love for Frances was the same as his own love for Helen. He remembered the day before he was married, when Helen had stayed at his parents' home - this was in fact rather atypical, though he'd thought little of it at the time. What had brought him back to reality was when he'd heard a loud shriek from Helen's bedroom. He'd hurried upstairs and was glad to wrap his arms around her.

"What's the matter, dear?" he asked.

"Look on my bed!" she panted.

Frank was somewhat taken aback by the size of the spider now sprawled out in detail upon Helen's bedcovers, presenting an excellent example of a sizeable English arachnid. He contemplated that whilst it might have been genuinely small compared to some of its South American cousins, it was certainly a magnificently large English specimen. He moved the creature outside.

He'd settled back to enjoy a peaceful preparation for the following morning, which basically amounted to watching Chelsea F.C. on the television with suitable friends. Again he'd heard an equally loud shriek from upstairs. This time the other women in the house had made it into Helen's bedroom before him, and he was surprised to view a second spider in almost exactly the same location on Helen's bedcovers.

"I thought I'd got rid of it?" he queried, as he escorted it outside.

"That's was the mummy!" Helen said exasperatedly. "The other one was the daddy."

"OK, well at least we've got rid of them now," he reassured her.

"Yes, but if that's the mummy and daddy, then what about the babies?" she inquired, looking more worried than she had done previously.

"Oh, don't worry about it dear," he replied. "They probably won't have had any little ones just yet."

"It's the 'probably' that I'm worried about," she continued.

The last part of the evening's action was announced by a third loud shriek from upstairs. Chelsea had just scored, so Frank wasn't too concerned by the latest distraction. He went back upstairs to investigate, and now there on the bedcovers were several smaller spiders moving playfully across towards Helen's pillow.

"I told you!" she shrieked equally loudly, and he had to admit she did have a good point. The smaller creatures proved slightly more troublesome to gather up, but in the end the whole family had been removed outside.

"I'm not sleeping in here tonight!" Helen protested.

"It's OK, don't worry, dear. They're all gone now," he pointed out.

"And what if they come back in?"

"Well they can't get in, because I've closed the door."

"So how did they get into my bedroom in the first place?"

Frank wasn't quite sure how to answer this one. He quickly juggled with the problem for a short period of time. "It'll take them ages to figure out how to get back in," he suggested.

"So there is a way in then?" she remonstrated.

"No, not really, dear. They might try to find a way back in, but they won't be able to, because I've put them all outside in a totally different place, so they won't have a clue where they are, and by the time they've spent days wandering around, we'll be on our honeymoon," he explained. He was very pleased with his new escapology skills, since they were suddenly very much needed.

"And what happens if a different spider finds the same way in?" she replied.

He decided to ditch the escapology, but instead plumped for a rapid response approach. Multiple minutes and an assortment of responses later, he was no longer convinced he was actually making progress.

"OK, you can leave now!" Helen announced.

He wasn't sure he'd heard things quite right.

"Sorry, dear?"

"Go on... out now!"

He rapidly left as directed, although not particularly confident he wouldn't be resummoned any time soon.

His marriage to Helen the following morning was one of the most satisfying events of his life. He was exceptionally lucky, and he remembered the feeling well. What he didn't remember though was to go up to bed before he fell asleep, accordingly when he did go up to bed, which was at three o'clock in the morning, he discovered how socks had become a bedtime fixture. He realised it in the morning.

-

Frank enjoyed discussing ideas with Helen and the family. He found that sharing thoughts or insights with each other, not only broadened their perspectives but also tended to answer one another's questions.

"What do we say if scientists create a form of life, or make these robots they've been developing into some type of thinking creations?" Helen had asked one day, seemingly worried.

"I'd say 'Well done!'" Frank replied.

"It's not funny!" Helen insisted.

"Why not?"

"Because it means they could possibly explain creation without God," Helen quickly added.

"Well that's good dear," Frank continued, suffering an indignant look from his wife. "I want our kids to learn or develop some decent ideas from us. In other words if men continue with an interest in creating things, albeit during time down here in mortality, at the end of the day it can only be a good thing. The science or art of creation have both been an inherent interest for all of us because they were initiated aeons ago, in the pre-existence. If people are explaining creation without God, it doesn't mean God didn't create things, it only means they're learning to create things independently."

Helen's glare had immediately softened. "Oh, I see," she said.

"There's usually a good reason or explanation for everything," Frank explained. "It's easier if you've come across the same question before, or gained a suitable answer."

Not long after, the reverse situation became apparent, since Frank had a question where Helen offered a possible answer.

"Why do we have to put up with other people's rubbish? I'd prefer to tell them exactly what I think of their ridiculous nonsense, usually right there and then."

"Sometimes we can't," Helen suggested. "The Jews couldn't complain during the Holocaust, or if they did, they were punished. The same applies to any suffering, because suffering is putting up with something unpleasant for the sake of others, or for the sake of doing good, or simply for what's good. That's why it's worthwhile."

He liked Helen's definition. He concluded from her ideas how every opinion was valid, even if sometimes, some people's opinions were just plain incorrect. All opinions were still valid though 'because everyone has a reason for doing something,' he concluded. 'Even if the hardest part can be listening to them.'

-

One Sunday they headed out to Church, sat down and after the weekly sacrament, began to listen to the speakers. One speaker, a local missionary, related how he'd been travelling door-to-door with his companion when they were advised by a resident not to bother making contact next door; apparently the occupant was deaf, therefore unlikely to be interested. The missionary had thanked the person for their advice, yet privately felt to make contact nevertheless. The lady occupant was indeed deaf, and in fact, true to the advice of the local resident, she wasn't interested in the missionary's message. However, a month later her son joined the Church organisation. Whilst the missionary couldn't determine what the future might hold for this small family, their association with the Church was a great source of eternal perspective as well as information, with a potential to assist them indefinitely. At the end of the day, even though the neighbour's opinion might have been subjectively incorrect, it was still valid, hence worth hearing. Frank subsequently developed an interest in listening to any reasonable opinion whenever it was offered, no matter how different it might turn out to be from his own.

Some opinions however, were worth heeding jolly quickly. When he was young, he'd gone up to London with his brothers to a dance event in Exhibition Road, where the parking was usually a problem. Their mother had kindly come along, keeping an eye on the family vehicle whilst they spent time at the event. It turned out to be thoroughly enjoyable. On their way out, his brother Edwin had retrieved the car before stopping in Exhibition Road to collect Frank and Oliver. Their mother had got out of the car to let Frank and Oliver get in the back, but after taking her time, Edwin encouraged her to speed up a little.

"Come on mum, we can't stay here too long. We're holding up the traffic."

"Just give me a moment," their mother had requested.

Edwin gave her a moment before driving forward. He hadn't looked back, choosing instead to concentrate on the road, resultantly as he drove off there was quite a loud shriek.

"You've just driven over my foot!" their mother yelled, justifiably annoyed.

"Oh sorry," Edwin replied. "But you should've got in quicker," he added, as he put the car into reverse, and drove back a little.

There was another equally loud shriek, at which point Edwin looked back.

"You've driven over my foot again!" their mother yelled.

"Oh, sorry," Edwin replied, changing gear then driving forward. The third loud shriek started to become farcical.

"The wheel's on my foot!"

When Edwin finally managed to park safely, their mother leapt into the car unexpectedly quickly.

'Yes, that was quite an event!' Frank chuckled, as he remembered the events of the night in London. There was however, an addendum to the incident, not unlike all decent shaggy-dog stories. As they drove out of London, several times Frank had noticed passengers of some other vehicles who'd been pointing towards the roof of their car, so eventually when they joined the motorway he mentioned it.

"Oh, my shoes!" their mother exclaimed. "I've left them on the roof!"

Edwin obligingly pulled onto the motorway's hard shoulder,

catching sight of a shoe which had now dropped onto the tarmac.

"Don't worry, I've seen one of them. It's behind us on the hard shoulder," Edwin announced. Frank jumped out of the car along with Oliver, perfectly positioned to save the day and retrieve the footwear.

"Where's the other one?" he questioned.

"There it is, over there in the slow lane," Oliver observed. Frank caught sight of the second shoe, and just in time, to see a large juggernaut run over it with every one of its numerous, nearside wheels. "I don't think she'll be wearing that one again," he suggested, as they both got back in. "We've managed to retrieve your shoe," Oliver announced.

"Well, where's the other one?" came back the reply.

"Slightly squashed by a lorry."

Edwin received a double tongue-lashing on the journey home, but at least Frank realised why their mother had been taking such a long time to get back into the car - she'd been changing footwear after she'd found a parking space for the car. By the time she'd actually found the nearby space, her sons had thoroughly enjoyed their time at the dance event. Things had worked out well, they concluded.

These were the type of experiences Frank remembered clearly from his youth. When he was young, he'd been closer to his sister Christina in age, and had initially spent more time with her than his older brothers. He'd found Christina to be kind-hearted as well as comical, thus wasn't surprised by a story which he later heard, as interestingly related by her husband. Apparently they'd been walking out in the countryside one weekend when suddenly Christina went missing.

"Where's she gone? She was here a second ago..."

Her husband looked all around but couldn't seem to find her anywhere, until eventually he glanced down to see a head popping out of some murky water just to one side of the path.

When the head disappeared again, he barely had enough time to reach down and grab the disappearing hair before it also vanished, and with a strong tug he managed to retrieve his wife from an ill-positioned slurry pit. He never did manage to figure out why a slurry pit was positioned alongside that country lane.

What impressed Frank greatly though was how Christina had remained upbeat, completely jovial about the whole event.

'I'd have been mega irate,' Frank reflected, yet Christina's character was different. She could usually appreciate a humorous side to life's foibles. It was always a jolly decent strength to possess.

Frank eventually began to record his family history experiences in journals, encouraged by his own wife. Helen had recorded them from around the time they were first married, forming quite an account of their married life together. He'd only preserved those events he could remember, rather than everyday happenings. Helen was good at the daily details, whereas he'd always struggled to remember a lot of the regular things. There was a useful role for different approaches, as was often the case in life. Despite those natural differences and remembering the discussion group's debate over Margaret Thatcher, he did still wonder how history could actually be manipulated over time. He thought back to what Adam had related over his experiences with the CVS.

"Beyond the efforts of historians or the work of judiciary for good or for bad, history and justice are most accurately discussed by the players involved," Adam had suggested.

How true Frank considered that to be. Apparently even the stenographers had made mistakes with transcripts, where Adam was apparently talking rapidly or they were unfamiliar with context or terminology. They'd asked him to slow down on occasions, which was ironic because the CVS cited his behaviour as unusual when he'd used time to think under questioning. Adam's concluding remarks though, he found more curious: "The reason God is the best judge of character is because He's seen all the different memories before, and He freely listens. The Father cares a lot about His kids."

'Not sure I'd be that patient,' Frank mentally noted.

"D'you think you'll still be listening to people's excuses throughout eternity, especially when they make the same crazy mistakes, over and over again?" he asked.

"I listen to your endless sagas about business, don't I?" Helen retorted.

He didn't have a comeback for her comment. Not this time.

CHAPTER 32

T hey'd agreed to meet up in Gavant before driving the forty miles to the meeting venue. One of Frank's students was taking part in a debate and he was interested to see how she'd fare. She'd come a long way since the first lectures, but he wasn't entirely sure whether she'd cope with the rigours of public engagement, so they were going along for moral support.

"Come on, hurry up you two," Frank encouraged, as Siggel and Adam bundled into the back to get out of the rain.

"What a day they've chosen!" Siggel commented.

"Yer, my wipers have been losing the battle against precipitation all evening."

"Precipitation?"

"Yer, the wet stuff!"

"Hold onto your horses! Getting all American on us, eh?"

"You're a fine one to talk with that Church of yours," Frank countered.

"You joined it first."

"I was pushed into it."

"We all were. Anyway, let's hope they've got some refreshments at this thing tonight."

"With veg," Adam added.

"Vegetables, please!" Frank corrected.

"How is veg uncouth, yet 'yer' isn't? How does that work?"

Siggel protested.

"The word 'vegetable' or 'vegetables' is firmly in my lexicon, but when it's shortened, it suddenly becomes foreign."

"D'you realise you're really becoming noticeably old?"

"Well even if it's remotely true, it's never being admitted."

They spent the next ten miles discussing merits of how to use the vernacular, deciding eventually they couldn't come up with a consensus of opinion. Opinions were ultimately divided, which duly set the scene for their evening's event.

The venue was without doubt splendid, commencing at a series of steps leading up to the entrance doors. They were wide, expansive, totally pristine, even to the degree where Frank would've been happy to eat an evening meal off them. He considered they probably had more marble than the Elgin statues, but in turn these were outshone by a couple of plush reception booths - the booths greeted all incoming visitors whenever they entered the conference centre. There were corridors branching off from the front entrance, spreading out equally in numerous directions, providing an excellent maze in which to get suitably lost. Finally, the conference room itself was a perfect example of a modern, purpose built auditorium with facilities which Frank judged, could only be understood by his kids. It was excellent.

They entered by a side entrance, before taking seats to the left-hand side of the auditorium. The session began with the usual formal introductions, and Frank was surprised to hear a couple of doctors being announced as speakers.

"I thought this was a straight forward debate?"

"Well, it is, isn't it?"

"Not when there's a couple of academics on the panel... for the opposition."

"Oh OK, I see what you mean," Siggel responded. "Then Joanna might be a little in over her head."

"You could well be right."

"Don't worry," Adam intervened. "We can provide some timely assistance if she needs it."

"We can't do that!" Frank insisted. "The rule of objectivity or impartiality is paramount on occasions such as these."

"Joanna can be objective, and we can be objective, but if she needs some help, our objectivities can duly meet up together," Adam suggested.

"That's not funny!"

"You might change your mind pretty soon."

"I don't think so."

"Well, the first doctor is up, even ready to speak now... whilst there's a second one next in line."

"Just sit back and listen. Joanna will be fine."

"OK."

"We can't get involved. Nor can we give any help."

"OK."

"That's final..."

"OK."

Twenty minutes later Siggel restrained Frank from standing up.

"Sit down, man. What are you intending to do?"

"The person there in the tweed jacket... he's really rather annoying!"

"Doctor Watson, you mean?"

"Doctor Whatsoeveryoulike, I don't mind!"

"What happened to your 'not getting involved' idea, or 'remaining objective and impartial'?"

"Don't be ridiculous. They've spent years at this stuff, yet they're pitting themselves against a young twenty-something year old girl. I'm not sitting back or accepting these tactics."

"So what do you suggest?"

"Just watch."

A ping rang out from a phone resting on the desk at the front of the conference room. Joanna picked up her phone, then after several moments, looked initially a little startled, but suddenly a smile crept across her face.

"That could help."

"Well, she'll need to put her incoming text notifications to silent," Siggel pointed out.

"It's not my problem."

"It could be hers though, if you continue sending down messages."

Whilst they proceeded with their private debate in the audience, Joanna took a few moments tending to her phone. Subsequently no further notification prompts were heard.

"Clever girl," Frank grinned. "She'll be fine."

Several minutes later Frank sent out another message.

"That could help."

The assistance was likewise noted.

"Joanna," intervened the Chairperson. "A point of order has been raised which I need to address. You're permitted one team coach and four debaters. Are you receiving assistance from any person without the rules of the debate?"

The young debater appeared unsure over how to respond, so after a brief pause Frank raised his hand.

"What are you doing, Frank?" Siggel chastised.

"I have a point of information," Frank responded loudly, carrying his voice towards the front of the conference hall.

"Can I ask you to state your name with your point of information, please?"

"Yes, I'm Frank Lewseed, and I'm on Joanna's team. My apologies for arriving late, but we were held up by the weather."

"How were we held up by the weather?" Siggel inquired.

"You took ages to get into the car," Frank replied, quietly yet quickly.

"If you'd like to come forward to take your seat at the front, we can conclude the point of order," suggested the

Chairperson, whereupon Frank stood up. He made his way to the front, accompanied by Siggel.

"What are you doing?"

"I'm coming along for moral support."

"I thought you told me not to get involved?"

"I did."

"So, why are you coming up here then?"

"You always need a hand."

Frank accepted the explanation. However, within a few moments, both of them suddenly noticed that Adam was also sitting alongside them.

"And what are you doing up here?" they asked in unison.

"I'm the coach."

"OK, fair enough." No more was said.

The following minutes became a game of musical chairs with various players on both sides of the debate, rising or reseating after addressing a thread of varied, detailed and debated matters arising. Frank considered the exchanges probably to be quite evenly balanced. He was more pleased though to observe how Joanna was managing her team, using everyone rather effectively.

"Here goes Dr. Watson," Siggel observed.

"Of course, human knowledge has evolved from the days of our primitive ancestors, who looked to the environment around them for gods or superstitions in explaining what they couldn't understand. Science over time has superseded the need to look for help from gods, because we now understand many things which we can easily take for granted, such as a round Earth. Primitive man struggled to evolve without the technology we have today, so we should remain grateful for the advances that great men such as Charles Darwin have given our world. Many suffered throughout history at the hands of religious inquisitors, and we owe them a great debt. The advances of science have benefitted mankind, not just in terms of our vast library of knowledge, but also in terms of our general living conditions as well as improved human welfare. We similarly have to be grateful for the important medical progressions made through science, along with the understandings of our very origin, or our future chances of colonising other planets. Somewhere man may find a second home, way out within the observable stellar cosmos which we're continually understanding. Science is increasingly revealing so much knowledge through more advanced and sophisticated technologies. Man's progress in technologies has become truly exponential."

Joanna invited Frank to respond.

"It's a pleasant thought how one day man could be out exploring the universe. Perhaps it could be on a starship Enterprise, following Star Trek's endless adventures into the unknown. At the end of such a journey, much fun would've been enjoyed. But science gadgets offer nothing more. In reality God governs science without any gadgets, and it's a key facet of how things work. Power and energy, creative evolution, the governance of time travel through speed... these things equate to a key, or primary source of scientific guidance. God doesn't need something else to do something for Him, nor for anyone else, because He does or can do everything that's needed for everyone within His domain. He remains completely powerful, completely knowledgable and completely in control of teaching His children how to evolve. Science describes God's work. Eschatology on the other hand is a wonderful setup, and one day humans won't need gadgets either... so long as they choose to continue evolving, permitting themselves to be directed carefully by God. But individuals retain the choice to cease evolving, because God won't force anyone to follow Him. Freewill is essential for all living individuals, whilst becoming clones isn't part of God's plan."

"What's eschatology?" Joanna asked, somewhat puzzled.

"I thought you might ask," Frank replied, grinning broadly. "I've brought along a book," he added, pulling it out from within his case before passing it over to her. The book would form a basis of private study for Joanna over the following five decades.

"Where did you get this from?" Joanna asked.

"Helen can probably do a better job of telling you a bit about it later," he replied.

"OK."

"Dr. Livingstone's up next," Siggel commentated.

"You say that god doesn't need anyone else to do anything for anyone else. Can I ask then what your god did for primitive man, when men lived without the comfort of today's technologies, or were fighting for survival amongst the harsh environments of prehistoric time periods?"

Joanna looked towards Siggel to respond for the team, and he duly obliged.

"You may believe ancient peoples were lacking knowledge or were primitive. When children observe more experienced individuals at work, their descriptions can at times seem simple, yet there's clarity in simplistic descriptions because they convey fundamental principles. Child-like observations remain different from the puerile. Science might balk at the idea of basic elements being entitled 'earth, wind, fire or water', and yet Psalms of the Bema describes ideas such as these. The same ideas would fit neatly into any scientific descriptions of temporally 'early' or developing cosmology. Ancient peoples necessarily described God's workings in simplistic terms, as we must still do today, although we'd do well to remember that observations of the ancients are just as valid now, as they were years ago. We need to logically fit the former, or observed descriptions into the science we've started to try and understand. 'Fire' fits neatly into a description of the centre of the Earth, or stars, or the formation of early planets, and supernovae. 'Earth' is an excellently simple planetary description. 'Water' and 'wind' are probably more interesting, since they bring to mind the idea of dark matter or dark energy, but these descriptions are inherently synonymous with fundamentally scientific observations. The science becomes fascinating when the ancient texts are trawled for methodology. Repositories, disposal areas, matter recycling and decontamination, all are constant themes. So too are the reports of multiply designed, engineered, and bespoke planetary bodies. Their physical blueprints unfold a story of an elementary transition from a harsh, uninhabitable or poisonous environment, towards an evolved reality of variety, with continually wondrous biological adaption and beautiful transformation. Creation becomes an evolution from function-free chaos, to a situation where instead, the greatest, most complex or refined physical creation, is human. The Apocalypse of Abraham provides an interesting text for more insights. One of the likely reasons ancients appeared backward, is due to the fact much antediluvian science didn't survive the deluge, but was lost. The deluge was a consequence of degenerative human depravity, with ancient records describing concurrent volcanic or seismic activity, as well as tsunamis, plus a shift in the earth's axis which initiated astronomical changes. Whilst anciently there were many practices which were far more advanced than we can currently recognise, or even therefore acknowledge, conversely antediluvian man had become significantly depraved or carnal, behaving in ways which we'd recognise or associate today with primitive man."

Dr. Watson rose in response to Siggel's remarks.

"You dream of a life after death but there is none. You place faith in a god you can't prove and have no evidence for, nor ever can have. You waste time as well as resources in make-beliefs which don't exist. Science deals with fact rather than children's fairy tales, and it takes courage to face up to reality, even when the reality might not be pleasant. I'd rather spend my life in reality dealing with facts, rather than dreaming it away amongst fanciful stories of strange events which will never occur."

Joanna invited Adam to respond for the team.

Adam paused a moment before commencing.

"Well, you've made your position clear for everyone to hear," he stated. "I guess we'll find out when we die." He paused somewhat longer. "I don't share your beliefs in the cessation of existence, because my experiences give me another perspective. I find the pursuit of personal evolution or personal preparation for the next dimension, to be worthwhile mortal activities. I enjoy it because it's pleasant. The positive feedback in real time is rather excellent. The joy from family life is real, the happiness gained in helping people is real, whilst the reward for trying to live a life with integrity is real. We all make mistakes, but I applaud anyone who seeks after good things, whether they're religious or otherwise. Free will is real for everyone living in mortality, but for me I choose to communicate with the most intelligent Being in the universe. I also choose to take advice from the most knowledgeable Being in the universe, and I choose to be helped by the most powerful Being in the universe. Do as you will. We'll find out about reality when we pass into the next dimension, because it's something none of us can avoid."

Frank considered Adam's testimony of deity to have been powerful, and he listened with interest. He found himself aligned with the concept that everyone has made mistakes in life, so the positivity of personal evolution he found particularly refreshing. He was still thinking about it as they made their way out of the conference centre and back to the car.

"Were you allowed to participate? I thought the coach could only coach."

"They didn't object, which I guess meant it was OK."

"Fair enough."

"It's still raining," Siggel moaned.

"This is England," Frank pointed out. "What d'you expect?"

"Some sun..."

"Now you're completely dreaming!"

"We get some sun."

"Yes, on a Saturday in March."

"It's a bit of an exaggeration."

"Although still a justified one..."

"I'm not too sure what's justified but let's get something to eat on the way back, can we?" Adam intervened.

"Sounds good to me."

"And me."

After their search for any nearby McDonalds had eventually ended in failure, they stopped at a local café, finding a table in one corner.

"I've been finding of late, how I need to record more family history events."

"What's brought this on then?"

"I'm not sure really. A premonition I suppose... it might be something useful I could do. I'm not entirely sure though. It'll probably just end up being another stack of papers in umpteen years time."

"It probably won't be paper. The world's headed towards a paperless society."

"Yer, good point."

"Is 'yer' uncouth?"

"I'm not answering that again. Anyway, I'm happy to record all sorts of things. Mind you, I'm not so comfortable with recording everything."

"Will tonight's venture make an entry?" Siggel probed,

mischievously.

"Probably. But some things are just too important to record."

"It's a contradiction in terms, isn't it?"

"No, not really. Everyone needs to gain their own knowledge regarding the really important stuff, and it can only come, as far as I can work out, from 'upstairs'."

"You mean from God?"

"I'd agree with his thinking," interjected Adam. "I have list 'B' experiences, ones I can be OK in sharing with people, and usually under most circumstances. Then there are a few list 'A' experiences, which generally I tend not to share."

"Give me an example of a list 'B' experience," Siggel requested, yet before Adam had a chance to respond, they were distracted by a small, rising commotion at a centre table in the middle of the café.

Years ago, Frank had watched a television series presented by Michael Buerk entitled '999 Lifesavers'. He hadn't expected though to see a real life incident playing out in front of him. A chap who'd been seated at the centre table stood up abruptly, unable to breathe, emitting an unusual gasping noise. There were a couple of other men at the table with him, and where they'd been talking together, these were probably a group of friends or acquaintances. The other men stood up together, trying a couple of different ways to relieve the difficulty. One manoeuvre involved turning the choking man upside down whilst slapping him hard on the back. Frank thought at the time how the slapping seemed a bit excessive, but under the circumstances no one was measuring their displayed force in Newtons. Another attempt appeared to be a Heimlich manoeuvre. Initially it didn't seem to be working so their efforts became more vigorous. Whilst the gasping continued for an age, after he'd gone through various shades of pale the tactic eventually began to work. It was all very dramatic. At the end of the incident the victim appeared to be jolly relieved.

"I guess that one could be included as a list 'B' experience?" Siggel inquired.

"Yes, I think perhaps it could," Adam replied. "Definitely life-changing, but possibly in a slightly different way though."

Siggel wasn't certain what kind of experiences Adam would class as list 'A'. He assumed they'd be personal. He didn't inquire.

CHAPTER 33

F rank's favourite dates with Helen were going for a meal or watching a film at the cinema. Recently though he'd grown tired of watching pointless films. Actions scenes could certainly be entertaining but without a storyline, a film seemed entirely pointless or pointedly tiresome. He wasn't quite sure which. It was nevertheless strange, because he enjoyed watching films.

"What are we doing this weekend, Helen?"

"We're going to the village fête."

"Oh, OK," he replied contentedly. She always had something rather good arranged for the weekends.

"Robert has entered some of his vegetables and I think he might win."

"Really?"

"Yes, they're big. Have you seen them?"

"No I haven't actually."

Ten minutes later Robert came down with the first runner bean he'd ever seen which didn't eventually have an end. It was accompanied by another example which was two inches longer, and in fact there were five of them.

"What else has he entered?" Frank inquired. The rest of the evening turned out to be rather interesting.

"You know, I think it's been OK how Robert's our last to get married."

"I don't want them to all get married," Helen quietly protested.

"Well Robert can't be the odd one out, dear."

"Yes, but I'm not ready for all the children to be gone yet."

He understood because this was Helen's day job. He knew she could turn it into a part-time post, so gradually her focus would probably turn more towards her horses. They'd both recognised that although keeping horses was a financial struggle, they'd been lucky how it had somehow worked out. Helen was lucky because it was her passion and probably always would be, whilst he was lucky because it kept Helen happy, which meant it was pleasantly, as well as definitely, worthwhile. Handling horses was also interesting.

"I saw a Church leader record the way he felt his favourite horse would be with him in Paradise," Frank remarked.

"I certainly hope so," Helen replied. "I'm not going unless they're with me!"

He didn't see any reason why it couldn't be the case, since he judged animals had psyches, similar to people.

"I wonder what Paradise is actually like?" he pondered vocally.

"It must be good, but I'm not sure."

"I hope it's not boring!"

"That's the world's thoughts about a place they can't see," Helen responded.

"Yes, I guess you're right. How can anyone accurately know what it's like from here?"

-

Two men stood together. They were dressed in white suits, white shoes and white ties and were deeply engaged in discussion.

"Shall we give them a hand?" John-Paul suggested.

"I don't see a reason why not," Charlie agreed.
"Shall we help out now?"
"I think it would be appropriate, yes."

-

Frank suddenly realised the fact his tour around Paradise was really quite unique. He couldn't remember how he'd come to be invited, yet he was going to make the most of it, thus he decided not to worry about the details.
"And where are we off to now then, John-Paul?"
"I'd like us to take a general look around, so you can see what it's like here."
"OK, that sounds good."
As they began the tour, the first thing he noticed was the way people looked cheerful rather than bored.
"Let's chat to a couple of people can we?"
"OK," John-Paul agreed obligingly.
Frank saw a woman sitting down on a lawned area surrounded by some trees, observing the wildlife around her. He was fascinated, hence they approached.
"Hi, do you mind if we join you?"
"Yes, please do," she responded.
"Can I ask what you're doing?"
"Certainly. I'm observing the birds around us."
Frank thought for a moment before deciding to change his follow-up question. "Do you ever get bored in Paradise?"
"No not at all. I was very interested in aviculture during my time in mortality, so this environment is ideal for me to observe birds or learn freely. There's plenty of work to do here, but there's also time for my interest in everything avian, and since we don't spend hours asleep, I have more time in Paradise to follow my interest."
"I see," Frank replied.

"Would you like to see some?"

"I think I would."

The woman opened the palm of her hand and outstretched her arm. A few moments later a couple of birds flew down, with one alighting on her hand whilst the other rested upon her forearm. He marvelled how these were real, live 'wild' birds, although he noted they weren't particularly wild in any way. They were extremely comfortable in coming close to the woman.

"You might be thinking this is unusual," she added, as the birds moved around on her arm. "But you see, there's no hunting here with no possibility of any danger, and without danger there's nothing for the birds to fear. It allows them to simply come down around us quite freely. They're still birds, acting or behaving in the same ways we can easily remember from mortality, but I observe them up close, and my interest or studies are so much more satisfying."

Frank had to admit, seeing wild birds this close was rather excellent. These two birds looked very similar to the European Robins he'd seen so frequently in his garden at home. They appeared to be respective cock plus hen birds, where he judged the male bird to have a darker hue on its crimson breast, with rather intriguing white and brown pied markings elsewhere. The beak was small and sturdy, whilst the eyes were round and alert. He'd always been amused by the Robins' confidence, full of pleasant song, especially during times he'd seen them in his garden, yet he mentally concurred this was significantly better close up.

"Yes, I can understand your interest," he acknowledged.

They thanked the woman then continued on their journey.

"What are those large, ornate buildings to the left John-Paul?"

"Those are schools. Many good people haven't enjoyed the same opportunities for education in mortality, whereby they have access to education and learn quickly over here."

"I see. What about the strong, large building with pillars to the right of them... what's that?"

"It's a government building."

"But there are people coming in or out freely, with no attendants nor restrictions at the entrances."

"Yes, everyone has access to the government building. There's always time for everyone to learn or share their thoughts, whilst the structure of the government remains highly ordered. The temple is positioned next to the government building because individuals are frequently going forward or coming back from the Father's home or other realms, generally with instructions or reports."

"That's interesting. What d'you mean by 'other realms'?"

"Other planets like our own are inhabited, and there are many of them. We all share information with each other, to improve or continue to evolve."

Frank considered it curious. He'd never imagined human psyches would evolve in the next dimension. He'd thought progress would have finished in mortality, yet clearly his idea needed adjusting. 'No worries though,' he concluded. 'I'm happy with the idea of progressing over here. It's interesting.'

"There aren't any hospitals, police stations, or fire stations, or even shops," he commented.

"Yes, we have no need for them," John-Paul replied.

As Frank continued to observe the environment which he was experiencing, he realised there weren't any banks because no one was using money, and everyone had access to the things they needed. Nobody looked ill, which meant hospitals weren't required, and individuals seemed to enjoy cooperating with each other, so the police didn't have a work to do. It was good how neither fire nor any catastrophes seemed to occur, and the environment was permanently pleasant. It was also truly peaceful.

"There are many things in mortality which really annoy

everyone," Frank stated, as a contrast to Paradise. "A great many of them though are simply brought about by the way people treat each other." Frank suddenly realised he'd stumbled upon a meaning for the statement 'Give unto Caesar, what is Caesar's', since it suggested cooperation or conformity. Compromise wasn't always possible in mortality, where countries, family and friends sometimes needed defending, yet returning good for evil now seemed to be a progressive approach. He'd previously read about a military leader who'd resigned when his country decided to attack an enemy rather than continuing to defend its homelands. He'd also heard of a modern, seemingly fashionable idea where pre-emptive killing of a few people in order to save many more, was deemed not only justifiable, but also the new way forward. That had always seemed a backward rather than a progressive step for him, since mortality was a test for every individual. He believed shortening mortal tests would usually be illogical, especially through displays of aggression. Physical defence remained defensible. Pre-emptive attacks would remain pre-emptive. He began to appreciate a cogency behind this rationale. The overall or good objective seemed to be a delay in any form of war.

They travelled on.

They travelled down onto a beachfront with beautiful golden sands and gently lapping waves, stretching out far into the distance in either direction. He loved the seaside, since it reminded him of times when the kids were small and Helen would arrange for them all to spend time at the beach. The kids were always excited, so the feeling was one of contentment alongside peacefulness, especially because Helen was good at arranging family outings. They were magical family times.

Slightly away from the beachfront, the countryside colours appeared somehow a lot more vivid than he was accustomed to, at least compared to when he'd been back in mortality. There were a variety of shades he'd probably not seen before, where everything seemed very real, almost more real than he'd ever come across. He felt very much alive, although time seemed to stand still in the moment and the moment was distinctly pleasant. He thought he'd experienced the feeling previously, but a long, long time ago. In fact, it was so long ago he wondered whether time had actually existed when he'd previously experienced it? He wondered how God controlled time. 'Does He need to control time? Time is just a series of events with a beginning and an ending. Does He want to control time? He allows freedom, so maybe He doesn't want to control it? But He must be able to... perhaps like most things though, there's a right place or a right time.'

His thoughts were interrupted by a seriously familiar sound. He'd heard the noise many times before, and it was getting louder. He'd observed how life was beautifully quiet in Paradise but this wasn't. It was quickly building, although John-Paul didn't appear to be paying any attention to it. It seemed rather bizarre. He looked around to where the noise was coming from and he saw slowly, coming into focus from a distance, the familiar sight of galloping horses with distinctively audible beats of hooves upon the ground as they raced towards him. It was a sight which fascinated him, since he enjoyed seeing horses moving, it didn't matter whether at a slow walk, or trotting, extended trot, canter or unleashed into full flowing gallop. They were pacing each other, gathering encouragement from the movement of the group, and as they neared he noticed the riders were in fact bareback riding. It reminded him of Helen's recent activities with her horses. She'd begun to ride bareback, and although at first he found the idea quite alarming, he'd watched her many times as she'd canter around very safely. He loved watching her ride, since her style was very pleasing to the eye. Maybe he just loved watching his wife, yet he appreciated natural ability when he saw it, and he could happily watch Helen ride for a long time. So as the riders came into view, he duly focused upon them. Helen's love was of long-distance riding where each rider had to cover a given distance, ten, twenty, thirty, forty or fifty miles, all within an allotted time period, with each returning horse showing suitable fitness through its measured heart rate. This was Helen's passion. The bookshelves at home contained many of her 'long-distance riding horsey' books.

As the group moved closer towards the beach, the noise of the hooves grew quieter, taking on a softer hue, matching the softness of the pleasant, golden sands. Some animals at the edges of the group threw up water as they willingly moved over into the shallow waves, working their way slowly up the beach. He noticed one horse amongst the rest, a mare and a grey, moving strongly within the centre of the field, slightly to the front. Again it looked familiar. Helen's horse was an Arab-Welsh grey mare, which was an ideal combination for long distance riding. He'd always thought how excellent it looked. The 'grey' reference was really only an indication of juvenile markings, since invariably the adult horse was pure white. This was true for Helen's mare, so his eye was naturally turned towards this grey in the centre of the field. Helen had often talked about bringing her grey down to the beach where she could ride her through the seaside waves. It was something she'd never had the opportunity to do, but she'd dreamed of the chance since they were first married, and he took notice to focus more closely upon the passenger of this grey. He could see the mount's rider was female, and with long flowing hair. It reminded him of the way Helen looked when he caught her playfully happy or relaxed. She was riding the mare in a very familiar style, a style so similar to the one Helen would adopt, with confident care, yet ability and lovely feminine grace. The rider noticed him, and then gently turning towards him, she smiled. It was Helen!

-

Frank woke up with a jolt. "I've had another dream!"
"Oh no, not again," Helen moaned as she turned back over. "What was it about this time?"
"Well I've been somewhere in a dream. I'm not sure about the timing or even how it works, but I've been somewhere."
Two minutes later they were deeply engaged in their own discussion. Two hours later a dawn chorus heralded the start of a new day.
"Isn't it strange that birds can be heard at sunrise, whilst they never seem to make any noise during the rest of the day?"
"Yes, well I need to be getting up and getting down to my horses," Helen announced.
He momentarily reflected on the years of his night owl work, which had simultaneously been unfolding alongside her skylark habits with the animals. They'd finally met somewhere in the middle.
"OK dear," he agreed. Helen was happy, which in the end translated into the fact he was therefore happy as well.

-

Two men stood together. They were dressed in white suits, white shoes and white ties and were deeply engaged in discussion.
"Do you think it helped?"
"Yes, I believe it did."
"Did they understand what it meant?"
"Whatever they didn't understand, they can still remember and then think about it, at a later date."
"Yes OK," John-Paul agreed, obligingly.

CHAPTER 34

"What d'you think the Christian message is?"

"About Christ, essentially."

"But there are many different religions with many good ideas. Are they all wrong?"

"I don't think they're necessarily wrong as Churches, even if they do get some things wrong, because doctrine can always be ironed out later. I think they just have different things to add. Atheism is wrong, but many churches bring many good things into the world."

"And many bad ones as well."

"Yes, with free agency that'll always be true. Free agency allows history to unfold, because without it there'd be zero history... just clones... but with free agency, there will always be history, and there'll always be interesting new stories to tell."

"I guess that's true," Frank reflected.

"What makes you ask, anyway?" Siggel inquired, as they walked away from the cinema after watching the latest instalment of the 'X-Men' trilogy.

"Well the Jean Grey character had the greatest powers in the film," Frank continued, taking a gentle grip of Helen's hand, something he loved to do as they walked together. "But seemingly, she was the most troubled of all the characters."

"I think it's basically wrong as an idea," Helen intervened.

"Someone has power when they've figured things out. Christ has power because He's figured it all out, but only after coming down here into mortality, with all of us."

"Helen has a good point," Siggel concurred. "Lucifer had power, yet he couldn't figure out how to be happy with what he had, so he's ended up destroying things, and it's continued throughout history. Christ stated the Father had given him 'a fullness of joy'. He relied upon the Father for direction or assistance. There's a message in Christianity which seems to be that we all need to find our own correct slots in life, because Christ slotted into a position under the Father, whilst mortals are slotted into positions below Christ, as well as the Father. Any ordered government will always have sensible 'slots' or positions for everyone, allowing it all to work out, or evolve properly."

"Atheism is the only religion which doesn't evolve. It ends up with nothing."

"And that's not logical because something exists."

"At the end of the day, everyone has faith in something. You just need to choose where your faith is placed. There'll finally be no need for faith after mortality, since we'll all find out what's real..."

"When we die!" the three of them vocalised in unison. Frank never grew tired of such a reminder. 'It's so real,' he reflected. "I'm not entirely sure though whether faith isn't just repositioned in the next dimension."

"What d'you mean?"

"Well, there'll still be new situations which will probably require new faith again."

"Maybe."

Helen squeezed his hand gently. He loved walking with her. It was also jolly decent to spend time with Siggel. It had been a good evening.

"I wonder what Christ and God are doing at the moment?"

Frank queried, as he drove the car out of the underground car park, leaving the cinema complex.

"Probably sorting out loads of problems," Siggel suggested.

"Don't they ever get fed up with sorting out problems?"

"I'm not sure they do."

"Well, I'd get jolly fed up with sorting out endless problems," Frank concluded.

"We're sorting family issues all the time," Helen suggested.

"I suppose you've made a good point," he agreed. "I can remember a cold, bleak night coming back across a deserted motorway out of Polgaria," he described, looking out of the window at the inclement weather outside. "It was mega chilly that night, and there were snowdrifts right across the motorway. Annoyingly, the thermostat for the car's heater had chosen to pack in."

"So what did you do?" Siggel asked.

"We had to put up with no internal heating, despite the snow. The weather was also threatening to strand us on the motorway, out in those hills."

"We had a prayer and got through," Helen explained.

"There were blankets with quilts in the back for the kids to wrap into, so I just kept driving until we came off the hills. It was strangely dark as well as super bleak up there, although the motorway looked brand new. I was impressed."

"There's usually a silver lining somewhere."

"Maybe. But I made sure we got the thermostat replaced asap, when we arrived back in England."

"Those kind of incidents are the ones we all remember."

"Yes, you're right." He stopped mid-sentence, staring intently ahead. "And this perhaps, could be another one!"

"What d'you mean?"

"Hold on a second..."

They were travelling around a gentle right-hand bend as they approached a dual carriageway, yet for some reason the car

307

was oversteering into the oncoming lane. Frank noticed how a car travelling in the opposite direction was coming towards them really quite fast, pushing him to correct their motion back towards the left-hand side. Nothing happened. He didn't want to pull too hard on the steering wheel, otherwise his vehicle might slide. He concluded they'd somehow hit a patch of 'black ice', which as far as he could remember was notoriously difficult to identify on any road surface, and he had no idea when it would end. His father had talked about the dangers of 'black ice' when he was significantly younger, whilst the whole scenario reminded him of a story someone had once told, but he couldn't quite remember it at that moment in time, nor under the current circumstances. Their onrushing problem was whether he could actually regain control of the steering before the other car reached them? He mentally assessed the various possibilities to avoid a collision. The best or only decent option he could come up with, was attempting to make it right across the other lane and onto the grass bank. The oncoming car had got a lot closer during the time he'd been thinking, and there was also no grass bank on the other side of the road, only trees. He was running out of options. He'd run out of time. At the last moment, the steering suddenly kicked back under his control, allowing him to pull the car over to the left-hand side, thankfully missing the oncoming vehicle. He was surprised the other driver hadn't leant on his horn. He was more surprised they'd avoided a collision.

"Well that was close!" Siggel observed. "What was going on there?"

Helen looked very pale.

"We must have hit a patch of black ice, because I had no control whatsoever with the steering for a while. We were just drifting round the bend into that other car."

"So what changed?"

"I'm not too sure. The steering just kicked back in."

"I think we were helped there," Helen commented.

"You're probably right, dear," Frank agreed. The whole experience felt like a déjà vu.

"Looks like the guardian angel department have been busy again!" Helen remarked.

Frank couldn't disagree.

-

Two men stood together. They were dressed in white suits, white shoes and white ties and were deeply engaged in discussion.

"There's never a dull moment with our family."

"Yes, I'd tend to agree."

"We've been kept quite busy."

Charlie had to admit, John-Paul had made rather a relevant point.

"I believe you're right."

"Will we always be this busy?"

"Perhaps."

"OK," John-Paul responded, and obligingly.

-

They travelled onwards joining a dual carriageway, which luckily covered quite a number of miles towards Siggel's house. Frank kept the speed down, just in case there was more black ice. He saw a car ahead of them, so he steadied his speed as he came up behind it to overtake. As he put his indicator on and moved over into the fast lane, he suddenly saw the other car massively decelerate, to the point where he passed it almost instantaneously.

"That chap was in a hurry to stop," he commented.

"I think you'd better pull over," Siggel suggested.

"Why's that?"

"He hasn't just stopped. The back end of his car has come right up into the air and his front bumper's hit the tarmac."

"Oh no!" Helen exclaimed. "Quickly dear, pull over in the lay-by here, and go back to see if he's alright."

He pulled into the lay-by, before jumping out of the car, meeting Siggel around the back. They both hurried along the road to see what assistance they could provide.

"Are you OK?"

"Yes, the car just suddenly stopped."

"It certainly looked dramatic."

"It certainly felt dramatic!"

"Yes, I bet it probably did."

"So what caused it? Did you have to brake hard?"

"No. It just stopped suddenly."

"Can you start it?" The driver attempted to turn over the engine but without success.

"I've been meaning to put some oil in for a while now, ever since the oil light came on."

"Aghhh. It could well be the answer."

They waited with the driver until the AA had been called, after pushing the vehicle onto the side of the road in neutral. Fortunately the AA assistance arrived quickly, which meant they could resume their homeward journey, knowing a decent resolution had been achieved.

"Now there's a very good reason why you should check your oil regularly!" Siggel announced.

"He'd had a good indication though when the warning light came on."

"Yep. It's not something you can leave until later."

"Was he OK? Will he get home OK?" Helen worried, as they both got back into the car.

"He'll be fine, dear. The AA truck is with him now."

Helen relaxed, and they made their way home.

-

The remainder of the trip was less eventful. They turned the corner at the end of Siggel's road, then pulled onto his front drive.

"Thanks for the lift," Siggel mentioned, before getting out of the car then making his way up the drive to his front door. He disappeared when the door closed behind him.

Driving along, Helen noticed something at the side of the road.

"Careful of the bird there," she said, pointing towards the kerbside. Frank pulled away from the kerb a little, as he drove past.

"Stop a minute, can you? I just need to check whether it's OK."

After pulling over they both got out to see what they'd avoided, which turned out to be a blackbird which had been sitting in the road, not far from the kerb but certainly far enough in, which meant it could probably get run over by local traffic. It flew over Frank's foot as they approached, taking up a new position in the middle of the road. Together they both coaxed the bird over towards a grass bank on the roadside, and following a short rest, it flew off into a nearby garden.

"It was probably stunned by a car which might have hit it," he suggested. "Luckily you spotted the bird, dear."

"Do you think it'll be OK?"

"Yes. Everything will be fine. They don't take long for recovery when they've been stunned. You've most likely saved that blackbird though."

He loved her care for animals. She was pleased the bird was now safe. He was also pleased that she was pleased. They drove on home.

-

Helen and Frank often took long walks along the bridleway paths, close to where she kept her horses. Strangely enough he enjoyed walking in the winter evenings just before it got dark, especially on occasions a little after dark, when everything was still and they could talk and walk along together. Sometimes the family would come along. These times were known as 'family evenings' or alternatively they took place on Sunday afternoons. Helen would try holding the family occasions at least once a week. Some weeks they watched a television series entitled 'The Waltons', or a Walt Disney film. Other times they'd read stories or play games. They also discussed different ideas as a family, typically about a theory or questions some of them might have, where the discussions were interesting as well as far-reaching. Frank enjoyed remembering the times when all the children were at home.

"What's the purpose of life?" Jane once asked.

"I guess it's seeing what we'll do when the boss isn't around."

"Who's the boss."

"God."

"OK, but why couldn't we do that in the pre-existence?"

"Because God was always present in the pre-existence."

"So why didn't we just go somewhere else?"

"We did, because we came to Earth."

"But that didn't mean we needed to come into a different dimension."

"Well, we needed a body."

"But we had a body in the pre-existence."

"Well, another body."

"Why did we need another body?"

"Because it could do things which the first psyche body

couldn't do."

"Like what?"

"Like having children and a family."

"What's so important about having a family?"

"Having a family is the start of following God as a father."

"And what about as a mother?"

"There's a father and a mother in every family."

"What's so important in being a father or mother?"

"It's an evolution. Having a family means every individual can evolve or progress. God wants everyone to become more like Him."

"So His family grows, as our families are formed."

"Yes, absolutely. We're all given the chance of becoming like Him, or evolving in eternity."

"But why would we want the chance of becoming like God?"

"Because God is perfectly good. Becoming better by evolving means we naturally copy Him, so we may as well also proactively copy Him."

"Then if we become like Him, how do we stay humble?"

"He'll always be our Father. It's a good thing when we're helping others become good. As we evolve we want to help others, which involves being pleasant or not wanting an egotistical attitude. In turn, we'll naturally become more humble, preferring kindness rather than feeling selfish or conceited."

Family discussions developed a life of their own. Some were short and concise, whilst others took on a more leisurely, elongated exploration of ideas or opinions. Family life with children would always be an exploratory adventure. Adventures were interesting.

-

As the years passed, the children grew, requiring the family

313

evenings to be constantly adapted. The older children seemed happier when the family went out for activities rather than staying indoors, whereby Helen became expert at arranging new things they'd do. Frank remembered a time when the family had walked along a pathway just across from their house, passing underneath a small group of trees adjacent to the local school. Frank could hear an owl calling, and he thought he'd previously heard the same call for several consecutive nights. He guessed it might be somewhere close. It sounded reasonably close, although he couldn't see it at all.

"Can you hear that owl?" he asked.

"Yes, I can."

"I can as well, but I can't see it."

"It's probably in the trees around the churchyard over there."

The local church was quite an historic building. It carried musket ball holes from times of the English civil war. The children had attended this school simply because it was opposite their house, and the school was actually affiliated with the local church. The entire area was rather picturesque with pleasant hillside walks and a mixture of ponds, meadows, shops, a library, wooded regions and a hospital. One of their favourite homes during their married years had also been close to the seaside, near Theirhead. It was a delightful place to live. Over the years, he'd felt the family was particularly lucky in the locations where they'd been privileged to find various homes. He was pleased how Helen shared his appreciation of the countryside, so whenever they'd moved home, it was usually into another country location.

"There it is dad," Daniel pointed out.

"Where?"

"Up there in the trees."

Frank was surprised that Daniel was now pointing directly above them, up into a large, expansive leaf canopy right over their heads. At first, he couldn't detect exactly where Daniel had been pointing, but slowly, as he scanned the area, sure enough he came upon a small, darkly coloured owl, sitting nonchalantly on a thick central bough in the treetop above.

"Well that's incredible! I wouldn't have thought it was so close," he remarked.

"I thought it sounded quite a distance away, as well."

"Where is it?" Jane asked.

"Over there in the middle, on that large bough... not far from the trunk."

"Oh, I see it."

Frank had kept aviary birds for years, but he always enjoyed seeing avian wildlife. He wasn't too sure though whether he enjoyed seeing birds of prey when they hunted, even to the point where he'd be rooting for any crows which would come down and mob them as they slowly swept across the countryside for prey.

He'd recently seen a couple of Magpies steal eggs from a Woodpeckers' nest, which also surprised him, because it was really quite late in the season.

Helen wasn't very keen on aviculture, because it meant birds were kept in captivity. It was something she didn't find useful. She'd similarly always put her horses out to pasture rather than keeping them indoors within stables, especially for any extended periods of time. Frank understood her reasonings. He was consoled over his concerns for aviculture, by the fact that captive-bred birds were not only a means of species conservation, but were also a way of protecting birds from the harsh realities of living wild. Wherever aviary birds had sufficient room to fly freely, he was comfortable with the idea of birds in captivity, relying upon a rationale that breeding birds were contented animals. He endeavoured to ensure all of his stock could breed at some point.

He remembered times as a teenager with Oliver, when they'd kept Alexandrine Parakeets in garden flights they'd built, along with Golden Mantled Rosellas, Ringnecks, Princess of Wales Parakeets, Redrumps and other species. On one occasion the Alexandrines had gnawed through the supporting beams of a flight to such an extent, one of the Ringnecks had escaped. Over the following decades, he'd heard about flocks of Ringnecks which had become native in regions near London, and he wondered whether their escapee had successfully survived. He doubted it, but it was still a possibility. Foreign birds seldom survived a release, or any escape from captivity. One of their Yellow Weaver Birds had unfortunately become lodged into a corner of a flight, and the next morning they found numerous wild birds pecking at something in the selfsame location. When they came down for a closer inspection, they were rather shocked to discover the wild birds had killed the Weaver. It could only be identified by its remaining bright plumage.

For the most part, Frank was contented with the hobby of aviculture. Some stock were jolly pleasant to keep, although sometimes less hardy against the English weather. He enjoyed their seasons with African birds, particularly the Fire Finches, Whydahs, Lavender Finches, and especially the St. Helena Finches. African species usually required rehousing within indoor flights or cages during the winter. Aviculture was a fascinating pastime. He'd always enjoyed it.

-

Frank couldn't figure out where the noise was coming from. He'd been tapping away on his computer for around an hour when he suddenly noticed the noise. In fact, the sound itself was a type of tapping or light knocking. He got up and moved across the room to the point where he thought he could hear something. He put his ear against the wall, yet it didn't get any louder. He looked out of the bedroom window, although he saw nothing. He didn't hear anything at all coming from outside which could perhaps explain this annoying tapping sound. For a while he subsequently heard nothing further, so after several minutes he went back over to his computer and continued with an article he'd been typing up.

The noise started again. Frank went back over to the same corner of his bedroom again. The disturbance disappeared again. Ten minutes later he gave up, then picked up his computer and went downstairs.

Three weeks later he heard the tapping noise in the same place, but a little later in the day. Over the next month he kept a careful note of the increasingly strange bedroom anomaly. It only occurred during the daytime, whereby he guessed it was probably an animal of some description, possibly not a nocturnal one though. Fortunately it also ruled out the likelihood of rats or mice in the loft.

'Phew!' he mentally acknowledged.

He followed the sound around to locate the loudest point once more, which similarly was in the same corner of the room.

Three months later he still hadn't figured out just exactly where the unusual tapping was coming from, until one day he was sitting in the dinning room. He heard a ticking coming from somewhere. One strange noise was annoying, whereas two strange noises most definitely had to be solved. After an hour of straining to hear the faint ticking, he followed it around the wall, up through the dining room hatch and into the kitchen, where he traced the source of the vexation to a kitchen clock. It was situated on a far wall, on the opposite side of the room.

"How did that come through the hatch?"

"What dear?" Helen asked.

"I could hear the kitchen clock ticking, but in the dining room. Somehow the ticking was travelling along the length of the whole dining room wall, just as clear as a bell."

"Or a clock..."

"Yes, quite... but unfortunately it doesn't explain how it came along several different walls, through the hatch, then over to me."

"It's no different to the Whispering Gallery in St. Paul's."

She was right. On one occasion he'd gone up to St. Paul's Cathedral with a friend, before he took the family up there, and he'd experimented with the acoustics in the Whispering Gallery. Sure enough, even without putting his ear to the wall he heard a distinct message all the way round from the other side – in fact, from directly opposite his position, right across the gallery. More relevantly though, it had occurred before he'd been ready.

"Can you hear me?"

"Don't be silly, you need to go around to the other side before you start calling out."

"I'm round the other side."

"What?" Frank looked up and was greatly surprised to see Brian gesticulating as well as grinning from across the dome.

So Helen had solved one mystery. There was one left.

Frank got up and walked out into the kitchen. He sat down on a stool quite close to where Helen was preparing the evening meal. He could just see the Bengalese Finches in the corner of the utility room as they congregated around a water container. He'd placed it to act as a water bath, whereas he'd previously been using various EasyFlo containers for their water supply. He enjoyed watching them. During a vigorous bathe, one of the finches caught its beak on the side of the container.

'Tap'.

Another finch summarily took its place, yet bathing just as vigorously.

'Tap'.

Frank was rather curious. He went upstairs and into his bedroom.

"Are you coming back down, dear?" Helen called.

"I'll be down in a second."

A few minutes later Frank re-entered the kitchen, wearing a distinctively broad grin.

"What's the matter?"

"Oh nothing. I've just realised where the other strange noise was coming from?"

"Where's that?"

"The finches."

"How's that then?" Helen asked.

"When they bathe, they knock their beaks against the water container, and it's what I can hear upstairs in our bedroom. Your idea about the Whispering Gallery got it all started off. If the kitchen clock could bend sounds around walls, then it was just as plausible the tapping from the finches was a noise I could hear up stairs."

"I'm glad you've found an answer," Helen replied sincerely. He went over and hugged her. He loved his beautiful wife.

-

The following evening Frank reflected upon the way he'd been distracted from what was real. In turn, it raised a question as to which organisations he truly trusted. He trusted the religious organisation he'd recently joined. However, his interactions with Adam Hut over the CVS corruption had left him dubious about the impartiality of regulatory bodies, and he'd similarly not trusted certain press reports after reading the stories covering Adam's case. The reports diverged from what he knew to be true, yet his daughter Jane was a reporter and she'd been able to report accurately, so he couldn't quite figure out why the press had become rather good at fabrication.

Realistically he knew less scrupulous individuals existed in any or probably every profession, so why should journalism be any different? His time abroad showed him how customs officials could also behave suspectly, and the corruption he'd observed in business dealings was similarly significant.

Consequently, Frank concluded it wasn't sensible to label any given organisation as generically corrupt, even if a member or members of that organisation had acted, or were acting unwisely. Firstly, every organisation would betimes have its own internal problems or difficulties, and should be allowed time to correct them. Secondly, even if the core of an organisation had become corrupted, where the mission statement of an organisation had originally been good, then it was something worth upholding. Any good principle was worth sustaining, if nothing else but for the sake of goodness per se. Thirdly Frank realised, no one was perfect and there'd only been one perfect mortal person. With such an idea in mind, individuals were on a journey of personal evolution, hopefully towards a better version of themselves, and that would always be something worthy of encouragement.

'I can believe or trust such an idea,' Frank resolved. 'Personal evolution is definitely worth encouraging.'

"That's correct Frank," came the reply.

-

"Well it was certainly interesting," Frank declared, waking up with a jolt.

"What was interesting?" Helen asked, rolling over slightly,

"Oh, just another dream."

"What was it this time?"

"Bit of a collage really. Things started off with our investigations into those mysterious noises. Then they spilled over into what is or isn't real. And finally there was a very graphic scene of psyches leaving the pre-existence, coming to this life of ours in mortality, and finally making permanent trips into the next dimension."

"So who goes first then? I don't want to go first. And if you go first then I'll look after the grandchildren and spend time with the kids. It'll be nice, because you can do what you like up there whilst I make sure the children are OK, and I'll help them raise their children. The men always go first. You should go first." Helen paused for breath.

Frank reasoned even though he enjoyed public speaking or presentations, Helen was better at social mixing. She'd a knack for introducing herself to people, and was naturally gregarious, so if there were already family members in the next dimension then it wouldn't take long for Helen to catch up with them all. If all those discussions were actually correct about genealogy or gathering family members, Helen could be the natural choice. On the other hand, he'd spent a while researching the genealogical records, yet the records were physical world items, leaving him to wonder whether records were kept in the next dimension? 'This rationale's getting a little convoluted,' he concluded.

"What happens though if you go first?" Frank asked, slightly concerned after realising he'd be rather lost without Helen. He'd spent twenty-eight years without her before they were married, delighting in twenty-eight years of being married to her (after an extra year of courtship). He didn't want to spend another twenty-eight annual cycles alone or without her again, exactly as his mother had done after his father had died.

"Well, we could hope for a notebook ending."

"A notebook ending?" he inquired.

"Don't you remember that film we watched the other week, called 'The Notebook'. The couple passed through the veil together."

"Yes, I do actually. I'm glad we saw it. The idea was a good one."

"But you don't have to worry, because the man usually goes first. But if it did somehow happen the other way round, you'd find a way of coping."

On July 25th 2022 Frank had been trying to find a way of coping for nearly five years, although he still hadn't come up with a solution. His darling wife had been very brave with cancer. She'd ended up sleeping for twenty-three hours a day, and when she did wake, where she'd slept so much she'd began to mix dreams up with reality - even television programmes they'd watched together were mixed with her dreams. That was understandable. Her reality was deeply focused within her constant dreaming. She remained kind, determined to be good right through until she passed into the next dimension. He'd watched in amazement as she'd succeeded in achieving her final desire.

When she'd passed through the veil into the next dimension on 25th November at 1.42pm, she'd been watching something for several minutes. Helen had come out of her coma just before she made the passing, which he noticed because she'd moved her arm about three inches. He'd spent every day in the living room at her bedside, sleeping next to her each night, yet for the past fortnight she hadn't moved, ever since the metastases had spread from her liver into her brain. On occasions if the family weren't available he'd take the dogs for a walk and Helen would phone him just so she could speak to him whilst he was away. At her bedside he'd constantly asked if she was in pain whenever she was awake. Other times they'd simply talk, although the conversations diminished significantly before she entered the coma after seven worrying seizures. Inevitably it was at the moment Helen moved her arm a second time, he was up from his bedside pouffe, asking how she was, whether she needed pain relief... and yet... and yet Helen didn't see him. She'd always slept or rested on her left-hand side, facing towards a picture of Christ on the living room wall. Eventually her left eye had become swollen most likely from the constant pressure placed upon it, leaving her with right eye vision as she emerged from the coma. He watched his beautiful wife scan an area of about six to eight feet at the bottom of her bed, right to left, left to right continually, intently, fixedly. It was as though he wasn't present. He stopped trying to gain her attention, and continued watching instead. Helen scanned something at the end of her bed for a few minutes. He didn't know what was there, however she was viewing something. It reminded him of the doctor who'd seen the psyche of a patient's dying wife, just as the patient himself had seen her psyche. Frank saw nothing. Gradually Helen's breathing slowed down from once every five seconds, to once every ten seconds, to twenty seconds, to thirty seconds, then his soulmate was gone.

Frank looked down at his wedding ring. He didn't want to take it off because he was still married to Helen through their temple sealing, which was extrapolated into the next dimension. His father never wore a wedding ring. During RAF days his dad's friend had caught a wedding band on the fuselage of a plane, which had ripped the finger off. Frank had once lost his ring on a hot summer's day when it simply flew off as he was closing a car door in a car park. A quick inquiry 'upstairs' meant the important item was quickly retrieved, although in the end at quite some distance from the car.

He didn't feel angry, and he similarly didn't feel jealous of anyone with a living spouse. He always loved success stories because it cheered him up immensely. The only feeling he could ascribe to the loss of beautiful Helen was a deep, and constant, or profoundly aching loss of happiness. He was lost amongst feelings of loss, knowing little he could actually do about it. He would give anything to turn back time, to live in those twenty-nine years with Helen. Life hadn't always been perfect and various problems had been their companions, but it was a happy and family life. He decided he wouldn't write again, or at least certainly not about their family history, not unless he could find an answer to losing Helen.

'Besides, for another family story there's always Jane... our professional reporter... or anyone in the family. They could write something. Who knows what they'll write. Someone will write something... someone needs to, and for the next and upcoming generation. Someone always does.' Frank sighed as he closed the last page, having finished with an emphatic fullstop.

He thought a moment on Helen's journals which she'd kept so faithfully, often wondering why she'd felt inspired to record them.

"You wrote them for me, my darling. You wrote them for me. They've kept me sane these past years, as I've had you with me, plus all the daily detail to remember and feel good about. You've made me want to be good, so they've reminded me how to be good. Maybe that's the secret to my loss of you, Helen..." He paused. "Striving to spread goodness. It's got to feel good, and if I feel good, maybe, just maybe I'll forget my loss of you?" he wondered. "I love you Helen... with all my heart, dear," Frank said, kissing the picture of his beautiful wife riding one of her beautiful horses. "We're married forever. I hope to see you soon darling. Good night."

Frank fell asleep, immersed in another day with Helen and all that a new day would bring. He was free again as he drifted into the reality of liberating sleep, free to hold her hand once more, and spend hours of normality with his perfect wife. Helen knew she wasn't perfect, but they both knew that she was perfect for Frank, and quite frankly it meant he'd always go straight into heaven every night, to join her for more uplifting adventures. Frank was happy again. Frank's favourite films were 'Meet Joe Black' and 'Chariots of Fire'.

Helen loved 'Love Story' and he used to enjoy it, but the only reason he couldn't think about her favourite film anymore, let alone contemplate watching it, was because her story became true.

The kids put at the bottom of their combined gravestone: 'Dad's gone home to mum and he's happy.'

-

Helen and Frank had completed their journey, completed their cycle or completed their test, coming out of the pre-existence, into mortality, then beyond and over to the Spirit World.

The next story would be for the next generation. That could definitely be interesting.

-

Three hundred people stood together. They were dressed in white suits and white dresses, and were deeply engaged in family discussion.

"Can you see now John-Paul why we had to train them?"

"Yes Charlie, I think I can."

"Good. Nothing would have been written otherwise, and without Helen's journals their story would have been lost in mortality. No journals, no family history. That's why premonitions are important. Now we have to work with the rest of the family, the ones still passing through mortality."

"But they've had even more children of their own!"

"And so the beautifully extended plan of evolution goes on. Evolving the one, whilst evolving them all! The Father's plan is rather perfect, don't you think?"

"Yes, I guess you're right."

"It was always His idea from the beginning," Charlie highlighted. "And we chose to follow Him, along with the

Firstborn."

"Yes we did!" Frank agreed, as he put his arm around John-Paul, and Helen wrapped herself around both of them. Charlie joined in, together with Patricia and scores upon scores of other family members.

"Not sure what I would've done without those journals your mum wrote son. She was still with me when she wasn't," he continued, as he gazed again at beautiful Helen. "And I don't know what I would have done if I hadn't been able to talk to you dear," Frank added.

"Well I was trying to catch your attention," Helen quickly responded. "Luckily John-Paul and Charlie helped out. That's why family are so important."

"I love you to the moon and back Helen."

"Hey, that's my line!" she protested.

"Well now, whatever I have is yours, and whatever you have is mine. And forever!"

"I need to show you around first..."

Their recaptured banter continued. Helen and Frank disappeared into the background, as Frank concluded his life was once more, truly perfect. This time though he had Helen forever, and they were both sealed to their own respective paternal and maternal families, as well as to each other. Frank also knew why Helen had made the jump into the Spirit World before him, because there were so many close family or loved ones who needed to make the transition from Prison to Paradise. It was easy to forget those family who were in Prison, yet they were still there, waiting, hoping for something else. Frank's separation from Helen was a rather large, 'no ginormous, inconvenience. But a necessary one I guess. Families can indeed be together forever,' he sighed. He concluded that although he found mortality interesting, he didn't want to do it again. He didn't have to. He was happy.

EPILOGUE

M ortal life is a reflection of who were really are, plus who we were in the pre-existence, plus who we can be with a little help from our friends, as well as family and most importantly deity. My concerns have led me to investigate evolution. The real evolution is our evolution of psyches, because psyches existed for aeons before our biological or physical bodies were formed, and will continue to live into unfolding future eternities. When we pass into the next dimension, we find out what's real or what's not real. It won't particularly matter how much money we've accumulated in mortality, nor how far up the social or status ladders we've climbed. What will be important is what we've done with what we've had, because in a few million years from now everyone will have had ample time to become the equivalent of a British Prime Minister or POTUS, or an ecclesiastical leader, just so long as we continue to evolve ourselves. Evolving means continuing to become good. The good part is our futures continue forever - we only have to remember the things we've learnt or the good we've practised in mortality. Evolution for humans has always been the plan of deity. My last and final question or possibly sub-questions, relate to the future or 'how can we write about it before it actually happens?' Perhaps I should call such possible things, 'Premonition'. If we receive premonitions, how can deity

know what will happen yet still allow everyone freewill? I
think it's perhaps a straight forward swap at times, because
it's not rocket science for God to know about any pandemic
which He's about to allow in the future. I see any infectious
illness as a way of bringing a group of His children back home
at the same time. Whether people would prefer or not prefer to
come back via a pandemic, or maybe choose a different
method, well I suppose it remains another question. I know of
one gentleman aged a hundred and three, who was pleased to
rejoin his wife in the next dimension during the pandemic, but
those who are left behind are sometimes left wondering about
the future. More to the point, if we're considering our future,
then what actually happened in our past, by which I mean far
back in the past, or the beginning of everything, or from the
beginning of our pre-existence? Essentially, both the future
and the beginning are different stories. Right now though, I
think I'm going off on holiday. After all, it's still summer.

Frank Lewseed
formerly E B Mad
formerly Abdem

A MESSAGE

"We have to come up with a message."
"Why?"
"There's always a message."
"Says who?"
"Says anyone who's read a book."
"Well, what type of message?"
"Any storyline which was developed throughout a book just has to have an overall message built in, otherwise it's been a waste of time reading the book."
"I said at the very beginning, anyone who reads this all the way through already has my apologies, because it was only going to be a huge, colossal chore to finish it right to the end."
"But what's the message? It's got to be usefully important."
"OK, fair enough. I know what the overall message could be."
"OK." There was an extended period of silence. "Well come on then, what is it?"
"What's what?"
"The message!"
"OK, sure. Yes, I've got it now."
"This is boring..."
"Well, at the end of the book the message is... don't write a book like this one!"
"Yer, brilliant."
"You like it?"

"No I don't! It's ridiculous!"

"Why?"

"Because you can't undo what you've only just done."

"Anything's possible."

"Yawn!"

"Anyway, this could be all the rage now, with things on the end of things and I like the idea. I think you're right. Let's come up with a message which can be stuck on the end of everything. But having said that, you can come up with a suggestion. What do you think's a good message?" There was no reply. "On the other hand, no one's ever going to read this, so they might as well go straight to the back, then read the message at the end. What we haven't thought about though, is what it'll do to James' role because he did go straight to the back when he was perusing the book, but only to read the epilogue. How's he going to find the epilogue if there's an extra message stuck on the end as well?"

"You worry too much."

"I reckon I'm probably justified on this one."

"Think of it this way. Did you actually see him read the very last page, or was he reading just somewhere around the back of the book?"

"I saw him turn the book over, go to the back, and immediately start reading."

"So you don't know."

"No."

"Then stop worrying about it."

"OK, what's the message going to be?"

"Well, I asked you."

"Now I'm asking you."

"I'm not sure."

"I thought the epilogue was a message."

"It's a summary of the storyline."

"The whole thing is merely a collection of stories. Helen and I collected them from the onset for our family."

"Everyday events can address everyday issues. Everyone has a story to tell, which makes all of our lives interesting. Let me ask you a question."

"OK."

"Name something of pressing concern in the world today."

"D'you want to hear something you think you want to hear, or d'you want to hear something other people might be interested in?"

"Both."

"No, you have to choose."

"Why?"

"Because it's either, or."

"Why can't it be both?"

"Because you probably won't think of something other people will be thinking of."

"Right, then go for something conventional."

"Fine. I choose world poverty."

"Good choice. Considering the things you've seen, what's the best way to solve world poverty?"

"There's a need to balance the ideal with the practicable. An ideal would be simply to work out how much those with wealth would need to give to those without wealth, then implement the principle until the world's resources are spread more fairly. On the other hand, any regimes which have already attempted such impositions, have proven the rationale isn't practicable, therefore neither is it idyllic because people generally fight against any loss of freewill."

"So what's the answer?"

"Wealth must be distributed fairly, but more importantly through free choice."

"Similar to charity work."

"Yes, I think that's a fair comment. People are good over charitable issues."

"What made you come to those conclusions?"

"I suppose it was mostly the time our family spent in Polgaria."

"Hence life's experiences can be helpful."

"Well yes, I think your comment's probably a good one."

"Which in turn, means it's worth writing journals."

"I take your point."

"Bearing our discussion in mind, let's return to the idea of a message."

"What message?"

"Exactly."

"We've done this before."

"Without a conclusion."

"Perhaps. Since we're now part of a Christian organisation, I'm thinking a message might have a religious theme."

"That's a start."

"And the best Christian message I can think of, straight off the cuff, is the message as given in Matthew twenty-two, verses thirty six to forty, also suggested as the most important advice for people, with two parts. Namely, for part one, it's important to love God, since God has seen it all before, hence following along with His suggestions remains a smart thing to do."

"But arguments then begin as to what God has or hasn't said, or what doctrines are real or just made up by man."

"I agree it's not straight forward. Generally life's never straight forward. The second part though is basically centred around caring for other people, because at the end of the day, we're all in mortality together, and we should all be helping each other out, as much as possible."

"There's still the issue though, over ongoing arguments concerning which Church is the correct one. Obviously we all have allegiances to any organisation we've personally joined, yet it's easy to see how other denominations believe theirs is the one which God favours."

"I tend to come back to near-death experiences or NDEs again on this one."

"What d'you mean?"

"Well if you think about it millions of people have experienced NDEs. Different messages are conveyed during various NDEs, especially between relatives but the most commonly repeated message given to people is an instruction to show love towards each other. This common message is usually delivered by a person emanating a substantial amount of light around them. The personage has been described as angelic, although many have reported or identified him as deity. The instruction or message relates to the second part of the biblical instruction from Christ 'to love one another'. It's a logical idea because cooperation is constructive, progressive, as well as satisfying."

"I agree. What I do wonder about though is why deity hasn't indicated which religion is correct during NDEs?"

"If anyone reported such an answer, would people believe it?"

"Probably not, which is a good point actually, since history has shown how people generally disregard religious messages. I guess deity has to help people in a different way."

"This raises another question. Why bother with any message if people won't listen?"

"Because we never know what good will come of anything good we try to do."

"Or bad..."

"What d'you mean?"

"Some people are mixing up real NDEs with false ideas, relating or suggesting how strange experiences can happen. These descriptions can sound like something out of an episode from a drug induced psychedelic trip, rather than NDEs recorded by organisations such as IANDS."

"Surely all experiences are valid. It's something you actually quoted a while back."

"Valid yes... but generally bad experiences are plainly or simply bad."

"So what's your idea then, around how to distinguish a legitimately correct and genuine experience, from an inappropriately false or bad one?"

"Anything good can ultimately be identified because it feels good, whilst anything bad can similarly be discerned because it will ultimately feel bad."

"Many would persuasively argue how people have been tricked into believing things which aren't true, based purely upon the way they felt at the time."

"When people can no longer distinguish right from wrong, then society has a problem. But I'm not totally convinced by the stories of people who choose evil ignorantly. It's generally quite straight forward to sense when something's wrong. If people are led to believe falsehoods, it rightly falls upon those doing the teaching, who clearly become responsible for the consequences of their teachings."

"I'd pretty much agree with your reasoning there."

"Our psyches have inherited an innate ability from deity, allowing them to always sense good as well as evil. It's innately similar to the way animals can stand up or walk, usually very soon after birth. Such abilities are natural protection or innate mechanisms given to our psyches."

"I'd have to agree with this latest point as well."

"Mind you, whenever we come up with a solution for one particular problem, pretty soon another one tends to surface all over again, simply to take its place."

"Which is giving a jolly decent basis for a message, or the reason we began this discussion in the first place."

"It's been a bit of a long discussion."

"All decent ones are."

"In light of your latest comment and added to the lateness of the hour, I think some abundant refreshments are now called for... perhaps more importantly post-haste."

"You do know we haven't come to any conclusion as yet though, don't you?"

"I can't see as it makes too much difference, to be honest."

"What d'you mean?"

"Whatever the message turns out to be, people will eventually find out about reality anyway."

"What, you mean when they die?"

"Yep!"

"Some would argue there's simply nothing to find out."

"Then I'd reply, they'll never know."

"Since you've already pointed out the fact we're part of a religious organisation now, we'd say we do know."

"And we do. As much as we can know anything."

"Some would again argue we're deluding ourselves."

"They'll discover what's delusional or what's real... when they pass into the next dimension."

"Yes, I've always remembered the near-death experience of an atheist. He was rather surprised, yet happy to find out there was indeed a 'next dimension' for him to go into after death."

"Which could present another angle on the message from Matthew chapter twenty-two, verses thirty six to forty. We all pass through mortality, then into the next dimension, and it involves a personal evolution or an evolution of the psyche."

"It sounds like an ongoing process."

"We'd all be bored without something to do."

"A lot of old people are lonely because they've no work to do when they retire."

"Well, you're retired."

"I've got things to do. Besides, we've discussed before how the definition of hell is probably having nowhere to go and nothing to do."

"You're right... it does sound boring."

"Does it mean you'll write again?"

"I'm not sure, to be honest."

"Peace is a personal thing. How long is it since Helen passed into the next dimension?"

"Nearly five years ago."

"When did you finish writing."

"About a year ago."

"So you've been writing for over four years without figuring it out."

"Hmmm, yer good point."

"Well I must say, I thought that particular line of argument was rather a good one. But you still haven't answered my question."

"No I haven't." A pause followed. A long pause.

"Shall we go?"

"Sure. Sounds like a rather excellent idea."

Frank and Siggel went off to the cafeteria. They were allowed because after all, they'd managed to convince themselves they were still middle aged.

They'd already forgotten about the message. Maybe someone else would have one.

Printed in Great Britain
by Amazon

83791822R00197